Dear Reader,

These three *Long, Tall Texans* reprints have a story
behind them.

Harden was special to me from the beginning. He
was the outcast in his own family, hard because he
never seemed to fit in, and a loner by nature. What it
took to get him out of his shell was a young woman
who temporarily needed nurturing, and a very poor
relationship with his mother that had to be resolved.
I loved doing his book.

Evan was a combination of ideas and situations that
were inspired by his appearance in *Connal*. He was a
lighthearted, funny man, but I kept wondering about
that comment that popped up, when Harden told
Pepi that he'd hate to see her disillusioned when
Evan threw somebody over a fence. A whole new set
of characteristics became possible, and Evan in love
was a holy terror.

Donavan was inspired by a song of Neil Diamond's
that I used to love to listen to—"Forever in Blue
Jeans." I kept picturing a poor little rich girl in a
rural bar surrounded by tough cowboys. Eventually,
I pictured one special cowboy who had to come to
her rescue. Donavan was born.

These stories truly came from the heart. I hope you
enjoy knowing something of how they came about,
and I also hope you enjoy reading them. My best to
all of you,

Diana Palmer

**Texas sure knows how to grow cowboys—
and Diana Palmer knows just how to
write about them!**

THE MEN OF
JACOBSVILLE, TEXAS

**LONG,
TALL
TEXANS I**
{
CALHOUN BALLENGER & ABBY CLARK
JUSTIN BALLENGER & SHELBY JACOBS
TYLER JACOBS & NELL REGAN

**LONG,
TALL
TEXANS II**
{
QUINN SUTTON & AMANDA CALLAWAY
ETHAN HARDEMAN & ARABELLA CRAIG
CONNAL TREMAYNE & PEPI MATHEWS

**LONG,
TALL
TEXANS III**
{
HARDEN TREMAYNE & MIRANDA WARREN
EVAN TREMAYNE & ANNA COCHRAN
DONAVAN LANGLEY & FAY YORK

AND THERE ARE STILL
MORE TO COME!

EMMETT (SR #910)
REGAN'S PRIDE (SR #1000)
THAT BURKE MAN (SD #913)
COLTRAIN'S PROPOSAL (SR #1103)

DIANA PALMER

LONG, TALL TEXANS III

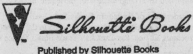

Silhouette Books

Published by Silhouette Books
America's Publisher of Contemporary Romance

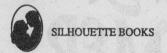

SILHOUETTE BOOKS

by Request
LONG, TALL TEXANS III

Copyright © 1997 by Harlequin Books S.A.

ISBN 0-373-20137-0

The publisher acknowledges the copyright holders of the individual works as follows:

HARDEN
Copyright © 1991 by Diana Palmer
EVAN
Copyright © 1991 by Diana Palmer
DONAVAN
Copyright © 1992 by Diana Palmer

Printed in U.S.A.

CONTENTS

DIANA PALMER
got her start in writing as a newspaper reporter and
published her first romance novel for Silhouette
Books in 1982. In 1993, she celebrated the
publication of her fiftieth novel for Silhouette
Books. *Affaire de Coeur* lists her as one of the top
ten romance authors in the country. Beloved by
fans worldwide, Diana Palmer is the winner of
numerous national Waldenbooks Romance
Bestseller awards and national B. Dalton Books
Bestseller awards.

HARDEN

Chapter One

The bar wasn't crowded. Harden wished it had been, so that he could have blended in better. He was the only customer in boots and a Stetson, even if he was wearing an expensive gray suit with them. But the thing was, he stood out, and he didn't want to.

A beef producers' conference was being held at this uptown hotel in Chicago, where he'd booked a luxury suite for the duration. He was giving a workshop on an improved method of crossbreeding. Not that he'd wanted to; his brother Evan had volunteered him, and it had been too late to back out by the time Harden found out. Of his three brothers, Evan was the one he was closest to. Under the other man's good-natured kidding was a temper even hotter than Harden's and a ferocity of spirit that made him a keen ally.

Harden sipped his drink, feeling his aloneness

keenly. He didn't fit in well with most people. Even his in-laws found him particularly disturbing as a dinner companion, and he knew it. Sometimes it was difficult just to get through the day. He felt incomplete; as if something crucial was missing in his life. He'd come down here to the lounge to get his mind off the emptiness. But he felt even more alone as he looked around him at the laughing, happy couples who filled the room.

His flinty pale blue eyes glittered at an older woman nearby making a play for a man. Same old story. Bored housewife, handsome stranger, a one-night fling. His own mother could have written a book on that subject. He was the result of her amorous fling, the only outsider in a family of four boys.

Everybody knew Harden was illegitimate. It didn't bother him so much anymore, but his hatred of the female sex, like his contempt for his mother, had never dwindled. And there was another reason, an even more painful one, why he could never forgive his mother. It was much more damning than the fact of his illegitimacy, and he pushed the thought of it to the back of his mind. Years had passed, but the memory still cut like a sharp knife. It was why he hadn't married. It was why he probably never would.

Two of his brothers were married. Donald, the youngest Tremayne, had succumbed four years ago. Connal had given in last year. Evan was still single. He and Harden were the only bachelors left. Theodora, their mother, did her best to throw eligible women at them. Evan enjoyed them. Harden did not.

He had no use for women these days. At one time, he'd even considered becoming a minister. That had gone the way of most boyish dreams. He was a man now, and had his share of responsibility for the Tremayne ranch. Besides, he'd never really felt the calling for the cloth. Or for anything else.

A silvery laugh caught his attention and he glanced at the doorway. Despite his hostility toward anything in skirts, he couldn't tear his eyes away. She was beautiful. The most beautiful creature he'd ever seen in his life. She had long, wavy black hair halfway down her back. Her figure was exquisite, perfectly formed from the small thrust of her high breasts to the nipped-in waist of her silver cocktail dress. Her legs were encased in hose, and they were as perfect as the rest of her. He let his gaze slide back up to her creamy complexion with just the right touch of makeup, and he allowed himself to wonder what color her eyes were.

As if sensing his scrutiny, her head abruptly turned from the man with her, and he saw that her eyes matched her dress. They were the purest silver, and despite the smile and the happy expression, they were the saddest eyes he'd ever seen.

She seemed to find him as fascinating as he found her. She stared at him openly, her eyes lingering on his long, lean face with its pale blue eyes and jet-black hair and eyebrows. After a minute, she realized that she was staring and she averted her face.

They sat down at a table near him. The woman

had obviously been drinking already, because she was loud.

"Isn't this fun?" she was saying. "Goodness, Sam, I never realized that alcohol tasted so nice! Tim never drank."

"You have to stop thinking about him," the other man said firmly. "Have some peanuts."

"I'm not an elephant," she said vehemently.

"Will you stop? Mindy, you might at least pretend that you're improving."

"I do. I pretend from morning until night, haven't you noticed?"

"Listen, I've got to—" There was a sudden beeping sound. The man muttered something and shut it off. "Damn the luck! I'll have to find a phone. I'll be right back, Mindy."

Mindy. The name suited her somehow. Harden twisted his shot glass in his hand as he studied her back and wondered what the nickname was short for.

She turned slightly, watching her companion dial a number at a pay phone. The happy expression went into eclipse and she looked almost desperate, her face drawn and somber.

Her companion, meanwhile, had finished his phone call and was checking his watch even as he rejoined her.

"Damn," he cursed again, "I've got a call. I'll have to go to the hospital right away. I'll drop you off on the way."

"No need, Sam," she replied. "I'll phone Joan and have her take me home. You go ahead."

"Are you sure you want to go back to the apartment? You know you're welcome to stay with me."

"I know. You've been very kind, but it's time I went back."

"You don't mind calling Joan?" he added reluctantly. "Your apartment is ten minutes out of my way, and every second counts in an emergency."

"Go!" she said. "Honest, I'm okay."

He grimaced. "All right. I'll phone you later."

He bent, but Harden noticed that he kissed her on the cheek, not the lips.

She watched him go with something bordering on relief. Odd reaction, Harden thought, for a woman who was obviously dating a man.

She turned abruptly and saw Harden watching her. With a sultry laugh she picked up the piña colada she'd ordered and got to her feet. She moved fluidly to Harden's table and without waiting for an invitation, she sat down, sprawling languidly in the chair across from him. Her gaze was as direct as his, curious and cautious.

"You've been staring at me," she said.

"You're beautiful," he returned without inflection. "A walking work of art. I expect everyone stares."

She lifted both elegant eyebrows, clearly surprised. "You're very forthright."

"Blunt," he corrected, lifting his glass in a cynical salute before he drained it. "I don't beat around the bush."

"Neither do I. Do you want me?"

He cocked his head, not surprised, even if he was oddly disappointed. "Excuse me?"

She swallowed. "Do you want to go to bed with me?" she asked.

His broad shoulders rose and fell. "Not particularly," he said simply. "But thanks for the offer."

"I wasn't offering," she replied. "I was going to tell you that I'm not that kind of woman. See?"

She proffered her left hand, displaying a wedding band and an engagement ring.

Harden felt a hot stirring inside him. She was married. Well, what had he expected? A beauty like that would be married, of course. And she was out with a man who wasn't her husband. Contempt kindled in his eyes.

"I see," he replied belatedly.

Mindy saw the contempt and it hurt. "Are you...married?" she persisted.

"Nobody brave enough for that job," he returned. His eyes narrowed and he smiled coldly. "I'm hell on the nerves, or so they tell me."

"A womanizer, you mean?"

He leaned forward, his pale blue eyes as cold as the ice they resembled. "A woman hater."

The way he said it made her skin chill. She rubbed warm hands over her upper arms. "Oh."

"Doesn't your husband mind you going out with other men?" he asked mockingly.

"My husband...died," she bit off the word. She took a sudden deep sip of her drink and then another,

her brows drawn together. "Three weeks ago." Her face contorted suddenly. "I can't bear it!"

She got up and rushed out of the bar, her purse forgotten in her desperate haste.

Harden knew the look he'd just seen in her eyes. He knew the sound, as well. It brought him to his feet in an instant. He crammed her tiny purse into his pocket, paid for his drink, and went right out behind her.

It didn't take him long to find her. There was a bridge nearby, over the Chicago River. She was leaning over it, her posture stiff and suggestive as she held the rails.

Harden moved toward her with quick, hard strides, noticing her sudden shocked glance in his direction.

"Oh, hell, no, you don't," he said roughly and abruptly dragged her away from the rails. He shook her once, hard. "Pull yourself together, for God's sake! This is stupid!"

She seemed to realize then where she was. She looked at the water below and shivered. "I...wouldn't really have done it. I don't think I would," she stammered. "It's just that it's so hard, to go on. I can't eat, I can't sleep...!"

"Committing suicide isn't the answer," he said stubbornly.

Her eyes glittered like moonlit water in her tragic face as she looked up at him. "What is?"

"Life isn't perfect," he said. "Tonight, this minute, is all we really have. No yesterdays. No tomorrows. There's only the present. Everything else is a memory or a daydream."

She wiped her eyes with a beautifully manicured hand, her nails palest pink against her faintly tanned skin. "Today is pretty horrible."

"Put one foot forward at a time. Live from one minute to the next. You'll get through."

"Losing Tim was terrible enough, you see," she said, trying to explain. "But I was pregnant. I lost the baby in the accident, too. I was...I was driving." She looked up, her face terrible. "The road was slick and I lost control of the car. I killed him! I killed my baby and I killed Tim...!"

He took her by the shoulders, fascinated by the feel of her soft skin even as he registered the thinness of them. "God decided that it was his time to die," Harden corrected.

"There isn't a God!" she whispered, her face white with pain and remembered anguish.

"Yes, there is," he said softly. His broad chest rose and fell. "Come on."

"Where are you taking me?"

"Home."

"No!"

She was pulling against his hand. "I won't go back there tonight, I can't! He haunts me...."

He stopped. His eyes searched her face quietly. "I don't want you physically. But you can stay with me tonight, if you like. There's a spare bed and you'll be safe."

He couldn't believe he was making the offer. He,

who hated women. But there was something so terribly fragile about her. She wasn't sober, and he didn't want her trying something stupid. It would lie heavily on his conscience; at least, that was what he told himself to justify his interest.

She stared at him quietly. "I'm a stranger."

"So am I."

She hesitated. "My name is Miranda Warren," she said finally.

"Harden Tremayne. You're not a stranger anymore. Come on."

She let him guide her back to the hotel, her steps not quite steady. She looked up at him curiously. He was wearing an expensive hat and suit. Even his boots looked expensive. Her mind was still whirling, but she had enough sense left to realize that he might think she was targeting him because he had money.

"I should go to my own apartment," she said hesitantly.

"Why?"

He was blunt. So was she. "Because you look very well-to-do. I'm a secretary. Tim was a reporter. I'm not at all wealthy, and I don't want you to get the wrong idea about me."

"I told you, I don't want a woman tonight," he said irritably.

"It isn't just that." She shifted restlessly. "You might think I deliberately staged all this to rob you."

His eyebrows rose. "What an intriguing thought," he murmured dryly.

"Yes, isn't it?" she said wryly. "But if I were

planning any such thing, I'd pick someone who looked less dangerous.''

He smiled faintly. "Afraid of me?" he asked deeply.

She searched his hard face. "I have a feeling I should be. But, no, I'm not. You've been very kind. I just had a moment's panic. I wouldn't really have thrown myself off the bridge, you know. I hate getting wet." She shifted. "I really should go home."

"You really should come with me," he replied. "I won't rest, wondering if you've got another bridge picked out. Come on. I don't think you're a would-be thief, and I'm tired."

"Are you sure?" she asked.

He nodded. "I'm sure."

She let him lead her into the hotel and around to the elevator. It was one of the best hotels in the city, and he went straight up to the luxury suites. He unlocked the door and let her in. There was a huge sitting room that led off in either direction to two separate bedrooms. Evan had planned to come up with Harden from Texas. At the last minute, though, there'd been an emergency and Evan had stayed behind to handle it.

Miranda began to feel nervous. She really knew nothing about this man, and she knew she was out of control. But there was something in his eyes that reassured her. He was a strong man. He positively radiated strength, and she needed that tonight. Needed someone to lean on, someone to take care of her, just this once. Tim had been more child than husband, always expecting her to handle things. Bills, telephone calls about broken appliances, the checkbook, groceries, dry cleaning, housekeeping— all that had been Miranda's job. Tim worked and came home and watched television, and then expected sex on demand. Miranda hadn't liked sex. It was an unpleasant duty that she tried to perform with the same resignation that she applied to all her other chores. Tim knew, of course he did. She'd gotten pregnant, and Tim hadn't liked it. He found her repulsive pregnant. That had been an unexpected benefit. But now there was no pregnancy. Her hand went to her stomach and her face contorted. She'd lost her baby....

"Stop that," Harden said unexpectedly, his pale blue eyes flashing at her when he saw the expression on her face. "Agonizing over it isn't going to change one damned thing." He tossed his hotel key on the coffee table and motioned her into a chair. "I keep a pot of coffee on. Would you like a cup?"

"Yes, please," she said with resignation. She slumped down into the chair, feeling as if all the life had drained out of her. "I can get it," she added quickly, starting to rise.

He frowned. "I'm perfectly capable of pouring coffee," he said shortly.

"Sorry," she said with a shy smile. "I'm used to waiting on Tim."

He searched her eyes. "Had you trained, did he?" he asked.

She gasped.

He turned. "Black, or do you like something in it?"

"I...I like it black," she stammered.

"Good. There's no cream."

She'd never been in a hotel penthouse before. It was beautiful. It overlooked the lake and the beach-front, and she didn't like thinking about what it must have cost. She got to her feet and walked a little unsteadily to the patio door that overlooked Chicago at night. She wanted to go outside and get a breath of air, but she couldn't get the sliding door to work.

"Oh, for God's sake, not again!" came a curt, angry deep voice from behind her. Lean, strong hands caught her waist from behind, lifting and turning her effortlessly before he frog-marched her back to her chair and sat her down in it. "Now stay put," he said shortly. "I am not having any more leaping episodes tonight, do you understand me?"

She swallowed. He was very tall, and extremely intimidating. She'd always managed to manipulate Tim when he had bad moods, but this man didn't look as if he was controllable any way at all. "Yes," she said through tight lips. "But I wasn't going to jump. I just wanted to see the view—"

He cut her off. "Here. Drink this. It won't sober you up, but it might lighten your mood a bit."

He pushed a cup and saucer toward her. The smell of strong coffee drifted up into her nostrils as she lifted the cup.

"Careful," he said. "Don't spill it on that pretty dress."

"It's old," she replied with a sad smile. "My clothes have to last years. Tim was furious that I wasted money on this one, but I wanted just one nice dress."

He sat down across from her and leaned back, crossing his long legs before he lit a cigarette and dragged an ashtray closer. "If you don't like the smoke, I'll turn the air conditioning up," he offered.

"I don't mind it," she replied. "I used to smoke, but Tim made me quit. He didn't like it."

Harden was getting a picture of the late Tim that *he* didn't like. He blew out a cloud of smoke, his eyes raking her face, absorbing the fragility in it. "What kind of secretary are you?"

"Legal," she said. "I work for a firm of attorneys. It's a good job. I'm a paralegal now. I took night courses to learn it. I do a lot of legwork and re- searching along with typing up briefs and such. It gives me some freedom, because I'm not chained to a desk all day."

"The man you were with tonight..."

"Sam?" She laughed. "It isn't like that. Sam is my brother."

His eyebrows arched. "Your brother takes you on drinking sprees?"

"Sam is a doctor, and he hardly drinks at all. He and Joan—my sister-in-law—have been letting me stay with them since...since the accident. But tonight I was going home. I'd just come from an office party. I certainly didn't feel like a party, but I got dragged in because everyone thought a few drinks might make me feel better. They did. But one of my co-workers thought I was feeling too much better so she called Sam to come and get me. Then I wanted to come here and try a piña colada and Sam humored me because I threatened to make a scene.'' She smiled. ''Sam is very straitlaced. He's a surgeon.''

''You don't favor each other.''

She laughed, and it was like silvery bells all over again. ''He looks like our father. I look like our mother's mother. There are just the two of us. Our parents were middle-aged when they married and had us. They died within six months of each other when Sam was still in medical school. He's ten years older than I am, you see. He practically raised me.''

''His wife didn't mind?''

''Oh, no,'' she said, remembering Joan's kindness and maternal instincts. ''They can't have children of their own. Joan always said I was more like her daughter than her sister-in-law. She's been very good to me.''

He couldn't imagine anybody not being good to her. She wasn't like the women he'd known in the past. This one seemed to have a heart. And despite her widowed status, there was something very innocent about her, almost naive.

''You said your husband was a reporter,'' he said when he'd finished his coffee.

She nodded. ''He did sports. Football, mostly.'' She smiled apologetically. ''I hate football.''

He chuckled faintly and took another draw from his cigarette. ''So do I.''

Her eyes widened. "Really? I thought all men loved it."

He shook his head. "I like baseball."

"I don't mind that," she agreed. "At least I understand the rules." She sipped her coffee and studied him over the rim of the cup. "What do you do, Mr. Tremayne?"

"Harden," he corrected. "I buy and sell cattle. My brothers and I own a ranch down in Jacobsville, Texas."

"How many brothers do you have?"

"Three." The question made him uncomfortable. They weren't really his brothers, they were his half brothers, but he didn't want to get into specifics like that. Not now. He turned his wrist and glanced at his thin gold watch. "It's midnight. We'd better call it a day. There's a spare bedroom through there," he indicated with a careless hand. "And a lock on the door, if it makes you feel more secure."

She shook her head, her gentle eyes searching his hard face. "I'm not afraid of you," she said quietly. "You've been very kind. I hope that someday, someone is kind to you when you need help."

His pale eyes narrowed, glittered. "I'm not likely to need it, and I don't want thanks. Go to bed, Cinderella."

She stood up, feeling lost. "Good night, then."

He only nodded, busy crushing out his cigarette. "Oh. By the way, you left this behind." He pulled her tiny purse from his jacket pocket and tossed it to her.

Her purse! In her desperate flight, she'd forgotten all about it. "Thank you," she said.

"No problem. Good night." He added that last bit very firmly and she didn't stop to argue.

She went quickly into the bedroom—it was almost as large as the whole of the little house she lived in—and she quietly closed the door. She didn't have anything to sleep in except her slip, but that wouldn't matter. She was tired to death.

It wasn't until she was almost asleep that she remembered nobody would know where she was. She hadn't called Joan to come and get her, as she'd promised Sam she would, and she hadn't phoned her brother to leave any message. Well, nobody would miss her for a few hours, she was sure. She closed her eyes and let herself drift off to sleep. For the first time since the accident, she slept soundly, and without nightmares.

Chapter Two

Miranda awoke slowly, the sunlight pouring in through the wispy curtains and drifting across her sleepy face. She stretched lazily and her eyes opened. She frowned. She was in a strange room. She sat up in her nylon slip and stared around her, vaguely aware of a nagging ache in her head. She put a hand to it, pushing back her disheveled dark hair as her memory began to filter through her confused thoughts.

She got up quickly and pulled her dress over her head, zipping it even as she stepped into her shoes and looked around for her purse. The clock on the bedside table said eight o'clock and she was due at work in thirty minutes. She groaned. She'd never make it. She had to get a cab and get back to her apartment, change and fix her makeup—she was going to be late!

She opened the door and exploded into the sitting room to find Harden in jeans and a yellow designer T-shirt, just lifting the lid off what smelled like bacon and eggs.

"Just in time," he mused, glancing at her. "Sit down and have something to eat."

"Oh, I can't," she wailed. "I have to be at work at eight-thirty, and I still have to get to my apartment and change, and look at me! People will stare...!"

He calmly lifted the telephone receiver and handed it to her. "Call your office and tell them you've got a headache and you won't be in until noon."

"They'll fire me!" she wailed.

"They won't. Dial!"

She did, automatically. He had that kind of abrasive masculinity that seemed to dominate without conscious effort, and she responded to it as she imagined most other people did. She got Dee at the office and explained the headache. Dee laughed, murmuring something about there being a lot of tardiness that morning because of the office party the night before. They'd expect her at noon, she added and hung up.

"Nobody was surprised," she said, staring blankly at the phone.

"Office parties wreak havoc," he agreed. "Call your brother so he won't worry about you."

She hesitated.

"Something wrong?" he asked.

"What do I tell him?" she asked worriedly, nibbling her lower lip. "'Hi, Sam, I've just spent the night with a total stranger'?"

He chuckled softly. "That wasn't what I had in mind."

She shook her head. "I'll think of something as I go." She dialed Sam's home number and got him instead of Joan. "Sam?"

"Where the devil are you?" her brother raged.

"I'm at the Carlton Arms," she said. "Look, I'm late for work and it's a long story. I'll tell you everything later, I promise..."

"You'll damned well tell me everything now!"

Harden held out his hand and she put the phone into it, aware of the mocking, amused look on his hard face.

She moved toward the breakfast trolley, absently aware of the abrupt, quiet explanation he was giving her brother. She wondered if he was always so cool and in control, and reasoned that he probably was. She lifted the lid off one of the dishes and sniffed the delicious bacon. He'd ordered breakfast for two, and she was aware of a needling hunger.

"He wants to talk to you," Harden said, holding out the phone.

She took it. "Sam?" she began hesitantly.

"It's all right," he replied, pacified. "You're apparently in good hands. Just pure luck, of course," he added angrily. "You can't pull a stunt like that again. I'll have a heart attack."

"I won't. I promise," she said. "No more office parties. I'm off them for life."

"Good. Call me tonight."

"I will. Bye."

She hung up and smiled at Harden. "Thanks."

He shrugged. "Sit down and eat. I've got a workshop at eleven for the cattlemen's conference. I'll drop you off at your place first."

She vaguely remembered the sign she'd seen on the way into the hotel about a beef producers seminar. "Isn't the conference here?" she stammered.

"Sure. But I'll drop you off anyway."

"I don't know quite how to thank you," she began, her silver eyes soft and shy.

He searched her face for a long, long moment before he was able to drag his eyes back to his plate. "I don't care much for women, Miranda," he said tersely, "So call this a momentary aberration. But next time, don't put yourself in that kind of vulnerable situation. I didn't take advantage. Most other men would have."

She knew that already. She poured herself a cup of coffee from the carafe, darting curious glances at him. "Why don't you like women?"

His dark eyebrows clashed and he stared at her with hard eyes.

"It won't do any good to glower at me," she said gently. "I'm not intimidated. Won't you tell me?"

He laughed without humor. "Brave this morning, aren't we?"

"I'm sober," she replied. "And you shouldn't carry people home with you if you don't want them to ask questions."

"I'll remember that next time," he assured her as he lifted his fork.

"Why?" she persisted.

"I'm illegitimate."

She didn't flinch or look shocked. She sipped her coffee. "Your mother wasn't married to your father." She nodded.

He scowled. "My mother had a flaming affair and I was the result. Her husband took her back. I have three brothers who are her husband's children. I'm not."

"Was your stepfather cruel to you?" she asked gently.

He shifted restlessly. "No," he said reluctantly.

"Were you treated differently from the other boys?"

"No. Look," he said irritably, "why don't you eat your breakfast?"

"Doesn't your mother love you?"

"Yes, my mother loves me!"

"No need to shout, Mr. Tremayne." She grimaced, holding one ear. "I have perfect hearing."

"What business of yours is my life?" he demanded.

"You saved mine," she reminded him. "Now you're responsible for me for the rest of yours."

"I am not," he said icily.

She wondered at her own courage, because he looked much more intimidating in the light than he had the night before. He made her feel alive and safe and cosseted. Ordinarily she was a spirited, independent woman, but the trauma of the accident and the loss of the baby had wrung the spirit out of her. Now it was beginning to come back. All because of this tall, angry stranger who'd jerked her from what he'd thought were the waiting jaws of death. Actually jumping had been the very last thing in her mind on that bridge last night. It had been nausea that had her hanging over it, but it had passed by the time he reached her.

"Are you always so hard to get along with?" she asked pleasantly.

His pale blue eyes narrowed. Of course he was, but he didn't like hearing it from her. She confused him. He turned back to his food. "You'd better eat."

"The sooner I finish, the sooner I'm out of your hair?" she mused.

"Right."

She shrugged and finished her breakfast, washing it down with the last of her coffee. She didn't want to go. Odd, when he was so obviously impatient to be rid of her. He was like a security blanket that she'd just found, and already she was losing it. He gave her peace, made her feel whole again. The thought of being without him made her panicky.

Harden was feeling something similar. He, who'd sworn that never again would he give his heart, was experiencing a protective instinct he hadn't been aware he had. He didn't understand what was happening to him. He didn't like it, either.

"If you're finished, we'll go," he said tersely, rising to dig into his pocket for his car keys.

She left the last sip of coffee in the immaculate china cup and got to her feet, retrieving her small purse from the couch. She probably looked like a shipwreck survivor, she thought as she followed him to the door, and God knew what people would think when they saw her come downstairs in the clothes she'd worn the night before. How ridiculous, she chided herself. They'd think the obvious thing, of course. That she'd slept with him. She flushed as they went down in the elevator, hoping that he wouldn't see the expression on her face.

He didn't. He was much too busy cursing himself for being in that bar the night before. The elevator stopped and he stood aside to let her out.

It was unfortunate that his brother Evan had decided to fly up early for the workshop Harden was conducting on new beef production methods. It was even more unfortunate that Evan should be standing in front of the elevator when Harden and Miranda got off it.

"Oh, God," Harden ground out.

Evan's brown eyebrows went straight up and his dark eyes threatened to pop. "Harden?" he asked, leaning forward as if he wasn't really sure that this was his half brother.

Harden's blue eyes narrowed threateningly, and a dark flush spread over his cheekbones. Instinctively he took Miranda's arm.

"Excuse me. We're late," he told Evan, his eyes threatening all kinds of retribution.

Evan grinned, white teeth in a swarthy face flashing mischievously. "You aren't going to introduce me?" he asked.

"I'm Miranda Warren," Miranda said gently, smiling at him over Harden's arm.

"I'm Evan Tremayne," he replied. "Nice to meet you."

"Go home," Harden told Evan curtly.

"I will not," Evan said indignantly, towering over both of them. "I came to hear you tell people how to make more money raising beef."

"You heard me at the supper table last month—just before you volunteered me for this damned workshop!" he reminded the other man. "Why did you have to come to Chicago to hear it again?"

"I like Chicago." He pursed his lips, smiling appreciatively at Miranda. "Lots of pretty girls up here."

"This one is off-limits, so go away," Harden told him.

"He hates women," Evan told Miranda. "He doesn't even go on dates back home. What did you do, if you don't mind saying? I mean, you didn't drug him or hit him with some zombie spell...?"

Miranda shifted closer to Harden involuntarily and slid a shy hand into his. Evan's knowing look made her feel self-conscious and embarrassed. "Actually—" she began reluctantly.

Harden cut her off. "She had a small problem last night, and I rescued her. Now I'm taking her home," he said, daring his brother to ask another question. "I'll see you at the workshop."

"You're all right?" Evan asked Miranda, with sincere concern.

"Yes." She forced a smile. "I've been a lot of trouble to Mr. Tremayne. I...really do have to go."

Harden locked his fingers closer into hers and walked past Evan without another word.

"Your brother is very big, isn't he?" Miranda asked, tingling all over at the delicious contact with Harden's strong fingers. She wondered if he was even aware of holding her hand so tightly.

"Evan's a giant," he agreed. "The biggest of us all. Short on tact, sometimes."

"Look who's talking," she couldn't resist replying.

He glared down at her and tightened his fingers. "Watch it."

She smiled, sighing as they reached his car in the garage. "I don't guess I'll see you again?" she asked.

"Not much reason to, if you don't try jumping off bridges anymore," he replied, putting up a cool front. Actually he didn't like the thought of not seeing her again. But she was mourning a husband and baby and he didn't want involvement. It would be for the best if he didn't start anything. He was still wearing the scars from the one time he'd become totally involved.

"I had too much to drink," she said after he'd put her in the luxury car he'd rented at the airport the day before and climbed in beside her to start the engine. "I don't drink as a rule. That last piña colada was fatal."

"Almost literally," he agreed, glancing at her irritably. "Find something to occupy your mind. It will help get you through the rough times."

"I know." She looked down at her lap. "I guess your brother thinks I slept with you."

"Does it matter what people think?"

She looked over at him. "Not to you, I expect. But I'm disgustingly conventional. I don't even jaywalk."

"I'll square it with Evan."

"Thank you." She twisted her purse and stared out the window, her sad eyes shadowed.

"How long has it been?"

She sighed softly. "Almost a month. I should be used to it by now, shouldn't I?"

"It takes a year, they say, to completely get over a loss. We all mourned my stepfather for at least that long."

"Your name is Tremayne, like your brother's."

"And you wonder why? My stepfather legally adopted me. Only a very few people know about my background. It isn't obvious until you see me next to my half brothers. They're all dark-eyed."

"My mother was a redhead with green eyes and my father was blond and blue-eyed," she remarked. "I'm dark-haired and gray-eyed, and everybody thought I was adopted."

"You aren't?"

She smiled. "I'm the image of my mother's mother. She was pretty, of course..."

"What do you think you are, the Witch of Endor?" he asked on a hard laugh. He glanced at her while they stopped for a traffic light. "My God, you're devastating. Didn't anyone ever tell you?"

"Well, no," she stammered.

"Not even your husband?"

"He liked fair women with voluptuous figures," she blurted out.

"Then he should have married one," he said shortly. "There's nothing wrong with you."

"I'm flat chested," she said without thinking.

Which was a mistake, because he immediately glanced down at her bodice with a raised eyebrow that spoke volumes. "Somebody ought to tell you that men have varied tastes in women. There are a few who prefer women without massive...bosoms," he murmured when he saw her expression. "And you aren't flat-chested."

She swallowed. He made her feel naked. She folded her arms over her chest and stared out the window again.

"How long were you married?" he asked.

"Well...four months," she confessed.

"Happily?"

"I don't know. He seemed so different before we married. And then I got pregnant and he was furious. But I wanted a baby so badly." She had to take a breath before she could go on. "I'm twenty-five. He was the first man who ever proposed to me."

"I can't believe that."

"Well, I didn't always look like this," she said. "I'm nearsighted. I wear contact lenses now. I took a modeling course and learned how to make the most of what I had. I guess it worked, because I met Tim at the courthouse while I was researching and he asked me out that same night. We only went together two weeks before we got married. I didn't know him, I guess."

"Was he your first man?"

She gasped. "You're very blunt!"

"You know that already." He lit a cigarette while he drove. "Answer me."

"Yes," she muttered, glaring at him. "But it's none of your business."

"Any particular reason why you waited until marriage?"

The glare got worse. "I'm old-fashioned and I go to church!"

He smiled. It was a genuine smile, for once, too. "So do I."

"You?"

"Never judge a book by its cover," he murmured. His pale eyes glanced sideways and he laughed.

She shook her head. "Miracles happen every day, they say."

"Thanks a lot." He stopped at another red light. "Which way from here?"

She gave him directions and minutes later, he pulled up in front of the small apartment house where she lived. It was in a fairly old neighborhood, but not a bad one. The house wasn't fancy, but it was clean and the small yard had flowers.

"There are just three apartments," she said. "One upstairs and two downstairs. I planted the flowers. This is where I lived before I married Tim. When he...died, Sam and Joan insisted that I stay with them. It's still hard to go in there. I did a stupid thing and bought baby furniture—" She stopped, swallowing hard.

He cut off the engine and got out, opening the door. "Come on. I'll go in with you."

He took her arm and guided her to the door, waiting impatiently while she unlocked it. "Do you have a landlady or landlord?"

"Absentee," she told him. "And I don't have a morals clause," she added, indicating her evening gown. "Good thing, I guess."

"You aren't a fallen woman," he reminded her.

"I know." She unlocked the door and let him in. The apartment was just as she'd left it, neat and clean. But there was a bassinet in one corner of the bedroom and a playpen in its box still sitting against the dividing counter between the kitchen and the dining room. She fought down a sob.

"Come here, little one," he said gently, and pulled her into his arms.

She was rigid at first, until her body adjusted to being held, to the strength and scent of him. He was very strong. She could feel the hard press of muscle against her breasts and her long legs. He probably did a lot of physical work around his ranch, because he was certainly fit. But his strength wasn't affecting her nearly as much as the feel of his big, lean hands against her back, and the warmth of his arms around her. He smelled of delicious masculine cologne and tobacco, and her lower body felt like molten liquid all of a sudden.

His fingers moved into the hair at her nape and their tips gently massaged her scalp. She felt his warm breath at her temple while he held her.

Tears rolled down her cheeks. She hadn't really cried since the accident. She made up for it now, pressing close to him innocently for comfort.

But the movement had an unexpected conse- quence, and she felt it against her belly. She stiffened and moved her hips demurely back from his with what she hoped was subtlety. All the same, her face flamed with embarrassment. Four brief months of marriage hadn't loosened many of her inhibitions.

Harden felt equally uncomfortable. His blood had cooled somewhat with age, and he didn't have much to do with women. His reaction to Miranda shocked and embarrassed him. Her reaction only made it worse, because when he lifted his head, he could see the scarlet blush on her face.

"Thanks again for looking after me last night," she said to ease the painful silence. Her hands slid around to his broad chest and rested there while she looked up into pale, quiet eyes in a face like stone. "I won't see you again?" she asked.

He shook his head. "It wouldn't be wise."

"I suppose not." She reached up hesitantly and

touched his beautiful mouth, her fingertips lingering on the full, wide lower lip. "Thank you for my life," she said softly. "I'll take better care of it from now on."

"See that you do." He caught her fingers. "Don't do that," he said irritably, letting her hand fall to her side. He moved back, away from her. "I have to go."

"Yes, well, I won't keep you," she managed, embarrassed all over again. She hadn't meant to be so forward, but she'd never felt as secure with anyone before. It amazed her that such a sweeping emotion wouldn't be mutual. But he didn't look as if he even liked her, much less was affected by her. Except for that one telltale sign...

She went with him to the door and stood framed in the opening when he went out onto the porch.

He turned, his eyes narrow and angry as he gazed down at her. She looked vulnerable and sad and so alone. He let out a harsh breath.

"I'll be all right, you know," she said with false pride.

"Will you?" He moved closer, his stance arrogant, his eyes hot with feeling. His body throbbed as he looked at her. His gaze slid to her mouth and he couldn't help himself. He wanted it until it was an obsession. Reluctantly he caught the back of her neck in his lean hand and tilted her face as he bent toward her.

Her heart ran wild. She'd wanted his kiss so much,

and it was happening. "Harden," she whispered helplessly.

"This is stupid," he breathed, but his mouth was already on hers even as he said it, the words going past her parted lips along with his smoky breath.

She didn't even hesitate. She slid her arms up around his neck and locked her hands behind his head, lifting herself closer to his hard, rough mouth. She moaned faintly, because the passion he kindled in her was something she'd never felt. Her legs trembled against his and she felt the shudder that buffeted him as his body reacted helplessly to her response.

He felt it and moved back. He dragged his mouth away from hers, breathing roughly as he looked down into her dazed eyes. "For God's sake!" he groaned.

He pushed her back into the apartment and followed her, elbowing the door shut before he reached for her again.

He wasn't even lucid. He knew he wasn't. But her mouth was the sweetest honey he'd ever tasted, and he didn't seem capable of giving it up.

She seemed equally helpless. Her body clung to his, her mouth protesting when he started to lift his. He sighed softly, giving in to her hunger, his mouth gentling as the kiss grew longer, more insistent. He toyed with her lips, teasing them into parting for him before his tongue eased gently past her teeth.

He felt her gasp even as he heard it. His hand smoothed her cheek, his thumb tenderly touching the corner of her mouth while his lips brushed it, calming her. She trembled. He persisted until she finally gave in, all at once, her soft body almost collapsing against him. His tongue pushed completely into her mouth and she shivered with passion.

The slow, rhythmic thrust of his tongue was so suggestive, so blatantly sexual, that it completely disarmed her. She hadn't expected this from a man she'd only met the day before. She hadn't expected her headlong reaction to him, either. She couldn't seem to let go, to draw back, to protest this fierce intimacy.

She moaned. The sound penetrated his mind, aroused him even more. He felt her legs trembling against his blatant arousal, and he forced his mouth to lift, his hands to clasp her waist and hold her roughly away from him while he fought for control of his senses.

Her face was flushed, her eyes half closed, drowsy with pleasure. Her soft mouth was swollen, still lifted, willing, waiting.

He shook her gently. "Stop it," he said huskily. "Or I'll have you right here, standing up."

She stared up at him only half comprehending, her breath jerking out of her tight throat, her heart slamming at her ribs. "What…happened?" she whispered.

He let go of her and stepped back, his face rigid with unsatisfied desire. His chest heaved with the force of his breathing. "God knows," he said tersely.

"I've…I've *never*…" she began, flustered with embarrassment.

"Oh, hell, I've 'never,' either," he said irritably. "Not like that." He had to fight for breath. He stared at her, fascinated. "That can't happen again. Ever."

She swallowed. She'd known that, too, but there had been a tiny hope that this was the beginning of something. Impossible, of course. She was a widow of barely one month, with emotional scars from the loss of her husband and child, and he was a man who obviously didn't want to get involved. Wrong time, wrong place, she thought sadly, and wondered how she was going to cope with this new hurt. "Yes. I know," she said finally.

"Goodbye, Miranda."

Her eyes locked with his. "Goodbye, Harden."

He turned with cold reluctance and opened the door again. He could still taste her on his mouth, and his body was taut with arousal. He paused with the doorknob in his hand. He couldn't make himself turn it. His spine straightened.

"It's too soon for you."

"I...suppose so."

There had been a definite hesitation there. He turned and looked at her, his eyes intent, searching.

"You're a city girl."

That wasn't quite true, but he obviously wanted to believe it. "Yes," she said.

He took a slow, steadying breath, letting his eyes run down her body before he dragged them back up to her face.

"Wrong time, wrong place," he said huskily.

She nodded. "Yes. I was thinking that, too."

So she was already reading his mind. This was one dangerous woman. It was a good thing that the timing was wrong. She could have tied him up like a trussed turkey.

His gaze fell to her flat belly and it took all his willpower not to think what sprang to his mind. He'd never wanted a child. Before.

"I'll be late for the workshop. And you'll be late for work. Take care of yourself," he said.

She smiled gently. "You, too. Thank you, Harden."

His broad shoulders rose and fell. "I'd have done the same for anyone," he said, almost defensively.

"I know that, too. So long."

He opened the door this time and went through it, without haste but without lingering. When he was back in the car, he forced himself to ignore the way it wounded him to leave her there alone with her painful memories.

Chapter Three

Evan was waiting for Harden the minute he walked into the hotel. Harden glowered at him, but it didn't slow the other man down.

"It's not my fault," Evan said as they walked toward the conference rooms where the workshop was to be held. "A venomous woman hater who comes downstairs with a woman in an evening gown at eight-thirty in the morning is bound to attract unwanted attention."

"No doubt." Harden kept walking.

Evan sighed heavily. "You never date anybody. You're forever on the job. My God, just seeing you with a woman is extraordinary. Tell me how you met her."

"She was leaning off a bridge. I stopped her."

"And...?"

Harden shrugged. "I let her use the spare room

until she sobered up. This morning I took her home. End of story."

Evan threw up his hands. "Will you talk to me? Why was a gorgeous girl like that jumping off a bridge?"

"She lost her husband and a baby in a car accident," he replied.

Evan stopped, his eyes quiet and somber. "I'm sorry. She's still healing, is that it?"

"In a nutshell."

"So it was just compassion then." Evan shook his head and stuck his big hands into his pockets. "I might have known." He glanced at his half brother narrowly. "If you'd get married, I might have a chance of getting my own girl. They all walk over me trying to get to you. And you can't stand women." He brightened. "Maybe that's the secret. Maybe if I pretend to hate them, they'll climb all over me!"

"Why don't you try that?" Harden agreed.

"I have. It scared the last one off. No great loss. She had two cats and a hamster. I'm allergic to fur."

Harden laughed shortly. "So we've all noticed."

"I had a call from Mother earlier."

Harden's face froze. "Did you?"

"I wish you wouldn't do that," his brother said. "She's paid enough for what she did, Harden. You just don't understand how it is to be obsessively in love. Maybe that's why you've never forgiven her."

Evan had been away at college during the worst months of Harden's life. Neither Harden nor Theo-

dora had ever told him much about the tragedy that
had turned Harden cold. "Love is for idiots," Harden said, refusing to let himself remember. He
paused to light a cigarette, his fingers steady and
sure. "I want no part of it."

"Too bad," Evan replied. "It might limber you
up a bit."

"Not much hope of that, at my age." He blew out
a cloud of smoke, part of his mind still on Miranda
and the way it had felt to kiss her. He turned toward
the conference room. "I still don't understand why
you came up here."

"To get away from Connal," he said shortly. "My
God, he's driving me crazy."

Harden lifted an amused eyebrow. "Baby fever.
Once Pepi gives birth, he'll be back to normal."

"He paces, he smokes, he worries about something going wrong. What if they don't recognize labor in time, what if the car won't start when it's time
to go to the hospital!" He threw up his hands. "It's
enough to put a man off fatherhood."

Fatherhood. Harden remembered looking hungrily
at Miranda's waist and wondering how it would feel
to father a child. Incredible thought, and he'd never
had it before in his life, not even with the one woman
he'd loved beyond bearing...or thought he'd loved.
He scowled.

He had a lot of new thoughts and feelings with
Miranda. This wouldn't do. They were strangers. He
lived in Texas, she lived in Illinois. There was no

future in it, even if she wasn't still in mourning. He had to bite back a groan.

"Something's eating you up," Evan said perceptively, narrowing one dark eye. "You never talk about things that bother you."

"What's the use? They won't go away."

"No, but bringing them out in the light helps to get them into perspective." He pursed his lips. "It's that woman, isn't it? You saved her, now you feel responsible for her."

Harden whirled, his pale blue eyes glaring furiously at the other man.

Evan held up both hands, grinning. "Okay, I get the message. She was a dish, though. You might try your luck. Donald and Connal and I can talk you through a date...and the other things you don't know about."

Harden sighed. "Will you stop?"

"It's no crime to be innocent, even if you are a man," Evan continued. "We all know you thought about becoming a minister."

Harden just shook his head and kept walking. Surely to God, Evan was a case. That assumption irritated him, but he wouldn't lower himself enough to deny it.

"No comment?" Evan asked.

"No comment," Harden said pleasantly. "Let's go. The crowd's already gathering."

Despite Harden's preoccupation with Miranda, the workshop went well. He had a dry wit, which he used to his advantage to keep the audience's attention while he lectured on the combinations of maternal and carcass breeds that had been so successful back home. Profit was the bottom line in any cattle operation, and the strains he was using in a limited cross-breeding had proven themselves financially.

But his position on hormone implants wasn't popular, and had resulted in some hot exchanges with other cattlemen. Cattle at the Tremayne ranch weren't implanted, and Harden was fervently against the artificial means of beef growth.

"Damn it, it's like using steroids on a human," he argued with the older cattleman. "And we still don't know the long-range effects of consumption of implanted cattle on human beings!"

"You're talking a hell of a financial loss, all the same!" the other argued hotly. "Damn it, man, I'm operating in the red already! Those implants you're against are the only thing keeping me in business. More weight means more money. That's how it is!"

"And what about the countries that won't import American beef because of the implants?" Harden shot back. "What about moral responsibility for what may prove to be a dangerous and unwarranted risk to public health?"

"We're already getting heat for the pesticides we use leaching into the water table," a deep, familiar voice interrupted. "And I won't go into environmentalists claiming grazing is responsible for global warming or the animal rights people who think branding our cattle is cruel, or the government bailing out the dairy industry by dumping their tough, used-up cows on the market with our prime beef!''

That did it. Before Harden could open his mouth, his workshop was shot to hell. He gave up trying to call for order and sat down to drink his coffee.

Evan sat back down beside him, grinning. ''Saved your beans, didn't I, pard?'' he asked.

Harden gestured toward the crowd. ''What about theirs?'' he asked, indicating two cattlemen who were shoving each other and red in the face.

''Their problem, not mine. I just didn't want to have to save you from a lynch mob. Couldn't you be a little less opinionated?''

Harden shrugged. ''Not my way.''

''So I noticed.'' Evan stood up. ''Well, we might as well go and eat lunch. When we come back we can worry about how to dispose of the carnage.'' He grimaced as a blow was struck nearby.

Harden pursed his lips, his blue eyes narrowing amusedly. ''And leave just when things are getting interesting?''

''No.'' Evan stood in front of him. ''Now, look here...''

It didn't work. Harden walked around him and right into a furious big fist. He returned the punch with a hard laugh and waded right into the melee. Evan sighed. He took off his Stetson and his jacket, rolled up the sleeves of his white cotton shirt and loosened his tie. There was such a thing as family unity.

Later, after the police came and spoiled all the fun,

Harden and Evan had a quiet lunch in their suite while they patched up the cuts.

"We could have been arrested," Evan muttered between bites of his sandwiches.

"No kidding." Harden swallowed down the last of his coffee and poured another cup from the carafe. He had a bruise on one cheek and another, with a cut, lower on his jaw. Evan had fared almost as badly. Of course, the competition downstairs looked much worse.

"You had a change of clothes," Evan muttered, brushing at blood spots on his white shirt. "I have to fly home like this."

"The stewardesses will be fascinated by you. You'll probably have to turn down dates all the way home."

Evan brightened. "Think so?"

"You look wounded and macho," Harden agreed. "Aren't women supposed to love that?"

"I'm not sure. I lost my perspective when they started carrying guns and bodybuilding. I think the ideal these days is a man who can cook and do housework and likes baby-sitting." He shuddered. "Kids scare me to death!"

"They wouldn't if they were your own."

Evan sighed, and his dark eyes had a faraway look. "I'm too old to start a family."

"My God, you're barely thirty-four!"

"Anyway, I'd have to get married first. Nobody wants me."

"You scare women," Harden replied. "You're the

original clown. All smiles and wit. Then something upsets you and you lose your temper and throw somebody over a fence.''

Evan's dark eyes narrowed, the real man showing through the facade as he remembered what had prompted that incident. ''That yellow-bellied so-and-so put a quirt to my new filly and beat her bloody. He's damned lucky I didn't catch him until he got off the property in his truck.''

''Any of us would have felt that way,'' Harden agreed. ''But you're not exactly what you seem to be. I may scare people, but I'm always the same. You're not.''

Evan dropped his gaze to his coffee, the smile gone. ''I got used to fighting when I was a kid. I had to take care of the rest of you, always picking on guys twice your size.''

''I know.'' Harden smiled involuntarily at the memories. ''Don't think we didn't appreciate it, either.''

Evan looked up. ''But once I put a man in the hospital, remember? Never realized I'd hit him that hard. I haven't liked to fight since.''

''That was an accident,'' Harden reminded him. ''He fell the wrong way and hit his head. It could have happened to anyone.''

''I guess. But my size encourages people to try me. Funny thing, it seems to intimidate women.'' He shrugged. ''I guess I'll be a bachelor for life.''

Harden opened his mouth to correct that impression, but the phone rang and claimed his attention.

He picked it up and answered, listening with an amused face.

"Sure. I'll be down in ten minutes."

He hung up. "Imagine that. They want me to do another hour. My audience has been bragging that this was the best workshop they'd ever attended. Not boring, you see."

Evan burst out laughing. "Well, you owe that to me."

Harden glared at him. "You can only come back if you promise to keep your mouth shut."

"Bull. You enjoyed it." He stretched hugely. "Anyway, it got your mind off the woman, didn't it?"

Harden was actually lost for words. He just stared at the bigger man.

"It's the timing, isn't it?" Evan asked seriously. "She's newly widowed and you think she's too susceptible. But if she was in that kind of condition, she sure as hell needs someone."

"It's still the wrong time," he replied quietly.

Evan shrugged. "No harm in keeping the door open until it is the right time, is there?" he asked with a grin.

Harden thought about what Evan had said for the rest of the afternoon, even after the other man had caught his flight back to Jacobsville. No, there wouldn't really be any harm in keeping his door open. But was it what he wanted? A woman like Miranda wasn't fit for ranch life, even if he went crazy and got serious about her. She was a city girl from Chicago with a terrible tragedy to put behind her. He was a loner who hated city life and was carrying around his own scars. It would never work.

But his noble thoughts didn't spare his body the anguish of remembering how it had been with Miranda that morning, how fiercely his ardor had affected both of them. All that silky softness against him, her warm, sweet mouth begging for his, her arms holding fast. He groaned aloud as he pictured that slender body naked on white sheets. As explosive as the passion between them was, a night with her would surpass his wildest dreams of ecstasy, he knew it would.

It was the thought of afterward that disturbed him. He might not be able to let her go. That was what stopped him when he placed his hand hesitantly over the telephone and thought about finding her number in the directory and calling her. Once he'd known her intimately, would he be capable of walking away? He stared at the telephone for a long time before he turned away from it and went to bed. No, he told himself. He'd been right in the first place. The timing was all wrong, not only for Miranda, but for himself. He wasn't ready for any kind of commitment.

Miranda was thinking the same thing, back at her own apartment house. But she had the number of the Carlton Arms under her nervous fingers. She stared at it while she sat on her sofa in the lonely apartment, and she wanted so badly to phone, to ask for Harden Tremayne, to...

To what? she asked herself. She knew she'd already been enough trouble to him. But she'd just finished giving her baby furniture to a charity group, and she was sick and depressed. Even though she wasn't in love with Tim anymore, she grieved for the child she was carrying. It would have been so wonderful to have a baby of her own to love and care for.

None of which was Harden's problem. He'd been reluctantly kind, as he would have been to anybody in trouble. He'd said as much. But she was remembering the way they'd kissed each other, and the heat of passion that she'd never felt with anyone else. It made her so hungry. She'd expected love and forever from marriage. She'd had neither. Even sex, so mysterious and complicated, hadn't been the wonderful experience she'd expected. It had been painful at first, and then just unpleasant. Bells didn't ring and the earth didn't move. In fact, she was only just able to admit to herself that she'd never felt any kind of physical attraction to Tim. She'd briefly imagined herself in love with him, but he'd been a stranger when they married. As she lived with him, she began to see the real man under the brash outgoing reporter, and it was a person she didn't like very much. He was selfish and demanding and totally insensitive.

Harden didn't seem to be that kind of man at all. He was caring, even if he was scary and cold on the surface. Underneath, he was a smoldering volcano of emotion and she wanted to dig deeper, to see how consuming a fire they could create together. With him, intimacy would be a wondrous thing. She knew it. Probably he did, too, but he was keeping his distance tonight. Either he wasn't interested or he thought it was too soon after her loss.

He was right. It was too soon. She crumpled the piece of paper where she'd written the number of the hotel. She was still grieving and much too vulnerable for a quick love affair, which was probably all he'd be able to offer her. He'd said he was a loner and he didn't seem in any hurry to marry. He'd been all too eager to get away from her, in fact. She put the paper in the trash can. It was just as well. She'd managed to get through work today without breaking down, and she'd manage the rest of her life the same way. It wasn't really fair to involve another person in the mess her mind was in.

She put on her nightgown and climbed under the covers. Finally she slept.

Chapter Four

Harden slept badly. When he woke, he only retained images of the torrid dreams that had made him so restless. But a vivid picture of Miranda danced in front of his eyes.

He was due to go home today. The thought, so pleasantly entertained two days before, was unpalatable today. Texas was a long way from Illinois. He probably wouldn't see Miranda again.

He dragged himself out of bed, hitching up the navy-blue pajama trousers that hung low on his narrow hips. He rubbed a careless hand over his broad, hair-matted chest and stared out the window, scowling. Ridiculous, what he was thinking. There were responsibilities at home, and he'd already told himself how impossible it was to entertain ideas about her.

Impossible. He repeated the word even as he

turned and picked up the telephone directory. He didn't know Miranda's maiden name, which made phoning her brother to ask where she worked out of the question. His only chance was to call her apartment and catch her before she left.

He found Tim Warren's name in the new directory and dialed the number before he could change his mind.

It rang once. Twice. Three times. He glanced at his watch on the bedside table. Eight o'clock. Perhaps she'd left for work. It rang four times. Then five. With a long sigh, he started to hang it up. Maybe it was fate, he thought with disappointment.

Then, just as the receiver started down, her soft voice said, "Hello?"

His hand reversed in midair. "Miranda?" he asked softly.

Her breath caught audibly. "Harden!" she cried as if she couldn't believe her ears.

His chest expanded with involuntary pleasure, because she'd recognized his voice instantly. "Yes," he replied. "How are you?"

She sat down, overcome with excited pleasure. "I'm better. Much better, thank you. How are you?"

"Bruised," he murmured dryly. "My brother helped me into a free-for-all at the workshop yesterday."

"Somebody insulted Texas," she guessed.

"Not at all," he replied. "We were discussing hormone implants and the ecology at the time."

"Really?"

He laughed in spite of himself. "I'll tell you all about it over lunch."

She caught her breath. It was more than she'd dared hope for. "You want to take me to lunch?" she asked breathlessly.

"Yes."

"Oh, I'd like that," she said softly.

He didn't want to have to admit how much he'd like it himself. He put on his watch. "When should I pick you up? And where?"

"At eleven-thirty," she said. "I go early so that we won't be all out of the office at the same time. It's in the Brant building. Three blocks north of your hotel." She gave him directions and the office number. "Can you find it?"

"I'll find it."

He hung up before she had time to reply. This was stupid, he told himself. But all the same, he had a delicious feeling of anticipation. He phoned the ranch to tell them he wouldn't be home for another day or two.

His mother, Theodora, answered the phone. "Harden?" she asked. "The car won't start."

"Did you put it in park before you tried to start it?" he asked irritably.

There was a long pause. "Just because I did that once...!" she began defensively.

"Six times."

"Whatever. Well, no, actually, I guess it's in drive."

"Put it in Park and it will start. Is Donald back?"

"No, he won't be home until next week."

"Then tell Evan he'll have to manage. I'm going to be delayed for a few days."

There was another pause. "Evan's got a split lip."

"I've got a black eye. So what? You have to expect a little spirit when you get a roomful of cattlemen."

"I do wish you wouldn't encourage him to get into fights."

"For God's sake, Theodora, he started it!" he raged.

"Can't you ever call me Mother?" she asked in an unconsciously wistful tone.

"Will you give the message to Evan?" he replied stiffly.

She sighed. "Yes, I'll tell him. You wouldn't like to explain what's going on up there, I suppose?"

"There's nothing to tell."

"I see. I don't know why I keep hoping for the impossible from you, Harden," she said dully. "When I know full well that you'll never forgive me."

Her voice was sad. He felt guilty when he heard that note in her voice. Theodora was flighty, but she had a big heart and a sensitive spirit. Probably he hurt her every time he talked to her.

"Evan can reach me here at the hotel if he needs me," he said, refusing to give in to the impulse to talk—to really talk—to her.

"All right. Goodbye, Son."

She hung up and he stared at the receiver, the dial

tone loud in his ears. He'd never asked her about his father, or why she hadn't thought of an abortion when she knew she was carrying him. Certainly it would have made her life easier. He wondered why that thought occurred to him now. He put down the receiver and got dressed.

At eleven-thirty sharp, he walked into the law office where Miranda worked. He was wearing a tan suit, a subdued striped tie, a pearly Stetson and handtooled leather boots. He immediately drew the eyes of every woman in the office, and Miranda got up from her desk self-consciously. She couldn't tear her eyes away from him, either.

In her neat red-patterned rayon skirt and white blouse with a trendy scarf draped over one shoulder she looked pretty, too. Harden glared at her because she pleased his senses. This whole thing was against his will. He should be on his way home, not hanging around here with a recently widowed woman.

Miranda felt threatened by the dark scowl on his face. He looked as if he'd rather be anywhere but here, and she felt a little self-conscious herself at what amounted to a date only weeks after she was widowed. But it was only lunch, after all.

"I'll just get my purse," she murmured nervously.

"I could go with you and carry it," Janet, her coworker, volunteered in a stage whisper. She grinned at Harden, but he had eyes for no one except Miranda. He gave the other employee a look that could have frozen fire.

"Thanks, anyway," Miranda murmured when

Janet began to appear threatened. She grabbed her purse, smiled halfheartedly at the other woman, and rushed out the door.

"Does your friend always come on to men like that?" he asked as he closed the door behind her.

"Only when they look like you do," she said shyly.

He cocked an eyebrow and pulled his hat lower over his eyes. "I don't take one woman out and flirt with another one."

"I'm absolutely sure that Janet won't forget that," she assured him.

He took her arm as they got into the elevator. "What do you feel like? Hamburgers, fish, barbecue, or Chinese?"

"I like Chinese," she said at once.

"So do I." He pushed the Down button and stared at her from his lounging posture against the wall as it began to move. Her hair was done in some complicated plait down her back, but it suited her. So did the dangly silver earrings she was wearing. His eyes slid down to the dainty strappy high heels on her pretty feet and back up again.

"Will I do?" she asked uncertainly.

"Oh, you'll do," he agreed quietly. His eyes narrowed with faint anger while he searched hers. "I'm supposed to be on a one o'clock flight home."

She swallowed. "Are you?" she asked, and her face fell.

He noticed her disappointment. It had to mean that she was as fascinated by him as he was by her, but it didn't do much for his conscience. This was all wrong.

"Do you have time to take me to lunch?" she asked worriedly.

"I canceled the flight," he said then. He didn't add that he hadn't yet decided when he was going home. He didn't want to admit how drawn he was to her.

Her silver eyes went molten as they met his and she couldn't hide her pleasure.

That made it worse, somehow. "It's insane!" he said roughly. "Wrong time, wrong place."

"Then why aren't you leaving town?" she asked.

"Why didn't you say no when I asked you out to lunch?" he shot right back.

She felt, and looked, uncertain. "I couldn't," she replied hesitantly. "I...wanted to be with you."

He nodded. "That's why I'm here," he said.

The elevator stopped while they were staring at each other. His pale blue eyes glittered, but he didn't make a move toward her, even though it was killing him to keep the distance between them.

The doors opened and he escorted her out the front door, his fingers hard on her upper arm, feeling the thinness through the blouse.

"You've lost weight, haven't you?" he asked as they walked down the crowded street toward the Chinese restaurant he'd seen on the way to her building.

"A little. I've always been thin."

A small group of people came rushing past them and knocked against Miranda. Even as she lost her footing, Harden's arm was around her, pressing her against him.

"Okay?" he asked softly, his eyes watchful, concerned.

She couldn't look away from him. He hypnotized her. "Yes. I'm fine, thanks."

His fingers contracted on her waist. She was wrapping silken bonds around him. He didn't know if he liked it, but he couldn't quite resist her.

Her heart hammered crazily. He looked odd; totally out of humor, but fascinated at the same time.

In fact, he was. His own helplessness irritated him.

Neither of them moved, and he almost groaned out loud as he forced himself to turn and walk on down the street.

Miranda felt the strength in his powerful body and felt guilty for noticing it, for reacting to it. She walked beside him quietly, her thoughts tormenting her.

The restaurant wasn't crowded. Miranda settled on the day's special, while Harden indulged his passion for sweet-and-sour pork. When he reached for the hot mustard sauce for his egg roll, she shuddered.

"You aren't really going to do that, are you?" she asked. "You might vanish in a puff of smoke. Haven't you ever heard of spontaneous combustion?"

"I like Tabasco sauce on my chili," he informed her, heaping the sauce on the egg roll. "I haven't had taste buds since 1975."

"I still can't watch."

He smiled. "Suit yourself."

He ate the egg roll with evident enjoyment while she sipped more hot tea. When he finished she stared at him openly.

"I'm waiting for you to explode," she explained when his eyebrows lifted in a question. "I think that stuff is really rocket fuel."

He chuckled. It had been a long time since he'd felt like laughing. It surprised him that Miranda was the catalyst, with all the grief she'd suffered so recently. He searched her eyes curiously as a new thought occurred to him.

"You forget when you're with me, don't you?" he asked. "That's why you came back to the hotel night before last instead of insisting that I take you home."

She stared at him. Finally she nodded. "I stop brooding when I'm around you. I don't understand why, really," she added with a quiet sigh. "But you make it all go away."

He didn't reply. He stared down at his cup with eyes that hardly saw it. She attracted him. He'd thought it was mutual. But apparently he was only a balm for her grief, and that disturbed him. He should have followed his instincts and gone home this morning.

"Did I even say thank you?" she asked.

"You said it." He finished his tea and studied her over the rim of the small cup. "When do you have to be back?"

She glanced at the big face of his watch. "At one-thirty." She hesitated. "I guess you think I'm only using you, to put what happened out of my mind," she said suddenly. "But I'm not. I enjoy being with you. I don't feel so alone anymore."

She might have read his mind. The tension in him relaxed a little. He finished his tea. "In that case, we'll go the park and feed the pigeons."

Her face lit up. That would mean a few more precious minutes in his company. It also meant that he wasn't angry with her.

"No need to ask if you'd like to," he murmured dryly. "Finish your tea, little one."

She drained the cup obediently and got up, waiting for him to join her.

They strolled through the park overlooking the lake. The wind was blowing, as it always did, and she enjoyed the feel of it in her hair. He bought popcorn from a vendor and they sat on a bench facing the water, tossing the treat to the fat pigeons.

"We're probably giving them high-blood pressure, high cholesterol, and heart trouble," she observed as the birds waddled from one piece of popcorn to the next.

He leaned back on the bench, one arm over the back, and looked down at her indulgently. "Popcorn is healthier than bread. But you could ask them to stop eating it."

She laughed. "I'd be committed."

"Oh, I'd save you." He tossed another kernel to the pigeons and stared out at the lake, where sailboats were visible in the distance. "Jacobsville doesn't have a lake this size,'' he murmured. ''We have a small one on the ranch, but we're pretty landlocked back home.''

''I've gotten used to seeing the sailboats and motorboats here,'' she sighed, following his gaze. ''I can see them out the office window on a clear day.'' She tucked loose strands of hair back behind her ear. ''The wind never stops. I suppose the lake adds to it.''

''More than likely,'' he replied. ''I used to spend a good bit of time down in the Caribbean. It blows nonstop on the beach as well.''

''And out on the plains,'' she murmured, smiling as she remembered her childhood on a ranch in South Dakota. Something she hadn't told him about.

''Pretty country,'' he said. ''We had an interest in a ranch up in Montana, a few years back. It folded. Bad water. Salt leaching killed the land.''

''What kind of cattle do you raise?'' she asked.

''Purebred Santa Gertrudis mostly. But we run a cow-calf operation alongside it. That means we produce beef cattle,'' he explained.

She knew that instantly, and more. She'd grown up in ranching country and knew quite a bit about how beef was produced, but she didn't say so. It was nicer to let him explain how it worked, to sit and listen to his deep, quiet voice.

Her lunch hour was up before she realized it. She got to her feet with real reluctance. ''I have to go,'' she said miserably.

He stood up beside her, his pale blue eyes on her

downbent head. He rammed his hands into his pockets and glowered at the dejected picture she made. He knew what he had to do, though.

"I'm going home, Miranda," he said shortly.

She wasn't surprised. He'd acted as if he was here against his better judgment, and she couldn't blame him. Her conscience was beating her over the head, because it didn't feel right to be going on a date when her husband was only dead a month.

She looked up. His expression gave nothing away, but something was flickering in his eyes. "I don't know what would have happened to me if it hadn't been for you," she said. "I won't forget you."

His jaw went taut. He wouldn't forget her, either, but he couldn't put it into words.

He turned, beginning the long walk back to her office. It shouldn't have felt so painful. In recent years, there hadn't been a woman he couldn't take in his stride and walk away from. But Miranda looked lost and vulnerable.

"I'm a loner," he said irritably. "I like it that way. I don't need anyone."

"I suppose I'm not very good at being alone," she replied. "But I'll learn. I'll have to."

"You were alone before you married, weren't you?" he asked.

"Not really. I lived with Sam and Joan. Then I decided that enough was enough, so I improved myself and found Tim." She sighed wearily. "But I guess I was alone, if you stop and think about it. Even after Tim and I got married, he always had someplace to go without me. Then I got pregnant, but that wasn't meant to be.'' She felt her body tauten. It was still hard to think about the child she'd lost; about her part in its loss. She felt a minute's panic at losing Harden, now that she'd begun to depend on him. She glanced at him. "I married too quickly and I learned a hard lesson: there are worse things than your own company."

"Yes." He let his pale eyes slide down to meet hers. "You've given me a new perspective on women. I suppose there are some decent ones in the world."

She smiled sadly. "High praise, coming from you."

"Higher than you realize. I meant it. I hate women," he said curtly.

That was sad. She knew it was probably because of his mother, and she wondered if he'd ever tried to understand how his mother had felt. If he'd never loved, how could he?

"You've been very kind to me."

"I'm not a kind man, as a rule. You bring out a side of me I haven't seen before."

She smiled. "I'm glad."

"I'm not sure I am," he said. "Will you be all right?"

"Yes. I've got Sam and Joan, you know. And the worst of it is over now. I'll grieve longer for the baby than I will for Tim, I'm afraid."

"You're young. There can be other babies."

Her eyes turned wistful. "Can there? I'm not so sure."

"You'll marry again. Don't give up on life because you had some hard knocks. We all have them. But we survive."

"I never found out what yours were," she reminded him.

He shrugged. "It does no good to talk about them." He stopped in front of her office building. "Take care of yourself, Miranda."

She looked up at him with quiet regret. He was a very special man, and she was a better person for having known him at all. She wondered how different her life would have been if she'd met him before Tim. He was everything Tim hadn't been. He was the kind of man a woman would do anything for. But he was out of her reach already. It made her sad.

"I will. You, too." She sighed. "Goodbye, Harden."

He searched her eyes for a long minute, until her body began to throb. "Goodbye."

He turned and walked away. She watched him helplessly, feeling more lost and alone than ever before.

Harden was feeling something similar. It should have been easy to end something that had never really begun, but it wasn't. She'd looked so vulnerable when he'd left her. Her face haunted him already, and he was only a few yards away.

If only his mind would stop remembering the softness of Miranda's silver eyes, looking up at him so trustingly. He'd never had a woman lean on him before. He was surprised to find that he liked it. He felt himself hesitating.

His steps slowed. He muttered a harsh curse as he turned. Sure enough, Miranda was still standing there, looking lost. He felt himself walking back to her without understanding how it happened. A minute later, he was towering over her, seeing his own helpless relief mirrored in her soft gray eyes.

Her eyes searched his in the silence that followed.

"What time do you get off—five?" he asked tersely.

She could hardly get the word out. "Yes."

He nodded. "I'll pick you up."

"The traffic is terrible…"

He glared at her. "So what?"

She reached out and touched his arm. "You came back."

"Don't think I wanted to," he told her flatly. "But I can't seem to help myself. Go to work. We'll find some exotic place for supper."

"I can cook," she volunteered. "You could come to my apartment."

"And let you spend half the night in the kitchen after you've worked all day?" he asked. He shook his head. "No way."

"Are you sure?"

He smiled faintly. "No. But we'll manage. I'll be out front when you get off. Are you usually on time?"

"Always," she said. "The boss is a stickler for

promptness, even when it comes to getting off from work.'' She stared up at him for a long moment, ignoring passers-by, her heart singing. "Oh, I'm glad you stayed!'' she said softly.

"Even if it was against my better instincts?''

"Will it help if I tell you that you might have saved my sanity, if not my life?'' she replied.

He studied her for a long moment. "It will help. I'll see you later.''

He watched her go inside the building, his face still taut with reluctant need. It surprised him that he could feel at all, when his emotions had lived in limbo for so long.

After he left her, he spent the rest of the day getting acquainted with the city. It was big and busy and much like any other city, but he enjoyed the huge modern sculptures and the ethnic restaurants and the museums. He felt like any tourist by the time he'd showered and changed and gone back to pick up Miranda.

She was breathless when she got to him in the lobby.

"I ran all the way,'' she panted, holding on to the sleeves of his gray suit coat as she fought for breath. "We were late today, of all days!''

He smiled faintly. "I would have waited.''

"I guess I knew that, but I hurried, all the same.''

He escorted her to the car and put her inside. "I found a Polynesian place. Ever had poi?''

"Not yet. That sounds adventurous. But I really would like to change first...''

"No problem." He remembered without being told where her apartment was. He drove her there, finding a parking spot near the house—a miracle in itself, she told him brightly.

He waited in the living room while she changed. His curiosity got the best of him and he browsed through her bookshelf and stared around, learning about her. She liked biographies, especially those that dealt with the late nineteenth century out West. She had craft books and plenty of specific works on various Plains Indian tribes. There were music books, too, and he looked around instinctively for an instrument, but he didn't find one.

She came out, still hurriedly fastening a pearl necklace over the simple black sheath dress she was wearing with strappy high heels. Her hair was loose, but neatly brushed, hanging over her shoulders like black silk.

"Is this all right?" she asked. "I haven't been out much. Tim liked casual places. If I'm overdressed, I can change, but you're wearing a suit and I thought—!"

He moved close to her during the rush of words and quietly laid his thumb square over her pretty lips, halting them.

"You look fine," he said. "There's no reason to be nervous."

"Isn't there?" she asked, forcing a smile. "I'm all thumbs. I feel as if I'm eighteen again." The smile faded. "I shouldn't be doing this. My husband has only been dead a few weeks, and I lost my baby. I shouldn't go out, I should still be in mourning," she stammered, trying to make sense of what was happening to her.

"We both know that," he agreed. "It doesn't help very much."

"No," she replied with a sad smile.

He sighed heavily. "I can go back to my hotel and pack," he said, "or we can go out to dinner, which is the best solution. If it helps, think of us as two lonely people helping each other through a bad time."

"Are you lonely, Harden?" she asked.

He drew in a slow breath and his hand touched her hair very lightly. "Yes, I'm lonely," he said harshly. "I've never been any other way."

"Always on the outside looking in," she murmured, watching his face tauten. "Yes, I know how it feels, because in spite of Sam and Joan, that's how it was with me. I thought Tim would make it all come right, but he only made things worse. He wanted what I couldn't give him."

"This?" he asked, and slowly, slowly, traced around the firm, full curve of her mouth, watching her lips part and follow his finger helplessly. She reacted to him instantly. It made his head spin with delicious sensations.

She caught his wrist, staying his hand. "Please," she whispered, swallowing hard. "Don't."

"Does it make you feel guilty to let me pleasure you?" he asked quietly. "It isn't something I offer very often. I meant what I said, I detest women, as a rule.''

"I guess I do feel guilty," she admitted. "I was driving and two lives were lost." Her voice broke. "It was *my* fault...!"

He drew her to him and enveloped her in his hard arms, holding her while the tears fell. "Give yourself time. Desperation won't solve the problem or stop the pain. You have to be kind to yourself."

"I hate myself!"

His lips brushed her temple. "Miranda, everyone has a secret shame, a searing guilt. It's part of being human. Believe me, you can get through the pain if you just think past it. Think ahead. Find something to look forward to, even if it's just a movie or eating at a special restaurant or a holiday. You can survive anything if you have something to look forward to."

"Does it work?"

"It got me through my own rough time," he replied.

She drew back, brushing at her tear-streaked cheeks. "Want to tell me what it was?" she asked with a watery smile.

He smiled back, gently. "No."

She sighed. "You're a very private person, aren't you?"

"I think that's a trait we share." He drew back, pulling her upright with him. The neckline of her dress was high and very demure and he lifted an eyebrow at it.

"I dress like a middle-aged woman, isn't that what you're thinking?" she muttered.

He laughed out loud. "I'm afraid so. Don't you have something a little more modern in your closet?"

She shifted her shoulders. "Yes. But I can't wear low necklines because…"

He tilted her chin up. "Because…?"

She flushed a little and dropped her eyes. "I'm not exactly overendowed. I, well, I cheat a little and if I wear something low cut, you can tell."

He pursed his lips and dropped his eyes to her bodice. "Now you've intrigued me."

She moved a little away from him, feeling shy and naive. "Hadn't we better go?"

He smiled. "Nervous of me, Miranda?"

"I imagine most women are," she said seriously, searching his hard face. "You're intimidating."

"I'll try not to intimidate you too much," he promised, and held the door open for her. As she passed him on the way out, he wondered how long he could contain his desire for her without doing something irrevocable.

Chapter Five

For the next few days, Harden tried not to think about the reasons he shouldn't be with Miranda. She was in his blood, a sweet fever that he couldn't cure. The more he tried to resist her, the more his mind tormented him. Eventually, he gave in to it, because there was nothing else he could do.

Work was piling up back at home because he wasn't there to help Evan. His mind was anywhere except on the job these days. More and more, his waking and sleeping hours were filled with the sight of Miranda's lovely face.

He hated his obsession with her. He was a confirmed bachelor, well able to resist a pretty face. Why couldn't he escape this one? Her figure was really nothing spectacular. She was pretty, but so were plenty of other women. No, it was her nature that drew him; her sweet, gentle nature that gave more than it asked. She enveloped him like a soft web, and fighting it only entangled him deeper.

During the past few days, they'd been inseparable. They went out to dinner almost every night. He took her dancing, and last night they'd gone bowling. He hadn't done that in years. It felt unfamiliar to be throwing balls down alleys, and when he scored, Miranda was as enthusiastic as if she'd done it herself.

She laughed. She played. He was fascinated by the way she came out of her shell when she was with him, even if he did get frequent and disturbing glimpses of the anguish in her silver eyes.

He didn't touch her. That was one luxury he wouldn't allow himself. They were too explosive physically, as he'd found out the morning he'd taken her home from the hotel. Instead, they talked. He learned more about her, and told her more about himself than he'd shared with anyone else. It was a time of discovery, of exploration. It was a time between worlds, and it had to end soon.

"You're brooding again," she remarked as he walked her to her door. They'd been out to eat, again, and he'd been preoccupied all night.

"I've got to go back," he said reluctantly. He looked down at her with a dark frown. "I can't stay any longer."

She turned and unlocked her door slowly, without glancing his way. She'd expected it. It shouldn't have surprised her.

"I'm a working man, damn it," he said shortly.

"I can't spend my life wandering around Chicago while you're in your office!"

She did look at him then, with soft, sad eyes. "I know, Harden," she said softly.

He shoved his hands into his pockets. "Can you write a letter?"

She hesitated. "A letter? Well, yes…I've never had anybody to write to, of course," she added.

"You can write to me," he said, his voice terse with impatience and irritation. "It isn't the same as having time to spend together, but it's better than phone calls. I can't talk on the phone. I can never think of anything to say."

"Me, too," she said, smiling up at him. Her heart raced. He had to be interested if he was willing to keep in touch. It lifted her spirits.

"Don't expect a letter a day," he cautioned her. "I'm not that good at it."

"I don't have your mailing address," she said.

"Get me a piece of paper. I'll write it down for you."

He followed her into the apartment and waited while she produced a pad and pen. He scribbled the ranch's box number and zip code in a bold, black scrawl and gave it to her.

"This is mine," she said, taking the pad and writing down her own address. She put the pad aside and looked up at him. "You've made life bearable for me. I wish I could do something that nice for you."

His teeth clenched. He let his eyes run down the length of the black strappy dress she was wearing to long legs encased in nylon and sling-back pumps with rhinestone buckles. His gaze came back up to her loosened dark hair and her soft oval face and her trusting silver eyes.

"You could, if you wanted to," he said huskily.

She swallowed. Here it was. She hadn't mistaken his desire for her, and now he was going to ask something that she didn't know if she could give.

"Harden...I...I don't like intimacy," she said nervously.

His eyebrows arched. He hadn't expected her to be so blunt. "I wasn't going to ask you to come to bed with me," he murmured dryly. "Even I have more finesse than that."

She took a steadying breath. "Oh."

"But while we're on the subject," he said, pushing the door shut behind him, "why don't you like intimacy?"

"It's unpleasant," she said flatly.

"Painful?" he probed.

She put her purse on a table and traced patterns on it, without looking at him. Harsh memories flooded into her mind. "Only once," she said hesitantly. "I mean unsatisfying, I guess. Embarrassing and unsatisfying. I never liked it."

He paused behind her, his lean hands catching her waist and turning her, so that she faced him.

"Did he arouse you properly before he took you?" he asked matter-of-factly.

She gasped. Her wide eyes met his as if she couldn't believe what he'd said.

He shrugged. "I don't find it uncomfortable to talk about. Neither should you, at your age."

"I haven't ever talked about it, though," she stammered.

"Your brother is a doctor," he pointed out.

"But, my goodness, Sam is worse than I am," she exclaimed. "He can't even say the word sex in front of people. He's a very repressed man. Straitlaced, isn't that the word? And Joan is a dear, but you can't talk to her about...intimacy."

"Then talk to me about it," he replied. "That first morning, when I kissed you, you weren't afraid of being intimate with me, were you?"

She nibbled her lower lip. "No," she said, her face flaming.

"Was it like that with your husband?"

She hesitated. Then she shook her head.

"There's a chemistry between people sometimes," he said, watching her face. "An explosive need that pulls them together. I haven't felt it often, and never quite like this. I gather that you've never felt it at all before."

"That's...fairly accurate."

He tucked his hand under her chin and lifted her shy eyes to his. "Sex, in order to be good, has to have that explosive quality. That, and a few other ingredients—like respect, trust, and emotional involvement. It's an elusive combination that most people never find. They settle for what they can get."

"Like I did, you mean," she said.

He nodded. "Like you did." He lifted one lean

hand to her face and very lightly traced her mouth, watching it part, watching her breathing change suddenly. "Feel it?" he asked softly. "That tightening in your body when I touch your mouth, the way your breath catches and your pulse races?"

"Yes." She swallowed. "Harden, do you feel it?"

"To the soles of my feet," he replied. He bent and lifted her, very gently, in his arms, his eyes on her face. "Let me make love to you. Set any limits you like."

The temptation made her heart race. She dropped her eyes to his thin mouth and wanted it beyond bearing. "Don't...don't make me pregnant," she whispered. "I don't have anything to use."

His body shuddered. It humbled him that she'd let him go that far. "I don't have anything to use, either, so we can't go all the way together," he said unsteadily. "Does that reassure you?"

"Yes."

He moved toward the bedroom, and stopped when he noticed her eyes darting nervously to the bed.

"He made love to you there," he said suddenly, his eyes blazing as he guessed the reason for her hesitation. He looked down into her face. "Was it always there?"

"Yes," she whispered.

"How about on the sofa?"

Her body tensed with anticipated pleasure. "No."

He whirled on his heel and carried her to the long, cushy sofa. He put her down on it and stood looking at the length of her with eyes that made her body move restlessly.

She felt uneasy. He was probably used to women who were voluptuous and perfectly figured, and she had plenty of inhibitions about her body that Tim had given her. The padded bra had been his idea, because he never thought she was adequate.

Harden saw the hesitation in Miranda's big eyes and wondered at it. He unfastened his tie and tossed it into the chair beside the sofa. His jacket followed. He held her eyes while his hand slowly unbuttoned the white shirt under it, revealing the breadth and strength of his hair-matted chest. He liked the way Miranda's eyes lingered on his torso, the helpless delight in them.

"Do you like what you see?" he asked arrogantly.

"Can't you tell?" she whispered.

He sat down beside her, his hand sliding under her back to find the zipper of her dress. "We'll compare notes."

But her hands caught his arms as she realized what he was going to do. All her insecurities flamed on her face.

He frowned. And then he remembered. His thin mouth pulled into a soft, secretive smile. "Ah, I see. The padded bra," he whispered.

She blushed scarlet, but he only laughed. It wasn't a cruel laugh, either. It was as if he was going to share some delicious secret with her, and wanted her to enjoy it, too.

His hand slowly pulled the zipper down. He ignored the nervous hands trying to stop him. "Will it help if I tell you that size only matters to adolescent boys who never grow up?" he asked softly.

"Tim said…"

"I'm not Tim," he whispered as his mouth gently covered hers.

She felt the very texture of his lips as he brushed them lightly over and around hers. He caught her top lip between his teeth and touched it with his tongue, as if he were savoring the taste of the delicate inner flesh. Her breath stopped in her throat because it was very arousing.

And meanwhile, he was sliding the dress off her shoulders, along with her bra straps.

"You…mustn't," she protested just once.

He hesitated as the dress slid to the upper curves of her firm breasts. "Why?" he asked softly, his lips touching her mouth as he spoke.

"It's…it's too soon," she said, her voice sounding panicky.

"No, that's not the reason," he murmured. He lifted his head and searched her silver eyes. "You think I'll be disappointed when I look at you." He smiled. "You're beautiful, Miranda, and you have a heart as big as all outdoors. The size of your breasts isn't going to matter to me."

The color came into her cheeks again. Even Tim had never said anything so intimate to her.

"So innocent," he said solemnly, all the humor gone. "He didn't leave fingerprints, did he? But I promise you, I will." His hands moved, drawing the fabric away from her firm, high breasts, and he looked down at them with masculine appreciation.

She didn't even breathe. Her heart was racing madly, and she felt her nipples become hard under that silent, intent scrutiny. She might be small, but he wasn't looking at her as if he minded. His eyes were finding every difference in color, in texture, sketching her with the absorption of an artist.

"Sometimes I think God must be an artist," he said, echoing her silent thoughts. "The way He creates perfection with just the right form and mix of colors, the beauty of His compositions. I get breathless looking at a sunset. But I get more breathless looking at you." His eyes finally lifted to hers. "Why are you self-conscious about your size?"

"I..." She cleared her throat. Incredible, to be lying here naked from the waist up and listening to a man talk about her breasts! "Well, Tim said I was too little."

He smiled gently. "Did he?"

He seemed to find that amusing. His hands moved again, and this time she did protest, but he bent and gently brushed her eyelids shut with his mouth as he eased the rest of the fabric down her body. In seconds, he had her totally undressed.

He lifted his head then and looked at her, his eyes soft and quiet as she lay trembling, helpless.

"I won't even touch you," he whispered. "Don't be embarrassed."

"But...I've *never*—!" she stammered.

"Not even in front of your husband?" he asked.

"He didn't like looking at me," she managed unsteadily.

He sighed softly, his eyes on her breasts, the curve of her waist, her flat belly and the shadow of her womanhood that led to long, elegant legs. "Miranda, I fear for the sanity of any man who wouldn't like looking at you," he said finally. "I swear to God, you knock the breath right out of me!"

Her eyes fell in shocked delight, and landed on a point south of his belt that spoke volumes. She gasped audibly and averted her gaze to his chest.

"I've always tried to hide that reaction with other women," he said frankly. "But I don't mind very much if you see it. I want you very badly. I'm not ashamed of it, even if it is the wrong time. Look at me, Miranda. I don't think you've ever really looked at a man in this condition."

His tone coaxed her eyes back to his body, but she lifted her gaze a little too quickly and he smiled.

"Doesn't it make you uncomfortable?" she blurted out.

"What? Letting you look, or being this way?"

"Both."

He touched her mouth with a lean forefinger. "I'm enjoying every second of it."

"So am I," she whispered as if it were a guilty secret.

"Will you let me touch you?" he asked softly, searching her eyes. "It has to be because you want it. In this, I won't do anything that even hints of force or coercion."

Her head was whirling. She looked at him and fires kindled in her body. She wanted to know what it felt like to have his hands on her, to feel pleasure.

"Will I like it?" she whispered.

He smiled gently. "Oh, I think so," he murmured.

He bent, and very lightly brushed his lips over one firm breast, his teeth grazing the nipple.

She gasped and shivered. "You...didn't tell me you were going to do that!" she exclaimed, her silver eyes like saucers.

He lifted his head and searched them. "Didn't I?" He smiled again. "Is it all right?"

Having him ask her that made her go boneless. Tim had always taken, demanded, hurt her. The funny thing was that she'd thought it would be like pleading if a man asked first, but Harden looked impossibly arrogant and it didn't sound anything like pleading. Her whole body trembled with shocked pleasure.

"Yes," she whispered. "It's all right."

"In that case..."

His lean hands lifted her body in an arch so that his lips could settle and feed on her soft breasts. She couldn't believe what was happening to her. She'd never felt pleasure before. What she'd thought was desire had been nothing more than infatuation, and this was the stark reality. It was hot and sharp-edged and totally overwhelming. She was helpless as she'd never been, living only through the hard mouth that was teaching her body its most sensitive areas, through the hands that were so gently controlling her.

Her hands were in his thick, dark hair and his mouth was suddenly on hers, forcing her lips apart with a tender ferocity that made her totally his.

"Don't panic," he whispered.

She didn't understand until she felt him touch her in a way that even Tim never had. She cried out and arched, her body going rigid.

Harden looked down at her, but he didn't stop, even when he felt her hands fighting him. "Just this, sweetheart," he whispered, watching her eyes. "Just this. Let it happen. It won't hurt."

She couldn't stop. It was like going over a cliff. She responded because it was impossible not to, her face taut with panic, her eyes wild with it. She was enjoying it, and she couldn't even pretend not to. He watched her face, smiling when she began to whimper, feeling her responses, feeling her pleasure. When it spiraled up suddenly and arched her silky body, when she wept and twisted and then cried out, convulsing, he felt as if he'd experienced everything life had to offer.

He cradled her in his arms while she cried, his lips gentle on her closed eyes, sipping away the tears.

"Amazing, what a man can do when he sets his mind to it," he whispered against her mouth. "I'm glad to see that my instincts haven't worn out. Although I've read about that, I've never done it before."

Her eyes flew open. She was still trembling, but through the afterglow of satisfaction, she could see the muted pleasure in his eyes.

"Never?" she exclaimed.

"Why are you shocked?" he asked. "I'm no play-boy. Women are still pretty much a mystery to me. Less so now," he added with a wicked gleam in his eyes.

She blushed and hid her face in his throat. His hair-roughened chest brushed her breasts and she stiffened at the pleasurable sensations that kindled in her. Involuntarily she pressed closer, pushing her hard nipples into the thick hair so that they brushed his skin.

He went taut against her. "No," he whispered.

He sounded threatened, and she liked his sudden vulnerability. He'd seen her helpless. She wanted to see him the same way. She brushed against him, drawing her breasts sensually across his broad chest until she felt him shudder. His big hands caught her arms and tightened, but he didn't try to make her move away.

"Here." He lifted her, so that she sat over his taut body, facing him, and then his hands bruised her hips and pulled her closer, so that the force of his arousal was blatant against her soft belly. He wrapped her up, crushing her breasts into his chest, and sat rocking her hungrily.

"Harden," she whispered.

His jaw clenched. He was losing it. "Touch me, sweetheart."

Her hands smoothed over his chest.

"No," he ground out. "Touch me where I'm a man."

She hesitated. His mouth whispered over her closed eyes. He caught one of her hands and slowly smoothed it down over his flat stomach, his breath catching when he pressed it gently to him.

Her heart ran away with her. She'd never touched Tim like that. The intimate feel of Harden's body made her throb all over. She liked touching him. But when he began to slide the zipper down, she jerked her fingers away and buried her hot face in his throat.

"You're right," he said roughly, fastening it back. "I'm letting it go too far. Much too far."

He eased her away and got up, his tall body shivering a little with residual desire as he fumbled a cigarette out of his pocket and lit it. "Put your things back on, little one," he said huskily.

She stared at him with her black dress in her hands. "You don't want me to," she whispered.

His eyes closed. "My God, no, I don't want you to," he ground out. He turned, his face rigid with unsated passion, his body blatant with it. "I want to bury myself inside you!"

She trembled at the stark need. Her lips parted helplessly. "I...I'd let you," she said fervently.

His gaze dropped to her breasts and beyond it, to her flat belly. She'd had a baby there. She'd lost the baby and her husband, and he shouldn't be doing this to her. He shouldn't be taking advantage of her vulnerability.

He closed his eyes again and turned away. "Miranda, you aren't capable of making that kind of decision right now. It's too soon."

Too soon. Too soon. She came back to herself all at once. This was the apartment she'd shared with Tim. She'd been pregnant. She'd lost control of the car and killed her husband and her unborn child. And only minutes before, she'd been begging another man to make love to her.

She dragged the black dress over her head and fumbled the zipper up, her face white with reaction. She bundled up the rest of her things and pushed them down beside the sofa cushion, because she was shaking too hard to put them on. What had she done!

Harden had fastened his shirt and put his tie and jacket in place by the time she dressed.

He looked down at her with quiet, somber eyes in a face as hard as stone. "I won't apologize. It was too sweet for words. But it's too soon for lovemaking."

She couldn't meet his eyes. "But, we did…"

"I pleasured you," he replied quietly. "By lovemaking, I mean sex. If I stay around here much longer, you'll give yourself to me."

"You make me sound like a terrible weakling." She laughed mirthlessly.

He knelt just in front of her, his hands beside her hips on the sofa. "Miranda, it isn't a weakness or a sin to want someone. But you've got a tragedy to work through. By staying here, I'm only postponing your need to put it behind you, not to mention clouding your grief with desire. I want you, baby," he said huskily, his eyes fierce as they met hers. "I want you just as desperately as you want me, but you've got to be sure it's not just misplaced grief or a crutch. Sex is serious business to me. I don't sleep around, ever.''

She wanted to ask him if he ever had. He seemed very experienced, but he didn't sound as if sex was a minor amusement to him. He might be even more innocent than she was, and that made her feel less embarrassed about what she'd let him do.

She searched his face. ''Harden, I might not have acted like it, but it's serious business to me, too. Tim was the only man I ever slept with.''

''I know.'' He caught her hand and held the soft palm to his mouth hungrily. ''But he never satisfied you, did he?''

She swallowed. Finally she gave in to that blatant stare. ''Not like you did, no.'' She hesitated.

''You want to ask me something,'' he guessed from that odd look. ''Go ahead. What is it?''

''Would it feel like that if I gave myself to you? If we went all the way?'' she asked slowly.

His fingers clenched on hers. ''I think it might be even more intense,'' he said gruffly. ''Watching you almost sent me over the edge myself.''

She reached out and touched his face, adoring the strength of it under her cool fingers. ''You…had nothing,'' she exclaimed belatedly.

He only smiled. ''Don't you believe it,'' he said with a deep, somber look in his pale blue eyes. ''And now, I've got to go. I've put it off as long as I can.''

He got to his feet. Miranda let him pull her up and her heart was in her eyes as she gazed up at him.

"I'll miss you more than ever, now," she confessed.

He sighed. "I'll miss you, too, little one," he said curtly. "Write to me. I'm as close as the telephone, if you just want to talk. You'll get through this, Miranda. All you need is a little time."

"I know. You made it so much easier, though."

He brushed his fingers through her unruly hair and tilted her face up to his hungry eyes. "It isn't goodbye. Just so long, for a while."

She nodded. "Okay. So long, then."

He bent and kissed her, so tenderly that she almost cried. "Be good."

"I can't be anything else. You won't be here. Harden," she said as he opened the door.

He looked back, his eyebrow arching in a question.

"Just remember," she said with forced humor. "You saved my life. Now you're responsible for it."

He smiled gently. "I won't forget."

He didn't say goodbye. He gave her one long, last look and went out the door, closing it gently behind him. He hadn't really saved her life, she knew, because she hadn't meant to jump off the bridge. But it made her feel good to think that she owed it to him, that he cared enough to worry about her.

She had his address, and she'd write. Maybe when she was through the natural grieving process, he'd come back, and she'd have a second chance at happiness. She closed her eyes, savoring the intimacy she'd shared with him. She wondered how she was going to live until she saw him again.

Chapter Six

Harden was grumpy when he got home. Not that anybody noticed, because he was *always* grumpy. His irritation didn't improve, either, when his brother Connal showed up.

"Oh, God, no, here he comes again!" Evan groaned when the car pulled up just as he and Harden were coming down the steps.

"That's no way to talk about your brother," Harden chided.

"Just wait," the bigger man said curtly.

"I can't stand it!" Connal greeted them, throwing up his hands. "We get all the way to the hospital, I make all the necessary phone calls, and they say it's false labor! Her water hasn't even broken!"

Evan and Harden exchanged glances.

"He needs help," Evan said. "Broken water?"

"You wouldn't understand," Connal said heavily,

his lean, dark face worn and haggard. "I've just left her sleeping long enough to ask Mother to come back with me. Pepi needs a woman around right now."

"We'll starve," Evan said miserably.

"No, you won't," Harden muttered. "We have a cook, remember."

"Mother tells Jeanie May what to cook. You'd better worry, too," Evan said shortly. "Even if you don't live here, you're always around when the food goes on the table."

"Don't you two start, I've got enough problems," Connal muttered darkly.

Evan's eyebrows arched. "Don't look at me. You're the one who made Pepi pregnant.

"I wanted children. So did she."

"Then stop muttering and go home."

Connal glared at the bigger man. "Your day will come," he assured Evan. "You'll be walking the streets dreading your own Waterloo in the delivery room, wait and see!"

Evan's face clouded. His usual carefree expression went into eclipse. "Will I?" he asked on a hard laugh. "Don't bet on it."

Connal started to question that look, but Harden stepped in.

"Theodora's in the study looking up something about how to repair bathrooms," he said.

"The plumber will love that," Connal said knowingly. "Don't worry, I'll have her out of here before she bursts another pipe."

"Last one flooded the back hall," Evan recalled.

"I opened the door and almost got swept down to the south forty."

"She's got no business trying to fix things. My God, she had a flat tire on the wheelbarrow!" Harden exclaimed.

"Takes talent," Evan agreed. "But don't keep her too long, will you? She takes my side against him," he jerked a thumb at Harden.

"That's nothing new," Harden said, lighting a cigarette. "She knows how I feel about her."

"One day you'll regret that," Connal said. It wasn't something he usually mentioned, but Harden's attitude was getting to him. Part of the reason he'd come for Theodora was that he'd noticed her increasing depression since Harden had come home from his unexplained stay in Chicago.

"Tell Pepi we asked about her," Harden said easily, refusing to rise to the bait.

"I'll do that."

Connal asked about Donald, who was away again with his wife, and after a minute he said goodbye and went into the house, leaving Harden and Evan to go about their business.

Harden climbed behind the wheel before his brother could protest.

"I'm not riding with you," he told Evan flatly. "Your foot's too heavy."

"I like speed," Evan said bluntly.

"Lately, you like it too much." Harden glanced at him and away. "You haven't been yourself since that girl you were dating broke up with you."

Evan's face set and he glanced out the window without speaking.

"I'm sorry," he told Evan. "I'm sorry as hell. But there has to be a woman for you somewhere."

"I'm thirty-four," Evan said quietly. "It's too late. You used to talk about being a minister. Maybe I should consider it myself."

"A minister isn't necessarily celibate," his brother replied. "You're thinking of a priest. You aren't Catholic," he added.

"No, I'm not. I'm the giant in Jack and the Beanstalk," he said wearily. He put his hat back on. "I'm sorry I don't smoke," he murmured, eyeing Harden's smoke. "It might keep me as cool as it seems to keep you."

"I'm not cool." Harden stared out the windshield. "I've got problems of my own."

"Miranda?" Evan asked slowly.

Harden stiffened. His dreams haunted him with the images of Miranda as she'd let him see her that last night at her apartment. The taste of her mouth, the exquisite softness of her body made him shiver with pleasure even in memory. He missed her like hell, but he had to be patient.

He glanced at Evan. He sighed, then, letting it all out. Evan was the only human being alive he could talk to. "Yes."

"You came home."

"I had to. She's so damned vulnerable. I could never be sure it was me she wanted and not a way to avoid coping with the grief."

"Do you want her?"

Harden took a draw from the cigarette and turned his head. His eyes were blazing as the memories washed over him. "Like I want to breathe," he said.

"What are you going to do?"

The broad shoulders lifted and fell. "I don't know. I'll write to her, I guess. Maybe I'll fly to Chicago now and again. Until she's completely over her grief, I don't dare push too hard. I don't want half a woman."

"Strange," Evan said quietly, "thinking about you with a woman."

"It happens to us all sooner or later, didn't Connal say?"

Evan smiled. "Well, Miranda's a dish. When you finally decide to get involved, you sure pick a winner."

"It's more than the way she looks," came the reply. "She's...different."

"*The* woman usually is," Evan said, his dark eyes sad in his broad face. "Or so they say."

"You'll find out yourself one day, old son."

"Think so? I can hope, I suppose."

"What we both need is a diversion."

Evan brightened. "Great. Let's go to town and wreck a bar."

"Just because you hate alcohol is no reason to do a Carrie Nation on some defenseless bar," his brother told him firmly.

Evan shrugged. "Okay, I'm easy. Let's go to town and wreck a coffee shop."

Harden chuckled softly. "Not until my eye heals completely," he said, touching the yellowish bruise over his cheekbone.

"Spoilsport. Well, I guess we can go to the hardware store and order that butane we need to heat the branding irons."

"That's better."

Harden got his first letter from Miranda the very next day. It didn't smell of perfume, and it was in a perfectly respectable white envelope instead of a colorful one, but it was newsy and warm.

She mentioned that she'd had dinner with her brother and sister-in-law twice, and that she'd started going to their church—a Baptist church—with them on Sunday. He smiled, wondering if he'd influenced her. She wasn't a Baptist, but he was; a deacon in his local church, where he also sang in the choir. She missed seeing him, her letter concluded, and she hoped that he could make time to write her once in a while.

She was going to be shocked, he decided as he pulled up the chair to his desk and started the word processing program on his computer. He wrote several pages, about the new bulls they'd bought and the hopes he had for the crossbreeding program he'd spoken about at the conference in Chicago. When he finished, he chuckled at his own unfamiliar verbosity. Of course, reading over what he'd written, he discovered that it was a totally impersonal letter. There was nothing warm about it.

He frowned, fingering the paper after he'd printed
it out. Well, he couldn't very well say that he missed
her like hell and wished he was still in Chicago. That
would be overdoing it. With a shrug, he signed the
letter with a flourish and sealed it before he could
change his mind. Personal touches weren't his style.
She'd just have to get used to that.

Miranda was so thrilled when she opened the letter
two days later that she didn't at first notice the impersonal style of it. It was only after the excitement
subsided that she realized he might have been writing
it to a stranger.

Consequently she began to wonder if he was really
interested in her, or if he was trying to find a way of
letting her down, now that they were so far apart.
She remembered how sweet it had been in his arms,
but that had only been desire on his part. She knew
men could fool themselves into thinking they cared
about a woman when it was only their glands getting
involved. She'd given Harden plenty of license with
her body, and it still made her uneasy that she'd been
that intimate with him so soon after Tim and the
baby. Her own glands were giving her fits, because
she couldn't stop remembering how much pleasure
Harden had given her. She missed him until it was
like being cut in half. But this letter he'd written to
her didn't sound like he was missing her. Not at all.

She sat down that night as she watched television
and tried to write the same sort of note back. If he
wanted to play it cool, she'd do her best to follow

his lead. She couldn't let him know how badly she wanted to be with him, or make him feel guilty for the physical closeness they'd shared. She had to keep things light, or she might inadvertently chase him away. She couldn't bear that. If he wanted impersonal letters, then that's what he'd get. She pushed her sadness to the back of her mind and began to write.

From there, it all began to go downhill. Harden frowned over her reply and his own was terse and brief. Maybe she was regretting their time together. Maybe grief had fed her guilt and she wanted him to end it. Maybe what they'd done together was wearing on her conscience and she only wanted to forget. He'd known he was rushing her. Why hadn't he taken more time?

Once he was back at his apartment in Houston, he was putting things into prospective. There was no future with someone like Miranda, after all. She was a city girl. She'd never fit into ranching. He had his eye on a small ranch near Jacobsville and he'd already put a deposit on it. The house wasn't much. He was having it renovated, but even then it wouldn't be a showplace. It was a working ranch, and it would look like one. Miranda would probably hate the hardship of living on the land, even if he did make good money at it.

He stared out his window at the city lights. The office building where the family's corporate offices were located was visible in the distance among the glittering lights of downtown Houston. He sighed wearily, smoking a cigarette. It had been better when he'd kept to himself and brooded over Theodora's indiscretion.

For the first time, he allowed himself to wonder if his mother had felt for his father the way he felt with Miranda. If her heart had fallen victim to a passion it couldn't resist. If she'd loved his father so much that she couldn't refuse him anything, especially a child.

He thought about the child Miranda had lost, and wondered how it would be to give her another, to watch her grow big with it. He remembered her soft cries of pleasure, the look of utter completion on her face. His teeth ground together.

He turned away from the window angrily. Miranda wrote him the kind of letter his brothers might, so how could he imagine she cared? She was closing doors between them. She didn't want him. If she did, why hadn't her later letter been as sweet and warm as that first one?

The more he thought about that, the angrier he got. Days turned to weeks, and before he realized it, three months had passed. He was still writing to Miranda, against his better judgment, but their letters were impersonal and brief. He'd all but stopped writing in the past two weeks. Then a client in Chicago asked Evan to fly up and talk to him.

Evan found an excuse not to go. Connal, a brand-new father with a baby boy to play with, was back on the ranch he and Pepi's father owned in West Texas. Donald and Jo Ann were just back from overseas, and Harden's youngest brother said flatly that he wasn't going anywhere for months—he and Jo Ann had had their fill of traveling.

"Looks like you're elected," Evan told Harden with a grin. "Call it fate."

Harden looked hunted. He paced the office. "I need to stay here."

"You need to go," Evan said quietly. "It hasn't gotten better, you know. You look terrible. You've lost weight, and you're working yourself to death. She's had time to get herself back together. Go and see if the magic's still there."

"She writes me business letters. She's probably dating somebody else by now."

"Go find out."

Harden moved irritably. The temptation was irresistible. The thought of seeing Miranda again made him feel warm. He studied the older man. "I guess I might as well."

"I'll handle things here. Have a good trip."

Harden heard those words over and over. He deliberately put off calling Miranda. He met the client, settled his business, and had lunch. He went to a movie. Then, at five, he happened to walk past her office building just about time for her to come out.

He stood by a traffic sign, Western looking in a pale gray suit with black boots and Stetson, a cigarette in his hand. He got curious, interested looks from several attractive women, but he ignored them. He only had eyes for one woman these days, even if he wasn't sure exactly how he felt about her.

A siren distracted him and when he glanced back, Miranda was coming out of the entrance, her dark hair around her shoulders, wearing a pale green striped dress that made his temperature soar. Her long legs were encased in hose, her pretty feet in strappy high heels. She looked young and pretty, even if she was just as thin as she'd been when he left her.

She was fumbling in her purse for something, so she didn't look up until he was standing directly in her path.

Her expression told him everything he wanted to know. It went from shock to disbelief to utter delight in seconds, her huge silvery eyes like saucers as they met his.

"Harden!" she whispered joyously.

"No need to ask if you're glad to see me," he murmured dryly. "Hello, Miranda."

"When did you get here? How long can you stay? Do you have time to get a cup of coffee with me...!"

He touched his forefinger to her soft mouth with a smile, oblivious to onlookers and pedestrians and motorists that sped past them. "I'll answer all those questions later. I'm parked over here. Let's go."

"I was fumbling for change for the bus," she stammered, red-faced and shaken by his unexpected appearance. Her eyes adored him. "I didn't have it. Have you been here long?"

"A few minutes. I got in this morning." He looked down at her. "You're still thin, but you have a bit more color than you did. Is it getting easier?"

"Yes," she said, nodding. "It's amazing what time can accomplish. I think I have things in perspective now. I'm still sad about the baby, but I'm getting over it."

He paused at his rented Lincoln and opened the passenger door for her. "I'm glad."

She waited until he got in beside her and started the car before she spoke. "I didn't know if I'd see you again," she confessed. "Your letters got shorter and shorter."

"So did yours," he said, and his deep voice sounded vaguely accusing.

"I thought maybe my first one made you uncomfortable," she confessed with a smile. "I sort of used yours as a pattern."

He smiled, too, because that explained everything. Now he understood what she'd done, and why.

"I don't know how to write a letter to a woman," he said after a minute, when he'd pulled into traffic and was negotiating lanes. "That was the first time I ever had."

Her face brightened. "I didn't know."

He shrugged. "No reason you should."

"How long can you stay?"

"I had to see a client," he replied. "I did that this morning."

"Then, you're on your way home. I see," she said quietly. She twisted her purse on her lap and stared out at traffic. Disappointment lined her face, but she didn't let him see. "Well, I'm glad you stopped by, anyway. It was a nice surprise."

He cocked an eyebrow. Either she was transparent, or he was learning to read her very well. "Can't wait to get rid of me, can you?" he mused. "I had thought about staying until tomorrow, at least."

Her face turned toward his, and her eyes brightened. "Were you? I could cook supper."

"I might let you, this time," he said. "I don't want to waste the whole evening in a restaurant."

"Do you need to go back to your hotel first?" she asked.

"What for? I'm wearing the only suit I brought with me, and I've got my wallet in my pocket."

She laughed. "Then we can just go straight home."

He remembered where her apartment house was without any difficulty. He parked the car as close to it as he could get, locked it, and escorted her inside.

While she was changing into jeans and a pink knit top, he wandered around her living room. Nothing had changed, except that there were more books. He picked up one of the paperbacks on the table beside the couch and smiled at her taste. Detective stories and romance novels.

"I like Erle Stanley Gardner," he remarked when she was busy in the kitchen.

"So do I," she told him, smiling over her shoulder as she put coffee on to perk. "And I'm crazy about Sherlock Holmes—on the educational channel, you know."

"I watch that myself."

He perched himself on a stool in front of her

breakfast bar and folded his arms on it to study her trim figure as she worked. She produced an ashtray for him, but as she put it down, he caught her waist and pulled her between his legs.

"Kiss me," he said quietly, holding her gaze. "It's been a long, dry spell."

"You haven't been kissed in three months?" she stammered, a little nervous of the proximity.

He smiled. "I hate women, remember? Kiss me, before you start on the steak."

She smiled jerkily. "All right." She leaned foreward, closed her eyes, and brushed her mouth softly against his.

His lean hand tangled in her long hair and held her there, taking over, parting her lips, deepening the kiss. His breath caught at the intensity of it, like a lightning bolt in the silence of the kitchen.

"It isn't enough," he said tersely, drawing back just long enough to crush out his cigarette. Both arms slid around her and brought her intimately close, so that her belly was against his, her face on an unnerving level with his glittery blue eyes. "I've missed you, woman," he whispered roughly.

His mouth met hers with enough force to push her head back against his hand. He was rough because he was starved for her, and it was a mutual thing. She hesitated only for a second before her arms went around his neck and she pressed close with a soft moan, loving the warm strength of his body as she was enveloped against it. She could hear his breath sighing out as his mouth grew harder on hers, bruising her lips, pushing them apart to give him total access to their moist inner softness.

All at once, his tongue pushed past her lips and into her mouth, and a sensation like liquid fire burst in her stomach. It was as intimate as lovemaking. She felt her whole body begin to throb as he tasted her in a quick, hard rhythm. She made a sound she'd never heard from her throat in her life and shuddered as she moved closer to him, her legs trembling against his.

"Yes," he breathed unsteadily into her mouth. "Yes, sweetheart, like...that...!"

He stood up, taking her with him, one lean hand dropping to her hips to grind them into his own. She stiffened at his fierce arousal, but he ignored her instinctive withdrawal.

"It's all right," he whispered. "Relax. Just relax. I won't hurt you."

His voice had the oddest effect on her. The struggle went out of her all at once, and she gave in to him with an unsteady sigh. Her hands pressed gently into his shirt front and lingered there while the kiss went on and on and she felt a slight tremor in his own powerful legs.

He lifted his head finally and looked down at her, breathing unsteadily, fighting to control what he felt for her.

His hands at her waist tightened and the helpless, submissive look on her soft face pushed him over the edge. "Is there anything cooking that won't keep for a few minutes, Miranda?" he asked quietly.

She swallowed. "No. But..."

He bent and lifted her gently into his arms and carried her out of the kitchen. "Don't be afraid, little one," he said quietly.

"Harden, I don't...I'm still not using anything," she stammered.

He didn't look at her as he walked into her bedroom. "We won't make love."

Her lips parted. They felt sore and they tasted of him when she touched them with her tongue. He laid her down on the bed and stood looking at her for a long moment before he sat down beside her and bent to take her mouth softly under his once again.

The look in his eyes fascinated her. It was desire mingled with irritation and something darker, something far less identifiable. His gaze fell to the unsteady rise and fall of the knit top she was wearing and his hand moved to smooth down her shoulder to her collarbone.

"No bra tonight?" he asked bluntly, meeting her eyes.

She flushed. "I..."

He put a long forefinger on her lips. "What we do together is between you and me," he said solemnly. "Not even my own brothers know anything about my personal life. I want very badly to touch you again, Miranda. I think you want it just as much. If you do, there isn't really any reason we can't indulge each other."

She searched his eyes quietly. "I couldn't sleep,

for dreaming about how it was between us, last time," she whispered.

"Neither could I," he replied. His hands moved to her waist and brought her into a sitting position. Gently he removed the pink knit top and put it aside, letting his eyes adore her pink and mauve nudity. He smiled when her nipples went hard under the scrutiny.

Her hands touched his lean cheeks hesitantly and she shivered as she drew his face toward her, arching her back to show him what she wanted most.

"Here?" he whispered, obliging her.

She drew in her breath as his mouth opened over her breast, taking almost all of one inside. The faint suction made her tremble, made her nails bite into the shoulders of his suit jacket.

"Too…many clothes, Harden," she whispered.

He lifted his head and pressed a soft kiss on her mouth before he stood up. "Yes. Far too many."

He watched her while he removed everything above his belt, enjoying the way her eyes sketched over him.

"Harden," she began shyly, her eyes falling to the wide silver belt.

"No," he said, reading the question in her eyes. He sat down beside her and drew her gently across his lap, moving her breasts into the thick mat of hair over his chest. "If I take anything else off, we'll be lovers."

"Don't you want to?" she asked breathlessly.

"Yes," he said simply. "But it's still too soon for

that.'' He looked down where her pale body was
pressed to his darkly tanned one. ''I want you to
come home with me, Miranda.''

Chapter Seven

Miranda didn't believe at first that she'd heard him. She stared at him blankly. "What?"

He met her eyes. "I want you to come home with me," he said, shocking himself as much as he was obviously shocking her. "I want more than this," he added, dragging her breasts sensually against his bare chest. "As sweet as it is, I want to get to know all of you, not just your body."

"But...my job," she began.

"I have in mind asking you to marry me, once we've gotten used to each other a little more," he said then, driving the point home. "And don't look so shocked. You know as well as I do that we're going to wind up in bed together. It's inevitable. I'm no more liberated than you are, so we have to do something. Either we get married, or we stop seeing each other altogether. That being the case, you have to come home with me."

"And stay...with you?" she echoed.

"With Theodora. My mother," he clarified it. "I'm buying a place in Jacobsville, but it isn't ready to move into. Even if it was," he added with a rueful smile, "things aren't done that way in Jacobsville. You'd stay with Theodora anyway, to keep everything aboveboard. Or didn't I mention that I was a deacon in our Baptist church?"

"No," she stammered. "You didn't."

"I thought about being a minister once," he murmured, searching her rapt eyes. "But I didn't feel called to it, and that makes the difference. I still feel uncomfortable with so-called modern attitudes. Holding you like this is one thing. Sleeping with you— my conscience isn't going to allow that."

"I was married," she began.

"Yes. But not to me." He smiled gently, looking down to the blatant thrust of her soft breasts with their hard tips brushing against his chest. "And it didn't feel like this, did it?"

"No," she admitted, going breathless when he brushed her body lazily against his. "Oh, no, it didn't feel anything like this!" She pressed even closer, gripping his shoulders tightly. "But you say you hate women. How are you going to manage to marry me?"

"I didn't say I hated you," he replied. His hands tangled in her hair and raised her face to his quiet eyes. "I've never wanted anyone like this," he said simply. "All I've done since I left Chicago is brood over you. I haven't looked at another woman in all that time.''

She drew back a little, tingling with pleasure when the action drew his eyes immediately to her breasts. She didn't try to hide them this time.

After a minute, he lifted his eyes to hers and searched them, reading with pinpoint accuracy the pride and pleasure there. "You like it, don't you?" he asked quietly. "You like my eyes on you."

"Yes," she said hesitantly.

"Shame isn't something you should feel with me," he told her. "Not ever. I know too much about you to think you're easy."

She smiled then. "Thank you."

His lean hands smoothed down to her waist, and he shook his head. "I can't imagine being able to do this anytime I please, do you know that?" he said unexpectedly. "I've never had...anyone of my own before." It surprised him to realize that it was true. He'd thought he had, once, but it had been more illusion than reality and he was only discovering it.

"Actually, neither have I," she said. Her eyes ran over his hair-roughened chest down to the ripple of his stomach muscles above his belt and back to the width of his shoulders and his upper arms. "I love to look at you," she said huskily.

"It's mutual." His fingers brushed over the taut curve of one breast, tracing it lovingly. "Don't you *ever* put on a padded bra again," he said shortly, meeting her eyes. "Do you hear me, Miranda?"

She laughed breathlessly. "Yes."

He laughed, too, at his own vehemence. "Too small. My God. Maybe he was shortsighted." He stood up, drawing her with him, his eyes eloquent on her body. "I don't suppose you'd like to cook supper like that…" He sighed heavily.

"Harden!"

"Well, I like looking at you," he said irritably. "Touching you." His fingers brushed over her breasts lovingly, so that she gasped. "Kissing you…"

He bent, caressing her with his mouth until she began to burn. Somehow, they were back on the bed again, and his mouth was on her breasts, his hands adoring her while he brushed her silky skin with his lips.

"It won't…be enough," she moaned.

"My God, I know that," he said unsteadily.

He moved, easing his body over hers so that she could feel his arousal, his eyes holding hers as he caught his weight on his forearms and pressed his hips into hers.

"You'd let me, right now, wouldn't you?" he asked roughly.

"Yes." She let her hands learn the rigid muscles of his back, delighting in the slight roughness of his skin.

His mouth bent to hers and nibbled at her lower lip. "This is really stupid."

"I don't care. I belong to you."

He shuddered. The words went through him with incredible impact. He actually gasped.

"Well, I do," she whispered defensively. Her mouth opened under his. "Lift up, Harden."

He obeyed the soft whisper, feeling her hands suddenly between them. His shocked eyes met hers while she worked at the fastening of his belt. "My God, no!" he burst out. He caught her hand and rolled onto his back, shivering.

She sat up, her eyes curious. "No?"

"You don't understand," he ground out.

Her soft eyes searched his face, seeing the restraint that was almost gone. "Oh. You mean that if I touch you that way, the same thing will happen to you that happened to me when...when you did it?"

"Yes." His cheeks went ruddy. He stared at her with desire and irritation and pain mingling. "I can't let you do that."

"Why?" she asked quietly.

"Call it an overdose of male pride," he muttered, and threw his long legs off the side of the bed. "Or a vicious hang-up. Call it whatever the hell you like, but I can't let you."

She watched him get to his feet and come around the bed, his eyes slow and quiet on her bare breasts as she sat watching him. "I let you," she pointed out.

"You're a woman." He drew in a jerky breath. "My God, you're all woman," he said huskily. "We'll set the bed on fire our first time."

She flushed. "You're avoiding the issue."

"Sure I am." He pulled her up, grabbed her knit top, and abruptly helped her back into it. "I'm an old-fashioned man with dozens of hang-ups—like being nude in front of a woman, like allowing myself to be satisfied with a woman seeing me helpless, like… Well, you get the idea, don't you?'' he asked curtly. He shouldered into his shirt and caught her hand, tugging her along with him. "Feed me. I'm starving."

Her head whirled with the things she was learning about him as he led her into the kitchen. He was the most fascinating man she'd ever known. But she was beginning to wonder just how experienced he was. He didn't act like a ladies' man, even if he kissed like one.

The memory of the baby still nagged at the back of her mind. She was sorry about Tim, too, but as she went over and over the night of the wreck, she began to realize that no one could have done more than she had. She was an experienced driver, and a careful one. And Tim had been drinking. She couldn't have allowed him behind the wheel. The roads were slick, another car pulled out in front of her without warning, and she reacted instinctively, but a fraction of a second too late. It was fate. It had to be.

He watched her toy with her salad. "Brooding?" he asked gently.

She lifted her gray eyes to his and pushed back a long strand of disheveled dark hair. "Not really. I was thinking about the accident. I've been punishing myself for months, but the police said it was unavoidable, that there was nothing I could have done. They'd know, wouldn't they?"

"Yes," he told her gently. "They'd know."

"Tim wasn't good to me. All the same, I hate it that he died in such a way," she said sadly. "I regret losing my baby."

"I'll give you a baby," he said huskily, his pale eyes glittering with possession.

She looked up, surprised, straight into his face, and saw something that she didn't begin to understand. "You want children?" she asked softly.

His eyes fell to her breasts and back up to her mouth. "We're both dark haired. Your eyes are gray and mine are blue, and I'm darker skinned than you are. They'll probably favor both of us."

Her face brightened. "You...want a child with me?" she whispered.

He wondered about that wide-eyed delight. He knew she was still grieving for her child. If he could give her another one, it might help her to get over it. Even if she didn't love him, she might find some affection for him after the baby came. If he could get her pregnant. He knew that some men were sterile, and he'd never been tested. He didn't want to think about that possibility. He had to assume he could give her a child, for his own peace of mind. She was so terribly vulnerable. He found himself driven to protect her, to give her anything she needed to keep going.

"Yes," he said solemnly. "I want a child with you."

She beamed. Her eyes softened to the palest silver as they searched his hard face.

"But not right away," he said firmly. "First, you and I are going to do some serious socializing, get to know each other. There are a lot of hurdles we have to jump before we find a minister."

Meaning her marriage and her loss, she assumed. She managed a smile. "All right. Whatever you say, Harden."

He smiled back. Things were going better than he'd ever expected.

Miranda was nervous when he drove from the airport back to the Tremayne ranch. She barely heard what he said about the town and the landmarks they passed. His mother was an unknown quantity and she was half afraid of the first meeting. She'd seen Evan, his eldest brother, at the hotel, so he wouldn't be a stranger. But there were two other brothers, and both of them were married. She was all but holding her breath as Harden pulled the car onto the ranch road and eventually stopped in front of a white, two-story clapboard house.

"Don't fidget," Harden scolded gently, approving her white sundress with its colorful belt and her sexy high-heel sandals. "You look pretty and nobody here is going to savage you. All right?"

"All right," she said, but her eyes were troubled when he helped her out of the car.

Theodora Tremayne was hiding in the living room, peeking out of the curtains with Evan.

"He's brought a woman with him!" she burst out. "He's tormented me for years for what happened, first about his real father and then about that...that girl he loved." She closed her eyes. "He threatened once to bring me a prostitute, to get even, and that's what he's doing right now, isn't he, Evan? He's going to get even with me by bringing a woman of the streets into my home!"

Evan was too shocked to speak. By the time he finally realized that his mother knew nothing about Miranda, it was too late. He could even understand why she'd made such an assumption, because he'd heard Harden make the threat. Miranda was a city girl, and she dressed like one, with sophistication and style. Theodora, with her country background, could easily mistake a woman she didn't know for something she wasn't.

The front door opened and Miranda was marched into the living room by Harden.

"Miranda, this is my mother, Theodora," he said arrogantly, and without a word of greeting, which only cemented Theodora's horrified assumption.

Miranda stared at the small, dark woman who stood with clenched hands at her waist.

"It's...very nice to meet you," Miranda said, her voice shaking a little, because the older woman hadn't said a word or cracked a smile yet. She looked intimidating and furiously angry. Miranda's face flushed as she recognized the blatant hostility without understanding what had triggered it. "Harden's been kind to me..."

"I'll bet he has," Theodora said with uncharacteristic venom in her voice.

Miranda wasn't used to cruelty. She didn't quite know how to handle it. She swallowed down tears. "I...I guess I really should go, Harden," she blurted out, flushing violently as she met Harden's furious eyes. "I..."

"What kind of welcome is this?" he asked his mother.

"What kind did you expect?" Theodora countered, her eyes flashing. "This is a low-down thing to do to me, Harden."

"To you?" he growled. "How do you think Miranda feels?"

"I don't remember extending any invitations," Theodora replied stiffly.

Miranda was ready to get under the carpet. "Please, let's go," she appealed to Harden, almost frantic to leave.

"You just got here," Evan said shortly. "Come in and sit down, for God's sake."

But Miranda wouldn't budge. Her eyes pleaded with Harden.

He understood without a word being spoken. "All right, little one," he said gently. His hand slid down to take hers in a gesture of quiet comfort. "I'm sorry about this. We'll go."

"Nice to...to have met you," Miranda stammered, ready to run for it.

Harden was furious, and looked it. "Her husband was killed in a car wreck a few months back," he told his mother, watching her face stiffen with surprise. "She lost the baby she was carrying at the same time. I've been seeing her in Chicago, and I wanted her to visit Jacobsville. But considering the reception she just got, I don't imagine she'll miss the introductions."

He turned, his fingers caressing Miranda's, while Evan fumed and Theodora fought tears.

"Oh, no! No, please…!" Theodora spoke in a rush, embarrassed at her unkindness. The younger woman looked as if she'd been whipped, and despite Harden's lack of courtesy in telling her about this visit, she couldn't take it out on an innocent person. It was her own fault that she'd leaped to conclusions.

"I really have to go home," Miranda replied, her red face saying far more than the words. "My job…!"

Harden cursed under his breath. He brought her roughly to his side and held her there, his eyes protective as they went from her bowed head to his mother's tormented face.

"I asked Miranda down here to let her get to know my family and see if she likes it around here," he said with a cold smile. "Because if she does, I'm going to marry her. We can accomplish that without imposing on your hospitality," he told Theodora. "I'm sure the local motel has two rooms to spare."

Miranda looked up into Harden's face. "Don't," she said softly. "Please, don't. I shouldn't have come. Take me to the airport, please. I was wrong to come."

"No, you weren't," Evan said curtly. He glared at Theodora and then at Harden. "Look at her, damn it! Look what you're doing to her!"

Two pairs of eyes saw Miranda's white face, her huge, tragic eyes with their unnatural brightness.

"Evan's right," Theodora said with as much dignity as she could gather. "I'm sorry, Miranda. This isn't your fight."

"Which is why she's leaving," Harden added. He drew Miranda against him and turned her, gently maneuvering her out the door and back to the car.

"Where are you going?" Theodora asked miserably.

"Chicago," Harden said without breaking stride.

"She hasn't met Donald and Jo Ann, or Connal and Pepi," Evan remarked from the porch. He stuck his big hands into his pockets. "Not to mention that she hasn't had time to say hello to the bulls in the barn or learn to ride a horse, or especially, to get to know me. God knows, I'm the flower of the family."

Harden raised his eyebrows. "You?"

Evan glowered at him. "Me. I'm the eldest. After I was born, the rest of you were just an afterthought. You can't improve on perfection."

Miranda managed a smile at the banter. Evan was kind.

Theodora came down the steps and paused in front of her son and the other woman. "I've done this badly, and I'm sorry. You're very welcome in my home, Miranda. I'd like you to stay."

Miranda hesitated, looking up at Harden uncertainly.

"You'll never get to see all my sterling qualities if you leave now," Evan said.

She smiled involuntarily.

"And I just baked a chocolate cake," Theodora added with an unsteady smile. "And made a pot of coffee. You probably didn't have much to eat on the plane."

"We didn't," Miranda confessed. "I was too nervous to eat."

"Not without cause, either, it seems," Harden said with a glare at his mother.

"Cut it out, or we'll go for a walk behind the barn," Evan said with a smile that didn't touch his dark eyes. "Remember the last one?"

"You lost a tooth," Harden said.

"I was thinking about your broken nose," came the easy reply.

"You can't fight," Theodora told them. "Miranda probably already thinks she's been landed in a brawl. We should be able to be civil to each other if we try."

"For a few days, anyway," Evan agreed. "Don't worry, honey, I'll protect you from them," he said in a stage whisper.

She did laugh, then, at the wicked smile on his broad face. She clung to Harden's hand and went back into the house.

Theodora was less brittle after they'd had coffee,

but it wasn't until Evan took Harden off to see some new cattle that she really warmed up.

"I'm sorry about all his," she told Miranda earnestly. "Harden…likes to make things difficult for me, you see. I didn't know you were coming with him."

Miranda paled. "He didn't tell you?!"

Theodora grimaced. "Oh, dear. You didn't know, did you? I feel even worse now." She didn't, couldn't add, that she'd thought Miranda was a woman of the streets. That tragic young face was wounded enough without adding insult to injury.

"I'm so sorry…I can get a room in the motel," she began almost frantically.

Theodora laid a gentle hand on her arm. "Don't. Now that Donald and Jo Ann have their own home, like Connal and Pepi, I never have much female company. I'll enjoy having someone to talk to." She studied Miranda's wan face. "Harden's never brought a woman home."

"He feels sorry for me," Miranda said bluntly. "And he wants me." Her thin shoulders rose and fell. "I don't know why he wants to marry me, really, but he's relentless, isn't he? I was on the plane before I knew it."

Theodora smiled. "Yes, he's relentless. And he can be cruel." She drew in a steadying breath. "I can't pretend that he doesn't have a reason for that. I…had an affair. Harden was the result."

"Yes, I know." She replied, her voice gentle. "He told me."

Theodora's eyes widened. "That's a first! I don't think he's ever told anyone else."

"I suppose he isn't on his guard so much with me," Miranda said. "You see, I haven't had much spirit since the accident."

"It must have been terrible for you. You loved your husband?" she asked.

"I was fond of him," Miranda corrected. "And sorry that he had to die the way he did. It's my baby that I miss the most. I wanted him so much!"

"I lost two," Theodora said quietly. "I understand. Time will help."

Miranda's eyes narrowed as she looked at the older woman. "Forgive me, but it's more than just the circumstances of Harden's birth between the two of you, isn't it?" she asked very gently. "There's something more..."

Theodora caught her breath. "You're very perceptive, my dear. Yes, there is something more."

"I don't mean to pry," Miranda said when Theodora hesitated.

"No. It's your right to know. I'm not sure that Harden would ever talk about it." She leaned forward. "There was a girl. They were very much in love, but her parents disapproved. They had planned to elope and get married." Theodora's eyes went dull and sad with the memory. "She called here one night, frantic, begging to speak to Harden." She grimaced. "He'd gone to bed, and I thought they'd had a quarrel or something and it could wait until morning. Harden and I have never been really close, so I knew nothing of their plans to elope, or even that he was honestly in love with her. She seemed to be forever calling at bad times. I was trying to finish up in the kitchen because it was late, and I was tired. I lied. I told her that he didn't want to talk to her at the moment, and I hung up.''

Miranda frowned slightly, not understanding.

Theodora looked up. ''Her parents had found out about the elopement and were making arrangements to send her to a school in Switzerland to get her away from Harden. I can only guess that having Harden refuse to speak to her, as I made it sound, was the last straw. She walked out onto the second-story balcony of her house and jumped off, to the stone patio below. She died instantly.''

Miranda's eyes closed as she pictured how it would have been for Harden after that. He was sensitive, and deep, and to lose someone he'd loved that much because of a thoughtless phone call must have taken all the color out of his world.

''Yes, you understand, don't you?'' Theodora asked quietly. ''He stayed drunk for weeks afterward.'' She dabbed at tears. ''I've never forgiven myself, either. It was twelve years ago, but it might as well have been yesterday as far as Harden is concerned. That, added to the circumstances of his birth, has made me his worst enemy and turned him against women with a vengeance.''

''I'm sorry, for both of you,'' Miranda said. ''It can't have been an easy thing to get over.''

Theodora sipped coffee before she spoke. "As you see, Miranda, we all have our crosses," she mused.

"Yes." She picked up her own coffee cup. "Thank you for telling me."

Theodora's eyes narrowed. "Do you love him?"

The younger woman's face flushed, but she didn't look away. "With all my heart," she said. It was the first time she'd admitted it, even to herself.

"Harden is very protective of you," Theodora observed. "And he seems to be serious."

"He wants me very badly," Miranda said. "But whether or not he feels anything else, only he knows. Desire isn't enough, really."

"Love can grow out of it, though. Harden knows how to love. He's just forgotten." Theodora smiled. "Perhaps you can reeducate him."

Miranda smiled back. "Perhaps. You're sure you don't mind if I stay with you? I was serious about the motel."

"I'm very sure, Miranda." Theodora watched the young face relax, and she was glad she hadn't made the situation worse than it was.

Evan and Harden were on their way back to the house before Evan said anything about Miranda's arrival.

"I can't believe you brought her home," he murmured, grinning at his younger brother. "People will faint all over Jacobsville if you get married."

Harden shrugged. "She's young and pretty, and we get along. It's time I married someone." His eyes ran slowly around the property. "Even if there are four of us, we'll need sons to help us keep the place. I'd hate to see it cut up into subdivisions one day."

"So would I." Evan shoved his big hands into his pockets. "Mother thought you were bringing that streetwalker you threatened her with once. Not that I expect you'd know a streetwalker if you saw one," he murmured dryly, "considering your years of celibacy."

Harden let the insinuation go, as he always did, but he frowned. "You didn't tell Theodora who Miranda was?"

"I started to, but there wasn't time." His expression sobered. "You should have called first. No matter what vendettas you're conducting against Mother, you owe her a little common courtesy. Presenting her with a houseguest and no advance notice is unforgivable."

Harden, surprisingly, agreed. "Yes, I know." He broke off a twig from the low-hanging limb of one of the pecan trees as they passed through the small orchard and toyed with it. "Has Theodora ever talked about my real father?" he asked suddenly.

Chapter Eight

Evan's eyebrows shot up and he stopped walking. Harden had never once asked anything about his real father. He hadn't even wanted to know the man's name.

"What brought on that question?" he asked.

Harden frowned. "I don't know. I'm just curious. I'd like to know something about him, that's all."

"You'll have to ask Mother, then," Evan told him. "Because she's the only one who can tell you what you want to know."

He grimaced. "Wouldn't she love that?" he asked darkly.

Evan turned. "She'll die one day," he said shortly. "You're going to have to live with the way you treat her."

Harden looked dangerous for a minute, but his eyes calmed. He stared out over the land. "Yes, I know," he confessed. "But she's got some things to deal with herself."

"I have a simpler philosophy than you," Evan said quietly. "I believe that the day we die is pre-ordained. That being the case, I can accept tragedy a little better than you can. If you think Theodora played God that night, think again. You of all people should know that nobody can interfere if God wants someone to live."

Harden's heart jumped. He scowled, but he didn't speak.

"Hadn't considered that, had you?" Evan asked. "You've been so eaten up with hatred and vengeance that you haven't even thought about God's hand in life. You're the churchgoer, not me. Why don't you try living what you preach? Let's see a little for-giveness, or isn't that what your religion is supposed to be all about?"

He walked ahead of Harden to the house, leaving the other man quiet and thoughtful.

Supper that evening was boisterous. Donald and Jo Ann were live wires, vying with Evan for wise-cracks, and they made up for Harden's brooding and Theodora's discomfort.

Donald was shorter and more wiry than his broth-ers, although he had dark hair and eyes like Evan. Jo Ann was redheaded and blue-eyed, a little doll with a ready smile and a big heart. They took to Miranda at once, and she began to feel more at home by the minute, despite Harden's lack of enthusiasm for the gathering.

After the meal, Harden excused himself and went outside. He didn't ask Miranda to join him, but she did.

He glanced back at her, startled. "I thought you were having the time of your life with the family."

She smiled at his belligerence. It was uncanny, how well she understood him. He was the outsider; he didn't fit in. He was on his guard and frankly jealous of the attention she was getting from the family he pretended he wasn't a part of. She couldn't let on that she knew that, of course.

She moved to join him on the porch swing, where he was lazily smoking a cigarette.

"I like your family very much," she agreed. "But I came here because of you."

He was touched. He hadn't been wrong about her after all. She seemed to know things about him, emotionally, that he couldn't manage to share with her in words.

Hesitantly he slid his free arm around her and drew her close, loving the way she clung, her hand resting warmly over his chest while the swing creaked rhythmically on its chains.

"It's so peaceful here," she said with a sigh.

"Too peaceful for you, city girl?" he teased gently.

She started to tell him about her background, but she decided to keep her secret for a little longer. He had to want her for herself, not just because she could fit in on a ranch. She didn't want to prejudice his decision about marrying her until she was sure of his feelings.

"I travel a good deal. And I'll keep the apartment in Houston. You won't get too bored," he promised her. He stared at her dark head with new possession. "Lift your face, Miranda," he said, his voice soft and deep in the quiet. "I'm going to kiss you."

She obeyed him without conscious thought, waiting for his mouth. It was smoky from the cigarette, and still warm from the coffee he'd had with supper. But most of all, it was slow, and a little rough, and very thorough.

A soft moan broke the silence. She lifted her arms, startled by the onrush of passion that made her desperate for more of him than this.

If she felt it, so did he. The cigarette went over the banister as he lifted her across him, and the kiss went from a slow exploration to a statement of intent in seconds.

She heard him curse under his breath as he fought the buttons of her shirtwaist dress, and then his hand was on her, possessive in its caressing warmth.

"Miranda," he whispered into her mouth. His hand was faintly tremulous where it traced the swollen contours of her breast.

He lifted his head and drew the dress away from her body, but the porch was too dark to suit him. He stood up with Miranda in his arms and moved toward the settee against the wall, where the light from the living room filtered through the curtains onto the porch.

"Where are we going?" Miranda asked, dazed by the force of her own desire.

"Into the light," he said huskily, "I have to see you." He sat down with Miranda in his arms, turning her so that he could see her breasts. "I have to look at you... Yes!"

"Harden?" She barely recognized her own high-pitched voice, so shaken was she by the look on his face.

"You're beautiful, little one," he whispered, meeting her eyes. His hand moved and she shivered. His head bent to her mouth, brushing it tenderly. "Do you have any idea what you do to me?"

"The same thing you do to me, I hope," she whispered. Her body arched helplessly. "Harden," she moaned. "Someone could come out here. Oh, can't we go somewhere...?"

He caught his breath and looked around almost desperately. "Yes." He got up and buttoned her deftly back into her dress, only to catch her hand and lead her along with him. His mind was barely working at all. Nowhere in the house was safe, with that crowd. Neither was the barn, because two calving heifers were in there, being closely watched as they prepared to drop purebred calves.

His eyes found his car, and he sighed with resignation as he drew Miranda toward it. He put her inside and climbed in with her, turning her into his arms the instant the door was closed.

"Now," he breathed against her waiting mouth.

He unbuttoned the dress again and found her with his hands, and then with his mouth. Her arms clung to him, loving the newness of being with him like this, of enjoying physical intimacy. She slid her hands inside his shirt and found the hard, hair-roughened warmth of his chest, liking the way he responded to her searching touch.

"Here," he said curtly, unfastening the shirt all the way down. He gathered her to him inside it, pressing her soft breasts into the hard muscles of his chest. He lifted his head and looked down at where they touched, at the contrasts, in the light that glared out of the barn window.

He moved her away just a little, so that he could see the hard tips of her breasts barely touching him, their deep mauve dusky against his tanned skin. His forefinger touched her there, and his blue eyes lifted to her silvery ones when she gasped.

"Why do you...watch me like that?" she whispered.

"I enjoy the way you look when I touch you," he said softly. "Your eyes glow, like silver in sunlight." His gaze went to her swollen mouth, down her creamy throat to her breasts. "Your body...colors, like your cheeks, when I touch you intimately. Each time is like the first time you've known a man's love-making. That's why."

"It's the first time I ever felt like this," she replied. "It always embarrassed me with Tim. I felt...in-adequate." she searched his narrow eyes. He looked very sensuous with his shirt unbuttoned and his hair disheveled by her hands. "I've never been embarrassed with you."

"It's natural, isn't it?" he asked quietly. "Like breathing." His forefinger began to trace the hard nipple and she clutched his shirt and shuddered. "Addictive and dangerous," he whispered as his mouth hovered over hers and his touch grew more sensual, more arousing. "Like...loving..."

His mouth covered hers before she could be certain that she'd heard the word at all, and then it was too late to think. She gave him her mouth, all of her body that he wanted, abandoned and passionately in love, totally without shame.

"No, don't!" she wept frantically when he pulled back.

He stilled her hands and drew her close, rocking her against him. He was shivering, too, and his voice was strained. "I hurt, little one," he whispered. "Be still. Let me calm down."

She bit her lower lip until she almost drew blood, trembling in his arms. He whispered to her, soothed her with his voice and his hands until she calmed and lay still against him, trying to breathe.

He let out a long breath. "My God, it's been a long time since I've been that excited by a woman. A few more seconds and I couldn't have pulled back at all."

She nuzzled her face into his hot throat. "Would it be the end of the world if we went all the way?" she whispered boldly.

"No. Probably not. But as my brother Evan reminded me about something else tonight, it's time I started practicing what I preach. I want a ring on your finger before I make love to you completely."

"You're a hopeless Puritan," she murmured dryly.

"Yes, I am," he agreed. He raised his cheek from her dark hair. "And a pretty desperate one. Name a date."

She stared at him worriedly. She was sure. But it was his body that wanted her most, not his heart. "Harden, you have to be sure."

"I'm sure."

"I know how badly you want me," she began, frowning uncertainly. "But there has to be more than just that."

He didn't listen. He was looking down his nose at her with glittery blue eyes. "You can have two weeks to make up your mind."

"And, after that?" she asked slowly.

"After that, I'll pick you up, fly you down to Mexico, and you'll be married before you have time to argue about it."

"That's not fair!" she exclaimed.

"I don't feel fair," he shot back. "My God, I'm alive, really alive, for the first time in my life, and so are you. I'm not going to let you throw this away."

"But what if it's all just physical?" she groaned.

"Then it's still more than four out of five couples have. You'll get used to me. I won't pretend that it's

going to be easy, but you will. I'll never lift a hand
to you, or do anything to shame you. I won't stifle
you as a person. All I'll expect from you is fidelity.
And later, perhaps, a child.''

"I'd like to have a family," she said quietly. She
lowered her eyes. "I suppose sometimes we do get
second chances, don't we?"

He'd been thinking the same thing. His fingers
touched her cheek, smoothing down to her mouth.
"Yes. Sometimes we do, Miranda." He brushed her
lips gently with his before he rearranged their disheveled clothing and led her back to the house.

Miranda felt like an actress playing a part for the
next few days. Determined to find out if Harden
could accept her as he thought she was, she played
the city ingenue to the hilt. Leaving the jeans and
cotton shirts she'd packed still in their cases, she
chose her best dress slacks—white ones, of course—
and silk blouses to wear around the ranch. She did
her makeup as carefully as if she were going to work.
She acted as if she found the cattle smelly and frightening.

"They won't hurt you," Harden said, and it was
taking a real effort not to react badly to this side of
her. He didn't know what he'd expected, but it
wasn't to find her afraid of cattle. That was a bad
omen. Worse, she balked when he offered to take her
riding.

"I don't like horses," she lied. "I've only been

on them once or twice, and it's uncomfortable and scary. Can't we go in the truck?''

Harden had to bite his tongue. "Of course, we can," he said with gentlemanly courtesy. "It doesn't matter."

It did, though, she could tell. She clung to his arm as they walked back from the barn, because she was wearing high heels.

"Honey, don't you have some less dressy slacks and some flat shoes?" he asked after a minute, frowning down at her. "That's really not the rig to wear around here. You'll ruin your pretty things."

She smiled at the consideration and pressed closer. "I don't care. I love being with you."

His arm slid around her, and all his worries about her ability to fit in disappeared like fog in sunlight. "I like being with you, too," he said quietly. He held her against his side, aware of mingled feelings of peace and riotous desire and pleasure as he felt her softness melt into his strength so trustingly.

"It bothers you, doesn't it, that I'm not a country girl?" she asked when they reached the truck.

He frowned. His pale blue eyes searched her gray ones. "It isn't that important," he said stubbornly. "After all, you won't be expected to help me herd cattle or pull calves. We have other common interests."

"Yes. Like walks in the park and science fiction movies and quiet nights at home watching television," she said, grinning up at him.

The frown didn't fade. He couldn't put it into

words, but it was a little surprising that a woman who liked the park and loathed parties wouldn't be right at home on a ranch.

He shrugged it off and put her into the cab of the truck beside him, driving around to where Old Man Red, their prize-winning Santa Gertrudis bull lived in air-conditioned luxury in his own barn.

Miranda had to stifle a gasp of pure pleasure when she saw the enormous animal. He had the most beautiful conformation she'd ever seen, and she'd seen plenty in her childhood and adolescence on her father's South Dakota ranch. She knew Old Man Red's name from the livestock sale papers, from the annual breeders' editions. He was a legend in cattle circles, and here he stood, close enough to touch. His progeny thrived not only in the United States, but in countries around the world.

"He's so big," she said, sighing with unconscious delight.

"Our pride and joy," Harden replied. He reached out and smoothed the animal's muzzle affectionately. "He's been cosseted so much that he's nothing but a big pet these days."

"An expensive one, I'll bet," she said, trying not to give away her own knowledge of his value.

"He is that." He looked down at her. "I thought you didn't like cattle, city girl," he murmured. "Your eyes sure sparkle when you look at him."

She reached up to his ear. "Roast beef," she whispered. "I'm drooling."

"You cannibal!" he burst out, and laughed.

The sound was new, and pleasant. Startled, she laughed, too. "I'm sorry. That was unforgivable, wasn't it?" she mused.

"I'd rather eat my older brother Evan than put a fork to Old Man Red!"

Her eyebrows went up. "Poor Evan!"

"No, poor me," he replied. "He'd probably take weeks of tenderizing just to be digestible."

She slid her fingers into his and followed him down the wide aisle of the barn, happier than she could ever remember being. "Did you grow up here?"

He nodded. "My brothers and I used to play cowboy and Indian."

"You always got to be the Indian," she imagined.

He frowned. "How did you know that?"

"You're stoic," she said simply. "Very dignified and aloof."

"So is Connal. You'll meet him tonight. He's bringing Pepi and the baby over." He hesitated, staring at her expression. "It's going to hurt, isn't it?"

She turned, looking up at him. "Not if you're with me."

His breath caught. She made him feel so necessary. He caught her by the arms and drew her slowly to him, enfolding her. He laid his cheek against her dark hair and the wind blew down the long aisle, bringing the scent of fresh hay and cattle with it.

"I suppose you played with dolls when you were a little girl," he murmured.

"Not really. I liked to—" She stopped dead, because she couldn't admit, just yet, that she was riding in rodeos when she was in grammar school. Winning trophies, too. Thank God Sam had kept those at his house, so Harden hadn't seen them when he came to her apartment.

"You liked to...?" he prompted.

"Play dress-up in mother's best clothes," she invented.

"Girl stuff," he murmured. "I liked Indian leg wrestling and chasing lizards and snakes."

"Yuuck!" she said eloquently.

"Snakes are beneficial," he replied. "They eat the mice that eat up our grain."

"If you say so."

He tilted her face up to his dancing eyes. "Tenderfoot," he accused, but he made it sound like a caress.

"You'd be happier with a country girl, wouldn't you?" she asked softly. "Someone who could ride and liked cattle."

He drew in a slow, even breath and let his eyes wander slowly over the gentle oval of her face. "We don't get to pick and choose the qualities and abilities that make up a person. Your inner qualities are much more important to me than any talent you might have had for horseback riding. You're loyal and honest and compassionate, and in my arms, you burn. That's enough." He scowled. "Am I enough for you, though?"

"What a question!" she exclaimed, touched by the way he'd described her.

"I'm hard and unsociable. I don't go to parties and I don't pull my punches with people. There are times when being alone is like a religion to me. I find it difficult to share things, feelings." His broad shoulders lifted and fell, and he looked briefly worried. "Added to that, I've been down on women for so many years it isn't even funny. You may find me tough going."

She searched his eyes quietly. "You didn't even like me when we first met, but you came after me when you thought I might be suicidal. You looked after me and you never asked for anything." She smiled gently. "Mr. Tremayne, I knew everything I needed to know about you after just twenty-four hours."

He bent and brushed his mouth over her eyelids with breathless tenderness. "What if I fail you?" he whispered.

"What if I fail you?" she replied. She savored the touch of his mouth on her face, keenly aware of the rising tide of heat in her blood as his hands began to move up her back. "I'm a city girl...."

His breath grew unsteady. "I don't care," he said roughly. His mouth began to search for hers, hard and insistent. His hands went to her hips and jerked them up into his. "My God, I don't care what you are!" His mouth crushed down against her parted lips, and his last sane thought was that she was every bit as wild for him as he was for her.

Heated seconds later, she felt his mouth lift and her eyes opened slowly, dazed.

"Harden," she breathed.

His teeth delicately caught her upper lip and traced it. "Did I hurt you?" he whispered.

"No." Her arms linked around his neck and she lay against him heavily, her heartbeat shaking her, her eyes closed.

"We can live in Houston," he said unsteadily. "Maybe someday you'll learn to like the ranch. If you don't, it doesn't matter."

Her mind registered what he was saying, but before she could respond to it, his mouth was on hers again, and she forgot everything....

Connal and his wife, Pepi, came that night. They brought along their son, Jamie, who immediately became the center of attention.

Pepi didn't know about Miranda's lost baby, because nobody had told her. But she noticed a sad, wistful look on the other woman's face when she looked at the child.

"Something's wrong," she said softly, touching Miranda's thin hand while the men gathered to talk cattle and Theodora was helping Jeanie May in the kitchen. "What is it?"

Miranda told her, finding something gentle and very special in the other woman's brown eyes.

"I'm sorry," Pepi said afterward. "But you'll have other babies. I know you will."

"I hope so," Miranda replied, smiling. Involuntarily her eyes went to Harden.

"Connal says he's never brought a woman home

before," Pepi said. "There was something about an engagement years ago, although I never found out exactly what. I know that Harden hates Theodora, and he's taken it out on every woman who came near him. Until now," she added, her big eyes searching Miranda's. "You must be very special to him."

"I hope I am," Miranda said earnestly. "I don't know. It's sort of like a trial period. We're getting to know each other before he decides when we'll get married.

"Oh. So it's like that," Pepi said, grinning.

"He's a bulldozer."

"All the Tremayne brothers are, even Donald, you just ask Jo Ann." Pepi laughed. "I used to be scared to death of Harden myself, but he set me right about Connal once and maybe saved my marriage."

"He can be so intimidating," Miranda agreed. "Evan's the only even-tempered one, from what I see."

"Get Harden to tell you about the time Evan threw one of the cowboys over a fence," Pepi chuckled. "It's an eye-opener. Evan's deep, and not quite what he seems."

"He's friendly, at least," Miranda said.

"If he likes you. I hear he can be very difficult if he doesn't. Don't you love Theodora?"

"Yes, I do," Miranda replied. "We got off to a rocky start. Harden brought me down without warning Theodora first, but she warmed up after we were properly introduced. I'm enjoying it, now."

Pepi frowned. "I thought you didn't like ranch life."

"I'm getting used to it, I think."

"You'll like it better when you learn to ride," the other woman promised. "I hear Harden's going to teach you how."

Miranda's silver eyes opened wide. "He is?" she asked with assumed innocence.

"Yes. You'll enjoy it, I know you will. Horses are terrific."

"So I hear."

"Just never let them know you're afraid of them, and you'll do fine." The baby cried suddenly, and Pepi smiled down at him, her eyes soft with love. "Hungry, little boy?" she asked tenderly. "Miranda, could you hold him while I dig out his bottle?"

"Oh, of course!" came the immediate reply.

Pepi went to heat the bottle, and Miranda sighed over the tiny laughing face, her own mirroring her utter delight.

She wasn't aware of Harden's stare until he knelt beside her and touched a tiny little hand with one big finger.

"Isn't he beautiful?" Miranda asked, her eyes finding his.

He nodded. His eyes darkened, narrowed. His body burned with sudden need. "Do you want me to give you a child, Miranda?" he asked huskily.

Her face colored. Her lips parted. Her soft eyes searched his and linked with them in the silence that followed.

"Yes," she said unsteadily.

His eyes flashed, glittering down at her. "Then you'd better make up your mind to marry me, hadn't you?"

"Admiring your nephew?" Pepi asked as she joined them, breaking the spell.

"He's the image of Connal," Harden mused.

"Isn't he, though?" Pepi sighed, smiling toward her husband, who returned the look with breathless tenderness.

"Stop that," Harden muttered. "You people have been married over a year."

"It gets better every day," Pepi informed him. She grinned. "You ought to try it."

"I want to, if I could get my intended to agree," he murmured dryly, watching Miranda closely. "She's as slow as molasses about making up her mind."

"And you're impatient," she accused him.

"Can't help it," he replied. "It isn't every day that a man runs across a girl like you. I don't want Evan to snap you up."

"Did you mention my name?" Evan asked, grinning as he towered over them. "Nice job, Pepi," he said. "Now, how about a niece?"

"Don't rush me," she said. "I'm just getting used to making formula."

"You're a natural. Look at the smile on that little face."

"Why don't you get married and have kids?"

Connal asked the eldest Tremayne as he sauntered over to the small group.

Evan's expression closed up. "I told you once, they trample me trying to get to him." He stuck a finger toward Harden.

"They'll have to get past Miranda now, though," Connal replied. "Harden will go on the endangered species list."

"Evan has been on it for years," Harden chuckled. "Except that Anna can't convince him she's serious competition."

"I don't rob cradles," Evan said coldly. His dark eyes glittered, and his usual good nature went into eclipse, giving a glimpse of the formidable man behind the smiling mask.

"Your mother was nineteen when she married, wasn't she?" Pepi asked him.

"That was back in the dark ages."

"You might as well give up," Connal said, sliding a possessive arm around his wife as he smiled down at her. "He's worse than Harden was."

"Meaning that Harden is improving?" Evan asked, forcing a smile. He studied Harden closely. "You know, he is. He's actually been pleasant since he's been home this time. A nice change," he told Miranda, "from his first few days home from Chicago, when he took rust off old nails with his tongue and caused two wranglers to quit on the spot."

"He was horrible," Connal agreed. "Mother asked if she could go and live with Donald and Jo Ann."

Evan chuckled. "Then she took back the offer because I threatened to load my gun. She's fonder of Harden than she is of the rest of us."

Harden's face went taut. "That's enough."

Evan shrugged. "It's no big family secret that you're her favorite," he reminded the other man. "It's your sweet nature that stole her heart."

Once, Harden would have swung on his brother for that remark. Now, he actually smiled. "She should have hit you harder while she had the chance."

"I grew too fast," Evan said imperturbably.

"Are you sure you've stopped yet?" Connal mused, looking up at the other man.

Evan didn't answer him. His size was his sore spot, and Connal had been away long enough to forget. He turned back to Harden. "Did you ever get in touch with Scarborough about that shipment that got held up in Fort Worth?"

"Yes, I did," Harden said. "It's all ironed out now."

"That's a relief."

The men drifted back to business talk, and Pepi and Miranda played with the baby until Theodora rejoined them. Dinner was on the table shortly, and all the solemnity died out of the occasion. Miranda couldn't remember when she'd enjoyed anything more.

Harden noticed how easily she fit in with his family, and it pleased him. She might not be the ideal ranch wife, but she was special, and he wanted her.

They'd have a good marriage. They'd make it work. But one thing he did mean to do, and that was to show Miranda how to ride a horse. Tomorrow, he promised himself. Tomorrow, he was going to ease her onto a tame horse and coax her to ride with him. Once she learned how, she was going to love it. That would get one hurdle out of the way.

The rest would take care of themselves. He watched Miranda with an expression that would have knocked the breath out of her if she'd seen it. The flickering lights in his pale blue eyes were much more than infatuation or physical interest. They were the beginnings of something deep and poignant and real.

Chapter Nine

The next morning, Harden knocked on her door earlier than he had since they'd been at the ranch.

"Get up and put on some jeans and boots and a cotton shirt," he called. "If you don't have any, we'll borrow some of Jo Ann's for you—she's about your size."

"I've got some," she called back. "What are you up to?"

"I'm going to teach you to ride. Come on down to the stables when you finish breakfast. I've got to go and get the men started."

"Okay," she called with silent glee. "I'd just love to learn how to ride!"

"Good. Hurry up, honey."

His booted footsteps died away, and Miranda laughed delightedly as she dressed. Now that he was ready to accept the city girl he thought she was, it was time to let him in on the truth. It was, she anticipated, going to be delicious!

It was like going back in time for Miranda, who was right at home in jeans and boots and a red-checked cotton shirt. Harden met her at the stables, where he already had two horses saddled.

"You look cute," he said, grinning at the ponytail. "Almost like a cowgirl."

And you ain't seen nothin' yet, cowboy, she was thinking. "I'm glad I look the part," she said brightly. "What do we do first?"

"First, you learn how to mount. Now, there's nothing to be afraid of," he assured her. "This is the gentlest horse on the place. I'll lead you through the basics. Anyone can learn to ride. All you have to do is pay attention and do what I tell you."

He made it sound as if she'd never seen a horse. Of course, he knew nothing about her past, but still, her pride began to sting as he went through those basics in a faintly condescending tone.

"The hardest part is getting on the horse," he concluded. "But there's nothing to it, once you know how. It'll only take a minute to teach you the right way to do it."

"Oh, I'd love to learn the right way to get on a horse!" she exclaimed with mock enthusiasm. "Uh, would you hold the reins a minute?" she asked with twinkling eyes.

"Sure." He frowned as he took them. "What for?"

"You'll see." She walked away from him, trying

not to double up with mischievous laughter as she thought about what she was going to do.

"Got him?" she called when she was several yards away.

"I've got him," he said impatiently. "What in hell do you want me to do with him?"

"Just hold him, while I show you how I've *been* getting on horses." She got her bearings and suddenly took off toward the horse at a dead run. She jumped, balanced briefly on her hands on the horse's rump, and vaulted into the saddle as cleanly and neatly as she'd done it in rodeos years ago.

The look on Harden's face was worth money. Evan had been standing nearby, and he saw it, too, but he didn't look as if he trusted his eyes.

Miranda shook back her ponytail and laughed delightedly. "Gosh, you look strange," she told Harden.

"You didn't tell me you could do that!" he burst out.

She shrugged. "Nothing to it. I took first prizes in barrel racing back in South Dakota, and Dad used to say I was the best horseman he had on the place."

"What place?" he asked explosively.

"His ranch," she replied. She grinned at his shell-shocked expression. "Well, you're the one who said I was a city girl, weren't you?"

Harden's face wavered and broke into the most beautiful smile she'd ever seen. His blue eyes beamed up at her with admiration and pride and something more, something soft and elusive.

"Full of surprises, aren't you?" he asked, laying a lean hand on her thigh.

"I reckon I am," she chuckled. "Got a hat I can borrow?"

"Here." Evan tossed her one, barely concealing a chuckle. "My, my, they must have lots of horses in Chicago. You sure do look experienced at getting on them."

"She's a South Dakota ranch girl," Harden told him dryly. "Nice of her to share that tidbit, wasn't it?"

"Noting like the element of surprise," Miranda said smugly, putting the oversize hat on. She glowered at Evan with it covering her ears. "If you'll get me a handle, I can use it for an umbrella."

Evan glared at her. "I do not have a big head."

"Oh, no, of course not," she agreed, flopping the hat back and forth on her head. She grinned at Evan.

"Okay," Evan said. "I'll relent enough to admit that you have a very small head."

"How long have you been riding?" Harden asked her.

"Since I was three," she confessed. "I still go riding in Chicago. I love horses."

"Can you cut cattle?" he persisted.

"If you put me on a trained quarter horse, you bet," she replied. "With all due respect, this rocking horse isn't going to be much good in a herd of cattle."

Harden chuckled. "No, he's not. I'll saddle Dusty for you. Then we'll go work for a while."

"Surprise, surprise," Evan murmured as he joined his brother.

"The biggest hurdle of all was her city upbringing," Harden said with pure glee. "And she turns out to be a cowgirl."

"That lady's one of a kind," Evan mused. "Don't lose her."

"No chance. Not if I have to tie her to the bedpost."

Evan gave him a dry look. "Kinky, are you?"

Harden glared at him and strode off into the barn.

For the next three days, Miranda discovered more in common with Harden than she'd ever imagined. But in the back of her mind, always, was the woman he'd loved and lost. He couldn't be over her if he still held such a bitter grudge against his mother. While his heart was tangled up, he couldn't love anyone else. And if he didn't love her, their marriage would have very little chance of success.

She watched Harden work on one of the purebred mares in foal, fascinated by the tenderness with which he helped the mare through her ordeal. For all his faults, when the chips were down, he was the coolest, most compassionate man she'd ever known. In an emergency, he'd be a good man to have around.

"One more week," he reminded her when he was through with the mare. "Then I'll take the decision right out of your hands."

"You can't force me to marry you," she said stubbornly.

His eyes ran down her body with possession and barely controlled desire. "Watch me."

"I'd have to be out of my mind to marry you," she exploded. "I couldn't call my soul my own!"

He lifted his head and smiled at her arrogantly, his pale eyes glittery. "I'll have you, all the same. And you'll like it."

"You arrogant, unprincipled, overbearing—"

"Save it up, honey," he interrupted, jerking his hat down over one eyebrow. "I've got a man waiting on a cattle deal."

He dropped a hard kiss on her open mouth and left her standing, fuming, behind him.

Harden had given her permission to ride any of his horses except an oversize, bad-tempered stallion named Rocket. Normally, she wouldn't have gone against him. But he was acting like the Supreme Male, and she didn't like it. She saddled the stallion and took him out, riding hell for leather until she and the horse were too tired to go any farther.

She paused to water him at a small stream, talking to him gently. His reputation was largely undeserved, because he was a gentle horse as long as he had a firm hand. In many ways, he and she were kindred spirits. She'd left behind her unbridled youth, and Tim had made her uncomfortable with her femininity. She'd felt like a thing during most of her marriage, a toy that Tim took off the shelf when he was bored. But with Harden, she felt wild and rebellious. He brought all her buried passions to the surface, and some of them were uncomfortable.

When she glanced at her watch, she was surprised to find how much time had elapsed since she'd taken Rocket out of the barn. At a guess, she was going to be in a lot of trouble when she got back.

Sure enough, Harden was marching around the front of the barn, a cigarette in his hand, his normally lazy stride converted into a quick, impatient pacing. Even the set of his head was dangerous.

Miranda got out of the saddle and led Rocket the rest of the way. Her jeans were splattered with mud, like her boots, and her yellow cotton shirt wasn't much cleaner. Her hair, pinned up in a braid, was untidy. But her face was alive as never before, flushed with exhilaration, her gray eyes bright with challenge and excitement.

Harden turned and stiffened as she approached. Evan was nearby, probably to save her from him, she thought mischievously.

"Here," she said, handing him the reins. She lifted her face, daring him. "Go ahead. Yell. Shout. Curse. Give me hell."

His face was hard and his eyes were glittery, but he did none of those things. Unexpectedly he jerked her into his arms and stood holding her, a faint tremor in his lean, fit body as he held hers against it.

The action shocked her out of all resistance, because it told her graphically how worried he'd been. The shock of it took the edge off her temper, made her relax against him with pure delight.

"I forgot the time," she said at his ear. "I didn't

do it on purpose." She clung to him, her eyes closed. "I'm sorry you were worried."

"How do you know I was?" he asked curtly.

She smiled into his warm neck. "I don't know. But I do." Her arms tightened. "Going to kiss me?" she whispered.

"I'd kiss you blind if my brother wasn't standing ten feet away trying to look invisible. That being the case, it will have to wait." He lifted his head. His face was paler than usual. "Monday, we're getting married. I can't take anymore. Either you marry me, or you get out of my life."

She searched his eyes. It would be taking a huge chance. But she'd learned that they were pretty compatible, and she knew he was beginning to feel something besides physical attraction for her. At least, she hoped he was. They got along well together. She knew and enjoyed ranch life, so there wouldn't be much adjustment in that quarter. Anyway, the alternative was going back to Chicago to live with her ghosts and try to live without Harden. She'd tried that once and failed. She wasn't strong enough to try it again. She smiled up at him softly. "Monday, then," she said quietly.

Harden hadn't realized that he'd been holding his breath. He let it out slowly, feeling as if he'd just been handed the key to the world. He looked down at her. "Good enough. But just for the record, honey, if you ever, ever, get on that horse again without permission," he said in a seething undertone, "I'll feed him to you, tail first!"

She lifted her eyebrows. "You and whose army, buster?"

He grinned. He chuckled. He wrapped her up and gave her a bear hug, the first really affectionate gesture of their turbulent relationship.

They were married the following Monday. Miranda's brother, Sam, gave her away, and Evan was best man.

Joan, Sam's wife, managed to get a radiant Miranda alone long enough to find out how happy she really was.

"No more looking back," Joan said softly. "Promise?"

"I promise," Miranda replied with a smile. "Thank you. Did I ever just say thank you for all you and Sam have done for me over the years?"

"Twice a week, at least." Joan laughed, and then she sobered. "He's a tiger, that man," she added, nodding toward Harden, who was standing with his brothers and Sam. "Are you sure?"

"I love him," Miranda said simply.

Joan nodded. "Then it will be all right."

But would it, Miranda wondered, when Harden didn't love her.

"What a bunch," Sam said with a grin as he joined them. He put an affectionate arm around his sister. "At least you're no stranger to horses and ranch life," he said. "You'll fit right in here. Happy, kitten?"

"So happy," she assured him with a hug.

"Well, Harden will take care of you," he said. "No doubt about that. But," he added with a level stare, "no more leaping on horses' backs. I'm not sure your new husband's nerves will take it!"

She laughed, delighted that Harden had shared that incident with Sam. It meant that he liked her, anyway. He wanted her, too, and she was nervous despite the intimacy they'd shared. She didn't know if she was going to be enough for him.

Evan added his congratulations, along with the rest of the family. Theodora hugged her warmly and then looked with bitter hopelessness at Harden, who'd hardly spoken to her.

"He'll get over it one day," Miranda said hesitantly.

"Over the facts of his birth, maybe. Over Anita? I don't think he ever will," she added absently, oblivious to the shaken, tragic look that flashed briefly over Miranda's features before she quickly composed them.

Suddenly aware of what she'd said, Theodora turned, flushing. "I can't ever seem to say the right thing, can I?" she asked miserably. "I'm sorry, Miranda, I didn't mean that the way it sounded."

"You don't need to apologize to me," she told the older woman quietly. "I know he doesn't love me. It's all right. I'll try to be a good wife, and there will be children."

Theodora grimaced. Harden joined them, gathering Miranda with easy possessiveness under his arm to kiss her warmly.

"Hello, Mrs. Tremayne," he said softly. "How goes it?"

"I'm fine. How about you?" she asked.

"I'll be better when we get the reception out of the way. I had no idea we were related to so many people," he chuckled. Then he glanced at Theodora, and the laughter faded. "Few of them are related to me, of course," he added cuttingly.

Theodora didn't react. Her sad eyes searched his. "Have a nice honeymoon, Harden. You, too, Miranda." She turned and walked away, ignoring her son's hostility.

Miranda looked up at him worriedly. "You can't keep this up. You're cutting her to pieces."

His eyes narrowed. "Don't interfere," he cautioned quietly. "Theodora is my business."

"I'm your wife," she began.

"Yes. But that doesn't make you my conscience. Let's get this over with." He took her arm and led her into the house, where the caterers were ready for the reception.

The reception was held at the ranch, but Theodora ran interference long enough for the newlyweds to get away.

Connal and Pepi showed up for the wedding, and Miranda found that she and Pepi were fast becoming friends. Connal reminded her a lot of Evan, except that he was leaner and younger. Pepi was an elf, a gentle creature with big eyes. She and Connal had little Jamie Ben Tremayne with them, and he warmed Miranda's heart as he had the night they'd had supper with the rest of the family. But he made her ache for the child she'd lost. That, along with Theodora's faux pas put the only dampers on the day for her, and she carried the faint sadness along on their honeymoon.

They'd decided that Cancun was the best place to go, because they both had a passion for archaeology, and some Mayan ruins were near the hotel they'd booked into. Now, as her memories came back to haunt her, she wished again that she'd waited just a little longer, that she hadn't let Harden coax her into marriage so quickly.

What was done was done, though, and she had to make the best of it.

Harden had watched the joy go out of Miranda at the wedding, and he guessed that it was because of Connal and Pepi's baby. He almost groaned out loud. He should have carried her off and eloped, as he'd threatened. Now it was too late, and she was buried in the grief of the past. As if to emphasize the somber mood that had invaded what should have been a happy time, it began to pour rain.

Chapter Ten

Miranda hesitated in the doorway of their hotel room. It really hadn't occurred to her that they'd be given anything except a room with double beds. But there, dominating the room with its ocean view, was a huge king-size bed.

"We're married," Harden said curtly.

"Yes, of course." She stood aside to let the bellboy bring the luggage in and waited while Harden tipped him and closed the door.

She walked out onto the balcony and looked out over the Gulf of Mexico, all too aware of Harden behind her. She remembered the night at the bridge, and the way he'd rushed to save her. Presumably her action—rather, what he perceived to be a suicide attempt—had brought back unbearable memories for him. Suicide was something he knew all too much about, because the love of his life had died that way.

Was it all because of Anita? Was he reliving the affair in his mind, and substituting Miranda? Except this time there was no suicide, there was a marriage and a happy ending. She could have cried.

Harden misattributed her silent brooding to her own bitter memories, so he didn't say anything. He stood beside her, letting the sea air ruffle his hair while he watched people on the beach and sea gulls making dives out of the sky.

He was still wearing the gray suit he'd been married in, and Miranda was wearing a dressy, oyster-colored suit of her own with a pale blue blouse. Her hair, in a chignon, was elegant and sleek. She looked much more like a businesswoman than a bride, a fact that struck Harden forcibly.

"Want to change?" he asked. "We could go swimming or just lay on the beach."

"Yes," she replied. Without looking at him, she opened her suitcase on its rack and drew out a conservative blue one-piece bathing suit and a simple white cover-up.

"I'll change in the bathroom," he said tersely, carrying his white trunks in there and closing the door firmly behind him.

It wasn't, Miranda thought wistfully, the most idyllic start for a honeymoon. She couldn't help remembering that Tim had been wild to get her into bed, though, and how unpleasant and embarrassing it had been for her, in broad daylight. Tim had been selfish and quick, and her memories of her wedding day were bitter.

Harden came back in just as she was gathering up her suntan lotion and dark glasses. In swimming trunks, he was everything Tim hadn't been. She paused with her hand in her suitcase and just stared, taking in the powerful, hair-roughened length of his body, tapering from broad, bronzed shoulders down a heavily muscled chest and stomach to lean hips and long legs. A male model, she thought, should look half as good.

He lifted an eyebrow, trying not to look as self-conscious as that appraisal made him feel. Not that he minded the pure pleasure on her face as she studied him, but it was beginning to have a noticeable effect on his body.

He turned. "Ready to go?" He didn't dare look too long at her in that clingy suit.

She picked up the sunglasses she'd been reaching for. "Yes. Should we take a towel?"

"They'll have them on the beach. If they don't, we'll buy a couple in that drugstore next to the lobby."

She followed him out to the beach. There was a buggy with fresh towels in it, being handed out to hotel patrons as they headed for the small palm umbrellas that dotted the white sand beach.

"The water is the most gorgeous color," she sighed, stretching out on a convenient lounger with her towel under her.

"Part of the attraction," he agreed. He stretched lazily and closed his eyes. "God, I'm tired. Are you?"

"Just a little. Of course, I'm just a young thing myself. Old people like you probably feel the— oh!"

She laughed as he tumbled her off the lounger onto the sand and pinned her there, his twinkling eyes just above her own. "Old, my foot," he murmured. His gaze fell to her mouth and lingered.

"You can't," she whispered. "It's a public beach."

"Yes, I can," he whispered back, and brought his mouth down over hers.

It was a long, sweet kiss. He drew back finally, his pale eyes quiet and curious on her relaxed face. "You were disturbed when we left the house. Did Theodora say something to you?"

She hesitated. Perhaps it would be as well to get it out into the open, she considered. "Harden," she began, her eyes hesitant as they met his, "Theodora told me about Anita."

His face froze. His eyes seemed to go blank. He lifted himself away from Miranda, and his expression gave away nothing of what he was feeling. Damn Theodora! Damn her for doing that to him, for stabbing him in the back! She had no right to drag up that tragedy on his wedding day. He'd spent years trying to forget; now Miranda was going to remind him of it and bring the anguish back.

He sat down on his lounger and lit a cigarette, leaning back to smoke it and watch the sea. "I suppose it's just as well that you know," he said finally. "But I won't talk about it. You understand?"

"Shutting me out again, Harden?" she asked

sadly. "Is our marriage going to be like that, each of us with locked rooms in our hearts where the other can't come?"

"I won't talk about Anita, or about Theodora," he replied evenly. "Make what you like of it." He put on his own sunglasses and closed his eyes, effectively cutting off any further efforts at conversation.

Miranda was shattered. She knew then that she'd made another bad marriage, another big mistake, but it was too late to do anything about it. Now she had to live with it.

They had a quiet supper in the hotel restaurant much later. Harden was quiet, so was she. Conversation had been held to a minimum ever since they'd been on the beach, and Miranda's sad face was revealing her innermost thoughts.

When they got back to their room, Miranda turned and faced her husband with an expression that almost drove him to a furious outburst. It was so filled with bitter resignation, with determination to perform her wifely duties with stoic courage, that he could have turned the air blue.

"I want a drink," he said icily. "By the time I get back, you should be asleep and safe from any lecherous intentions I might have left. Good night, Mrs. Tremayne," he added contemptuously.

Miranda glared at him. "Thank you for a perfect day," she replied with equal contempt. "If I ever had any doubts about making our marriage work, you've sure set them to rest."

His eyes narrowed and glittered. "Is that a subtle hint that you want me, after all? In that case, let me oblige you."

He moved forward and picked her up unexpectedly, tossing her into the center of the huge bed. He followed her down, covering her with his own body, and unerringly finding her soft mouth with his own.

But she was too hurt to respond, too afraid of what he meant to do. It was like Tim...

She said Tim's name with real fear and Harden's head jerked up, his eyes glazing.

"You're just like him, really aren't you?" she choked, her eyes filled with bitter tears. "What you want, when you want it, always your way, no matter what the cost to anyone else."

He scowled. She looked so wounded, so alone. He reached down and touched her face, lightly, tracing the hot tears.

"I wouldn't hurt you," he said hesitantly. "Not that way."

"Go ahead, if you want to," she said tiredly, closing her eyes. "I don't care. I know better than to expect love from a man who can't forgive his mother a twelve-year-old tragedy or even the circumstances of his birth. Your mother must have loved your father very much to have risked the shame and humiliation of being pregnant with another man's child at the same time she was married to your stepfather." She opened her eyes, staring up at him. "But you don't know how to love, do you, Harden? Not anymore. All you knew of love is buried with your Anita. There's nothing left in here.'' She put her hand against his broad chest, where his heart was beating hard and raggedly. ''Nothing at all. Only hate.''

He jerked back from her hand and got to his feet, glaring down at her.

''Why did you marry me?'' she asked sadly, sitting up to stare at him. ''Was it pity, or just desire?''

He couldn't answer her. In the beginning, it had been pity. Desire came quickly after that, until she obsessed him. But since she'd been at the ranch, he'd had other feelings, feelings he'd never experienced even with Anita. His hand went to his chest where she'd touched it, absently rubbing the place her hand had rested, as if he could feel the warm imprint.

''You love me, don't you?'' he asked unexpectedly.

She flushed, averting her eyes. ''Think what you like.''

He didn't know what to say, what to do, anymore. It had all seemed so simple. They'd get married and he'd make love to her whenever he liked, and they'd have children. Now it was much more complicated. He remembered the day she'd gone riding, and how black his world had gone until she'd come back. He remembered the terror, the sick fear, and suddenly he knew why. Knew everything.

''Listen,'' he began quietly. ''This has all gone wrong. I think it might be a good idea—''

''If we break it off now?'' she concluded mistakenly, her gray eyes staring bravely into his. ''Yes, I think you're right. Neither of us is really ready for this kind of commitment yet. You were right when you said it was too soon.''

"It isn't that," he said heavily. "And we can't get a divorce on our wedding day.''

She gnawed her lower lip. ''No. I guess not.''

"We'll stay for a couple of days, at least. When we're home…we'll make decisions.'' He turned, picked up his clothes, and went into the bathroom to dress.

She changed quickly into a simple long cotton gown and got under the covers. She closed her eyes, but she needn't have bothered, because he didn't even look at her as he went out the door.

The rest of their stay in Cancun went by quickly, with the two of them being polite to each other and not much more. They went on a day trip to the ruins at Chichen Itza, wandering around the sprawling Maya ruins with scores of other tourists. The ruins covered four miles, with their widely spread buildings proving that it was a cult center and not just a conventional city. A huge plaza opened out to various religious buildings. The Mayan farmers would journey there for the year's great religious festivals; archaeologists also assumed that markets and council meetings drew the citizens to Chichen Itza.

The two most interesting aspects of the ancient city to Miranda were the observatory and the Sacred Cenote—or sacrificial well.

She stood at its edge and looked down past the underbrush into the murky water and shivered. It was nothing like the mental picture she had, of some small well-like structure. It was a cavernous opening that led down, down into the water, where over a period of many years, an estimated one hundred human beings were sacrificed to appease the gods in time of drought. The pool covered almost an acre, and it was sixty-five feet from its tree-lined edge down limestone cliffs to the water below.

"It gives me the screaming willies," a man beside Miranda remarked. "Imagine all those thousands of virgins being pushed off the cliff into that yucky water. Sacrificing people because of religion. Is that primitive, or what?"

"Ever hear of the Christians and the lions?" Harden drawled.

The man gave him a look and disappeared into the crowd.

If things had been less strained, Miranda might have corrected that assumption about the numbers, and sex, of the sacrificed Mayans and reminded the tourist that fact and fiction blended in this ancient place. But Harden had inhibited her too much. Sharing her long-standing education in the past of Chichen Itza probably wouldn't have endeared her to the tourist, either. Historical fact had been submerged in favor of Hollywood fiction in so many of the world's places of interest.

Miranda wandered back onto the grassy plaza and stared at the observatory. She knew that despite their infrequent sacrificial urges, the Maya were an intelligent people who had an advanced concept of astronomy and mathematics, and a library that covered the entire history of Maya. Sadly Spanish missionaries in 1545 burned the books that contained the Maya history. Only three survived to the present day.

Miranda wandered back to the bus. It was a sobering experience to look at the ruins and consider that in 500 B.C. this was a thriving city, where people lived and worshiped and probably never considered that their civilization would ever end. Just like us, she thought philosophically, and shivered. Just like my marriages, both in ruins, both like Chichen Itza.

She was somber back to the hotel, and for the rest of their stay in Cancun. She did things mechanically, and without any real enjoyment. Not that Harden was any more jovial than she was. Probably, she considered, he'd decided that there wasn't much to salvage from their brief relationship. And maybe it was just as well.

When they got back to Jacobsville, Theodora insisted that they stay with her until their own home was ready for occupancy—a matter of barely a week. Neither of them had the heart to announce that their honeymoon had resulted in a coming divorce.

Evan, however, sensed that something was wrong. Their first evening back, he steered Miranda onto the front porch with a determined expression on his swarthy face.

"Okay. What's wrong?" he asked abruptly.

She was taken aback at the sudden question. "W-what?"

"You heard me," he replied. "You both came

home looking like death warmed over, and if anything except arguing took place during the whole trip, I'll eat my hat."

"The one that could double as an umbrella?" she asked with a feeble attempt at humor.

"Cut it out. I know Harden. What happened?"

Miranda sighed, giving in. "He's still in love with Anita, that's all, so we decided that we made a mistake and we're going to get it annulled."

He raised an eyebrow. "Annulled?" he emphasized.

She colored. "Yes, well, for a man who seemed to be bristling with desire, he sure changed."

"You do know that he's a virgin?" Evan asked.

She knew her jaw was gaping. She closed her mouth. "He's a what?"

"You didn't know," he murmured. "Well, he'd kill me for telling you, but it's been family gossip for years. He wanted to be a minister, and he's had nothing to do with women since Anita died. A ladies' man, he ain't."

Miranda knew that, but she'd assumed he had some experience. He acted as if he had.

"Are you sure?" she blurted out.

"Of course I'm sure. Look, he's backward and full of hang-ups. It's going to be up to you to make the first move, or you'll end up in divorce court before you know it."

"But, I can't," she groaned.

"Yes, you can. You're a woman. Get some sexy clothes and drive him nuts. Wear perfume, drop handkerchiefs, vamp him. Then get him behind a locked door and let nature take its course. For God's sake, woman, you can't give up on him less than a week after the wedding!''

"He doesn't love me!''

"Make him,'' he said, his eyes steely and level. "And don't tell me you can't. I saw him when you were late getting back on that killer stallion. I've never seen him so shaken. A man who can feel that kind of fear for a woman can love her.''

She hesitated now, lured by the prospect of Harden falling in love with her. "Do you really think he could?''

He smiled. "He isn't as cold as he likes people to think he is. There's a soft core in that man that's been stomped on too many times.''

"I guess I could try,'' she said slowly.

"I guess you could.''

She smiled and went back inside, her mind whirling with possibilities.

The next day, Miranda asked Theodora to take her shopping, and she bought the kind of clothes she'd never worn in her life. She had her hair trimmed and styled, and she bought underwear that made her blush.

"Is this a campaign?'' Theodora asked on the way home, her dark eyes twinkling.

"I guess it is,'' she sighed. "Right now, it looks as if he's ready to toss me back into the lake.''

"I'm sorry that I mentioned Anita on your wed-

ding day,'' the older woman said heavily. ''I could
see the light go out of you. Harden and I may never
make our peace, Miranda, but I never meant to put
you in the middle.''

''I know that.'' She turned in the seat, readjusting
her seat belt. ''Does Harden know anything about his
real father?''

Theodora smiled. ''No. He's never wanted to.''

''Would you tell me?''

The older woman's eyes grew misty with remem-
brance. ''He was a captain in the Green Berets, actually,'' she said. ''I met him at a Fourth of July
parade, of all things, in Houston while my husband
and I were temporarily separated. He was a farm boy
from Tennessee, but he had a big heart and he was
full of fun. We went everywhere together. He spoiled
me, pampered me, fell in love with me. Before I
knew it, I was in love with him, desperately in love
with him!''

She turned onto the road that led to the ranch,
frowning now while Miranda listened, entranced.
''Neither of us wanted an affair, but what we felt
was much too explosive to… Well, I guess you know
about that,'' she added shyly. ''People in love have
a hard time controlling their passions. We were no
different. He gave me a ring, a beautiful emerald-
and-diamond ring that had been his mother's, and I
filed for divorce. We were going to be married as
soon as the divorce was final. But he was sent to
Vietnam and the first day there, the Viet Cong attacked and he was killed by mortar fire.''

"And you discovered you were pregnant," Miranda prompted when the other woman hesitated, her eyes anguished.

"Yes." She shifted behind the wheel. "Abortion was out of the question. I loved Barry so much, more than my own life. I'd have risked anything to have his child. I didn't know what to do. I got sick and couldn't work, and I had nowhere to go when I was asked to leave my apartment for nonpayment of rent. About that time, Jesse, my own husband, came and asked me to come back to the ranch, to end the separation. Evan was very young, and he had a governess for him, but he missed me."

"Did your husband love you?" Miranda asked softly.

"Yes. That made it so much worse, you see, because he was jealous and overpossessive and overprotective—that's why I left him in the first place. But perhaps the experience taught him something, because he never threw the affair up to me. He brought me back home and after the first few weeks, he became involved with my pregnancy. He loved children, you know. It didn't even matter to him that Harden wasn't his own. He never let it matter to anyone else, either. We had a good life. I did my grieving for Barry in secret, and then I fell in love with my husband all over again. But Harden has made sure since Anita's death that I paid for all my old sins. Interesting, that the instrument of my punishment for an illicit affair and an illegitimate child is the child himself."

"I'm sorry," Miranda said. "It can't be easy for you."

"It isn't easy for Harden, either," came the surprising reply. Theodora smiled sadly as they reached the house. "That gets me through it." She looked at Miranda with dark, somber eyes. "He's the image of Barry."

"I wish you could make him listen."

"What's the old saying, 'if wishes were horses, beggars could ride'?" Theodora shook her head. "My dear, we're all walking these days."

Later, like a huntress waiting for her prey to appear, Miranda donned the sexy underwear and the incredibly see-through lemon-yellow gown she'd bought, sprayed herself with perfume, and exhibited herself in a seductive position on the bed in the bedroom they'd been sharing. Harden made sure he didn't come in until she was asleep, and he was gone before she woke in the morning. But tonight, she was waiting for him. If what Evan said, as incredible as it seemed, was true, and Harden was innocent, it was going to be delicious to seduce him. She had to make allowances for his pride, of course, so she couldn't admit that she knew. That made it all the more exciting.

It was a long time before the door swung open and her tired, dust-stained husband came in the door. He paused with his Stetson in his hand and gaped at her where she lay on the bed, on her side, one perfect small breast almost bare.

"Hi, cowboy," she said huskily, and smiled at him. "Long day?"

"What the hell are you dudded up for?" he asked curtly.

She eased off the bed and stood up, so that he could get a good view of her creamy body under the gauzy fabric of her gown. She stretched, lifting her breasts so that the already hard tips were pushing against the bodice.

"I bought some new clothes, that's all," she murmured drowsily. "Going to have a shower?"

He muttered something under his breath about having one with ice cubes and slammed the bathroom door behind him.

Miranda laughed softly to herself when she heard the shower running. Now if only she could keep her nerve, if only she could dull his senses so that he couldn't resist her. She pulled the hem of the gown up to her thighs and the strap off one rounded shoulder and lay against the pillows, waiting.

He came out, eventually, with a dark green towel secured around his hips. She looked up at him, her eyes slitted, her lips parted invitingly while his eyes slid over her body with anything but a shy, innocent appraisal. The look was so hot, she writhed under it.

"Is this what it took for your late husband?" he asked, his own eyes narrow and almost insulting. "Did you have to dress up to get him interested?"

Her breath caught. She sat up, righting her gown. "Harden..." she began, ready to explain, despite her intention not to.

"Well, I don't need that kind of stimulation when I'm interested," he said, controlling a fiercely subdued rage over her behavior. She must think him impotent, at the least, to go so far to get him into bed. Which only made him more suspicious about her motives.

"You used to be interested," she stammered.

"So I did, before you decided that I needed reforming, before you started interfering in my life. I wanted you. But not anymore, honey, and all those cute tricks you're practicing don't do a damned thing for me."

He pulled her against him, "Can't you tell?"

His lack of interest was so blatant that she turned her eyes away, barely aware that he was pulling clothes out of drawers and closets. Tears blinded her. She hid under the covers and pulled them up to her blushing face, shivering with shame. This had been Tim's favorite weapon, making her feel inadequate, too little a woman to arouse him. Her pride lay on the floor at Harden's feet, and he didn't even care.

"For future reference, I'll do the chasing when I'm interested in sex," he said, glaring down at her white face. "I don't want it with you, not anymore. I told you it was over. You should have listened."

"Yes. I should have," she said hoarsely.

He felt wounded all over. She'd loved him, he knew she had, but she couldn't just be his wife, she had to be a reformer, to harp on his feud with Theodora, to make him seem cruel and selfish. He'd been stinging ever since Cancun, especially since some of those accusations were right on the money. But this was the last straw, this seductive act of hers. He'd had women come on to him all his adult life, their very aggressiveness turning him off. He hadn't expected his own wife to treat him like some casual stud to satisfy her passions. Was she really that desperate for sex?

He turned and went out of the room. It didn't help that he could hear Miranda crying even through the closed door.

Evan heard it, too, and minutes later he confronted his brother in the barn, where Harden was checking on one of the mares in foal.

The bigger man was taking off his hat as he walked down the wide, wood-chip-shaving-filled aisle between the rows of stalls, his swarthy face set in hard lines, his mouth barely visible as his jaw clenched.

"That does it," he said, and kept coming. "That really does it. That poor woman's had enough from you!"

Harden threw off his own hat and stood, waiting. "Go ahead, throw a punch. You'll get it back, with interest," he replied, his tone lazy, his blue eyes bright with anger.

"She goes shopping and buys all sorts of sexy clothes to turn you on, and then you leave her in tears! Doesn't it matter to you that she was trying to make it easy for you?" he demanded.

Harden frowned. Something wasn't right here. "Easy for me?" he prompted.

Evan sighed angrily. "I wasn't going to tell you, but maybe I'd better. I told her the truth about you," he said shortly.

"About what?"

"You know about what!" Evan growled. "It was her right to know, after all, she's your wife."

"What did you tell her, for God's sake?" Harden raged, at the end of his patience.

"The truth." Evan squared his shoulders and waited for the explosion as he replied, "I told her you were a virgin."

Chapter Eleven

For a minute Harden just stood staring at his brother, looking as if he hadn't heard a word. Then he began to laugh, softly at first, building into a roar of sound that echoed down the long aisle.

"It isn't funny," Evan glowered at him. "My God, it's nothing to be ashamed of. There are plenty of men who are celibate. Priests, for instance..."

Harden laughed louder.

Evan wiped his sleeve across his broad, damp forehead and sighed heavily. "What's so damned funny?"

Harden stopped to get his breath before he answered, and lit a cigarette. He took a deep draw, staring amusedly at his older brother.

"I never bothered to deny it, because it didn't matter. But I ought to deck you for passing that old gossip on to Miranda. I gave her hell upstairs for what she did. I had no idea she was supposed to be helping me through my first time!''

Evan cocked his head, narrowing one eye. ''You aren't a virgin?''

Harden didn't answer him. He lifted the cigarette to his mouth. ''Is that why she went on that spending spree in town, to buy sexy clothes to vamp me with?''

''Yes. I'm as much help as Mother, I guess,'' Evan said quietly. ''I overheard her telling Miranda that you'd never get over Anita.''

Harden frowned. ''When?''

''At the reception, before you left on your honeymoon.''

Harden groaned and closed his eyes. He turned to the barn wall and hit it soundly with his fist. ''Damn the luck!''

''One misunderstanding after another, isn't it?'' Evan leaned a broad shoulder against the wall. ''Was she right? Are you still in love with Anita?''

''No. Maybe you were right about that. Maybe it was her time, and Mother was just a link in the chain of events.''

''My God,'' Evan exclaimed reverently. ''Is that really you talking, or do you just have a fever?'' he asked dryly.

Harden glanced up at the lighted window of the room he shared with Miranda. ''I've got a fever, all right. And I know just how to get it down.''

He left Evan standing and went up to the bedroom,

his eyes gleaming with mischief and anticipated pleasure.

But the sight that met him when he opened the door wasn't conducive to pleasure. Miranda was fully dressed in a pretty white silk dress that was even more seductive than the nightgown she'd discarded, and she was packing a suitcase.

She turned a tearstained face to his. "Don't worry, I'm going," she said shortly. "You don't have to throw me off the place."

He closed the door calmly, turned the lock, and tossed his hat onto a chair before he moved toward her.

"You can stop right there," she said warningly. "I'm going home!"

"You are home," he said evenly.

He swept the suitcase, clothes and all, off the bed onto the floor into a littered heap and bent to lift a startled Miranda in his hard arms.

"You put me down!" she raged.

"Anything to oblige, sweetheart." He threw her onto the bed and before she could roll away, he had her pinned against the disheveled covers, one long leg holding her thrashing body. She fought him like a tigress until he caught her wrists and pressed them into the mattress on either side of her head.

Her hair was a dark cloud around her flushed face as she stared up at him furiously, her silver eyes flashing at him.

"I've had enough of damned men!" she raged at him. "It was bad enough having Tim tell me I wasn't woman enough to hold a man without having you rub my face in it, too! I have my pride!"

"Pride, and a lot of other faults," he mused. "Bad temper, impatience, interfering in things that don't concern you..."

"What are you, Mr. Sweetness and Light, a pattern for perfect manhood?!"

"Not by a long shot," he said pleasantly, studying her face. "You're a wildcat, Miranda. Everything I ever wanted, even if it did take me a long time to realize it, and to admit it."

"You don't want me," she said, her voice breaking as she tried to speak bravely about it. "You showed me...!"

"I had a cold shower, remember," he whispered, smiling gently. "Here. Feel."

He moved slowly, sensuously, and something predictable and beautiful happened to him, something so blatant that she caught her breath.

"I want you," he said softly. "But it's much, much more than wanting. Do you like poetry, Miranda?" he breathed at her lips, brushing them with maddening leisure as he spoke. "'Shall I compare thee to a summer's day? Thou art more lovely, and more temperate...'" He kissed her slowly, nibbling at her lower lip while she trembled with pleasure. "Shakespeare couldn't have been talking about you, could he, sweetheart? You aren't temperate, even if you are every bit as lovely as a summer's day...!"

The kiss grew rough, and deep, and his lean hands

found her hips, grinding them up against his fierce arousal.

"This is how much I want you," he bit off at her lips. "I hope you took vitamins, because you're going to need every bit of strength you've got."

She couldn't even speak. His hands were against her skin, and then his mouth was. She'd never in her wildest dreams imagined some of the ways he touched her, some of the things he whispered while he aroused her. He took her almost effortlessly to a fever pitch of passion and then calmed her and started all over again.

It was the sweetest kind of pleasure to feel him get the fabric away from her hot skin, and then to feel his own hair-roughened body intimately against her own. It was all of heaven to kiss and be kissed, to touch and be touched, to let him pleasure her until she was mindless with need.

"Evan said...you were...a virgin," she whispered, her voice breaking as she looked, shocked, into the amused indulgence of his face when the tension was unbearable.

He laughed, the sound soft and predatory. "Am I?" he whispered, and pushed down, hard.

She couldn't believe what she was feeling. His face blurred and then vanished, and it was all feverish motion and frantic grasping and sharp, hot pleasure that brought convulsive statisfaction.

She lay in his arms afterward, tears running helplessly down her cheeks while he smoked a cigarette and absently smoothed her disheveled hair. She was still trembling in the aftermath.

"Are you all right, little one?" he asked gently.

"Yes." She laid her wet cheek against his shoulder. "I didn't know," she stammered.

"It's different, every time," he replied quietly. "But sometimes there's a level of pleasure that you can only experience with one certain person." His lips brushed her forehead with breathless tenderness. "It helps if you're in love with them."

"I suppose you couldn't help but know that," she said, her eyes faintly sad. "I always did wear my heart on my sleeve."

He nuzzled her face until she lifted it to his quiet, vivid blue eyes. "I love you," he said quietly. "Didn't you know?"

No, she didn't know. Her breath stopped in her throat and she felt the flush that even reddened her breasts.

"My God," he murmured, watching it spread. "I've never seen a woman blush here." He touched her breasts, very gently.

"Well, now you have, and you can stop throwing your conquests in my face— Oh!"

His mouth stopped the tirade, and he smiled against it. "They weren't conquests, they were educational experiences that made me the perfect specimen of male prowess you see before you."

"Of all the conceited people..." she began.

He touched her, and she gasped, clinging to him.

"What was that bit, about being conceited?" he asked.

She moaned and curled into his body, shivering. "Harden!" she cried.

"I'll bet you didn't even know that only one man out of twenty is capable of this...."

The cigarette went into the ashtray and his body covered hers. And he gave her a long and unbearably sweet lesson in rare male endurance that lasted almost until morning.

When she woke, he was dressed, whistling to himself as he whipped a belt around his lean hips and secured the big silver buckle.

"Awake?" he murmured dryly. He arched an eyebrow as she moved and groaned and winced. "I could stay home and we could make love some more."

She caught her breath, gaping at him. "And your brother thinks you're a virgin!" she burst out.

He shrugged. "We all make mistakes."

"Yes, well the people who write sex manuals could do two chapters on you!" she gasped.

He grinned. "I could return the compliment. Don't get up unless you want to. Having you take to your bed can only reflect favorably on my reputation in the household."

She burst out laughing at the expression on his face. She sat up, letting the covers fall below her bare breasts, and held out her arms.

He dropped into them, kissing her with lazy affection. "I love you," he whispered. "I'm sorry if I was a little too enthusiastic about showing it."

"No more enthusiastic than I was," she murmured softly. She reached up and kissed him back. "I wish you could stay home. I wish I wasn't so...incapacitated."

"Don't sound regretful," he chuckled. "Wasn't it fun getting you that way?"

She clung to him, sighing. "Oh, yes." Her eyes opened and she stared past him at the wall, almost purring as his hands found her silky breasts and caressed them softly. "Harden?"

"What, sweetheart?"

She closed her eyes. "Nothing. Just...I love you."

He smiled, and reached down to kiss her again.

When he went downstairs to have Jeanie May take a tray up to Miranda, Evan grinned like a Cheshire cat.

"Worn her out after only one day? You'd better put some vitamins on that tray and feed her up," he said.

Harden actually grinned back. "I'm working on that."

"I gather everything's going to be all right?"

"No thanks to you," Harden said meaningfully.

Evan's cheeks went ruddy. "I was only trying to help, and how was I to know the truth? My God, you never went around with women, you never brought anybody home... You *could* have been a virgin!"

Harden smiled secretly. "Yes, I could have."

The way he put it made Evan more suspicious than ever. "Are you?" he asked.

"Not anymore," came the dry reply. "Even if I was," he added to further confound the older man. The smile faded. "Where's Theodora?"

"Out feeding her chickens."

He nodded, and went out the back door. He'd said some hard things to Theodora over the years, and Miranda was right about his vendetta. It was time to run up the white flag.

Theodora saw him coming and grimaced, and when he saw that expression, something twisted in his heart.

"Good morning," he said, his hands stuffed into his pockets.

Theodora glanced at him warily. "Good morning," she replied, tossing corn to her small congregation of Rhode Island Reds.

"I thought we might have a talk."

"Why bother?" she asked quietly. "You and Miranda will be in your own place by next week. You won't have to come over here except at Christmas."

He took out a cigarette and lit it, trying to decide how to proceed. It wasn't going to be easy. In all fairness, it shouldn't be, he conceded.

"I...would like to know about my father," he said.

The bowl slid involuntarily from Theodora's hands and scattered the rest of the corn while she stared, white-faced, at Harden. "What?" she asked.

"I want to know about my father," he said tersely.

"Who he was, what he looked like." He hesitated. "How you...felt about him."

"I imagine you know that already," she replied proudly. "Don't you?"

He blew out a cloud of smoke. "Yes. I think I do, now," he agreed. "There's a big difference between love and infatuation. I didn't know, until I met Miranda."

"All the same, I'm sorry about Anita," she said tightly. "I've had to live with it, too, you know."

"Yes." He hesitated. "It...must have been hard for you. Having me, living here." He stared at her, searching for words. "If Miranda and I hadn't married, if I'd given her a child, I know she'd have had it. Cherished it. Loved it, because it would have been a part of me."

Theodora nodded.

"And all the shame, all the taunts and cutting remarks, would have passed right off her because we loved each other so much," he continued. "She'd have raised my child, and what she felt for him would have been...special, because a love like that only happens once for most people."

Theodora averted her eyes, blinded by tears. "If they're lucky," she said huskily.

"I didn't know," he said unsteadily, unconsciously repeating the very words Miranda had said to him the night before. "I never loved...until now."

Theodora couldn't find the words. She turned, finding an equal emotion in Harden's face. She stood there, small and defenseless, and something burst inside him.

He held out his arms. Theodora went into them, crying her heart out against his broad chest, washing away all the bitterness and pain and hurt. She felt something wet against her cheek, where his face rested, and around them the wind blew.

"Mother," he said huskily.

Her thin arms tightened, and she smiled, thanking God for miracles.

Later, they sat on the front porch and she told him about his father, bringing out a long-hidden album that contained the only precious photographs she had.

"He looks like me," Harden mused, seeing his own face reflected in what, in the photograph, was a much younger one.

"He was like you," she replied. "Brave and loyal and loving. He never shirked his duty, and I loved him with all my heart. I still do. I always will."

"Did your husband know how you felt?"

"Oh, yes," she said simply. "I was too honest to pretend. But he loved children, you see, and my pregnancy brought out all his protective instincts. He loved me the way I loved Barry," she added sadly. "I gave him all I could, and hoped that it would be enough." She brushed at a tear. "He loved you, you know. Even though you weren't blood kin to him, he was crazy about you from the day you were born."

He smiled. "Yes. I remember." He frowned as he looked at his mother. "I'm sorry. I'm so damned sorry."

"You had to find your way," she said. "It took a long time, and you had plenty of sorrow along the way. I knew what you were going through in school, with the other children throwing the facts of your birth up to you. But if I had interfered, I would have made it worse, don't you see? You had to learn to cope. Experience is always the best teacher."

"Even if it doesn't seem so at the time. Yes, I know that now."

"About Anita…"

He took her thin, wrinkled hand in his and held it tightly. "Anita's people would never have let us marry. But even now, I can't really be sure that it was me she wanted, or just someone her parents didn't approve of. She was very young, and high-strung, and her mother died in an asylum. Evan said that if God wants someone to live, they will, despite the odds. I don't know why I never realized that until now."

She smiled gently. "I think Miranda's opened your eyes to a lot of things."

He nodded. "She won't ever forget her husband, or the child she lost. That's a good thing. Our experiences make us the people we are. But the past is just that. She and I will make our own happiness. And there'll be other babies. A lot of them, I hope."

"Oh, that reminds me! Jo Ann's pregnant!"

"Maybe it's the water," Harden said, and smiled at her.

She laughed. The smile faded and her eyes were eloquent. "I love you very much."

"I...love you," he said stiffly. He'd said it more in two days than he'd said it in his life. Probably it would get easier as he went along. Theodora didn't seem to mind, though. She just beamed and after a minute, she turned the page in the old album and started relating other stories about Harden's father.

It was late afternoon before Miranda came downstairs, and Evan was trying not to smile as she walked gingerly into the living room where he and Harden were discussing a new land purchase.

"Go ahead, laugh," she dared Evan. "It's all your fault!"

Evan did laugh. "I can't believe that's a complaint, judging by the disgustingly smug look on your husband's face," he mused.

She shook her head, as bright as a new penny as she went into Harden's arms and pressed close.

"No complaints at all," Harden said, sighing. He closed his eyes and laid his cheek against her dark hair. "I just hope I won't die of happiness."

"People have," Evan murmured. But his eyes were sad as he turned away from them. "Well, I'd better get busy. I should be back in time for supper, if this doesn't run late."

"Give Anna my love," Harden replied.

Evan grimaced. "Anna is precocious," he muttered. "Too forward and too outspoken by far for a nineteen-year-old."

"Most of my friends were married by that age," Miranda volunteered.

Evan looked uncomfortable and almost haunted for a minute. "She doesn't even need to be there," he said shortly. "Her mother and I can discuss a land deal without her."

"Is her mother pretty?" Miranda asked. "Maybe she's chaperoning you."

"Her mother is fifty and as thin as a rail," he replied. "Hardly my type."

"What does Anna look like?" Miranda asked, curious now.

"She's voluptuous, to coin a phrase," Harden answered for his taciturn brother. "Blonde and blue-eyed and tall. She's been swimming around Evan for four years, but he won't even give her a look. He's thirty-four, you know. Much too old for a mere child of nineteen."

"That's damned right," he told Harden forcibly. "A man doesn't rob cradles. My God, I've known her since she was a child." He frowned. "Which she still is, of course," he added quickly.

"Go ahead, convince yourself," Harden nodded.

"I don't have to do any convincing!"

"Have a good time."

"I'm going to be discussing land prices," he said, glaring at Harden.

"I used to enjoy that," Harden said, shrugging. "You might, too."

"That will be the day. I..."

"Harden, want a chocolate cake for supper?" Theodora called from the doorway, smiling.

Harden drew Miranda closer and smiled back. "Love one, if it's not too much trouble."

"No trouble at all," she said gently.

"Mother!" he called when she turned, and Evan's eyes popped.

"What?" Theodora asked pleasantly.

"Butter icing?"

She laughed. "That's just what I had in mind!"

Evan's jaw was even with his collar. "My God!" he exclaimed.

Harden looked at him. "Something wrong?"

"You called her Mother!"

"Of course I did, Evan, she's my mother," he replied.

"You've never called her anything except Theodora," Evan explained. "And you smiled at her. You even made sure she wouldn't be put to any extra work making you a cake." He looked at Miranda. "Maybe he's sick."

Miranda looked up at him shyly and blushed. "No, I don't think so."

"I'd have to be weak if I were sick," he explained to Evan, and Miranda made an embarrassed sound and hid her face against his shoulder.

Evan shook his head. "Miracles," he said absently. He shrugged, smiling, and turned toward the door, reaching for his hat as he walked through the hall. "I'll be back by supper."

"Anna's a great cook," Harden reminded him. "You might get invited for supper."

"I won't accept. I told you, damn it, she's too young for me!"

He went out, slamming the door behind him.

Harden led Miranda out the front door and onto the porch, to share the swing with him. "Anna wants to love him, but he won't let her," he explained.

"Why?"

"I'll tell you one dark night," he promised. "But for now, we've got other things to think about. Haven't we?" he added softly.

"Oh, yes." She caught her her breath just before he took it away, and she smiled under his hungry kiss.

The harsh memories of the wreck that had almost destroyed Miranda's life faded day by wonderful day, as Miranda and Harden grew closer. Theodora was drawn into the circle of their happiness and the new relationship she enjoyed with Harden lasted even when the newlyweds moved into their own house.

But Miranda's joy was complete weeks later, when she fainted at a family gathering and a white-faced Harden carried her hotfoot to the doctor.

"Nothing to worry about," Dr. Barnes assured them with a grin, after a cursory examination and a few pointed questions. "Nothing at all. A small growth that will come out all by itself—in just about seven months."

They didn't understand at first. And when they did, Miranda could have sworn that Harden's eyes were watery as he hugged her half to death in the doctor's office.

For Miranda, the circle was complete. The old life was a sad memory, and now there was a future of brightness and warmth to look forward to in a family circle that closed around her like gentle arms. She had, she considered as she looked up at her handsome husband, the whole world right here beside her.

* * * * *

EVAN

To my very special friend Suzanne Hewstone

Chapter One

It wasn't that he minded the dinner so much, or the business talk that followed it. What bothered Evan Tremayne was the way Anna sat and watched him.

She was nineteen, blond, buxom and blue-eyed, a statuesque young woman with long tanned legs that looked incredible in shorts. Evan had tried for the past year not to notice her, despite the fact that he and her mother did a lot of business together. At thirty-four, he was the eldest of four brothers, and he had almost total responsibility for their mother. The family business was mostly under his control and his life was one long tangle of cattle, personnel problems and financial headaches. Anna was the last damned straw.

Especially, he thought, in that pale blue dress that showed too much of her golden tan and her full breasts. Surely her mother should have said some-

thing about that. He wondered if Polly Cochran noticed how fast her daughter was growing up. Polly
was never home, though. She seemed always to be
busy with some new facet of her real estate business.
Anna's father was an airline pilot, but he and Polly
had separated years ago. He lived in Atlanta, Georgia, while they lived in Texas. In fact, Anna had been
given most of her upbringing by Lori, the family
housekeeper. Nobody seemed to have had much time
for her.

Polly had excused herself to take a phone call, and
Evan was left uncomfortably alone with Anna.

"Why have you been glowering at me for the past
ten minutes?" Anna asked softly. Her blond hair was
piled on top of her head, and she looked sophisticated
and very mature for a change.

"Because that dress shows too much of you,"
Evan replied with customary bluntness. His dark eyes
glanced from her face to the swell of her breasts.
"Polly shouldn't have bought it for you."

"She didn't," Anna said with a grin. "It's one of
hers. I borrowed it when she wasn't looking. She
hasn't even noticed that I'm wearing it. You know
how unobservant she is. Everything with Mama is
business."

"Your mother's dresses are too old for you," he
replied, softening the words a little with a smile. He
tended to be more abrasive with Anna than with anyone else in his life because of his unwanted attraction
to her. "You should wear something more appropri-
ate for your own age."

She took a slow breath and her eyes gently worshiped him before they dropped to the table. "Do I really seem so young to you, Evan?"

"I'm thirty-four, little one," he said, his voice deep and slow in the silence of the dining room. "Yes, you seem young."

Her blue eyes settled on her folded hands. "Mama's giving a party Friday night to celebrate the opening of that new mall in Jacobsville that she sold the property for," she said. "Are you coming?"

"Harden and Miranda might," he murmured. "I stay busy."

She looked up, her eyes searching his dark, broad face relentlessly. "You could dance one dance with me. It wouldn't kill you."

"Wouldn't it?" he asked with graveyard humor. He touched his linen napkin to his wide, chiseled mouth and laid it down beside his plate. He got to his feet, towering over her. He was a giant of a man, all muscle and streamlined, from the broad wedge of his chest to his narrow hips and long, powerful legs. "I have to go."

She stood up. "Not yet," she pleaded.

"I've got things to do," he said.

"No, you haven't," she said, pouting. "You just don't want to be alone with me. What are you afraid of, Evan, that I'll assault you on the table?"

He lifted an eyebrow over twinkling brown eyes. "And get mashed potatoes all over my back?"

She let out an irritated breath. "You won't take me seriously."

"I wouldn't dare," he said, fending her off with the ease of years of practice. "Tell Polly I'll see her tomorrow at the office."

"I could be dying of love for you," she said quietly. "And you don't even care that you're breaking my heart."

He grinned. "Hearts don't break, especially at your age."

"Yes, they do." Her eyes ran up and down his big body, lingering on his broad chest. "You might at least kiss me goodbye."

"Let Randall do that," he replied. "He's still at the experimenting age, like you."

"And you're over the hill, I guess?"

He chuckled. "Feels like it sometimes," he confessed. "Good night, little girl."

She colored delicately, which heightened the blue of her eyes. "I'm not a child!"

"You are to me." He picked up his Stetson from the sideboard without looking at her. "Give my apologies to your mother. I can't wait for her. Thanks for dinner."

Before she could come up with a reply, he was out the door and gone, without even seeming to hurry.

The hell of it was that he was fiercely attracted to her. In fact he could probably fall head over heels in love with her. But she was much too young for a serious relationship. At her age she was likely to fall in and out of love weekly. Besides, she was almost certainly a virgin. Evan was six-four and weighed over two hundred and thirty pounds. A brief love affair had ended in near tragedy because, in his desire for the woman he loved—an innocent woman, like Anna—he hadn't been able to control his great strength. Louisa had run from him, terrified. It had scarred him, made him hopelessly wary of innocents like Anna. His size had been a sore spot with him ever since childhood, when he was forever coming to the defense of his three brothers. He'd always had to pull his punches. He'd even put a man in the hospital once when he'd underestimated his strength. The risk with a sheltered girl like Anna was just too great. No, he couldn't afford another episode like that, he couldn't take the chance. Better to stick to experienced women who weren't afraid of him.

Back at the brick mansion, Anna was raging over the things Evan had said. He was treating her like a teen with a crush, when she was dying of unrequited love for him!

"Where's Evan?" her mother asked, pausing in the doorway. She was tall and thin and fiftyish, dark, where Anna was fair like her father.

"He left," Anna said curtly. "He was afraid I might bend him over the table and seduce him in the green beans and mashed potatoes."

"What?" Polly asked, laughing.

"He's afraid to be alone with me," Anna muttered. "I suppose he thinks I'll get him pregnant."

"Child, do watch your language," Polly chided. "Never mind Evan. You've already got a beau, much closer to your own age."

Anna sighed. "Good old Randall," she mused.
"With the wandering eyes. I like him a lot, but he
flirts with every woman he sees. I can't believe he's
serious about me."

"He's only in his twenties," Polly said. "Plenty
of time to get serious when you're older. Marriage
is for the birds, honey."

Anna glared at her. "Just because you and Daddy
weren't happy together doesn't mean that I can't
have a good marriage."

Polly's eyes darkened and she turned away to light
a cigarette, ignoring Anna's disapproving glance as
she reached for an ashtray. "Your father and I were
very happy at first," her mother corrected. "Then he
started flying overseas routes and I got into the real
estate business. We never saw each other." She
shrugged. "Just one of those things."

"Do you still love him?"

The older woman cocked a perfect dark eyebrow.
"Love is a myth."

"Oh, Mama," Anna sighed.

Polly just laughed. "Dream your dreams, child.
I'll settle for CDs in the bank and plenty of stocks
and bonds in my safety deposit box. Where did you
get that dress?"

The younger woman grinned. "It's yours."

Her mother gave her a mock glare. "How many
times have I told you to stay out of my closet?"

"Only twenty. You won't buy me anything this
sexy."

"I suppose you wore it to tempt Evan," Polly

mused. "Well, you might as well give up. Evan's too old for you, and he knows it, even if you don't. Go and change. I'll treat you to a movie."

"Okay."

It was nice to have a mother who was also a good friend, Anna thought as she complied with the request. But nobody seemed inclined to take her feelings for Evan seriously. Especially Evan himself.

Sometimes Anna thought it would be nice if she had a job that would put her in constant contact with Evan. But she couldn't work cattle and she knew nothing about bookkeeping or finance. The best she'd been able to manage was secretarial work at her mother's real estate office. That did bring her into fairly frequent contact with Evan, because the Tremayne brothers were always looking for investment properties. Since Evan was the eldest and headed the company, he was the one her mother saw most frequently. That meant Anna got to see him. She was working on the premise of water dripping on stone. If he was around her enough, he might notice her more.

There were, of course, better ways than just sitting around hoping. Anna had the pursuit of Evan down to a science. She could wrangle invitations to parties he'd attend, she found ways to track him down at lunch and accidentally run into him. She occasionally waylaid him at the post office or the feed store. Most people found her relentless chase amusing, but more and more she sensed that it was affecting Evan. If only he'd just look at her!

It was a well-known fact that Evan hated alcohol. He had an intense aversion to it for reasons nobody understood. So all Anna had to do to attract his interest at her mother's office the next day was to sit two bottles of unopened whiskey on her desk before he was due at the realty company.

He stopped dead when he saw them, his dark brows knitting over deep-set brown eyes shaded by the brim of the Stetson pulled low over his forehead.

"What the hell is that for?" he demanded, gesturing toward the bottles.

"Medicinal purposes," Anna said smugly. She was wearing a white linen suit with a pink blouse, her hair in a plait, and she looked both businesslike and feminine.

He glared at her. "Try again."

She glanced around to make sure none of the other women in the office were listening, and she leaned forward. "It's to treat snakebite."

The scowl got worse. "There aren't any rattlers in here."

She grinned. "Yes, there are." She pulled open her bottom drawer to reveal two huge plastic snakes with realistic fangs.

Evan's eyes widened. "Good God!"

"These are for people who need an excuse to drink the whiskey."

"Are you out of your mind?"

"If I was, how could I be using it to talk to you?"

He gave up and went past her, shaking his head. Anna watched him, her blue eyes lazily adoring on his tall, powerful body. He was perfectly built, with broad shoulders tapering to slender hips and long legs. He had a rodeo rider's physique, except for his great size. Evan had hands the size of plates. He was even intimidating to some of the women in the office, who made innuendoes that Anna was too sheltered to understand. But Anna found nothing frightening about him at all. She loved him.

He was aware of that silent stare, but he didn't react to it. She was playing games again, he knew it. She had to be aware that the whiskey would draw his attention. It had worked. He had to be more careful from now on, not to fall into her little traps.

But it wasn't that easy. When he came out of Polly's office, Anna wasn't at her desk. He found her outside near his car, on her hands and knees beside the small white Porsche her mother had bought her, looking through a small toolbox.

"Looking for something?" he asked.

"Yes. For my left-handed Johnson wrench."

He sighed impatiently. "There's no such thing."

"There is so. Johnson is the local mechanic and he's left-handed. I borrowed his wrench and now I've lost it."

He threw up his hands. "What's gotten into you today?"

"Maddened passion," she said, standing up, her eyes wide and theatrical, like her audible breathing. "I'm dying for you!" She threw her arms wide and sprawled against the side of the car. "Go ahead, ravish me!"

He was having to choke back laughter. "Where?" he asked, glancing around the big car park.

"On the hood of the car, in the trunk, I don't care!" She was still holding the pose, her eyes closed.

"The hood would break under your weight, never mind mine, and I don't think I could get my head and shoulders in that tiny trunk."

She opened her eyes and glared at him. "On the pavement?"

He shook his head. "Too hard."

"The grass."

"Chiggers and fire ants." He folded his arms over his chest, and his eyes ran down her body slowly and without his usual detachment. In fact, the bold gaze unnerved her. No one, not even Randall, had ever looked at her in that particular glittery way, as if he knew what she looked like with her clothes off.

Defensively, she folded her arms across her jacket. "Don't do that," she said softly.

"You started it, honey," he reminded her, and moved deliberately closer, threatening her with his size and strength. She looked nervous now, which was what he intended. Playing games with grown men could be dangerous. Someone needed to prove it to her.

"Evan..." she said uneasily.

The car park was deserted, and Anna's bravado was quickly disappearing. Flirting was one thing, but she still wasn't quite sure of herself in any intimate situation. She could handle Randall, but Evan had an untamed look about him. He might seem like a big teddy bear at times, but the Tremayne brothers were a fiery bunch and he was the eldest. Probably Connal, Harden and Donald had learned all they knew from his example.

"What's the matter?" he asked with a mocking smile when she backed against the car like a kitten at bay. "Not as safe as you thought?"

She didn't know what she thought anymore. He smelled of cologne and soap, and his height and size were intimidating.

"It's broad daylight," she pointed out.

"I know that." He pursed his wide lips and smiled down at her, but it wasn't any kind of smile she'd ever seen on his lips before. Or on any other man's, come to think of it. It was sensuous and masculine and very arrogant, as if he knew that her knees were weak and her heart was beating her to death.

"I really have to go, Evan," she said, sounding frantic.

He could have pushed it. He almost did. Her very vulnerability attracted him as her blatant flirting never had. His eyes fell to her high, full breasts and narrowed. She was voluptuous in the very best way, well-endowed enough to almost fill hands even the size of his. He started at the direction his thoughts were taking. Anna was a virgin. He reminded himself of that silently and forced his eyes back up to her flushed, stunned face.

"I thought you wanted to get ravished," he said

softly, the velvety depth of his voice a threat in itself. "Running away before we even get started?"

She swallowed down her fear and eased away from him, laughing nervously. He made her feel young and totally green. "I'll need to take a lot of vitamins first, to get in shape," she said, glancing at him as she opened the door of her car and climbed in. "Hold that thought, though."

He laughed gently at her grit. She had courage, and she bounced back fast. If she'd been a few years older, anything might happen. "Okay, rabbit, hit the road. But next time, be sure you know what you're asking for," he added, and his eyes were serious. "A man won't usually turn down a blatant invitation, even if it's against his better judgment."

"You've been turning me down for years," she reminded him, catching her breath. "You're experienced."

His dark eyes narrowed on her face. "Yes, I am," he said quietly. "Keep that in mind. You're still at the stage where you think a man's appetite can be satisfied by a few soft kisses. Mine can't."

She glared at him. "I wasn't offering...!"

"Weren't you?"

She averted her gaze to her fingers on the key in the ignition. "No, I wasn't," she said curtly. "I was only teasing."

"That kind of teasing can be dangerous. Practice on Randall. He's safer than I am."

"At least he wants me," she muttered, and she abruptly started the car.

"Good for him," he replied. "Don't speed in that toy car."

She moved the toolbox from the passenger seat to the floorboard. "I never speed," she lied.

He watched her fasten her seat belt. "Through for the day already?" he taunted softly.

"I'm having lunch with my best friend," she said evasively.

He lifted his eyebrows. "I didn't know you had one."

She didn't answer him. She backed out of the parking spot and managed to take off without stripping the gears. Tears glittered in her eyes, but he wouldn't see them.

She stopped at a nearby restaurant and had a hamburger, all by herself. She had no girlfriends. She liked Randall very well. He was a resident at the hospital, the son of the local doctor, and not bad looking. Of course, he did have a wandering eye, but Anna got along with him and didn't feel threatened by him. Her heart was Evan's, sadly enough. How terrible, to love a man who treated you like a child and made fun of you when you offered yourself to him. She could have bawled. Actually, everything was bravado with her, where Evan was concerned. She'd teased him just to get his attention. But having gotten it, she didn't know what to do with it. He was experienced, and she wasn't. She didn't know how to handle a man like that. She'd just been shown graphically that she was totally out of her element with Evan.

She went back to the office late, and her heart wasn't in her work for the rest of the day. Polly didn't even notice. Anna wondered sometimes if her mother paid much attention to anything that she didn't want to see.

The party her mother gave to celebrate the opening of the new Jacobsville mall gave Anna an excuse to dress to the back teeth. Not, she told herself, that Evan was going to notice. He'd already said he probably wouldn't come. Randall would be there, though. She could certainly dress up for him.

She wore a witchy, silver, crystal-pleated dress that fell in layers to just below her knees. She let her blond hair waft loosely around her shoulders, straight and heavy, and she wore sexy little high-heeled sandals on her feet. She knew she looked good, but the evening felt flat. She added a hint of pastel lipstick to her full lips and brushed her hair, but her heart wasn't in her preparations. Without Evan, her whole life was flat and uninteresting.

Downstairs Randall was waiting for her, looking very trendy in his sports coat and neatly pressed slacks. He wore wire-rimmed glasses, and he was very dignified. Not a hair out of place, although what he had was thinning above his forehead. He wasn't handsome. But women loved him. He had a gentle, caring demeanor and he was good company, even if he did have the worst kind of wandering eye. Anna liked him, and the feeling was mutual.

"You look very nice," he told her, glancing

around at the very elegant crowd Polly was enter-
taining. "Your mother knows everybody, doesn't
she?"

"Everyone who moves in her circles," Anna replied. Randall's interest in the wealthy set disturbed
her. Anna had never mixed with people simply because of their wealth or social status. Neither did the
Tremaynes. Randall was thinking ahead to the time
when he would be in practice, she was sure. His pref-
erence for an uptown medical practice was something he made no secret of.

He took Anna's arm and guided her through to the
canapé table, where ruby punch and savories were
being offered to the guests. "I'm starved. I had to
forego lunch for exams. I wish this was a sit-down
affair."

"Lori did honey chicken and salmon croquettes,"
she told him, gesturing toward platters of food. "And
there are little blueberry muffins, too. If you load
enough on your plate, you'll get full."

He smiled at her. "I guess so."

She noticed the couples moving to the soft music
of the live band. She loved to dance, but Randall
couldn't. He had no desire to learn, even though
she'd offered to teach him.

"You wouldn't like to shuffle around the floor?"
she tried yet once more.

He shook his head. "Sorry. I'm tired. I want to
get off my feet, not on them!"

She lifted her shoulders as if she didn't care. She
got a cup of punch, looking around for familiar faces.

When she spotted Harden and Miranda Tremayne, her eyes went helplessly past them, hoping for a glimpse of Evan. But he wasn't there. Her face fell, even as she smiled a greeting at the couple.

Miranda was wearing a black maternity dress with flowing lace, and she had a radiant Harden beside her. Anna had always felt a little sorry for Harden, because he'd seemed so alone. But these days, he smiled a lot, and the old coldness was gone from his blue eyes.

He had a possessive arm around Miranda's swollen waist, and he looked devastating in a dinner jacket. Almost, Anna thought, as good as Evan looked similarly clothed.

"Nice turnout," Harden murmured dryly. "Your mother outdid herself."

"Indeed she did," Anna said, grinning. "Do I get introduced? I've seen Miranda, but I've never actually gotten to meet her."

"Miranda, this is Anna Cochran," Harden obliged. "You met Polly at the Chamber of Commerce banquet a few days ago. Polly sold the property for the new mall and helped coax in some new businesses."

"I'm very glad to meet you," Miranda said, smiling back, her silvery eyes almost the color of Anna's dress. "I've heard a lot about you."

Anna sighed. "About my relentless pursuit of Evan, I guess," she murmured ruefully. "It's a hopeless cause, but I can't seem to get out of the habit.

One day he'll marry somebody and I can give up with good grace.''

"That doesn't seem likely," Harden replied on a sigh. "Evan is sure he's doomed to perpetual bachelorhood. He's forever moaning that women won't give him the time of day."

"His excuse used to be that they trampled him trying to get to Harden." Miranda laughed, swinging her long, dark hair. "Nowadays, he's convinced that he's too old to appeal to anyone."

"Thirty-four and ready for 'the home,'" Harden agreed. He shook his head. "Save him, Anna."

"I'm trying," she laughed. "But he won't let me put away my baby dolls and my play tea set. He thinks I'm a mere child."

"He wouldn't if he saw you in that dress," Miranda said with a conspiratory smile. "You look very elegant."

"At least Randall noticed," Anna grimaced. "Want to meet him?"

She turned to drag Randall over by one arm while he nibbled on chicken wings. "This is Randall Wayne," she told them. "He's a medical student."

"I'm a resident, thank you very much," Randall said, glowering at her. "Only a short leap from my own practice, when I finish my residency next year," he added, grinning at them. "Remember me if you break anything."

"I'll do that," Harden promised.

"Oh, Randall," Anna sighed. "You're hopeless."

"Patients are scarce for young doctors," he reminded her. "Can't blame a man for trying to drum up business in advance."

"Certainly not," Miranda said laughing.

Anna didn't want to ask, but she couldn't quite help it. "I don't suppose any of the rest of the family came with you?" she asked.

"Just Evan," Harden murmured reluctantly, watching the way her eyes brightened. "He's parking the car." He didn't want to tell her the rest. Anna's helpless attraction to Evan was so obvious that he was already hurting for her.

"He may be out there all night," Randall pointed out. "It took me thirty minutes to find someplace to leave my car."

"Evan's resourceful," Harden said. He glanced regretfully at Anna. She was going to need time to steel herself before Evan came in. He owed her that. "And Nina's with him. She's a whiz at finding the impossible."

Chapter Two

Anna didn't know how she managed to respond to that casual comment, but she saved her pride with a smile and an offhand remark. Evan had made it abundantly clear that he didn't want her adulation, now he was pushing the knife home. He'd brought Nina, whom everyone knew was his old flame. The woman was now a successful fashion model in Houston, and she was visiting locally. Probably she was doing her best to rekindle those embers. If Evan had brought her to Polly's party, he had to be encouraging her.

"My brother is an idiot," Harden told Miranda as they moved away, his blue eyes glittering. "My God, did you see what it did to her? Evan thinks she's a child, but the kind of hurt I saw in her face isn't juvenile."

"Doesn't he feel anything at all for her?" Miranda asked.

"I don't know. If he does, he's buried it. He's stubborn, and he can be cruel when he's pushed. Anna's made a game of it, playing at flirting and teasing. He thinks that's all there is to it. He doesn't think she's serious."

"But she is."

He nodded. "I'm sure of it. It's a camouflage. After all, the safest way to hide your feelings is to exaggerate them. Poor little thing. Randall isn't a patch on Evan, but she'll wind up marrying him out of unrequited love for my brother."

"Such a waste." Miranda sighed.

He pulled her closer. "Indeed it is. Thank God, we're past all that uncertainty."

She smiled, lifting radiant eyes to his. "I love you."

His blue eyes kindled. He bent and kissed her softly. "I can send that back, multiplied."

"Yes," she whispered, pressing close. "I know. We have so much, Harden."

His lean hand lightly touched the soft swell of her belly and his eyes blazed into hers. "More than I ever dreamed," he whispered. "Did I ever tell you that you're my life?"

Miranda was too choked with emotion to even answer. She pressed close against his side while his lips brushed her forehead with exquisite tenderness.

Anna, watching them covertly, wanted to cry. What they felt for each other was almost tangible. She'd never known that kind of intimate caring. She probably never would. Randall's idea of romance was a few kisses punctuated with groping. He might make an excellent doctor, but he had a long way to go as even a lukewarm lover. And he wasn't, could never be, Evan.

She sipped her punch while Randall spoke to someone he knew from the hospital. She wouldn't look at the door, she absolutely wouldn't. She wasn't going to give Evan the satisfaction of knowing that he was killing her with his indifference.

"Finally, something to drink!" came a husky, purring voice from behind her. "Hello, Anna!" Nina Ray said, smiling faintly. "I hope that punch is spiked. I really need a drink. Evan had to park almost in the pond! My feet are killing me from so much walking."

"That's nothing unusual is it, for a model?" Evan taunted.

Anna couldn't meet his eyes. She glanced at his white shirt and black tie and dinner jacket and averted her gaze to gorgeously dark Nina in a white and black gown that put everyone else's dresses to shame.

"You look great," Anna said sincerely. "I see you all the time in fashion magazines. For a small-town girl, you sure hit it big."

"I had a lot of help, lovey," Nina mused. She glanced up at Evan with a self-confident sexiness that made Anna grind her teeth in frustration. She'd never learn how to do that.

"Where's Polly?" Evan asked as he filled punch cups for Nina and then himself.

"Circulating," Anna said, smiling. "She's very much the lady of the hour."

"She deserves it," Evan replied. "That mall will bring in a lot of new businesses, and plenty of revenue."

"Everything helps to swell the tax base," Randall remarked, joining them. He smiled at Nina. "You look lovely!" he enthused, and Anna could have hit him. He hadn't been half that vocal about her own appearance.

"Thank you. And who's this?" Nina asked, her dark eyes flirting with Randall.

"Randall Wayne," he said, taking her slender hand in his. He actually kissed the knuckles, just above the red-painted nails. "Nice to meet you, Miss Ray."

Nina beamed. "You know who I am?"

"Everyone does. Your face is unmistakable. I see it on magazine covers all the time."

"Yes." Nina sighed complacently. "My career has taken off since Evan helped me find that new agency."

"Anything to help," Evan said suavely. He was trying not to notice Anna and failing miserably. In that silver gown, her exquisite skin was displayed almost too blatantly. Her honey-brown tan made her complexion even prettier and emphasized her big blue eyes. It was an effort to keep away from her.

"The band is very good," Nina remarked. "Evan, do let's dance!"

She took his hand and headed for the dance floor

without giving him time to speak to Randall or Anna. Not that he would have, anyway, Anna thought. He was giving her a blatant message—hands off. She lifted her cup of punch to her lips with a sigh.

"This punch needs help," one of the guests remarked, slipping a bottle of whiskey from under his dinner jacket. "Here goes!"

Anna watched him fill the bowl with a wry grin. She knew one of the guests would have hives if he saw that. Evan didn't like punch, though, so there was little likelihood that he'd imbibe. He hated alcohol. Anna had heard that he actually took a glass of wine back to the kitchen one night when he was having dinner with Justin and Shelby Ballenger.

She mentioned that to Randall after the punch spiker had sampled his handiwork and retired to the dance floor with his partner.

"Yes, I heard about that," Randall remarked. "Justin and Shelby have three boys now, haven't they?"

"Yes. They're neck and neck with Calhoun and Abby."

"They have two boys and a girl," he reminded her. "I heard Harden and Evan's brother Connal mention it at a party I attended a week ago."

She laughed gently. "Connal insisted that Calhoun and Abby had a daughter just after their second child was born. They don't. They have a son named Terry, and when Connal heard the name, he assumed they'd gotten the daughter they wanted. He knows better now, of course, but it's become something of a family joke. Not that anybody mentions it to Calhoun or Abby.''

"Terry is kind of a unisex name," Randall said.

"It's short for Terrance, which isn't," she corrected. "Imagine that—two brothers and six sons and not a girl in the bunch." She shook her head.

"What about Shelby's brother, Tyler?"

"He and his wife can't have children," Anna said with quiet regret. "But they've adopted five! Nell was very upset, but Tyler involved her in one of those foster parent programs. In no time, she was knee-deep in kids who'd had no real home at all. They said the children are the greatest miracle of their lives.''

"A unique solution," Randall agreed. "One couple in seven is infertile. It must be difficult, although they seem to have found a way to cope with the loss.''

Anna lowered her eyes to the punch table and thought about never having Evan's children. Not that she would, because he had Nina. It was sad and sobering.

"I suppose if you love each other, no obstacle is insurmountable," she said dimly.

"I suppose. Here. Try some of this. It's rather good.''

He handed her a cup of spiked punch and she sipped it, wincing at the sting of the alcohol on her tongue. The ice fruit ring hadn't diluted the whiskey very much, and Anna seldom drank.

"That's strong stuff," she remarked.

"Only if you aren't used to it." He chuckled. "You're just like Evan about alcohol, aren't you?"

She averted her face. He obviously had no idea how much that remark hurt her. "I don't like alcohol," she said absently.

"Yes, I've noticed."

She didn't hear the faint mockery in his tone. Her eyes had been drawn against her will to Evan. He was so tall and husky that he dwarfed almost every other man in the room. He had the lovely Nina close in his big arms and he was holding her with casual intimacy. Both her slender arms were looped around his neck; his hands on her waist held her carelessly close. He'd never held Anna like that. Probably he never would.

Her eyes softened and saddened at the sight of him. In evening clothes, he was devastating. His dark tan was emphasized by the white shirt he wore, and the black tie, dinner jacket and slacks made him look taller and very dignified. Just looking at him made Anna feel warm and safe, like coming home. If only he felt that way about her. It would be heaven.

Evan felt her rapt gaze and met it across the room. It was like lightning striking. His body tautened helplessly, and his eyes narrowed. Anna again, he thought angrily, playing with matches. She didn't know what she was doing. At nineteen she was just beginning to feel her power as a woman, and she was using it blatantly with every man who came close to her. That was all it was, so he'd better remember.

He tore his gaze away and bent to kiss Nina in front of the whole assembly. He did it thoroughly and with fierce need, to banish the sight of Anna's wounded face.

Nina was breathless when he let her go, and Anna had vanished. At least he'd accomplished that much.

"Want to take me home right now, big man?" Nina asked huskily. "I'm willing."

But Evan wasn't. He shook his head. "We'd better not vanish before Polly makes her speech," he said with forced humor.

Nina sighed. "You still don't really want me, do you?" she asked quietly. "I can't get you within a mile of my apartment."

"We're friends," he reminded her, smiling. "Otherwise, why would I be giving your career a helping hand?"

"To make some other woman jealous, I'm beginning to think," she said candidly, watching his eyelids flinch. "Or to use me as camouflage. Because you certainly don't want me just for myself. You hardly ever take me out."

He smiled. "I keep busy."

"Not that busy, and you don't go out with many women. That's right," she nodded when she saw his puzzled expression, "I still have friends in Jacobsville who keep me up-to-date on who's seeing whom. You don't date anyone regularly. The gossip is that Anna Cochran has been seen pursuing you everywhere except up a tree."

He drew in a heavy breath. "That's partially true."

"So that's why you brought me here. Probably why you kissed me, too." She smiled lazily. "Okay, lover. If you need protection, here I am. Do your worst. We'll say it's for old times' sake."

"You're very generous," he mused.

"You've been that," she replied seriously. "I'll help you scrape the kid off, no problem."

He didn't like it put that way, as if Anna was a leech. He frowned.

"She's a babe in the woods, isn't she?" Nina was saying, her eyes on Anna standing at the punch bowl with Randall. "Is she going to marry the medical student, do you think?"

"How should I know?" he asked irritably. He'd never thought of Randall as much of a threat to Anna's maidenhood, but she was spending a lot of time with the younger man lately.

"She's well-to-do. Or her mother is," Nina mused, thinking aloud. "A young doctor going into practice needs a rich wife."

Evan stiffened. "Anna isn't that stupid."

"Darling, she's a teenager. What does she know about men? My God, I'll bet she's even a virgin!"

Evan didn't want to think about that. It made his blood run hot. He turned Nina to the rhythm. "Anna is Randall's business, not mine. Dance. Help me get her off my neck."

Nina smiled warmly. "My pleasure."

Anna watched them dance and took another sip of

her punch, and then another. "I wish you could dance, Randall," she said, the words sounding a little slurred. She felt very relaxed.

"So do I, sometimes. Want to try it?" he asked, putting down his cup. "I feel pretty loose right now."

"Good."

She went into his arms and taught him the basic two-step. He began to grin, and his hands brought her gently closer.

"This is nice," he said wonderingly.

"So it is." She lay her cheek on his chest and closed her eyes, barely moving as the music continued. The devil with Evan, she told herself. She didn't care if he made love to his old flame right there on the dance floor. She just wouldn't look.

"Having a good time, Anna?" one of Polly's friends asked as she danced nearby with her husband.

"Oh, yes," Anna replied politely. "I hope you are."

"It's lovely. Evan's brought someone with him, I see," the woman added with a faintly mocking smile. "Warding you off, is he?"

Anna flushed. Over the years she'd gotten used to being teased about her pursuit of Evan, but tonight it stung. "Nina's an old friend of his," she pointed out.

"Yes, but he doesn't usually come to Polly's parties with a woman in tow. In fact," she said cattily, "he doesn't usually come at all these days, does he?

I suppose he's really desperate if he has to look up old flames to discourage you.''

Anna pulled away from Randall, who was openly scowling, and moved back to the punch bowl, leaving the woman with her mouth open.

"What are you so upset about?" Randall asked, joining her there. "Everybody knows that you used to chase Evan. You're not doing it now, so why let people bother you?" He slid an arm around her waist. "You've got me, now."

Had she really? Every time a new woman came into the room, she could see Randall's eyes sizing her up. He was a born flirt, and despite his lack of conventional good looks, he could be utterly charming.

"I guess I didn't realize how blatant I must have seemed," Anna said quietly, her eyes downcast. "I was only playing." She hadn't been, but it salvaged some of her pride to pretend she was.

"I know that," Randall said. "So do most other people. Don't worry about gossip. I've been ignoring it for weeks."

Her head jerked up. "What have you heard?"

He shrugged and smiled a little. "Just that you'd been madly pursuing Evan all over town. Accidental meetings that weren't accidental, hanging around him at parties and flirting shamelessly, that kind of thing. They said Evan couldn't go anywhere in Jacobsville without your turning up there. I thought it was funny."

"Evan didn't," she said miserably. "I went overboard and he's finally reached the end of his rope. I wish I'd realized sooner how silly I was behaving."

"Was that woman right? Did he bring the lovely Nina to ward you off?"

She nodded, feeling conspicuous now. "I'm sure of it. Poor Evan."

"I don't know," Randall murmured, smiling at her. "It must be flattering to be chased by a pretty young woman."

"It must be exasperating, you mean," she said, suddenly understanding. How could she have let things go that far without realizing the position she was putting Evan in? She'd teased and flirted, hoping to make him notice her. But all she'd accomplished was to scare him off. What an idiot she'd been!

As if realizing that wasn't bad enough, she had to face the fact that everyone knew that his squiring of Nina was to keep her at bay. It was humiliating to have him publicly reject her like this. As she glanced around, she caught people looking at her and began to notice the faint pity in their eyes.

She had to fight tears as the evening wore on. Evan danced with no one except Nina and was so attentive to her that speculation on the rekindling of the old relationship ran rampant. The way he avoided Anna spoke volumes. Nobody noticed that Anna was doing her best to avoid him as well. She clung to Randall like a leech.

Polly gave a speech and introduced two of the mall's main backers, along with the merchants who were already committed to opening businesses in it.

The speech was well received, and it did divert Anna from her misery.

But despite Randall's company, Anna felt dejected and empty inside. She put on a good front, laughing and glittering, so that no one would guess how badly hurt she was.

When the crowd started to dwindle, Polly paused beside her daughter with an affectionate smile. "I thought it went rather well. How are you doing, darling?"

"Marvelous, thanks," Anna said airily, forcing a smile. "It's been lovely, hasn't it, Randall?"

Randall was watching her narrowly. "How many times have you hit that punch bowl, Anna?"

"Only three," she said, blinking. "Why?"

He exchanged a knowing look with Polly.

"Somebody spiked the punch," Polly guessed.

"How did you know?"

"Evan smelled his punch and put it down with a vicious glare in my direction," Polly said dryly.

"I should have known he'd notice it first," Randall laughed. He checked his watch. "Goodness, I've got to go. I'm on call at the hospital from midnight, and it's almost that. I'll be in touch tomorrow or the next day, as soon as I get some free time. 'Night," he murmured, brushing a careless kiss across Anna's forehead.

She watched him go with no real interest. Polly put an affectionate arm around her shoulders.

"It's killing you, isn't it?" she asked with unusual protectiveness. "You'll survive, my darling. We all do. Evan just isn't the type to settle down. You've always known that."

"I was only ever flirting," Anna said stubbornly. "It wasn't for real. I thought he knew it."

Polly didn't contradict her daughter. She recognized the anguish in those blue eyes, though. Her arm contracted. "Let's go and listen to the band. Randall will phone tomorrow. Maybe he'll take you out to eat. You stay home too much."

"I guess I do. Randall's nice."

"You'll learn one day that we have to take what we can get out of life and not wish for the impossible things too hard," Polly said gently. "One day at a time, pet."

Anna smiled. "Yes." But she was thinking of how many days it was going to take to get over tonight.

Evan and Nina gravitated toward them, and Anna had to fight the urge to cut and run.

"It was a lovely party. Thank you for asking me," Nina said with a smile in Polly's direction.

"It was my pleasure," the older woman replied. "Evan, I'm glad you came, too. I didn't really expect you. If Nina managed to pry you out of your office, good for her."

"I plan to pry him out a lot more often, now," Nina purred, leaning against Evan's shoulder. Anna didn't speak or look at him, and after a minute, he stared at her openly.

"How much of that punch have you had?" Evan demanded of Anna, his dark eyes sparking.

She didn't look at him. "Only a little," she lied. "I know it's spiked."

"You should have poured it out and made more," he told Polly bluntly. "Anna isn't allowed to drink hard liquor, surely?"

Polly started. "Evan, she's nineteen, going on twenty," she said with urbane amusement. "Of course she's allowed to drink."

"Alcohol can kill," he persisted. "Especially if she ever gets in the habit of driving under the influence. She could go to jail..."

"I don't drink and drive, Evan," Anna said solemnly. "I never would. If the alcohol bothers you so much, why don't you go home?"

She poured herself another cup—her fourth, actually—and lifted it to her lips, draining it while her blue eyes defied the angry dark ones glaring at her.

"Can't you do anything with her?" he demanded of Polly.

Anna's eyebrows arched. "My mother doesn't tell me what to do anymore."

Evan's own eyebrows arched. That didn't sound like Anna. Not at all. "You're not used to liquor," he began.

She smiled coldly. "Watch me get used to it," she replied, still smarting from his public humiliation of her and wanting to hurt back. "Nothing I do is any of your damned business. You remember that."

She whirled on her heel, a little wobbly, and went toward the staircase. The whiskey in the punch was lying heavily on her stomach and she felt nausea ris-

ing in her throat. But she felt as if she'd just declared
independence, and it wasn't a bad feeling at all. Evan
wasn't going to be her fatal weakness anymore. Even
if she'd deserved his rejection, he could have simply
spoken to her in private. He didn't have to do it like
this.

Evan stared after her, scowling. It was the first
time in memory that Anna had talked back to him.
He was used to blind adoration from her, or at worst,
pert, flirting comments. Stark hostility was new and
all too exciting. His body was reacting to her antag-
onism in ways he'd never expected.

"She's a bit tipsy, I think, Evan. Don't mind anything she says," Polly said, waving it off. "By the
way, I've got a new investment property that you
might be interested in. Want to stop by the office
sometime next week and look over a prospectus?"

"Yes, I'd like that," Evan said, preoccupied.

"Let's go," Nina coaxed. "I'm so tired, and I've
got a show in the morning."

"Sure. Good night, Polly," Evan said.

She nodded, smiling curiously at the way Evan's
eyes kept going to the staircase. His possessive attitude toward Anna startled and amused her. Of
course, Evan was thirty-four, too old to be taking any
real masculine interest in her poor, lovesick daughter.
She turned and went back to her remaining guests,
thrusting his odd behavior to the back of her mind.
Anna would get over him. It was just a crush.

Anna was sick most of the night, and not just from
the alcohol. It had been an eye-opening experience

to have Evan flaunt a woman in front of her. For all of the two years, she'd been madly pursuing him, he'd never used that counterattack before. Probably now that he knew it bothered her, it wouldn't be the last time he resorted to it.

Well, she told herself, that was that. If he was desperate enough to throw himself into the arms of an old flame to escape Anna, it was time to retreat. She'd always known somehow that he was never going to take her seriously. She should have given up long ago.

The next morning she braided her long blond hair, put on her shorts and halter top and went out to set up her easel in the garden. She loved to paint. She was quite good at landscapes, having even sold a few. It gave her something to do when she wasn't working.

Polly was at the office today—she sometimes worked seven days a week. But Anna worked five and painted the other two. Now she was toying seriously with the idea of quitting the office. She loved art and she had an eye for investment paintings. She could ask the owner of the local art gallery, who was a friend of the family, to give her a job. It would get her away from the office, where she was all too likely to run into Evan. He wanted her out of his life, so she decided that she'd give him a helping hand. It was the least she could do after having pestered him for two years. Cold sober, she could even understand why he'd brought Nina to the party last night. Poor man. He must have been at the very end of his rope.

As she dabbed paint on the canvas, she considered her options. She didn't really want to leave home, but even that might be a good idea. She was going on twenty years old. It was time she had a life of her own, apart from her mother's. She had to start thinking about her future. Marrying Randall was hardly an option, even though he'd been hinting that he wouldn't be averse to the idea. Considering Polly's wealth, it would be a strategic move on his part. It would give him the financial wherewithal to buy into an established practice, because certainly Polly would be willing to help her new son-in-law.

The landscape she was working on was a study of sunflowers against the sky. She was using a huge sunflower in the garden as a model. It was a lazy summer day with only a slight breeze, and the sun felt like heaven on her skin.

A car door slammed. She didn't look up. It was almost lunchtime and she was expecting her mother.

"I'm out back," she called. "If you're ready, there's a pasta salad in the fridge. I want to finish this before I come in."

Footsteps answered her shout, but they didn't belong to a woman. They were too heavy.

Her head turned just as Evan came around the side of the house. He was wearing work clothes—jeans and a dust-stained blue plaid shirt, with disreputable boots and a Stetson that was battered almost beyond recognition. She stiffened with hurt indignation, but she couldn't afford to let it show. She turned back to her painting.

"Where's Polly?" he asked without preamble.

So much for the forlorn hope that he might have come to see her, to apologize for dragging her pride through the dust the night before. She kept her eyes on the canvas, so that he wouldn't see the disappointment in them.

"If she isn't at the office, she's on her way here for lunch, I guess," she said.

His dark eyes slid over her with reluctant interest. "She was supposed to leave a prospectus for me on a new piece of land. Know anything about it?"

She shook her head. "Sorry." She traced a sunflower petal with maniacal accuracy, to keep her mind off her breaking heart. "If you'd like to wait, Lori can make you some iced tea."

Anna was so unlike her usual self that he felt out of his element. "What? No invitation to ravish you among the sunflowers?"

"I've decided to grow up," she said without looking at him. "Chasing after unwilling men is for adolescents. From now on, I'm only going after men I think I can catch."

"Like Randall?" he asked.

She shrugged. "Why not?"

Her attitude disturbed him. He leaned against the fence that surrounded the small garden. "I didn't know you painted."

"At the speed you always go around me, I'm not surprised," she said imperturbably and dotted more yellow on the canvas. "No more games, Evan," she said, looking up at him quietly. "I got the message last night. If you really came here to make it clear, there's no need." She managed a smile. "I'm sorry I made your life so difficult. I won't embarrass you anymore, I promise."

He felt empty. His eyes narrowed as she turned back to her canvas. She didn't sound like herself. In fact, he mused, she didn't look like the kid he'd always thought her. Those long, tanned legs were a woman's, like the full breasts under that skimpy halter. She was delectable.

He quietly watched her. "Are you and Polly going to the Ballenger barbecue next week?"

"I don't know." She glanced at him shyly. "If you're going to be there, probably not. I don't want to do your social life any more damage than I already have. No wonder you've been staying away from local social occasions. I had no idea how difficult I'd made things for you until the gossip started to get back to me."

He started. That didn't sound like Anna. He opened his mouth to speak, but before he could deny the insinuation, Polly's car roared up the driveway. Seconds later she came around the corner, having seen Evan's car. "There you are!" she said, laughing. "I've brought the prospectus. I was going to run it out to you. Anna, is lunch ready?"

"Lori said it's on the table," Anna replied. "I'll be in later. I want to finish this while the light's right."

"Artists," Polly sighed. "Okay, honey. Evan, stay

and eat with me, since Anna's bent on being eccentric."

Evan's dark eyes lingered on Anna's profile. "I have to get back to work myself," he said hesitantly. "We're moving in new cattle today, so everybody's out in the yards helping—even mother."

"In a few years, you'll have plenty of help," Polly laughed. "All those babies coming along."

"Yes." He turned and took the prospectus Polly was holding out. "I'll run through this with Harden and the others and give you a call when we decide."

"Fine. Sure you won't stay for lunch?"

He waited for Anna to say something, to second her mother's offer at least. But she didn't. She said nothing. She didn't look up. After a minute, he shrugged and made his excuses.

When he was gone, Polly considered her daughter with open curiosity.

"Have you and Evan argued?" she asked softly.

"Of course not," Anna said. She turned, smiling, to her mother. "I've just decided to stop making his life miserable. Having me dog him at every step must have been wearing."

Polly relaxed a little. "I'm sure he realizes it's just a stage you're going through, darling," she replied gently. "Evan's not a bad man. He's just a card-carrying bachelor. You're a marrying type of girl. Even if you weren't years too young for him your goals are too different."

"You're right, of course," Anna said, trying not to choke on the words.

"I imagine he'll be pleased to be off the endangered list, all the same." She laughed. "You were getting pretty relentless. I, uh, heard about the whiskey bottles and the plastic snakes."

"Another ploy in my relentless campaign that failed." Anna sighed, managing not to reveal how hurt she really was. She concentrated on her canvas. "Well, it's over now. He did look relieved, didn't he?"

Polly nodded, but her eyes were saying something else. She wasn't sure exactly how Evan had looked, but relief wasn't the word she would have chosen. She had the oddest feeling that Anna had shocked him.

Chapter Three

In fact, *perplexed* was more the way Evan felt as he drove back to the Tremayne ranch. He hadn't slept well, remembering the way Anna had looked when he and Nina left the party. He'd used the prospectus as an excuse to come over and see how much damage he'd done.

What he'd found had surprised him. Anna was apparently indifferent to his presence and not at all anxious for his company. After two years of being pursued, teased, flirted with and vamped, it was shocking to have Anna treat him like a stranger.

He pulled up at the house and went inside, scowling.

"Something bothering you?" Harden asked from the study doorway.

Evan went in and closed the door. He could talk to Harden as he could to no one else, and he needed a sympathetic ear right now.

"Anna's bothering me," he said shortly.

"That's nothing new," Harden replied. "You've been complaining about Anna for as long as I can remember."

Evan scowled, turning. "No," he said. "You don't understand. She's ignoring me."

Harden's blue eyes twinkled. "A new ploy?"

Evan sat perched on the edge of the desk. "She hasn't been the same since last night. She's decided that she's been ruining my life, so she's giving me up."

"Nice of her," Harden commented.

"It's the way she's doing it that worries me," came the quiet reply. "She's too calm."

"You didn't see the way she looked when she saw you with Nina," Harden replied. "It cut her up."

Evan cursed under his breath. "I thought I was doing the right thing. I didn't want to hurt her. I just wanted to get her off my back."

"You did. So what's the problem?"

The bigger man sighed wearily. "I didn't know how it was going to feel, having her ignore me completely."

"Quite an admission from you, isn't it?"

"I guess it is." He studied his worn boot. "But I still think I did the right thing. She's years too young."

"So you keep saying. I guess she finally listened."

"I guess."

"Nina seems smitten all over again. Is it serious?"

Evan's dark eyes met his brother's blue ones. "I

don't want Nina. That was over years ago. I financed some new publicity for her and she's paying me back."

"I see," Harden murmured. "She's helping you fend off Anna."

"Unnecessarily, as it happens. Anna's dropped her mad pursuit. She said the game was over. Was that what it was all along to her—a game?"

"Maybe you're the one who was taking it too seriously," Harden said gently. "Anna played with you, brought you out of your shell. There were times when you almost seemed to enjoy it. Then you'd get your back up and complain that she was hounding you."

True enough, Evan thought, because just occasionally he felt a raging desire for Anna that he had to quell. It had been building for a long time, but lately it was explosive. Nina had been an act of desperation, as Anna had said. But the action seemed to be backfiring. He was the one who'd been burned.

"Anna's a virgin," Evan said shortly. "I'm almost certain of it. I had a rough experience with an innocent woman. These days, I look for sophistication."

"I know that," Harden replied kindly. "But that woman wasn't Anna. If she loved you, really loved you..."

"Anna isn't old enough to be that serious about a man."

"I hope you're right," he murmured. "Because if

she really cared, and you've killed it, you may have cost yourself the brightest star in your sky."

Evan scowled. "I told you, she said it was only a game!"

"Would she be likely to confess undying love when you'd just thrown one of your old conquests in her face?"

Of course not. This was getting him nowhere. "I'll get back out to the stockyard. Coming?"

"In a minute. I've got to drive Miranda in to the doctor," he said, grinning.

Evan shook his head. "First Pepi, now Miranda and Jo Anne. I'm surrounded by pregnant women."

"Uncle Evan," Harden mocked.

The big man smiled gently. "I love kids. I guess it's going to be up to mother and me to spoil them all."

"You might have some of your own one day."

Evan's eyes grew quiet and sad. "That isn't on the books."

"Anna's not afraid of you, for God's sake!" Harden growled.

"Of course she isn't, I've never made a heavy pass at her!" Evan replied levelly, his dark eyes unblinking. "Louisa was fine until I tried to take her to bed!"

Harden stared at him. "Nothing ventured, nothing gained."

"Even if Anna was old enough, I'd never have the nerve, don't you see?" He stuck his hands in his pockets and stared out the window. "That one experience spoiled intimacy for me. I lost control and hurt Louisa. I've been afraid ever since that I'd do it again. I put Randy Hardy in the hospital when we got into that brawl a few years back, didn't I?'' he added to emphasize his concern.

"Accidentally."

"Yes. Well, I could do the same thing to a woman if I lost my head," Evan returned hotly. "My size is no joke."

"You're big," Harden agreed. "And strong as a bull. Nobody's arguing with that. But you're giving yourself a complex, and it's not necessary. Just because one hysterical woman accused you of breaking her ribs…"

"I did bruise them pretty badly," Evan said miserably.

"She bruised them by trying to fight you and falling out of bed," Harden reminded him harshly. "She was half your size and all bones, and a terrified virgin into the bargain. Anna is a big girl, tall and sturdy and voluptuous. She's much more your type."

"I don't want Anna!" Evan returned.

"Suit yourself. She'll probably marry the honorable physician and have ten kids."

"If that's what she wants." His blood ran cold at the thought of Randall giving her children. He stuck his hat over his eyes and walked out of the room.

Harden, watching him, shook his head. He couldn't talk to Evan anymore. The older man was running scared, even if he wouldn't admit it. If he wasn't careful, he was going to make a mess of not only his life, but Anna's as well.

In the days that followed, Evan noticed a difference in his life. He went to town, and there was no more Anna peering over his shoulder in the hardware store or peeking out of her mother's office window to grin and wave at him. He went to a local social gathering, and Anna hadn't begged an invitation so that she could flirt with him. He took the precaution of taking Nina with him, just in case, but it hadn't been necessary.

He should have been jubilant, but somehow it wounded him that Anna didn't want him anymore. All his arguments against the relationship didn't help.

Two weeks after the party, Anna was shopping at the local boutique when Nina danced in, wafting expensive perfume and looking on top of the world.

"Well, hello!" she greeted Anna, smiling. "So Evan did finally beat you off! We didn't see a sign of you at the Andersons' get-together night before last! He spent the first few minutes peeking around corners in case you showed up. You really gave him a complex."

Anna felt sick at the way Nina had put it. "Yes. Well, I'm devoting myself to Randall these days."

"The doctor with the wandering eye, hmm?" Nina mused, fingering one of the more expensive dresses in the shop. "He won't be easy to hold, I'm afraid. I don't suppose you know he took Cindy Grayson to the swimming party at the Fords' Monday? Or that she didn't get home until daylight?"

Anna glared at the older woman. "Is all this malice really necessary? You've got Evan. What more do you want?"

Nina's delicate eyebrows levered up. "I haven't 'got' Evan at all," she said. "He only asked me out to keep you away from him. He said he'd do anything to scrape you off." Her eyes darkened as they studied Anna haughtily. "You should have known that his type of man doesn't like being chased. You cut your own throat."

"Well, he's safe now," Anna said, almost choking.

Nina shrugged. "I doubt he'll believe it. Not that I mind," she added cattily. "Because the longer he feels you're a threat, the longer I'll have with him. He's quite something in bed," she said deliberately, watching Anna blush.

Anna left the dress she was looking at and went out the door of the boutique as if her jeans were on fire. Nina watched her for a minute and then turned back to the dress racks. That had been easy enough. She didn't like the way Evan was preoccupied since Anna's defection. Only if Anna was kept away would Nina have a clear shot at Evan. The fiction of sleeping with him seemed to do the trick, though. She was actually humming by the time she left the shop.

For the rest of the afternoon Anna barely knew what was going on around her. She left early and went to the Taylor Gallery.

Brand Taylor was elderly, with a keen eye for art

and a thorough knowledge of the market for it. He'd known Anna since she was a child, and he'd followed her interest in art with pleasure.

"I've been hoping you might approach me for a job one day," he told her honestly when she asked about it. "I'm here alone, and it's a bit of a grind sometimes. It would be nice to have an assistant. You have an eye for detail, and I can teach you how to evaluate paintings, how to predict the market. But it will be hard work. Nothing like sitting in your garden and painting."

She smiled. "I'd like to try it, nevertheless."

He nodded. "All right. When can you start?"

"Monday," she said. Her mother had never really needed her. A job had been created for her, but they both knew she was redundant.

"Won't Polly mind?" he asked.

She shook her head. "On the contrary, I imagine she'll be delighted."

Polly was delighted and surprised. "I didn't think you'd want to leave the office," she admitted.

"Because Evan spends a lot of time there," Anna murmured dryly. "That's the very reason I want to leave. If I'm going to let go, I need to do it wholeheartedly. I'm very fond of Mr. Taylor, and I do like the idea of a career."

"I'd hoped you might think of marriage as one," Polly said quietly. "God knows, I'd have done that if your father had been able to settle down with me. He was too much a wanderer, though. He still is."

"You've never really dated anyone else," Anna ventured.

"Neither has he," Polly said with a smile. "Maybe someday he'll get it out of his system and come home. I never stop hoping. Meanwhile, I have a career I enjoy and I'm making gobs of money."

"That's what I want to do," Anna said seriously. "I want to do something useful with my life. Marriage—maybe someday. But not yet."

"Good girl. You're young. You have plenty of time."

"Plenty," she echoed. Her eyes were sad, but she wasn't going to moon around the house. "How about going out to eat tonight?"

"Delightful," Polly agreed. "The Beef Palace?"

Evan's favorite hangout. Anna shook her head. "How about that new Chinese restaurant, for a change?"

Polly smiled her approval. "Nice. Very nice."

As they were leaving the restaurant that night, talking animatedly about Anna's upcoming new job, Evan spotted them as he drove past with Nina. Odd, Anna eating Chinese food. He was sure she didn't like it.

"That's Polly and Anna, isn't it?" Nina murmured dryly. "I expected to have to ward Anna off at the Beef Palace tonight. They say she usually tracks you there."

Evan glowered at her. "It isn't necessary to ridicule her," he said quietly.

She stared at him blankly. "Why not? Everyone

else does. It's common knowledge that she's made an utter fool of herself over you. She knows it, too.''

His eyes narrowed. "You haven't said anything to her?"

She crossed her elegant legs. "I simply told her that you'd had enough of her," she replied carelessly. "She knew that already."

He winced inwardly. He knew Nina, and he couldn't imagine that she'd put it that kindly to Anna. "For God's sake," he muttered.

"She won't fare much better with her doctor friend, I'm afraid," Nina added with frank nonchalance. "He's got a wandering eye, and he'll sleep with anything in skirts. Still, it's her business."

Evan didn't say another word. He didn't even want to think about Anna.

But the next week, when he went to take the prospectus back to Polly and discuss the family's decision with her, there was no one at Anna's desk.

Polly greeted him, gesturing him into a chair as she closed the office door and slipped into her own chair behind the desk. "What did you decide?" she asked pleasantly.

He scowled. "Where's Anna? She isn't sick or anything?"

Polly stared. He actually sounded as though he was worried. "Why, she's got another job, Evan," she said haltingly. "Brand Taylor hired her."

"At the art gallery?" He sat back in the chair with a rough sigh. "She's going to take this thing to the limit, isn't she?" he asked curtly. "For God's sake, she didn't have to banish herself on my account!"

Polly wisely didn't say anything. She lowered her eyes to the prospectus he'd tossed on the desk. He didn't know the half of it. Anna was also discussing moving out. A local boarding house had a vacancy and she thought she might take it, she'd told Polly over the weekend.

"The job came open unexpectedly," Polly murmured.

"Did she mention talking to Nina lately?" he persisted, leaning forward, his dark eyes steady and unblinking on her face.

"No," she replied. "Why?"

"Apparently Nina said some harsh things to her on my behalf," he replied heavily. "I didn't put her up to it, but Anna won't know that."

"It's just as well, Evan," Polly said seriously. "You and I both know that there's no future in Anna wearing out her heart on you. She'll get over you and marry Randall. It will be the best thing all around."

"Randall is a playboy," he said shortly.

"If Anna loves him, it won't matter," she said, refusing to admit that it might. "If he loves her, he'll stop chasing other women."

"Men like that don't stop, ever," he said with narrow eyes. "And you know it."

She smiled sadly. "Randall wouldn't be my first choice, either, Evan, but it's Anna's life. I have no right to interfere."

He leaned back again and scowled, his expression preoccupied.

"What did you decide about the prospectus?" she asked again, hoping to change the subject.

"We're going to invest," he said absently. He named a figure and abandoned his fears about Anna's future temporarily to finish discussing business.

But what she'd done bothered him. When he left Polly's office, he found himself heading straight for Taylor's Gallery.

Brand had gone to Houston for a show, leaving a nervous Anna in charge. She'd done well so far, and she was enjoying her work. But it was nerve-racking to have complete charge of the gallery by herself.

She looked lovely, Evan thought, watching her through the plate-glass window front before he entered the store. She was wearing a beige silk suit with a delicately embroidered white blouse, and her hair was in a neat French plait behind her head. She wore high heels that emphasized the graceful curve of her ankles and calves, and the fit of her suit made it apparent in the nicest of ways that she had an exquisite figure.

He opened the door and walked in, setting the bell tinkling.

Anna turned, a smile on her face that abruptly vanished when she saw him.

He felt a terrible emptiness at her expression. Always before, her eyes had brightened with gladness when she looked at him. Now it was more dread than delight that was mirrored in her blue eyes.

"Can I help you, Evan?" she asked with formal courtesy.

He moved into the gallery, glancing approvingly at the huge No Smoking sign on the wall. He stuffed his big hands into the pockets of his gray slacks and stared at her through narrowed dark eyes.

"Was it necessary to leave your mother short-handed to avoid me?" he asked with blatant sarcasm, because her new attitude hurt him.

She lifted her delicately rounded chin to stare at him. "Since I didn't do much there in the first place except wait for you to walk in, I'd hardly call her 'left shorthanded.'"

He smiled faintly. "Is that why you're here? You don't think I have any interest in art?"

She finished dusting the frame she was holding and returned it to its position against the wall. "I don't know what your interests are aside from making money, Evan," she replied. "Did you want something?"

"I wanted to make sure Nina hadn't hurt you."

She turned, her eyebrows arching. "What difference would that make?" she asked.

He drew in a slow breath. "I didn't send her to you with any messages," he said.

"It would have served me right if you had, I guess," she confessed quietly, dropping her gaze to the floor. "I've given you a hard time."

The way she spoke made him uncomfortable. He moved closer, so that he could look down on her bright head. His hands came out of his pockets and gently framed her face to lift it to his. God, she was pretty, he thought reluctantly. Eyes like a September sky. Peaches and cream complexion. Bow lips, very pink and full and moist. Helplessly, his eyes traced them with such intensity that they parted abruptly.

"Anna," he whispered gruffly.

Her eyes widened at his tone. She'd never heard him speak that way. His gaze was hot and glittery on her mouth, and his big, warm hands had contracted around her face, tilting it up to his. With awe, she watched his head bend and his mouth come within a whisper of her lips.

"Come close," he said, his voice deep and rough. He could hear her breathing change, and all his caution vanished in a fierce rush of need. His thumbs forced her chin up as years of helpless longing knocked him off balance. "Damn it, come here!"

Trembling, her legs obeyed him even against her will, so that her slender body could feel the strength and heat of him. His suit jacket was open. His cologne drifted in to her nostrils even as she felt his chest quite suddenly against the thrust of her breasts. Contact with him was violently arousing, even through all the layers of cloth.

Her fingers pushed nervously into the soft folds of his cotton shirt and touched hard muscles. Her eyes saw nothing except the wide, hard curve of his mouth as it poised just over hers, his coffee-scented breath mingling with her own.

"Do you know how to kiss, Anna?" he asked, his head spinning with this new experience of her, his reason abruptly gone in the heat of his need for her mouth.

"Y-yes," she breathed.

"Show me."

The words went into her parted lips as his mouth suddenly crushed down over hers and took possession.

She tasted him in the sudden silence of the gallery, her body tensing, her breath stilling in her throat as she felt his hard mouth on hers for the very first time and almost fainted from the shock of pleasure its warm, expert touch gave her. He was breathing roughly. The sigh of his breath brushed her cheek. Against her breasts, his heartbeat was irregular and very hard.

Her fingers curled into his chest as she moved closer.

"Anna," he moaned hungrily.

His arms slid around her and brought her breasts crushing against him. He was very strong, and the embrace was bruising. But Anna hardly noticed in the fever he was kindling along her veins.

She lifted closer, her arms sliding under his, under the jacket, to lie against his long back. He was warm, so warm, and the feel of his powerful body was narcotic. She fed on his mouth, moaning softly as its hard crush became more insistent. She pushed upward, opening her mouth for him. When she felt his tongue accept the blatant invitation, a rush of heat made her shudder in his arms.

Evan couldn't think, couldn't breathe. This was

Anna, he thought dazedly. Anna, who was too young for him. He'd pushed her away, and now he was encouraging her in the most blatant way. But he couldn't fight his own hunger. His tongue thrust fiercely into her mouth, and with each intimate thrust he imagined her body under his in bed, accepting him with this same headlong passion, her femininity yielding its secrets to him as he initiated her into lovemaking.

With a harsh groan, he lifted her against him, building the kiss into a frenzy that he almost couldn't stop in time.

Ages later he let her down again, and slowly, slowly lifted his head to look down into wide, dazed blue eyes below which her red, crushed mouth still trembled from his hot possession.

She could barely stand. He held her lightly around the waist to keep her from falling, and all the time his heartbeat sounded like a bass drum in his chest.

"You kissed me," she managed unsteadily.

"You kissed me back," he returned. His jaw clenched. He let his eyes run down her body to the opened jacket to her silk suit. Ruthlessly he moved one big hand forward to pull it aside, revealing the thrust of her breast and something more—the hard, taut nipple that signaled her arousal.

"Did you need to see…that I wanted you?" she asked tearfully. "Couldn't you tell without look-ing?"

"Yes, I could tell." He caught her by the waist and his hands contracted while he fought to get himself back under control. "You're nineteen," he began.

"And you're thirty-four," she said, swallowing as she managed to breathe properly again. "You don't need to explain anything to me, Evan, I know how you feel. You want me, but I'm not in the running."

His eyes darkened. "Anna..."

"Nina's more your style," she said bitterly, pushing at his chest. "She's experienced and sophisticated. I'll bet she knows as much as you do!"

She was assuming that he was sleeping with Nina. He let her keep her illusions. It wouldn't do to start making confessions now. He'd just done enough damage.

"Have you had a man yet?" he asked huskily.

She lowered her eyes, but he thrust a huge fist under her chin and made her look at him. "I said," he repeated curtly, "have you had a man?"

His eyes were a little frightening. "Don't you know?" she asked in a whisper.

She was trembling. His fist opened and he drew the backs of his fingers slowly down her arched throat and onto her soft breast, lingering while she tensed and stared at him.

"You haven't," he said with certainty. His eyes fell to his knuckles. He teased around the hard nipple, watching her body shiver and then slowly, helplessly, try to lift toward him.

"I hate you," she whimpered.

His mouth eased down to brush hers open. "Say my name," he breathed.

The nearness, the teasing, were impossible to resist, even if she really had hated him, and his hand was driving her crazy. "Evan," she moaned, lifting.

His lips opened on hers even as his hand suddenly swallowed her breast, roughly caressing her in a silence that magnified her heartbeat and his harsh breathing.

Her nails bit into his shoulders, and he shivered with pleasure. His hand contracted. She moaned into his mouth, and he wrapped one long, powerful leg around her as he moved close enough to let her feel the force of his desire.

She bit him, so aroused that she hardly realized what she was doing until she felt him groan.

Shocked, she drew back, her eyes wide and startled. "I...I didn't mean to do that," she whispered brokenly. She tried to move away, but his leg was preventing her. She felt his blatant arousal and sucked her breath in again.

He had to fight to let her go, to unwrap his body from hers. His face was hard and faintly flushed, but his eyes were angry.

"What?" he asked unsteadily.

"I...I bit you."

"And clawed me," he murmured quietly. His lips twisted into an odd smile. "You'd rip my back open in bed with those nails."

She gasped, and he suddenly realized not only what he was saying, but to whom he was saying it.

He shook his head, as if to clear it, and his brows jerked together. "Anna. For God's sake...!"

"Yes, Anna," she whispered brokenly, backing away from him. She was disheveled and wide-eyed, and shocked that she could have allowed him such liberties after the way he'd treated her. Not only allowed them, but encouraged and returned them. And in the shop, where anyone could see them! It was fortunate that the shop fronted a side street that wasn't much traveled at this time of day. It was even more fortunate that a huge painting of a Texas landscape was positioned between them and the window front. "Is Nina starving you, or is this some kind of revenge?" she asked.

He could hardly breathe. She'd been with him all the way, as passionate and fiery as he could have dreamed a woman would be. Whatever he'd kindled in her hadn't been fear. But she was nineteen, and it should never have happened.

"What do you think, honey?" he asked with faint insolence.

"I think you should go," she said quietly.

He pulled his Stetson down over his eyes. "So do I. Good luck with your new job. I'll give Nina your regards."

She didn't answer. He was out of sight and gone before she could stop trembling. If he wanted her out of his life, this was hardly the way to go about it, she thought blankly. She touched her mouth and tasted him there, shivering again with the ardor he'd aroused. Imagine being kissed like that in broad daylight, and by Evan, who didn't want her. She remembered the feel of his big body against her and flushed. Well, so much for that myth.

She went to the back of the shop long enough to fix her makeup and brush her hair, wondering if she'd ever get over what he'd done. Trying to get over him had been difficult without knowing how it felt to be held and kissed by him. From now on, it would be impossible. His body might want her, but it was patently obvious that his mind didn't. He'd probably just come to say goodbye, she kept telling herself. But why, she wondered for days afterward, had he kissed her?

Chapter Four

All the way back to the ranch Evan's head was spinning. He'd never felt anything like that in his life, and it had to be with Anna, of all people! He groaned inwardly at the fever of passion he'd kindled in her so effortlessly; at her sweet, headlong response. In bed she would satisfy him so fully that he'd never be able to touch another woman as long as he lived. And that knowledge drove him crazy.

He had to remember the reasons he couldn't—didn't dare—let himself become involved with her. She was nineteen and a virgin. He knew instinctively that until today she'd never let a man touch her as he had. If she was really as besotted with him as everyone said she was, she'd probably been saving it all up for him, waiting for him to kiss her, to touch her. He hit the steering wheel with fierce anger at the trick fate had played on him. It was impossible! He

was fifteen years her senior and a man to whom innocence was a kind of nightmare. He wanted her
until she obsessed him, but he couldn't have her. He
could never have her.

Innocence frightened him. Louisa's face had
haunted him for years, white and rigid as he'd turned
toward her after shedding his clothes. He'd thought
she loved him, but she'd fought him like a tigress,
screaming in terror that he was too big, too strong,
he was hurting her...

He went into the house with his face like a thun-
dercloud, his eyes blazing at the memory. Louisa had
been small and thin, a fragile girl-woman whom Harden had always sworn had only tolerated his ardor
because he was rich. He hadn't believed it. Louisa
had loved him, as he'd loved her. Her rejection had
damaged him. Although he still had the infrequent
lover, now his women were sophisticated and experienced. He'd never dated an innocent since Louisa.

Harden had reminded him that Anna was a big
girl, and he had to admit that she was certainly equal
to his ardor. He hadn't hurt her today, and for a few
seconds his strength had been unleashed when he'd
forced her body into the curve of his. He couldn't
believe he'd done that, gone against all his resolu-
tions and even been oblivious enough to show her
graphically how much he wanted her. He laughed
bitterly, remembering the shocked look on her face,
in her eyes, when he'd let her go. She'd probably
never felt a man's aroused body in her life. Well,
now she knew, he thought. He couldn't really imag-

ine her lukewarm Randall ever doing anything as bold as that. He wondered absently if Randall was even aroused by Anna, because he seemed oddly passive around her, hardly noticing her. Anna must surely know that all Randall was interested in was her mother's money, but it didn't seem to matter, because she kept seeing the man.

It was none of his business, he reminded himself. From now on he had to keep out of Anna's way. He'd made a terrible error in judgment today, letting her see that he found her physically attractive. He'd have to find a way to make her believe it was a fluke, or he'd have her chasing him all over again. He couldn't afford that. The temptation to let her catch him was much too alluring.

There was a conference in Denver on a new crossbreeding program, and he packed a bag and left his brothers Donald and Harden in charge. The change of scenery might do him good. He might even meet some classy lady in Denver who could take his mind off Anna.

He didn't know it, but Anna had already decided that he was getting even with her for ignoring her, playing on her weakness for him. She flushed, remembering how quickly his body had responded to hers. It should have shocked her, but she remembered only the delight of knowing she affected him. Could he have faked that? She knew men could get aroused by thinking about women they desired. What if he'd had the delectable Nina on his mind and had used Anna to assuage his hunger for her?

She was so confused that she didn't know how to
react. She didn't delude herself for a minute with
thoughts that her avoidance of him had triggered
those ardent kisses. He'd been so...so hateful, mocking her reactions! Almost as if he was punishing himself and her for his unexpected behavior. If only she
knew what had motivated him. If only it had been
because he missed her, because he cared. She could
have cried at her own stupidity. He hadn't even
treated her as if he respected her. Touching her that
way, holding her close enough to be shocked by the
vivid response of his body. Surely a man who cared
about a woman wouldn't treat her like...that!

"You're very quiet lately," Polly remarked several evenings later when they were sharing a quiet
supper. "Want to talk about it?"

"There's nothing, really," Anna said, forcing a
smile. "I've been working very hard. Mr. Taylor said
that if I'd like to do a couple of landscapes, he'll
even put them in the shop. He thinks I have a talent
worth developing."

"I've always thought that myself," Polly said en-
couragingly. She grimaced. "Although Randall
didn't seem too enthusiastic about your sunflowers.
He barely even looked at them, and after all the trouble I went to, having them properly matted and
framed."

"Randall isn't an art lover," Anna said, defending
him wanly. "He isn't musical, either."

"And you do love your classics, don't you, darling?" Polly sighed, frowning. "Anna, I don't like

to interfere, but you're seeing a lot of Randall lately. Two dates this week. It isn't because of Evan, is it?''

Anna started, her face coloring. "What do you mean?''

Polly's eyes narrowed shrewdly on her daughter's face. "Evan must have hurt you very badly at that party. But don't let hurt pride send you running to the first man who shows an interest, will you? Randall's a fine man, but he has an eye to the main chance and he's something of a playboy.''

"He might be, but he's not in Evan's league,'' Anna said bitterly.

"Evan at least sticks to women who know the score,'' came the dry reply. "He doesn't involve himself with innocents.''

Anna kept her eyes down. It wouldn't do to tell her mother just how involved he'd been with her that day in the art gallery. "Evan is past history. I'm not running after him in dogged pursuit anymore, and he seems to find that a relief. I haven't seen him in…ages.''

"He's been in Denver,'' Polly mentioned carelessly. "Some conference or other. Donald was supposed to go, Harden told me, but Evan packed a bag last Thursday and took off before he could argue. A very sudden trip.''

Anna had to fight not to give herself away. Last Thursday had been the day he'd kissed her so hungrily. Had he been obliged to run for fear that she might come hurrying after him for more? She flushed. Well, he needn't worry, she wasn't about to hassle him.

"Are you listening, darling?" Polly asked.

Anna lifted a serene face, smiling. "Of course."

"You worry me lately. You really do."

"No need. I'm just enjoying my new job, and growing up."

"You've done that, with a vengeance," Polly had to admit, noticing the elegant hairdo, the sleek silk pantsuit of a blue that matched Anna's eyes. "You've changed before my very eyes."

"I'm almost twenty," she reminded Polly.

"Yes. You make me feel old. I sent your father a photo of you just last month, to show him how elegant you look." The smile faded and she touched her water glass absently. "He's based in Atlanta now. He said they might move him back to Houston. If they do, he'll come and see you."

"He doesn't date," Anna mused. "You don't, either. But neither one of you will give an inch. Don't you miss him?"

"More than you know." Polly got up, all business. "But life goes on, my darling. I have to go over some figures in the study."

Anna watched her go with sad eyes. Polly had never gotten over her husband and never would. There was the hope that they might someday reconcile, but Anna knew it was a long shot. Meanwhile, she felt her mother's pain keenly.

She left the gallery after work the next day feeling oddly restless. Randall was supposed to take her out that evening, but he'd called to cancel their date with some vague mention of night duty. It didn't matter; she wasn't in love with him, but lately he seemed to make a habit of canceling dates at the last minute, and she wondered if he was really working that much.

Her car wouldn't start, for the first time in memory. She got out and glared at it, angrily kicking a tire. It was cloudy and drizzling rain, and now she'd have to walk all the way back to the gallery to use the phone.

The roar of a truck caught her attention, and she turned just in time to see Evan pull up beside her in one of the ranch pickups with the Tremayne company's emblem on the side in bold red lettering.

"Got problems?" he asked tersely, slamming his black Stetson over one eye as he joined her. He was in working gear, chambray shirt, tight jeans, black boots and leather batwing chaps. His spurs made a faint jingling sound as he paused beside her.

"No," she lied, avoiding his eyes. "I just forgot something in the office."

His dark eyes narrowed. He knew she was lying, he could see it in the way she hesitated. Incredible that she was actually trying to avoid him.

"Your car won't start," he said flatly. "No use lying about it. I was passing when you got out and kicked it."

Her face flamed. She wouldn't meet his eyes. "I'm going to call the garage. They'll get it started."

"I'll run you over there. Get in."

"I don't want—!"

He caught her arm roughly and drew her against him, so close that she could feel the powerful threat of his body as he looked down into her shocked eyes.

"You want me," he said harshly. "I know it and so do you. Avoiding me doesn't change that. I can feel it the minute I touch you."

Her lower lip trembled "Can't you just leave me alone?" she asked brokenly. "I know you don't want me! Do you have to make a point of it every time you see me?"

Her pain made him feel guilty. He didn't understand his own actions. The last thing he wanted to do was to hurt or humiliate her. But Denver hadn't rid him of his need for her. He hadn't been able to touch the woman who'd clung to him there. He'd intended to. He'd taken her back to his room, fed her drinks, flattered her. But when he'd pulled her into his arms and started kissing her, nothing happened. His body, for the first time, had failed him. He'd sent the woman away and cursed Anna until his voice had gone hoarse. All he could think about was the taste of her mouth. It had enraged him so much that he could hardly function for the rest of the conference, and he'd come home still fuming. His unfortunate passion for Anna was cramping his style in an unbelievable way.

His dark eyes fell to her mouth and lingered there, his fingers gripping her arm so tightly that they left bruises. "You'd give me anything I wanted," he said huskily. "Do you think I don't know how vulnerable you are?"

She shivered. This wasn't the Evan she knew. This man was a stranger, sensual, domineering, frightening. "This isn't fair, Evan," she choked.

"Is what you do to me fair?" he asked coldly.

"I...haven't done anything to you, except avoid you," she said miserably. "I thought that was what you wanted."

His other hand moved to her waist and drew her slowly against the powerful length of him, against lean muscle that rippled where she touched it. She gasped as her hand caught at his shirt, her eyes going involuntarily to the thick pelt of hair that showed in the opening at the collar.

"This is what I want," he said, his voice deep and quiet, as his hand slid to the base of her spine and moved her hips gently against his. He caught his breath audibly as the feel of her kindled the kind of arousal he hadn't felt since his sixteenth birthday. He laughed bitterly at the irony of it, because he couldn't seem to feel that with another woman, having had a taste of Anna.

"It isn't funny," she moaned, pushing at his chest with her face gone scarlet. "Evan, stop!"

His hand withdrew, but he still had her by the arm. "Funny, isn't it?" he asked, his eyes glittering. "The joke of the century, that a virgin should have that effect on me when an experienced woman can't even..." He bit off the words, suddenly pushing Anna away. He was breathing roughly, and his arousal was so obvious that Anna averted her eyes in something like panic. He saw her embarrassment, and it angered him.

"I have to go," she said unsteadily.

"Still seeing the beloved physician?" he asked.

She wouldn't look at him. "If you mean Randall, yes."

"Why don't you marry him? It would get you out of my hair, at least."

Tears stung her eyes. "I've been out of your hair for weeks, haven't you noticed?" she asked, glaring up at him. His eyes were shadowed, but she thought she saw the flicker of his eyelashes. "I haven't come near you! It's you who are harassing me!"

"Turn about," he said softly, his eyes glittery. "How do you like it?"

"I hate it!" she raged.

"So did I, baby," he replied coldly. "Every minute, every day that you hounded me. Thank God for Nina, she must have finally convinced you that it was never going to work. Even a man who cares about a woman can't stomach that kind of harrassment."

Her eyes closed, containing the tears. "You've made your point," she said in a haunted tone. "May I go, now?"

He felt sick all over when he looked at her face. He shouldn't be this cruel to her. It wasn't her fault that he wanted her to the exclusion of other women. She was just a child, despite her lovely curves, just a little girl. And he was savaging her. He came to his senses in a painful jerk.

"Anna..."

Her eyes opened, blue as the sky, wet with tears and pain. "I'm sorry!"

His teeth ground together in a grimace of anguish. He moved toward her, but she turned and started to run across the street, back toward the gallery.

Evan watched her until she was out of sight, his face drawn with guilt and remorse. He felt as if he'd just torn the wings from a butterfly.

Anna was pale and unnaturally quiet when she got home, having found a mechanic to fix her car. But Polly was out, to Anna's relief, and Anna managed to get to bed without being seen. Now that she knew what Evan really thought of her, she didn't know how she was going to stay alive. He seemed to actually hate her.

The next few weeks dragged by, with Evan taunting her at every corner. He brought Nina in to buy paintings at the gallery, making his attentiveness to her so evident that Anna wanted to scream. He was seen around town with her, and seemed to go out of his way to make sure that Anna saw them. As revenge went, it was pure mastery. Anna felt as if she'd been cut to pieces, even if she did manage to salvage a little pride by stepping up her dates with Randall.

A month after Evan had made his last cruel taunt, she went to a concert with Randall and found Evan and Nina sitting only three seats away from them. It hurt to see the two of them together, with Evan so loving and attentive to Nina that the other woman seemed actually to purr when he touched her.

During the intermission, Randall went to get punch for himself and Anna, and Nina went to the powder room. It was almost fate, Anna thought miserably, that threw her directly in Evan's path while their respective dates were missing.

"Enjoying yourself, honey?" Evan asked her with a smile that didn't begin to reach his eyes. "Or is the beloved physician just a poor substitute for me?"

She shivered, glaring at him. "Randall is good company."

"Is he?" he mused. "He seems to pay more attention to the music than he does to you. Or is that what you like?"

"It beats having him all over me," she blurted out, and then blushed furiously at Evan's soft, mocking laughter.

"Nina likes being touched," he said, his eyes holding hers. "She opens her mouth when I kiss her, and melts under my body...."

"Damn you," Anna choked, tears burning her eyes. "I've never hated anyone in my life as much as I hate you!"

It would have hurt less if she'd slapped him. His face hardened. "It beats having you run after me begging to be made love to," he returned hotly.

She whirled, shaking all over, and made her way to Randall. She held on to his sleeve as if she was afraid she'd drown if she turned it loose. Behind her a tall man with dark eyes flinched at his own merciless behavior, wondering how he could have allowed it to go this far. His hunger for Anna grew daily, until it was an ache that almost brought him to his knees. He'd been fighting a losing battle for weeks, and tonight, he lost it. Being cruel to her was the only protection he had left, but that was no longer bearable. He sighed wearily, his eyes lovingly tracing the long lines of her body, adoring her silently. She was so lovely. All his sweetest dreams rolled together.

It was no good, he admitted finally. He was only fooling himself that he could fight her hold on him. He smiled ruefully. Tomorrow, he'd go by the gallery and take her to lunch and admit defeat. He hoped she wouldn't be too unforgiving. He turned back to find Nina approaching him, his mouth set in a hard, uncompromising line.

Anna was silent for the rest of the concert. She didn't look toward Evan again, refusing to glance at him even though he seemed to spend the better part of the evening trying to force her to look his way. She clung to Randall and rushed him outside when the concert ended, desperate not to have to see Evan and Nina together again.

She and Randall walked home, because the civic center was just two blocks away from Anna's house.

"I'll go into private practice next year," Randall was telling her, his eyes dreamy. "I want to set up in Houston. There's an older, established doctor in one of the ritzier parts of town. I've already inquired about buying into his practice." He glanced down at her. "If we got married, say around December, we could move in by late January."

She stopped walking and looked up at him. "You mean, you could buy into the practice if my mother gave us a substantial cash wedding present," she said matter-of-factly. What he was hinting at was suddenly welcome. She wanted so desperately to get out of Evan's reach forever, to avoid any more heartbreaking torment from him.

He was taken aback at the calm way she said it. "Anna..."

"I know you're not dying of love for me, Randall," she said quietly. "I know that there have been other women. It doesn't matter. I might as well marry you as anybody else. Why not?"

He felt guilty for the first time as he saw the dead look in her eyes. He didn't love her, but he was fond of her. He frowned. "You make it sound like a business proposition."

"It is. My mother would stake us. You're ambitious, so you'll work hard and make a name for yourself. I can entertain. I'll find things to keep me busy. Maybe I'll paint." She put away her dreams of Evan and a houseful of children for the last time. She had to be practical.

"You'll marry me?" he asked.

She nodded.

He sighed, and drew her into his arms, holding her lightly. "You deserve something better than this," he said unexpectedly.

She laid her cheek against his chest and smiled. "Sometimes, Randall, you're a very nice man."

"Not often. I'm all too aware of my limitations. I

like women, and for some reason they like me, even if I'm not handsome." He smoothed her long hair. "I like being with you, because I can be myself. I'll take care of you, Anna. I'll try to be discreet…"

"It won't matter." And it wouldn't. He couldn't touch her heart, so she was safe. "We'll tell Mama when we get home."

He nodded. He took her hand and smiled down at her as they walked back toward the house. Anna smiled back, but nothing helped the ache inside her.

"You're getting married?" Polly stammered when they told her the news, automatically registering that neither of them seemed particularly ecstatic or over-joyed at the prospect.

"That's right," Randall said pleasantly. "I hope you'll wish us well, Mrs. Cochran. I'll take care of Anna."

It would have made Polly a little happier if he'd said he loved Anna. She glanced at her daughter and wanted to weep at the composed features, the dull eyes. Anna was only doing this because of Evan; she knew it. But her daughter was old enough to make her own decisions, however wrong they might be.

"Of course I'll congratulate you," Polly said, forcing a smile. "I hope you'll be very happy. Now when are you planning to be married?"

"At Christmas," Anna said quietly.

Randall nodded. "I can take a couple of days off and we'll have a brief honeymoon."

"Randall wants to buy into a practice in Houston," Anna added, thinking that Houston would be a good place to live, because she wouldn't ever have to see Evan again.

"I'll help with that, of course," Polly said brusquely, and watched relief shadow Randall's eyes. Damn him! She didn't want to buy her daughter a husband, but what could she say? Anna was living on her nerves already. Evan was obviously not interested in her, either. He was being seen everywhere with Nina, flaunting his relationship. He'd even brought the woman to Polly's office with him, making his interest in her so evident that half the staff must have mentioned it to Anna. She wondered if that had been his intention. He seemed to go out of his way lately to taunt Anna, right down to parading Nina past the art gallery at lunch every day.

Polly had never thought of Evan as a particularly cruel man, but Anna seemed to trigger it in him. Odd, when Anna was the type of woman who particularly needed kindness. She certainly wouldn't find any in Evan. Polly pursed her lips. This engagement might not be a bad idea, after all. Once he knew Anna was marrying, he might relent and stop hurting her.

"We'll have to go shopping for an engagement ring tomorrow," Randall told Anna, smiling. "What would you like?"

She smiled back. He was a good friend, even if she couldn't work up a grand passion for him. "I'd like an emerald solitaire," she said.

Randall's eyebrows arched. "Emerald?"

"I don't like traditional stones," she said gently. "And a small emerald and diamond wedding band.

Later, when you're wildly successful, you can buy me something big and flashy, okay?''

He grimaced. She made him feel mean and guilty. "Anna, I'd buy you a trunkful of diamonds if I had the money,'' he said, and suddenly meant it. "God knows, you're worth them.''

Polly raised her eyebrows and smiled. That sounded more promising. Randall might turn out to be a worthy son-in-law after all. If only Anna loved him.

"We could go from the gallery to pick it up,'' Anna suggested, "about noon.''

Noon. That was when Evan usually escorted Nina past her window. Polly turned, smothering a grin. Good for Anna. It wouldn't hurt to let Evan know that she wasn't pining away for love of him anymore.

"It's a date,'' Randall said, smiling. "Now, you'd better walk me to the door. I've got exams the rest of the week, so except for getting the ring, we won't see too much of each other.''

"That's okay,'' Anna said demurely. "We'll make up for it when we're together. There's a new exhibit at the zoo, tropical amphibians.''

"Fantastic!'' Randall enjoyed the study of herpetology as a hobby, and Anna shared his fascination with exotic frogs and lizards. It had been surprising, and pleasing, to find that they had a few things in common. He hated art and music, although he humored Anna by attending concerts. But he really enjoyed going to the zoo, and so did she. It was something to build on, at least.

Anna was thinking the same thing. She wouldn't have an ecstatic marriage, but she'd settle for a little harmony. God knew, she could never have had that with Evan. For a kind, pleasant man, he seemed to grow fangs when he came within a few feet of her. She affected him in a very negative way, so it was probably just as well that she was marrying Randall. But inside her, dreams died.

Chapter Five

Anna thought she'd never get through the next morning. Only the thought that Randall was coming for her made it bearable. If she had to watch Evan with Nina, it would be for the last time. Presumably when he heard about her engagement, he'd realize that she'd given up on him and maybe then he'd leave her alone and stop taunting her with what she couldn't have. The humiliation of knowing that Evan was totally aware of her helpless passion for him was unbearable. Having him flaunt Nina at her was worse.

Sure enough, at ten minutes before noon, Evan came past the window as he did now every day. But he was alone this time. Nina wasn't with him.

Anna clenched her hands together in front of her, grateful that Mr. Taylor was in the gallery, going over their frame inventory, when Evan walked in the door. At least she wasn't on her own.

"Well, hello, Evan," Brand Taylor said with a smile. "Nice to see you. Anything in particular you're looking for?"

Evan was taken aback. He hadn't planned on Taylor being in. Most days, when he went past the gallery Anna was alone. Today, of all days, she wasn't.

"No, I'm…browsing, thanks," Evan said.

"Go ahead, then. Anna can help you with prices, if you see something you like."

Anna wasn't looking at him, though. Her eyes were almost frantic, riveted to the front door. His face hardened. Was she hoping to be rescued? Remembering his recent treatment of her, he realized that he couldn't blame her. He'd tried so hard to resist his hunger for her, but he couldn't quite live without her. He'd cope somehow with his fears, he'd have to. But her face wasn't encouraging, and he had a flash of panic as he realized that he might already be too late. She looked…

He hesitated, his dark eyes sweeping over her. She'd lost weight. The beige suit she wore didn't fit as closely as it had, and there were new lines in that pretty face, new hollows under her high cheekbones. She looked elegant and brittle.

He moved toward her, hating the way she jerked around and took a step backward when she saw him coming. Had he hurt her so badly?

Her eyes glanced off his gray suit and pearly Stetson. He was dressed for travel, she imagined, not knowing that he'd worn his best clothes just to see her.

"Was there something you wanted to know?" she asked in a forcibly steady tone, and made herself look at him.

Her eyes were deep blue and full of pain. It hurt him to see it and know that it was because of him.

"Yes," he said, his voice almost hesitant. His eyes fell to her soft mouth and back up to hold her gaze. "Anna, I..."

The bell on the front door drew their attention. Randall came in, smiling at Mr. Taylor before he walked to Anna's side. He knew how she felt about Evan Tremayne, and protective instincts he didn't even know he had welled up inside him. He slid an arm around her waist and kissed her forehead with deliberate possession, not missing the flash of Evan's stormy eyes or the surprise on his dark face.

"Hello, darling," he told Anna gently. "Ready to go?"

"Yes," Anna choked. "I'll just get my purse."

"We're picking out the rings today," Randall told Evan levelly. "Anna and I are getting married at Christmas."

Getting married. Getting married. Getting married. Evan heard the words echo in his mind until he thought he'd gone mad. Anna was going to marry Randall. They were going to pick out rings. He'd come here today to apologize to her, on his knees if necessary, to ask her out on what would have been their first real date. He was going to try to build a relationship with her. But Randall had beat him to it. He'd hurt her, tormented her into accepting Randall's proposal. For the rest of his life, he'd have to live with that. She didn't love Randall or want him, but she was going to marry him.

"You might congratulate us," Randall prompted. "I'm going to make her happy. I swear I am."

How can you, Evan was wondering bitterly, when she loves me? But he didn't say it. He rammed his hands into his pockets, drawing the fine fabric of his slacks taut over powerfully muscled legs, and his eyes smoldered as they went to Anna's pale face.

"I'm ready when you are, Randall," Anna told him quietly, and Evan had to look hard even to recognize that she was the same woman he'd known only weeks ago. The bright spark, the impish nature might never have been. Anna had matured to middle-age overnight, gone calm and quiet and elegant. At that moment he'd have given anything to see her the way she was.

"I'm coming. See you around, Evan," he told the older man, smiling as he went to take Anna's arm.

Evan watched them go with dead eyes. She was going to marry Randall. And when she looked up and met his gaze, he knew why. She was doing it to show him that she wasn't chasing him anymore, that he was free of her, because that was what she thought he wanted. Heaven knew, he'd given her more than enough reason to think so.

"Oh, God, no!" he ground out in a tortured whisper and started toward them. He had to stop her.

But as he nodded to Taylor and left the shop, Nina drove up to the curb and called to him.

"There you are!" she waved gaily. "I missed you at the office, so I thought I'd meet you here!"

Anna heard her, but she didn't look back. What a good thing Randall had come for her. She'd thought, hoped, that Evan might have come just to see her, but he'd been meeting Nina there, flaunting her again. No wonder he'd been in such a rush to get out of the gallery, and she'd dared to dream he was coming after her! Well, so much for dead hopes.

She slid her hand into Randall's and walked along beside him, half-numb, listening while he told her what he'd planned for the weekend. He might as well have been giving her a weather report, for all the interest she showed.

That afternoon, after work, she went home alone. On an impulse, she stopped by the civic center to see what concerts were planned for the weekend. Randall's emerald solitaire winked in the soft light, gracing her long, slender hand. The symbol of his intention to marry her, and it didn't even touch her heart. She was saving Evan from herself, she thought bitterly, that was all. She didn't dare think about what marriage to Randall would be like, or she'd go mad.

Tears stung her eyes and began to roll down her cheeks while she stood there. And she suddenly realized, horrified, that Miranda Tremayne was standing beside her.

"Oh, Anna," the older woman said, grimacing. She put her arms around Anna without even thinking, comforting her.

It was so unexpected that Anna was totally without

a defense. She cried until her throat hurt, grateful that pedestrian traffic was almost nonexistent for the moment. She pulled away finally, and Miranda produced a tissue out of the pocket of her maternity dress.

"Feel better?" she asked gently. "It's Evan, isn't it?" she added with resignation, nodding at Anna's surprised look. "Yes, I know. We all know what he's been doing, throwing Nina in your face. I used to think that Evan was a big teddy bear, but Harden wasn't kidding when he told me Evan had fangs. I never dreamed he could be so cruel."

"I drove him to it," Anna sniffed. "It's my own fault."

"He could have stopped it anytime he wanted to, just by having a quiet word with you," Miranda said angrily. "This isn't like him. He's been terrible at home ever since he came back from Denver."

"He hates me," Anna said unsteadily. "I'm not kidding. I mean, he really hates me! He made fun of the way I felt about him and laughed at Randall...I'm marrying Randall," she added weakly, showing her ring. "Isn't it pretty? We're going to live in Houston." She burst into tears again. "Oh, I am sorry," she apologized, red eyed. "I didn't realize how much he hated me. It must have embarrassed him terribly when I ran after him!"

Miranda could have backed a truck over Evan with pure delight at the moment. She patted Anna's shoulder awkwardly. "That doesn't mean he has any right to hurt you like this."

"This is just the aftershock," Anna said stubbornly, dabbing at her eyes. "Once Randall and I are married, I'll be fine."

"Not if you love Evan," Miranda said sadly.

Anna ground her teeth together, but her lower lip trembled ominously. "I'll stop loving him," she choked. "I'll have to."

"Evan keeps secrets," Miranda said slowly. "I don't know what they are and Harden won't tell me. But there's some reason for the way he treats you."

"It's my age," Anna replied. "He thinks I'm a child."

"There's more to it than that, I'm sure of it," Miranda replied. "Anna, I wish there was something I could do."

Anna smiled at her. "You're very kind," she said. "Harden's so lucky, to have someone like you. He was worse than Evan, you know. Most women around here were scared to death of him. He could look right through you."

"He's mellowed." Miranda grinned, patting her stomach. "Not that he's tame. None of the Tremayne men are. But he's all I'll ever want."

"I think that would go double for him," Anna said softly and smiled. "I have to go. You won't…mention that I was standing out here bawling my head off?"

"I won't tell Evan anything, Anna," came the gentle reply. "But I do wish you'd reconsider what you're doing."

"I'm doing the only thing I can, short of joining

the French Foreign Legion,'' Anna sighed. ''I'll be happy with Randall.''

Miranda wanted to question that cool statement, but she couldn't. Anna was headstrong and stubborn, and she seemed perfectly capable of cutting off her nose to spite her face. As for Evan...

She went home fuming. Harden was sitting in the living room with his mother, Theodora, when Miranda walked in and flung her purse on a chair.

''Are you all right?'' Harden asked, immediately concerned.

''Oh, you mean the checkup,'' she said, preoccupied. ''Yes, I'm fine. The doctor says I'm progressing beautifully,'' she said and bent to kiss him gently. She smiled down at him, her love echoing back from his glittery blue eyes. ''The baby is just fine.''

''Thank God,'' he sighed. ''The way you looked when you came in spooked me.''

''I want to kill your brother,'' she told him.

''Which one?'' he returned.

Theodora chuckled as she worked her embroidery thread into a complicated floral design. ''Evan,'' she guessed.

''How did you know?'' he queried.

''He's the only bachelor left.''

''Good point,'' Miranda agreed, ''and I hope he gets to stay that way for life. If you could have seen Anna...''

''What about Anna?'' Harden asked softly.

''He's cut her to pieces. She was in tears. And

that's not the worst of it. She's going to marry Randall.''

Harden's face went taut. "She doesn't love him.''

"It's to show Evan that she's through chasing him, I know it is,'' Miranda said miserably. "She's running, and you know as well as I do that he's given her every reason in the world to want to get away from him. She's convinced that he hates her.''

"He acts like it lately,'' Harden had to admit.

Theodora looked up from her needlework. "Love and hate are twins, you know. You can't hate somebody unless you can love them.''

"He's never been in love, not really,'' Harden replied. "Oh, he thought he was. He had a bad experience, and it's blinded him to a lot of things. Anna's not his problem. It's all in his mind.''

"What are you talking about?'' Miranda chided.

"I can't tell you without breaking a confidence,'' he said. He smiled at her. "No secrets, I know, but this is Evan's, not mine. You'll have to let him deal with it.''

"He's waited too late,'' Theodora said sadly. "I'm sorry. Anna's very young, but she's sweet and generous and loving. He could do so much worse.''

"I hope Randall will be kind to her.'' Miranda sighed. "But I'm not sorry for Evan,'' she added angrily. "He didn't deserve her in the first place. I hope he marries that Nina of his, and I hope she gives him hell twice a day!''

Theodora laughed at her rage, but Harden didn't. He knew what Evan was afraid of, why he was run-

ning from Anna. What a pity that he couldn't face
the threat of his own strength and deal with it. Now
he'd lost the one woman in the world who'd ever
really loved him. Harden felt sorry for him.

For days after that, Evan kept to himself, not even
talking to the people around him. He threw himself
into ranch work with a zest that surprised and ex-
hausted his own men, because while he was punishing himself, they had to suffer with him. He pushed
them during the late summer roundup of bulls until
one of them quit, which was what finally brought him
to his senses.

"I've never seen so many cowboys in church on
Sunday," Theodora mused when they had supper
that night. "They all seem to say the same thing—
please, God, save us from Evan."

"Cut it out," Evan muttered. He didn't smile. He
hadn't for a long time. The lighthearted man Miranda
remembered from her first days at the ranch might
never have been.

"God, you remind me of myself," Harden remarked dryly, glancing down the table at him. "All
bristles and thorns lately."

Evan didn't answer him. He finished his coffee
and got up. "I'll see you later."

"Taking Nina out again?"

"Who else?" Evan replied without looking at him.
He kept walking.

Miranda just shook her head. He got worse by the
day.

Evan had taken Nina to a play in Houston, but he

was surprised and infuriated to find Randall there—with a woman who was definitely not Anna. This one was tall and brunette and wearing a dress that left nothing at all to the imagination.

He cornered the man at intermission, his dark eyes threatening.

"I thought you were engaged," he said curtly.

"I am," Randall replied. "This is my cousin Nell."

Evan glanced at the woman and laughed shortly. "Sure she is."

"Listen," Randall said curtly, "Anna and I have an arrangement which is none of your business."

"Does she know you're out with Cousin Nell?" Evan persisted.

"No, but she will, because I never had any intention of covering it up," Randall replied honestly. "At least Anna will be better off with me than she would with you," he added coldly. "I'll never cut her up the way you did."

Evan exploded. He actually reached toward the other man, but a crowd of returning patrons interrupted the movement and he regained his control. He turned on his heel, rejoining Nina.

"What was that all about?" Nina demanded petulantly. "Trying to live Anna's life for her again?"

He looked down at her with eyes that threatened. She actually backed away.

"Anna is my business, not yours," he said, every word measured and dangerous.

Nina swallowed. "Don't you mean, she's Randall's? After all, it's him she's engaged to."

He took her arm and escorted her back to their seats. He didn't say another word to her then or later.

The next day he stopped by Polly's office on the pretense of business. But once the door was closed and he was sitting comfortably in one of her wing chairs, he tossed his hat aside and leaned forward intently.

"Randall was out on the town in Houston last night with some brunette," he said shortly. "He's already two-timing Anna, and they aren't even married yet."

Polly was shocked, not only by the information, but by the anger in Evan's voice as he told her about it.

"What kind of marriage is it going to be, for God's sake?" he ground out. "Her pride won't stand that kind of treatment!"

"Evan, I appreciate your concern," Polly said quietly. "But it's Anna's life."

"My God, she's ruining it!" he exclaimed, throwing up his hands. "Don't you care?"

Polly's eyebrows lifted. "Aren't you the man who's been doing his best to chase her into Randall's arms for the past few months?"

He grimaced. "I thought it would be the best thing for her," he said shortly. "Randall's going to make a good doctor, a good provider. I figured once they got engaged, he'd at least be discreet about his affairs."

"He is," Polly replied. "Houston is a long way from Jacobsville."

"If I saw him, other people from here could."

Polly leaned back in her chair, studying his angry face. "Evan, how do you know the woman he was with wasn't his cousin?"

He let out a rough sigh and rested his forehead on his bunched hands. "My God, I don't. But you know what he's like."

"Yes. And so does Anna. She'll be amply provided for, and she'll keep busy in Houston. That's where they're going to live when they're married."

It was killing him. Killing him! He got to his feet with a harsh groan, grabbing up his Stetson.

"Anna thinks you hate her," she said, noticing that he didn't face her, that his back was rigid. "Do her a favor and let her keep on thinking it."

He twisted the Stetson in his hands. "Why shouldn't I?" he asked huskily. "It's the truth."

"Is it, really, Evan?" she asked softly.

He didn't answer her. He slammed the Stetson over one eye and went out, without ever looking back.

Polly watched him leave and felt a twinge of sorrow for all of them. Evan loved Anna. If she'd ever wondered about his feelings, she knew now. It was a raging, helpless kind of love that he was fighting with everything in him, tearing her to pieces to keep her from seeing how vulnerable he really was. And Anna loved him, deathlessly. But neither of them was going to give in, least of all Evan, who for reasons

of his own wanted no part of loving. Polly could
have wept. She wished she could tell her daughter,
but it would serve no purpose. Evan wasn't going to
give in to it, she knew that instinctively, but if Anna
went too close to him, he'd savage her. He might
have already done that. Polly knew he'd been taunting her. She was sure he hated her. It was just as
well. She could do worse than Randall, and perhaps
someday, she'd even get over Evan.

Sure, she thought bitterly, as she pulled out the
portrait of her husband, Duke, that she kept in her
desk drawer, just like I've gotten over you. He
looked a lot like Anna—blond and blue-eyed. He
was tall and slender, and Polly had loved him just as
passionately as Anna loved Evan. But they'd never
been able to live together, because he had wander-
lust. She didn't like remembering how she'd begged
to go with him, or how he'd told her, so gently, that
he couldn't drag her around the world with a baby
in her arms. Slowly she brought the picture to her
lips and kissed it before she put it away. So much
for looking back. She had work to do. She pushed
the intercom button and called her secretary in for
dictation.

Randall told Anna about the woman he'd taken to
the play, because he knew Evan would make sure
she found out. As he'd expected, she didn't bat an
eyelash.

"I don't see anything so terrible about it." She
shrugged. "Why did you feel obliged to tell me?"

"Because Evan was there and went crazy when he

saw me with another woman," he said shortly, ramming his hands in his pockets. "He very nearly threw a punch at me."

Anna's heart jumped, but she schooled her face not to betray the shock of pleasure she felt at Evan's displeasure. "He's very old-fashioned," she began.

"Like the rest of the Tremaynes, I know," he sighed. "Well, I'm never going to be Mr. Faithful, Anna," he added with a rueful smile. "I'm sorry. It's not in me."

"I know that." She changed the subject abruptly, offering him coffee. He watched her make it and was suddenly grateful that he didn't love her. If he had, seeing how indifferent she was to his amours would kill him. She was going to live and die in love with Evan Tremayne. He pitied her. He pitied Evan more. There were worse things for a man than marrying a woman who loved him passionately. Evan had thrown away a precious gift and didn't even know it.

Polly mentioned that Evan had been by the office and had talked about seeing Randall in Houston. It amazed Anna that he'd been so persistent. But she was even more surprised to find him waiting for her at the gallery when she went to open it the next morning in Mr. Taylor's absence.

"It's about time," Evan said curtly, glaring at her as she produced the key.

Her heart jumped, but she schooled her face not to show the dangerous excitement he fostered in her.

She'd learned the hard way to keep a poker face these days. "What do you want?" she asked quietly.

He followed her into the gallery, formidable in tan denims and a blue-checked Western shirt, his old black Stetson slanted arrogantly over one dark eye. "You know what I want. How long are you going to let Randall drag your pride through the dirt before you do something about it? Or don't you care that he's having women on the side?"

She put her purse down and turned on the lights, very elegant in her tailored gray suit, with her hair in a neat chignon. "Randall is a grown man. I don't mind if he takes another woman to the theater when I'm not available."

"Why weren't you available?" he demanded. "You're engaged, aren't you?"

"I had a headache," she said inadequately.

"Already?" he asked with a cold mocking smile. "I thought that came after your wedding night."

She turned on him like a wounded thing. "Get out!" she cried. "Leave me alone!"

He moved closer, the slowness of his movements imparting a sensual threat. "That isn't what you want," he said, his voice deep and slow and soft.

She backed away until the counter stopped her, her eyes wide and frightened as they met his.

He eased his hands onto the counter on either side of her, gently pinning her there with the threat of his body. He smelled of spice and leather and she had to close her eyes to keep her hands away from the expanse of broad, hair-roughened chest in front of

her, where the snaps had come apart at his collarbone.

"Does it bother you to look at me?" he asked
quietly.

Her eyes opened, and he read the vulnerability in
them, the helpless attraction. Her gaze went to his
chest and was jerked back to his eyes.

"So that's it," he said, almost to himself. He
moved one hand to his shirt and, holding her eyes,
ripped the snaps open down the front, baring the
bronze, muscular chest under its thick mat of dark,
curling hair. "Touch me," he said curtly.

Her lips parted. She couldn't believe this was happening, here in the gallery, in broad daylight.

"It's all right," he said quietly. He caught her
hands and put them inside his shirt, pressing them
gently into the thickness of body hair.

"Evan!" she moaned.

His breath caught as he pushed her hands closer.
"Oh, God," he managed as his body suddenly went
taut with violent arousal. "Pull, baby," he breathed,
bending to her mouth. "Get a handful of it and
pull...!"

She did, arching up to the open warmth of his
mouth even as it met hers. He groaned as her hands
grew bolder, caressing him, tugging at the thick
growth of hair, glorying in his masculinity, in his
size, his strength.

He lifted her suddenly onto the counter so that he
was between the folds of her full skirt, between her
thighs. His mouth bent, nuzzling under the jacket to

find the soft silk of her blouse and the softer warmth of her breast. His mouth opened on the hard tip, taking it inside his lips along with the fabric.

"Ev…an, no!" she cried, shuddering at the sheer ecstasy of his mouth on her body. But even as she protested, her head arched back and her hands went trembling into his thick brown hair, dislodging his hat, to hold him to her body.

"You're mine," he whispered, nibbling softly at her nipple. "You belong to me. I'm not giving you to Randall."

He lifted his head suddenly and moved back, breathing unsteadily, his eyes dark and smoldering as they met hers. He looked down at the damp fabric over her breast with pure masculine triumph. "Do you let Randall do that to you?" he asked mockingly.

She could barely breathe. The sight of him like that—his hair disheveled, his shirt open and wrinkled over his bare chest, his mouth faintly swollen from its hard pressure against her body made her dizzy. What he was saying finally registered, though, and made her flush scarlet. She'd actually let him touch her in that intimate way, given in without a fight, and he was mocking her for it. She felt a wave of shame.

"No, you don't," he answered his own question, his eyes blazing into hers. "You've never let anybody do to you what you'll let me. You never will."

She was trembling, but the bold statement wounded her pride. He was telling her that he owned her, and that wasn't true. She couldn't let him humiliate her again.

He lifted her down from the counter, kissing her with careless tenderness before he lazily resnapped the pearly buttons of his shirt. "Give Randall back the ring," he said with a satisfied smile.

She pulled the jacket over the wet spot on her blouse, red-faced. She could still feel his mouth on her there. He must think she was easy, to treat her like that, like some loose woman. "No," she said huskily.

His hands paused. "What?"

She moved away from him to the door, deliberately opening it. "You wanted to show me that I can't resist you. All right, you've done it. Now you can go and laugh about it with Nina. But I'm going to marry Randall."

"For God's sake, why?" he burst out angrily, almost crushing the Stetson in his big hand. "You don't love him!"

She lifted her eyes to his without flinching. "That *is* why," she said hoarsely. "Because I don't love him. Because he can never hurt me the way you have. Is your pride satisfied now, Evan?" she asked. "Has humiliating me healed it?"

He drew in a sharp breath. "Anna, that isn't why I came," he began.

"I'd like you to go, please."

"You don't understand," he said angrily, pausing in front of her. "I came to explain something to you."

She closed her eyes, tears threatening. "Please, can't you stop hurting me?" she whispered brokenly. "I'm getting married, I'm leaving Jacobsville because of you...isn't that enough?"

"Because of me?" He asked hesitantly, scowling.

Her face lifted, her eyes opening, tormented. "I can't help...what I feel," she sobbed. "Why must you keep punishing me for it?"

"Oh, baby, no," he said, horrified. "Anna, I didn't come here to hurt you!"

"I don't ever want to see you again, Evan," she whispered. "If your friendship with my mother and me ever meant anything to you, then, please just go away."

"And let you make the biggest mistake of your life by marrying that pill-peddling philanderer?"

"At least he never treated me like a tramp!" she all but screamed at him.

Evan stiffened. "I haven't. Not ever."

"What would you call what you just did to me?" she asked, clutching the jacket closer, horrified at her own actions, at her response.

He began to realize just how innocent she was, how untouched. He let out a slow breath. "Anna, what I did to you...that's part of lovemaking," he said gently. "It's nothing to be ashamed of."

She went scarlet. "If you don't leave, I'll scream," she threatened, her eyes wet now.

He threw up his hands. "All right. But this isn't the end of it," he said shortly.

"Yes, it is," she cried. "Go away!"

He went out the door, his mind already spinning with ways to pry her out of Randall's arms. But Anna closed the door and wept. She knew he didn't care about her now. He couldn't, and treat her like—like that! And worst of all was the memory that she'd let him. How could she ever face herself in the mirror again?

Chapter Six

Polly noticed how upset Anna was at supper. She didn't want to pry, but she was worried about the way her daughter was losing weight and brooding.

"Can I help?" she asked Anna gently.

Anna's head jerked up and she flushed. "Uh, no, but thank you."

"Something's wrong," Polly said. "Did Randall do something to upset you?"

Anna shook her head. "It wasn't Randall."

"Evan?"

Anna flushed.

Polly smiled gently. "I should have known. He went to see you, didn't he? And had plenty to say about Randall taking that woman to the theater."

"How did you know?" Anna asked.

"He came to see me, too," Polly said, smiling ruefully. "He'd worked himself into a real lather over it. Amazing how possessive he is about you, for a man who professes not to be interested in you." Her eyes narrowed shrewdly when Anna's flush got worse. "He did more than just talk, too, didn't he?"

Anna's lower lip trembled as she lifted her coffee cup to her lips and took a sip. "He treated me like some woman he'd picked up for the night," she said huskily.

Polly's eyebrows rose. That didn't sound like Evan. "He kissed you?"

"Yes, and then he put his mouth on my...my..." She broke off, unable to put it into words.

Polly only smiled. "Darling, I've sheltered you too much, haven't I?" She touched Anna's cold hand. "Anna, nothing is, or should be, taboo in love-making between a man and a woman, as long as they both enjoy it," she said gently. "Because a man touches you, or kisses you, in a less than conventional way, it doesn't mean he has a low opinion of you. Where did you get such ideas?"

"Well, you never talk about it," Anna mumbled.

"You've never asked me." She studied the tormented young face. "Did you enjoy what he did, Anna?"

The younger woman's eyes closed. "Oh, yes," she whispered. "But I shouldn't have let him, and he shouldn't have touched me like that. I'm engaged!"

"To a man who doesn't even want you," Polly said quietly. "I'd rather see you have a blazing affair with Evan than marry a man you don't love, Anna."

"Mama!"

"Well, I would," Polly said stubbornly. "At least Evan wants you. I can't imagine him going out with another woman if it was him you were engaged to. Can you?"

"He's not like Randall."

"No, he isn't. He's passionate and stubborn and more man than most women could ever handle." She searched Anna's face. "He's a very big man, Anna. There was some talk once about his having hurt a woman badly in bed."

Anna flushed, her eyes meeting Polly's. "Deliberately?" she whispered.

"Of course not. But he's uncommonly strong, and a man can't always control his passion when he's aroused. The woman he was dating was half his size, a fragile little thing and very innocent. I don't know if that has anything to do with his attitude toward you, but it's a possibility."

"I'm not small and fragile," Anna reminded her mother.

"I know. But you're very innocent. Virginity can be an impossible obstacle for some men, especially men who are already afraid of their strength. It's something to think about."

"He didn't seem very afraid of it this morning," Anna recalled.

"Kissing is one thing. Sex is quite another."

She cleared her throat. "I won't have an affair with Evan."

"I never thought you would," Polly replied

calmly. "But if he's really interested in you, it wouldn't hurt to reconsider marrying Randall. Evan's twice the man he is."

"Evan hates me," she said unsteadily. "He looks at me as if he could tear me limb from limb half the time."

"He wants you," Polly clarified. "Desire is violent, especially great desire that's been repressed too long. I've seen the way Evan looks at you. Believe me, it isn't hatred."

"He isn't a marrying man," Anna said wearily. "Even if he does want me, it isn't for keeps. I can't handle that kind of relationship. I'd hate myself."

"Is marrying a man you don't love any better?"

"Probably not," Anna had to admit. She put down her cup. "Randall and I are driving to Houston tomorrow for a party his parents are giving. We'll be late getting back. He wants to tell them about our engagement."

"All right. It's your life, Anna. I'll advise you, but I won't try to sway you again. You have to live with your own decisions, not mine."

Anna looked at the older woman quietly. "You're a terrific mother, did I ever tell you?"

Polly smiled gently. "Frequently. But I never tire of hearing it."

"I think I'll get to bed early tonight," Anna said. "I haven't been sleeping well lately."

"Do that, darling. Sleep tight."

"You, too."

But she didn't sleep. She lay awake, feeling over

and over again the heat of Evan's mouth on her
breast. She touched her bodice where the lace fell
away and felt her body tauten at just the memory of
his warm lips there. She shuddered, closing her eyes.
She could hear his voice, whispering, seductive,
teaching her how to touch him, to excite him, while
he made her body sing with his mouth. She'd never
dreamed she could feel so hungry, so wanton. But it
had been new and frightening and embarrassing, to
be so intimate with him. She'd reacted badly. He'd
gone away, as she'd asked, and he hadn't called or
come back. Perhaps she'd really driven him away
this time, and it might be for the best. Whatever her
life was like with Randall, she wouldn't be at the
mercy of her body, of needs she hadn't known she
had.

Evan wasn't sleeping, either. He lay wide awake
on his own bed, thinking of Anna, remembering the
softness of her under his lips. That had been an error
in judgment. He should have talked to her first, before he came on too strong and frightened her. He
hadn't known she was so innocent that she felt insulted by the soft loveplay they'd shared. Under different circumstances, he could have taken her in his
arms and explained it to her, gently coaxed her to
give in to him. But he'd chosen a bad time, an impossible place. Next time, he'd have to be more cautious. But somehow he had to get her away from
Randall before she married the man. Then what?
What would he do about Anna? She was very in-

nocent and the old fears still haunted him. What if he hurt her? What if his strength sent her running, as it had Louisa? Could he bear that?

He rolled over, closing his eyes. One step at a time, he thought bitterly. He'd done enough damage to her pride and her heart. Now he had to put it right. If he could.

Randall's parents lived in a middle-class suburban home in Houston, nothing really fancy, but nice. They were pleasant people. His father was a teacher, his mother a dietician, and they were kind to Anna. But she felt very much on display when their friends began to arrive, and it was almost a relief when Randall offered to go for more liquor later in the evening.

Anna went with him, despite his protests. The liquor store was in a bad part of town, he told her, and there was no drive-in. He'd have to leave her in the car.

She could lock it, she told him, laughing. He had nothing to worry about.

He gave in with obvious reluctance. Anna was wearing an expensive dress and a diamond pendant that Polly had bought for her. She looked as though she had money. But he couldn't talk her out of going with him, so he made her promise to stay in the car and keep the doors locked.

Ordinarily she would have done so. But a kitten wandering on the side street caught her attention. It was small and pitiful looking, and it headed right for the street. There wasn't a soul in sight, and the parking lot was well lighted. She got out of the car and went after the kitten.

Unexpectedly it darted away and she followed, calling it. Her soft voice attracted the attention of a vagrant on the other side of the street. He saw the way she was dressed and assessed the shiny pendant around her neck and the glittery ring on her hand.

He was on her before she knew what had hit her. She fought like a tigress, but her struggling only enraged him and made him much more dangerous than he would have been if she'd let him have the diamond and the emerald ring.

She felt stark terror as his big fist connected with her face, and she screamed, but he kept hitting her. She couldn't even get away. He was an enormous man, heavyset and vicious, and by the time she finally blacked out, she tasted blood and felt as though he'd broken her to pieces...

Randall came back to the car and when he found it empty, he panicked. Dropping the bag of liquor on the hood of the car, he ran down the street, calling her. A shadow moved, and he went toward it hesitantly, just in time to see a man's shape move quickly away. There was a dark blob on the ground, and Randall knew all too well what it had to be.

He rushed to Anna's side, groaning as he saw her bleeding, bruised face. He examined her quickly, professionally. Her dress was torn but, thank God, the man hadn't raped her. He might have, if Randall hadn't come along when he had. As it was, he'd left with her jewelry. Her pulse was weak, but still there. There was blood in her hair from where she'd hit the pavement and she was almost surely concussed.

"Anna, can you hear me?" Randall asked huskily.

She didn't answer. She was unconscious.

He pulled out his penlight and examined her eyes quickly, grateful for his medical training. Definitely concussion, he thought, and that could be serious. He lifted her and struggled to get her into the car. Then he drove like a madman to the emergency room of the nearest hospital.

Harden was the only one at home when the telephone rang. He picked up the receiver, expecting a business call. But it was Polly Cochran on the other end of the line, half hysterical and all but incoherent.

"Slow down, Polly," he said curtly. "What is it?"

"It's Anna! Oh, God, I've got to get to Houston, Harden. I can't...I can't drive. Is Evan there?"

"No, he's flown to Dallas for a meeting." He didn't add that Evan had raised hell when he had to go, because his plans for the day were focused on something much more important than business, but he hadn't said what. He'd gone, with furious reluctance. "What's happened to Anna?"

"She's been mugged. She's in the hospital and badly hurt," Polly said shakily. "I have to..."

"I'll get Miranda and we'll be right over. You're at home?"

"Yes. Thank you!"

"No need. You'd do it for us." He hung up and

went to find Miranda. Minutes later they picked Polly up at her house and headed toward Houston.

"She'll be all right, Polly," Miranda said gently, smiling reassuringly at her. "She's a strong girl."

"Oh, I hope so," Polly said huskily, fighting tears.

Anna was in the intensive care unit when they got to the hospital, attached to life support systems, her breathing labored, her eyes closed. Her face was a mass of bruises and cuts, one eye almost swollen shut. Randall came out of the unit to talk to them in the hall.

"She's had a bad time of it," he said quietly. "The concussion is what worries us most. For the rest, it's just bruises and cuts, and she'll heal."

"She wasn't raped?" Polly asked through her teeth.

Randall shook his head. "I got to her in time to frighten the man off." He sighed wearily. "Oh, God, I'm so sorry. It's my fault. We went out to get some more liquor for the party, and I told her to stay in the car, so that she'd be safe. I still don't understand what made her get out of it."

"Why did you take her with you?" Polly wailed.

"She insisted," Randall said helplessly.

If it had been Evan, she'd have stayed at home, Polly thought angrily. Evan would have protected her. But she didn't say it. Randall looked broken up enough as it was.

They went into the intensive care unit and Polly sat beside her daughter, holding her hand. She had to get well. She had to!

* * *

It was morning before Harden and Miranda got home. Polly had refused to leave, so Harden had promised to return later in the day with some things she needed. He told Donald and Theodora what was going on, then grabbed a few hours sleep. He got up early and did what he needed to do on the ranch before he went to Polly's house and filled an overnight case for her. Then he drove back to Houston.

It was suppertime when he returned. He was worn and haggard. Evan was home, but he'd been out most of the day and had just joined the family. Nobody had told him yet.

Harden didn't know that. He clapped Evan on the shoulder. "I'm sorry about Anna," he said quietly.

Evan shrugged. "One of those things," he said curtly and turned away.

Harden was shocked by Evan's lack of feeling, but perhaps he was still raw from her engagement and hiding it.

Harden sat down and waited for Theodora to say grace. While they ate, Evan talked about the meeting and what he'd learned.

Miranda had felt nauseated, so she was late getting downstairs. She'd been asleep when Harden came home, so he hadn't wanted to wake her. He smiled at her as she joined them, lifting his face for her soft kiss before she eased into the chair beside him, her pregnancy delightfully obvious.

"How is she?" she asked gently.

"There's no change," Harden said heavily. "I promised Polly I'd drive back up tomorrow, so that she won't be completely alone. She's tried to contact Duke, but he's out of the country. They expect him back tomorrow. I hope to God..."

"Do they have any idea who did it?" Theodora asked quietly.

"Not yet," Harden said. "They won't, unless he tries to fence the jewelry. That's a long shot, too."

"Maybe not," Miranda interrupted, aware of Evan's sudden interest. "That emerald solitaire would stand out, wouldn't it?"

"So it would," Harden agreed.

"What the hell are you talking about?" Evan asked. "Anna has an emerald solitaire."

"She did have," Harden said. "It was stolen."

"How?"

Harden sat very still. He glanced around the table, from Donald and Jo Anne to Theodora. "Hasn't anybody told him yet?" he asked softly.

"There wasn't time," Theodora said gently. She grimaced as she looked at Evan. "And I didn't quite know how—"

"Tell me what?" Evan ground out.

"Anna's in the hospital in Houston," Harden said quietly. "She was attacked and badly hurt. She's in a coma."

He hated doing that to Evan in front of the others. He alone had a good idea of how Evan really felt about Anna, and it was like stripping his pride naked.

Evan handled it well, though. Except for his sudden pallor and a certain awkwardness about his movements when he stood up, he looked perfectly normal.

"Let's go," he told Harden.

Harden knew when not to argue. He kissed Miranda. "Don't wait up. I'll be back when I can."

"Drive carefully," she said, smiling.

He nodded toward the others and followed Evan out.

"Give me a cigarette," the bigger man said when they were headed toward Houston in Harden's car.

"You don't smoke."

"I just started."

He handed Evan his cigarettes and matches. "I hate corrupting you. Next you'll want a drink."

"I already do. Tell me how it happened."

"I'd rather not."

"Why?"

"Because you're volatile enough already."

"It was that damned doctor, wasn't it? He let her out of his sight."

"In a nutshell, yes, but he did tell her to stay in the car. She got out, God knows why, and was attacked for her jewelry. Apparently she put up a hell of a fight, but judging from the beating she took, he was big and mean."

Evan cursed solidly for five minutes, going from anger to rage to murderous fury. Harden didn't try to stop him. He knew exactly how he'd feel if it was Miranda in that hospital room.

"What are her chances?" he asked finally, almost choking as he drew on the cigarette.

"Fifty-fifty. We'll have to wait and see."

"Does she want to live, do you think?" he asked, his voice haunted. "I've hurt her, Harden. I've really hurt her."

"It wasn't your fault that you wanted her out of your life," he reminded the other man.

"But I didn't," Evan said miserably. "I was afraid I might hurt her. After Louisa…"

"We've had this converation before. Anna isn't Louisa. You might have given her a chance."

"Yes. I know." He took another draw from the cigarette. "I was planning to. I thought I still might be able to take her away from Randall, if I tried."

"Glory be! You got intelligent!"

"I got desperate," he said huskily. "I had the sweetest taste of her you could imagine at the art gallery two days ago. I haven't slept since. I want her until my heart aches."

Harden glanced at his hard, set face. "I know how that feels," he said gently. "I hope it works out for you."

"I hope she lives," Evan said dully. "That's all I want, for the moment. That, and to kill the man who put her in that bed."

Harden didn't say a word. He understood.

An hour later Evan was allowed into the intensive care unit. He cursed silently at the sight of her poor, hurt face. He should have never forced her out of his life. He'd brought this on her, by letting Randall take her away without a fight. He couldn't bear it if she died.

He sat down by the bed and slid her slender, cool hand between his big warm ones.

"Anna," he whispered.

She didn't stir, but he could have sworn he saw her eyelashes flicker, just a hair.

"Anna, it's me. It's Evan. Can you hear me, baby?"

The endearment got a reaction. Her fingers moved slightly in the cradle of his hands.

"Yes, you can hear me, can't you, little one?" he asked softly. He got to his feet and bent down, so that there was no danger that anyone passing by the open door could hear him. "Do you remember what we did together in the art gallery, Anna?" he whispered, his warm breath stirring the soft blond hair at her ear. "Do you remember how, and where, I kissed you?"

She made a soft sound and her eyebrows jerked.

His lips brushed her earlobe. His teeth gently closed on it. "I loved the feel of your breast under my mouth, Anna," he whispered. "I want it again."

She moaned. He lifted his head, his eyes glittering with triumph as she began to move her head.

"That's it," he coaxed. "That's it, little one, come back. Come back to me."

Seconds later her eyes opened and focused on him. She grimaced and they closed again and she shivered.

He pushed the nurse's call button. When the nurse arrived, before she could speak, he said, "She's conscious."

That was all it took. He was escorted out into the hall while a team of white-coated people marched into her room.

"She came to," he told Polly, smiling. "She'll be fine."

"But, how?" Polly asked, hugging him, laughing. "What did you say to her?"

He cleared his throat and looked uncomfortable. "I just talked to her," he said evasively. He scowled suddenly, glancing around. "Where's Randall?" he asked.

"He's staying with his parents," Polly said. "He was tired, so he went to get some sleep."

"With her here?" Evan asked, outraged.

Harden caught his arm and pulled him aside while the doctor came out and spoke with Polly.

"You're waving a flag," Harden cautioned.

"I can't help it," Evan raged. "Damn it, doesn't he care?"

"Not the way you do," the other man replied quietly. "Or isn't that already obvious?"

Evan ran a rough hand through his hair. "She flinched. She looked at me and flinched. If she didn't hate me, she probably does now."

"She's disoriented and in pain," Harden replied. "Give it time."

"Time," Evan said on a heavy sigh. "Yes."

He pursed his lips. "What did you say to her?"

Evan actually flushed. He gave Harden a cold glare and went to listen to what the doctor was saying.

Anna was going to be all right, the doctor told them, but there would more than likely be some emotional trauma and she'd need counseling. Being overpowered and beaten by the man could affect her drastically. He was a big man, too, the doctor had added, and very strong. He glanced at Evan ruefully and said flatly that she might find Evan's presence frightening and even a little intimidating until she had time to recover from her ordeal.

Evan listened, but he didn't leave. If Randall wasn't going to assume his responsibility for Anna, Evan certainly was. He wouldn't go away and leave her, and he said so. The doctor only smiled.

Polly was grateful for Evan's company in the days that followed, because Randall had to go back to work. He walked wide around Evan, feeling more guilty than ever when the big man glared at him. Anna loved Evan, and Randall hated standing in the way of her happiness. His original reason for wanting to marry her had begun to disturb him more and more as he realized how unhappy Anna had been. They'd been friends, and he missed her old, bubbling personality. Now, more than ever, he wanted her to be happy. He knew he couldn't give her that. But Evan could. He was leaving the field clear for the man she really loved. When she was well again, he'd break off the engagement, as gently as he could, and hope that things would work out for her.

Evan didn't know about the rationale, so he spent the better part of the day cursing Randall for all he was worth. He cursed even more when Anna suddenly refused to see him.

He couldn't accept that. He waited until Polly went to get herself a cup of coffee in the hospital canteen, then he calmly walked into Anna's room and sat down in the chair beside her bed.

She stiffened at his approach, and her eyes grew huge. He knew she must be connecting his size with that of her assailant, but it was more than he could do to leave her now.

"Don't be afraid of me," he said quietly, searching her blackened eyes. "I'm not going to hurt you. Not ever."

She seemed to relax a little, but her posture was still rigid, and she didn't take her eyes off him.

"Where's Randall?" she asked, her voice slurred because of the medicine they were giving her.

"You can forget Randall," he said shortly. "Because the last thing in the world you're going to do is marry him."

Chapter Seven

Anna was certain that she couldn't possibly have heard him right. "What?" she faltered.

"I said, you're not marrying Randall," he replied matter-of-factly. He glanced at the tray they'd brought her for lunch. "You aren't eating. Do you want them to put those tubes back in and feed you intravenously?"

"I'm not hungry," she said, dazed.

He got up and uncovered the food dishes, his dark eyes glaring at her. "You've lost enough weight."

"I'm a big girl," she muttered.

"Hmm," he agreed absently, letting his eyes fall to the thrust of her breasts under the thin hospital gown. He smiled gently. "In places."

She flushed and her breath drew in.

Evan cocked an eyebrow. "Shocked? You remember how I pulled you back, don't you, little one?" he asked softly. "What I reminded you of."

She swallowed, feeling trapped and nervous of him, painfully shy. She lowered her eyes to the white sheet.

He wouldn't have that. He touched her bruised chin very gently and lifted her face to his, searching her eyes in a tense silence. He remembered then, vividly, how she'd reacted to the intimate caress, what she'd thought. He smiled gently. "Anna, what I did to you wasn't meant to make you feel cheap," he said, his voice deep and tender.

"I...I know, now," she said hesitantly, without adding that Polly had explained it to her. "It frightened me," she whispered.

"Yes, and I think I know why." He bent, his eyes falling to her soft lips. He brushed them gently with his. "Desire can be frightening. The way I want you scares the hell out of me. Now more than ever."

She trembled, her eyes closing as his lips touched hers with lazy expertise. Her hand went to his arm, the nails digging into the huge muscle, scraping gently as he played with her mouth.

"Oh, Evan, you shouldn't," she moaned helplessly at his lips. "I'm engaged..."

His mouth pressed down on hers hungrily, driving all thoughts of Randall and honor right out of her mind. She cried out, both hands trembling at his nape, curling into it while he forced her mouth open and his tongue thrust hungrily into it.

Her helpless shudder and the sounds she made under his mouth brought him back to sanity. She was weak and hurt. He had no right to torment her.

He lifted his head slowly, his eyes opening to search hers. "I'm sorry," he whispered. "But I needed that. Here, stop shaking, little one, or they'll think I'm torturing you."

"Aren't you?" she whispered back, her voice shaken.

His eyes darkened, his jaw went taut. "It felt like that, didn't it?" he asked huskily. "I wanted so much more than your lips, Anna." His eyes went to her breasts, where her taut nipples betrayed the emotion he'd summoned up in her. "Do they want my mouth on them?" he whispered. "With no fabric in the way to dull the warmth and moistness when I take you inside it?"

She moaned hoarsely.

He caught his breath, standing up abruptly. "God, I'm sorry!" he ground out.

She turned her head and found herself looking down the broad sweep of his chest and shoulder to the thick belt that held up his jeans. And then at the evidence of his uncontrollable response to their quick passion.

"Yes, I want you," he said curtly, following her eyes to his body. "I can't hide it, can I?"

She bit her lower lip, struggling for words.

"No need to agonize over it," he murmured, going back to the plates on her tray as he moved it across her lap. "It will subside eventually," he added with rueful humor.

He made it sound matter-of-fact, and he didn't seem to be embarrassed that she saw him like that.

She watched his face as he undid the lids from the plates.

"It doesn't embarrass you?" she asked in a whisper.

"Not particularly." He laughed shortly, glancing down at her. "In fact, it's a welcome change."

"I don't understand."

"Don't you?" He laid the lids aside. "It doesn't happen with other women lately," he said, turning to face her. "In fact, I can't make it happen with anyone else. Only you."

Her eyes spoke volumes, half-questioning, half-jealous.

He nodded. "That's right. I tried. I went to Denver on business after I'd kissed you that day in the gallery. I deliberately came on to one of the party girls I met there and took her upstairs with me. We drank and watched television, and I sent her away, because despite her beauty and her obvious expertise, I couldn't even pretend to be interested."

"You…were…?"

"The word is impotent," he said quietly. "Ironic, isn't it? All I have to do is look at you, and I'm so aroused I can't even hold a fork."

He drew her attention to it, to the fine tremor of his big hand as he dipped the fork into a creamy chicken dish. She hated the thought of him with another woman, even if it did make her feel warm all over to realize that he only wanted her.

"Open up," he said gently, lifting the food to her mouth.

"But, you don't have to do that," she protested. All the same, she opened her mouth and let him slide the forkful in.

"Yes, I do," he replied gently, searching her poor, bruised face. "I've hurt you more than I ever meant to. But that's over. I'm going to take the most exquisite care of you from now on, Anna."

Because he felt sorry for her. That, and desire. She could have cried.

"But, Randall," she whispered.

His eyes flashed at her from under thick brown eyebrows. "Randall can go to hell. He never should have taken you to that liquor store. And you haven't yet said why you got out of the car in the first place."

"There was a kitten," she said, her eyes softening with the memory. "It was lost and heading for the street."

His heart turned over. At that moment, he loved her with such passion that his body could barely contain it. He wanted to throw the tray aside and come down beside her on the bed.

She lifted her eyes, puzzled by his silence, and saw the vicious heat of his gaze. Her face froze.

"What is it?" he rasped.

"That look," she said, averting her gaze. "You looked as if you hated me."

He reached down and turned her face back to his. "That look is a raging desire that I can only just control," he said tightly. "Yes," he added when she stared at him. "It's every bit as violent as hatred, but I assure you, it isn't. And there's no need to be afraid of it, or me. Nothing is going to happen, Anna, least of all while you're lying there bruised and broken.''

"I'm not afraid of you," she said gently.

"Aren't you?" he asked curtly. "The doctor said that you were going to have some emotional trauma because of what happened. The man was about my size, he said."

Her eyes swept over him softly. "Yes," she agreed. "But he was a cold, brutal stranger who wanted my jewelry."

His heart leapt. "I see."

He lifted another forkful of chicken to her mouth, taking his time, feeding her as gently as if she'd been a child.

"My eye hurts," she said when he finished and moved the tray away.

"I don't doubt it. You've got a shiner."

She managed a smile. Her face hurt when it moved. "I can tell people I was in a brawl."

"You gave him a few bruises, I hear," he said, hating the thought of some man beating her.

"A few bites, too," she muttered angrily. "He could have just taken the jewelry, he didn't have to...to hit me like that!"

Evan was vibrating with equal anger. She looked up and saw his face. It calmed her down.

The painkillers made her oddly comfortable with him, as if she didn't have to fight her feelings or avoid personal questions.

"Evan, can I ask you something very personal?" she asked after a minute.

He was lighting a cigarette. He turned back to her, his dark hair falling roguishly onto his broad forehead, his jeans taut across his powerful legs as he leaned back against the wall beside the window and crossed them.

"Shoot," he invited.

"You're smoking!" she exclaimed.

His big shoulders rose and fell. "Just as well I couldn't leave you long enough to go to a bar, or I'd be drinking, too," he said.

"But why?"

"Because I was worried, of course," he said, staring at her as if she were demented. "Polly spoke to your father this morning, by the way," he added. "He returned to the States last night and got the message she'd left for him the night you were brought in. He's on his way out from Atlanta now."

"Daddy?" She smiled, delighted. "I haven't seen him for years."

"I know. Polly's pretty nervous herself."

"I wish they could make up," she murmured. "Neither of them wants anyone else, but they can't live together."

"Your father will get tired of wandering someday and come home," he told her. "Polly, I imagine, will be waiting." He stared at her, curls of smoke drifting up from his cigarette. "What did you want to ask me?"

"Oh. That." She studied his dark, unsmiling face. "You've been so different lately," she murmured. "Not the same man you were."

"How was I?"

"Lighthearted," she recalled. "Carefree and playful. You've changed. Is it because of Nina?"

"What do you think, baby?"

She blushed at the endearment, remembering how and when he'd said it.

"Was that what you wanted to know?"

She drew in a slow breath. "No." She studied her clasped hands. One was scraped raw where she'd fallen to the pavement during her struggle with her assailant. The experience had been terrifying, and she'd had nightmares since, but when Evan was around, she didn't think about it.

"Well?" he asked impatiently.

"I don't think I can."

He moved closer to the bed. "There is nothing, absolutely nothing, you can't ask me," he told her quietly.

"Even about...about that girl who said you hurt her?" she asked, repeating the gossip Polly had once told her.

He froze. His face stiffened as all his fears came back to torment him.

She looked up and winced. "I'm sorry. Evan, I'm sorry!"

He met her worried eyes and took a deep breath. "It was a long time ago," he said dully.

"And you don't want to talk about it," she said. "I shouldn't have said anything."

His brows drew together. "What did you want to know about it? How I hurt her?"

She went scarlet and dropped her eyes.

He laughed bitterly. "Is that what you think, Anna?" he asked on an expelled breath. "That I get my kicks from being cruel in bed?"

Her hands tightened together until the knuckles went white. "No!"

"What if I do?" he persisted, angry that she could think of him that way. He remembered his own roughness with her when he'd kissed her, and realized that he might have given her a foundation for her assumptions. He moved closer to the bed, his eyes glittery with temper. "What if I like it?"

She ground her teeth together. "I know you're not like that," she said stubbornly.

"Do you?" he leaned down, his eyes looking straight into hers, making her heart jump and run. "I bit you," he whispered. "Do you remember where?"

Her body trembled with the memory, her breasts going hard-tipped, betraying her. "Yes," she whispered. "But it...didn't hurt."

"It wasn't supposed to," he said quietly. His eyes searched hers. "You've never made love at all, have you? Not even with Randall."

"It always seemed so intimate," she replied nervously. "Almost distasteful."

"But not with me?"

Her lips parted as her gaze fell helplessly to his hard mouth, and she remembered how it felt to kiss him with her whole heart and have him kiss her back in that hungry, expert way. "Nothing could ever seem distasteful with you," she managed weakly, too shattered to lie, even to save her pride.

His hand pressed gently against her cheek, his thumb rubbing softly over her swollen lips. He bent and brushed his nose against hers.

"Louisa was very small," he whispered. "And as innocent as you are. We were going to become engaged, and I wanted her very badly. So I took her back to my apartment and undressed her. Then I pulled off my clothes and turned around...and she went white in the face."

Her eyes lifted to his, startled.

He nodded grimly. "She was half your size. She knew nothing of sex except what she'd gleaned from her romance novels. I was crazy to have her and I didn't realize how frightened she was. I thought I could coax her into my arms. For a few seconds I thought she was mine. Then I lost control, and she couldn't get free. She fought me and screamed. I came to my senses just as she fell off the bed and hurt her ribs." He stood up, his face pale. "She said some things..." He turned away, hiding the look in his eyes. "Anyway, that was my first and last experience of virgins. Since then I've avoided them like the plague."

"If you loved her enough to marry her, it must have been a terrible blow to your pride," she said quietly, understanding now his reluctance to become involved with her.

"It was." He sighed heavily and glanced at her gentle face, at its soft flush. "She'd never seen a naked man before, much less one as obviously aroused as I was." His eyes narrowed at her embarrassment. "You haven't either, have you, Anna?"

"No," she confessed huskily.

"She left Jacobsville soon afterwards. The last I heard she was married to some insurance agent and had two children." He laughed bitterly. "Maybe he had the good sense to get her drunk and turn the lights out first."

Her eyes widened. "You didn't have the lights out?"

She looked horrified. In spite of himself, he began to laugh. "Oh, my God, you don't think people only make love at night, in the dark?"

"Don't they?" she asked, trying to imagine how embarrassing it would be to lie down with a man like that in broad daylight.

He sat down heavily in the chair beside the bed. "Remind me to give you a copy of the Kamasutra for Christmas," he said ruefully.

She knew what the book was, even if she didn't own one. "Evan!"

"All right, keep your inhibitions." He pursed his lips as he flicked ashes into the ashtray on her bedside table. "Not that you had many, in the gallery that day," he remarked softly. "Or any other time I've touched you."

Her heart was going crazy. "You shouldn't talk to me like this," she began.

"Because of the beloved physician?" he asked sarcastically.

"Because...it's not decent," she said uneasily.

He just shook his head. "Baby, you are a case," he murmured. "So many repressions."

"Don't make fun of me," she said curtly. "It's no sin not to sleep around."

His eyebrows lifted. "Did I say it was?"

"You said I was repressed," she muttered.

His lips tugged into a reluctant smile. "Repressed, but passionate," he replied. "All you need is a few lessons."

She swallowed. "Randall can give them to me."

"That'll be the day," he said flatly. "I told you, consider your engagement broken. Randall's not getting you. Any lessons you get from now on will be from me."

"You don't want me!" she burst out.

"And you know better," he said quietly.

She glared at him in a frustrated fury. "You can't build a relationship on desire."

"I agree." He leaned back in the chair, his eyes dark and possessive. "But you can build one on love."

"I love Randall," she choked.

He only smiled. "No, you don't," he said softly. "You love me."

"You don't want me to," she replied miserably, not bothering to deny it. She lay back against the pillows and closed her eyes wearily. "I'm sleepy."

"Rest is the best thing for you. I'll go and find Polly." He put out his cigarette and adjusted the pillow under her head, pulling the sheet up to her breasts. The back of his knuckles brushed the tip of one and it went immediately taut.

She blushed, but he didn't tease her about it. If anything, his face grew more solemn.

"When you're out of here," he said, "we're going to start spending some time together."

"You don't have to do that," she murmured.

"I know. I want to." He bent and brushed his mouth gently across her forehead. "My poor bruised baby," he whispered. "I'm sorry he hurt you."

Tears threatened at his tenderness. He'd been every way with her, from teasing to cold to passionate, but he'd never been tender before.

"Nina won't like it," she said unsteadily. "And neither will Randall," she added.

"Neither of them matters," he said, dismissing them. He brushed his lips softly against hers. "Go to sleep. I'll be here when you wake up."

"But you don't want me around," she whispered as she began to doze. "You keep throwing Nina at me to prove it."

His face went rigid with self-contempt. "Every man's entitled to one stupid mistake."

"She's very pretty," she sighed.

"Go to sleep," he said gruffly.

She did, her last conscious thought that he sounded angry about something, but she was too sleepy to wonder what.

When she woke again, a tall man with graying blond hair and blue eyes was sitting in the chair where Evan had been, gravely concerned.

"Papa!" she exclaimed, and held out her arms.

He went into them with rough laughter, hugging her warmly. "And here I sat, worried to death about the kind of reception I'd get."

"Don't be silly. You're my dad. I love you."

"I'm sorry I wasn't here sooner," he said bitterly. "I was out of the country. I didn't know until last night. How are you?" He stood up, studying her. "They said you were badly concussed."

"I was, but I'm much better. Just a little battered."

"So I see. And the man, the one who did it?"

"They haven't caught him yet, but they may be able to trace him through the jewelry he took."

"If he was a junkie, that's not likely," he said heavily. "They have a network all their own for fencing goods. My poor little girl!"

"I'll be all right."

"No thanks to your so-called fiancé," he growled. "What possessed you to let yourself be talked into marrying that wimp?" he demanded. "I thought you were head over heels in love with Evan Tremayne!"

"She is," came a deep, amused drawl from the doorway as Evan sauntered in, carrying two cups of coffee. Anna flushed, and he grinned. "Still take it black, Duke?"

Duke Cochran chuckled, rising to take the cup from Evan and shake hands. "Yes, I still do. How are you?"

"Tired." He glanced past him at Anna, who was pale but looked at least a little better. "We all are. It's been a long week."

"I know. I'm sorry I wasn't here."

"Couldn't be helped."

"Yes, it could," Duke said angrily, running a restless hand through his hair. "I'm never around when I'm needed. Polly's right, my family's only been an afterthought, hasn't it, sweetheart?" he asked Anna.

"It hasn't," she disagreed, her eyes soft. "You just can't settle down. I understand. Most men love their freedom," she added without daring to look at Evan.

"Freedom can cost too much sometimes," Duke replied tersely.

"Amen," Evan said under his breath.

Polly came in the door and stopped, her hand going to her throat as she looked into blue eyes she hadn't seen for two long years. "Duke," she whispered.

"Hello, pumpkin," he said, smiling hesitantly. "Surprise, it's really me."

"You look…"

"If you say marvelous," Duke threatened dryly, "I'll smack you. Come here, woman, and give me a kiss. I've gone hungry too long already!"

"Oh, you!"

Polly blushed, but she went to him, lifting her face for a kiss that, when it came, made the other occupants of the room feel briefly like intruders. Polly was breathless when Duke let her go.

He chuckled huskily at her expression. "Worth the wait, wasn't it, pumpkin?" he asked. "Glad to see me? God, I'm glad to see you! You look more beautiful every year."

"You flatterer," Polly faltered. "You always did have the devil's own charm."

"Doesn't he look great?" Anna asked her mother.

"Yes, he does," Polly had to admit. He was tanned and slender, no beer belly or excess weight. She averted her eyes to Anna. "But you don't. How are you, darling?"

"Better," Anna said doggedly. "When can I come home?"

"Your doctor said tomorrow, if you feel like it," Polly said, beaming. "You'll have to take it easy, of course, and they do want you to have some counseling," she added.

"We can talk about that when I get home," Anna replied. "I really don't feel that traumatized."

"You save that for when you're asleep," Evan said quietly. "You've been having nightmares. Painful ones, judging by the way you thrash around."

"He's right," Polly agreed. "Maybe the trauma is buried in your subconscious, but it's still there."

Anna grimaced. "If I'd only stayed in the car like Randall told me to," she sighed. "Speaking of Randall, has anyone seen him today?"

"He phoned," Polly said. "But he's got exams and he can't come to see you. He asked if you needed anything."

"What a loving fiancé," Evan said with bitter mockery, his dark eyes narrow and cruel.

"You stop that," Anna muttered. "Exams are very important to him."

"More important than you are, obviously," he shot back.

She glared at him. "My personal life is none of your business!"

"It is, when you do stupid things like agreeing to marry fools!"

"Now, now," Polly chided, getting between them. "Anna needs rest. So do you, Evan. You haven't slept more than an hour or two since the day after it happened."

"Good suggestion," Duke seconded. He clapped Evan on the shoulder. "Thanks for the coffee."

Evan was reluctant to leave, but he was feeling the strain. He glanced at Anna, grimaced and let himself be persuaded out the door by Duke.

Polly smiled at her daughter. "He's very antagonistic about Randall, I'm afraid," she mused. "He's said some things I won't even repeat to you."

"Randall is none of his business," she said doggedly.

"He won't believe that. He's very possessive, isn't he?" she asked with a twinkle in her eyes. "He hasn't left you since they brought you in, except to sleep."

She knew that. It warmed her, somehow. Randall's behavior was unexpected. He had compassion, and she knew he cared about her, but he was deliberately staying away. She couldn't help but wonder why.

"Evan knows how I feel," she told Polly. "Do

you think it's some game he's playing, trying to turn me against Randall? Or is it a case of dog in the manger?'' She sighed miserably. ''Oh, Mama, he just feels sorry for me, that's all it is. Once I'm well, he'll take off like a rocket, you wait and see.''

''Evan is deep,'' Polly said. ''Let the future take care of itself. Right now, you concentrate on getting well.''

''All right. It's nice to have Papa home, isn't it?''

Polly sighed with more feeling than she realized. ''Oh, yes. It is, indeed.''

Anna didn't say another word, but she smiled. She refused to let herself think about Evan's odd behavior and the hungry way he'd kissed her. Perhaps he enjoyed the feeling of power it gave him to know that she cared so deeply for him. About his own feelings, he'd said nothing. For all she knew, he could be planning to marry Nina. She didn't recognize the man he'd become lately. Of course, she thought dazedly, he'd never treated her like a woman until very recently. A man was one way with friends and family, but a totally different way with a woman he desired. She flushed remembering how helplessly he wanted her.

Could it be just desire driving him? She knew men could fool themselves about their emotions when their glands were involved. She didn't dare trust anything Evan said or did right now, while she was flat on her back. If it was only pity, or even only desire, she couldn't risk breaking her heart on him again.

Chapter Eight

Randall came to see Anna an hour later, looking remorseful and quiet.

"I hope you're better," he said, sitting down beside her. He searched her bruised face and grimaced. "I feel terrible about what happened."

"I know. But it really wasn't your fault," she said gently. "I got out of the car."

"Why?"

She told him, ruefully, and he just shook his head. "How did exams go?"

"Well, I hope," he said, smiling just faintly as he looked at her. "My heart wasn't in it. I was worried about you."

"I'll be all right," she assured him.

He crossed his legs and leaned back. "I see that Evan's very much in residence."

She flushed a little and averted her eyes. "Yes."

He smiled. "Don't be embarrassed. I've always known how you felt about him. This engagement of ours isn't going to work, Anna. You can't marry me when you're in love with someone else."

Her eyes were sad as they met his. "I guess not."

"We were friends," he reminded her. "I like the girl you were—the impulsive, happy, bubbling girl who played jokes and never stopped laughing. I don't like the middle-aged woman I've made you into."

"But, Randall, you haven't!" she protested.

He held up a hand, silencing her. "Probably some of it was because of Evan, but being engaged to me hasn't improved you. I want you to be happy again. I want us to be friends again." He grimaced. "I don't know that I'm ready to settle down yet. Evan was right. If I'd cared enough, I couldn't have gone out with anyone except you. And if you cared enough, you'd have been furious."

She couldn't argue, because he was right. She sat up against the pillows, drawing her knees up so that she could rest her hands on them. "Yes."

"Besides," he said with an amused smile, "Evan just got through telling me I couldn't have you."

Her eyes flashed. "He has no right...!"

"I'm afraid he thinks he does," Randall mused. "You can argue the point with him."

"He just feels sorry for me," she said heavily, staring at her slender hands. "Once I'm back on my feet again, he'll be lying awake nights trying to think of ways to discourage me, just the way he used to."

Randall didn't think so, but he didn't argue with her.

"I'm sorry about my beautiful engagement ring," she said.

"It was insured," he said easily. "I'm only sorry about the way you lost it. Poor little thing."

"I'm not little, and I'm getting stronger every day. When I'm well, I'm signing up for karate," she said angrily. "I'll learn to pulverize muggers."

"That's a good idea," he agreed. "Self-defense should be part of every woman's repertoire."

They talked for a long time, and when Randall left, promising to keep in touch, it was if a weight had been lifted from her head. The engagement had been a mistake, but she couldn't regret it. Randall had saved her pride after Evan's vicious rejection.

Evan had gone home to change his clothes, simmering with fury because he'd encountered Randall in the corridor. He'd sent the man off with a cold warning, but it might be too little too late. He was sure that Anna loved him, but he'd treated her pretty badly. She might very well marry Randall out of desperation. He had to stop her, but how?

He could, of course, marry her himself. His face went blank as he considered that possibility for the first time. Marriage had never been one of his personal priorities, but he was crazy about Anna and he wanted her. They could have children. He drew in a slow breath. The thought appealed to him. Anna, children, a home of his own. Anna in his bed... His heart began to thunder in his chest as he considered marriage and found that it wasn't the terror he'd once thought. His fear of hurting her would be an obstacle, of course, as would her fear of big men. But in time, they could work that out. If she'd have him now.

He groaned inwardly at his own stupidity in turning away from her. She didn't trust him because he'd hurt her so badly, rejected her not only fiercely but in public. He must have savaged her pride. After their argument the night before, he wasn't sure he could even get into her room without a struggle. She might rush right into Randall's arms for protection. The thought made him miserable all the way back to Jacobsville.

"How is she?" Harden asked almost as soon as Evan got in the door of the Tremayne house. Because of Evan's absence, and that of Jo Anne and Donald, Harden and Miranda were staying with Theodora to help with ranch business.

"Better," Evan said tersely, tossing his hat on the hall table. "Her fiancé showed up just as I left."

Harden lifted an eyebrow. "I thought you approved of her engagement."

"So did I."

He stared at the older man quietly, his blue eyes seeing the lines in Evan's face, the tautness. "You look like hell."

"It's been touch and go for a while. She's only just beginning to pick up. How are things here?"

"We're handling them just fine. I assume you're going back?"

"I'll have to," Evan said curtly, his dark eyes

stormy, "or she may let herself be talked into a hospital wedding by that pill-pushing wimp."

Harden had to bite back a grin. "He's not bad."

"Not when he's a hundred miles away from Anna," Evan agreed.

Harden's blue eyes searched the other man's face. "You said that she was too young. That you didn't want her. But I don't think you realize how you've changed since Anna hasn't been around." He shook his head slowly. "Honest to God, I hardly know you these days."

"Anna said that," he admitted. He jammed his big hands into his pockets with a rough curse. "She'll be even more fragile after what's happened to her, and I don't know how I'm going to handle my own doubts. But leaving her to the mercies of young Dr. Randall isn't something I can live with. I'm not perfect, but she'd be better off with me. At least I won't drive her around strange cities at night hunting muggers."

Harden had to bite back laughter at the disgust in that deep voice. "I thought you were afraid of your own strength."

Evan gazed at him evenly. "I was. I am. I don't know how I'll handle that, either." His big shoulders lifted. "She makes me shake like a boy. God knows I'll probably send her running when things heat up, but I can't push her away again. Not now."

"You may underestimate Anna's feelings," Harden reminded him. "And Anna's no shrinking violet. If she loves you, everything will be all right."

"She loves me, all right," Evan said quietly. "That's the only thing I'm still sure of. But she thinks I just feel sorry for her, and Randall's handy." He looked up. "I told him he couldn't have her."

Harden smiled. "Good for you. But have you told Anna?"

"I will." He moved into the living room and went to speak to his mother before he caught up on business and started back to Houston.

It was almost dark when Evan returned to Anna's hospital room. She'd been sure he wasn't coming back, but surprisingly, he showed up with a huge white teddy bear under one arm. He slung it beside her on the bed, his dark eyes accusing.

"What...!" Anna exclaimed, her eyes beaming as she lifted the enormous, soft bear. She'd been ready for a fight, but he'd stolen her thunder. The bear was beautiful, and it touched her that he'd cared even enough to bring her a present.

"His name's Hubert," he told her irritably. "You can be engaged to him."

She laughed, cuddling the bear beside her. "He's beautiful," she said shyly, knowing that she'd treasure it for the rest of her life. "Thank you."

He shrugged. His eyes narrowed. "What did Randall want?"

Her eyebrows jerked up. "To see how I was, of course."

"Did you break the engagement?" he persisted.

"No, I did not," she shot at him. That was true.

Randall had broken it, but her pride wouldn't let her tell Evan.

He moved to her side and bent over her, his dark face threatening as his gaze fell to her mouth. "What was that?"

The closeness made her dizzy. He was wearing a yellow knit shirt with tight-fitting jeans. He was enormous, lean and muscular and he smelled of expensive cologne. His head was bare, dark brown hair neatly combed, his face freshly shaven. He was so sensuous that her mouth ached for his, but she wasn't about to be taken in a second time.

"My engagement is none of your business," she said stubbornly. He was too close. She clutched the bear for protection, knowing all too well that he could touch her and knock every one of her barriers spinning. He probably knew it. She was too green to hide the effect he had on her.

"Suppose I make it my business?" he asked quietly, holding her gaze. "Suppose I tell you that I'm jealous as hell and I don't want another man's hands on you?"

Her heart ran away, but she wasn't going to be taken in. "I've been hurt and you feel sorry for me," she said shortly. "You don't have to throw out your arms and profess love eternal just because I got mugged, Evan."

His face colored angrily. "It isn't pity."

"What else could you ever feel for me?" she asked bitterly.

He drew in his breath sharply and stood up, his

hands jammed deep in his pockets. He'd been living on his nerves for too long, he supposed, because her harsh question made him sick inside. His self-confidence took a nosedive. Apparently she'd decided not to believe anything he told her from now on. How could he convince her that he'd had a sincere change of heart about her place in his life?

"That's right," she muttered darkly, "stand there and glare at me. At least that would be honest."

"What's gotten into you?" he asked flatly.

"I've seen the light, dear man," she returned. "Maybe I've even grown up a little as well. I've just gone off hero worship, Evan."

His hands clenched in his pockets, but his face gave nothing away. "Is that all it was?"

"I'm nineteen," she reminded him. "Too young for undying love and commitment, isn't that what you thought?"

His face tautened with strain. "It wasn't just your age."

"Then what was it?"

"Louisa," he said quietly.

She remembered what he'd told her about the other woman and her face softened. She could only imagine the scars that the experience had left on him. Her eyes fell to the bear and she stroked the soft fake fur gently.

"If she'd really loved you, Evan, nothing would have frightened her," she said, her voice subdued.

"Are you sure?"

He sounded mocking, cynical. She glanced at him,

her eyes faintly adoring. He looked so tired. "I would have been glad to prove it to you, once," she said.

His eyes flashed in a face like stone. "Think so?" he asked on a hard laugh. "You don't even know what it's all about. The way you react to me, I doubt if Randall's ever made you feel desire."

Denying that was beyond her. Her fingernails curled absently into the bear. "Nobody ever did, until that day in the gallery," she confessed.

His breath caught audibly, and his teeth ground together. "I lie awake at night, remembering how your hands felt on me," he said huskily.

She could have said the same thing to him. It would have been a perfect memory, except for what came afterward. The light went out of her eyes as she remembered Nina.

"Mine, or Nina's?" she asked dully.

He moved closer to the bed, leaning over her with one big hand resting beside her head on the thick pillow. "I'm not sleeping with Nina," he said, almost able to read the thoughts as they passed through her mind.

"Ever?" she asked cynically.

His eyes fell to her soft body and then to the bear. "I won't talk about old conquests to you, Anna," he said finally. "What happened in the past has no bearing on the present, or the future."

"Nina isn't in the past," she said, fighting not to show what his nearness was doing to her pulse.

"You've made sure that everybody knew it, too, not just me."

His gaze pinned hers and he looked faintly threatening. "I've been running from you for a long time," he said shortly. "It got to be a habit, but just lately, I look at you and get so damned aroused that I can hardly function. Keeping away from you was the only thing that saved you."

Her eyebrows arched. "You're not keeping away now," she began.

"You're flat on your back in bed," he said simply. "I'm no threat to you now."

"Oh. I see," she said dully.

"You see nothing!" he raged. "My God, a blind woman…!"

"I know you want me," she burst out. "It would be hard to miss. But I want more than five feverish minutes in bed with you, Evan!"

"*Five* minutes?" he asked suggestively. "Is that how long you think it takes?"

One of her school friends had intimated as much. Actually, she didn't know how long it took, and she didn't want him to know that.

She averted her eyes. "Never mind."

He caught her chin and tilted her face up to his dark, sensuous eyes. "In five minutes I could satisfy myself," he said softly. "But I'd need another twenty to satisfy you as well."

The color came into her cheeks despite all her frantic efforts to stop it. She swallowed. "That's not fair."

He drew in a slow breath as he tried to imagine Anna in passion. He drew his thumb gently over her cheek. "No," he agreed. "It isn't. Anna...I wish you knew more about men," he added heavily. "I wouldn't have you experienced, but it would make things easier."

"You think I'll be afraid of you," she replied. "Evan, I think every woman is secretly afraid of the first time. It's like stepping into the unknown, and all the reading in the world doesn't really prepare you for it. But you've blown that natural fear up in your mind until it's completely out of proportion."

"Have I?" His eyes grew hard. "You don't know how it was for me that night," he said roughly. "You don't know what she said...!"

His anguish made her sad. She caught the big, lean hand lying beside her on the bed and drew it gently to her breast, catching her breath as she felt its warm weight. He jerked back, caught off guard, but she held his hand there, cradling it with both of hers.

"What are you doing?" he asked huskily.

"Letting you feel how frightened I am," she whispered, and pressed the heel of his hand against the furious throb of her heart.

His lips parted as he struggled to breathe normally. He looked down at his hand and began to move it, very gently, against her breast through the thin fabric of the hospital gown. The nipple went hard at once and she drew in her breath as she felt its instant response to the slow caress of his big thumb.

"You really are a big girl," he whispered sensuously.

"Do…you mind?"

"You fill my hands," he said softly. He leaned closer, his breath on her lips. "Would you like to fill my mouth, too?"

Her fingers bit into his broad shoulders. "Yes!"

He felt his body tighten, and his breath almost strangled him. His mouth brushed softly over hers, feeling its exquisite response while his hand suddenly tightened on her breast and swallowed it. His free hand went under her nape to arch her throat, and his mouth opened on hers in a kiss that was almost a statement of intent.

He tore his mouth away seconds later and stood up, visibly shuddering with frustrated desire, his face dark with it, his eyes glittering with it.

Anna stared at him hungrily, without fear, helplessly pleased at the evidence of his desire for her.

"You can see how terrified of you I am, can't you?" she whispered unsteadily. Her hands blatantly drew the gown taut around her breasts so that he could see their hard tips.

He had to swallow before he could even speak. His face was rigid as he looked at her body. "You don't understand," he said shortly. "There's more to it than this."

She moved her hands beside her head and sighed as she looked up at him. "But I'll never know, will I, because you're afraid to make love to me completely."

He laughed harshly, moving away from her to drag a cigarette out of his pocket and light it. He fumbled, because his hands were shaking so badly. "This is hardly the time or place."

"Randall wants to marry me," she lied, because she hadn't told him yet that their engagement was off. "He's not afraid to be intimate with me!"

He whirled, his eyes frightening.

She met his furious gaze evenly. "I thought it was what you wanted, to have me out of your hair for good."

"So did I," he returned curtly.

"Then you shouldn't mind if I get married and have children."

His jaw went taut. "Randall is the worst mistake you've ever made," he said. "He won't make you happy. Every time you turn around, he'll be out with some other woman."

"At least he won't be able to hurt me."

He took a long draw from the cigarette. "You don't love him. You love me."

"Isn't that just a little conceited?" she asked irritably.

"Probably, but it's true," he said quietly. He looked at her hungrily. "I don't know how I'm going to cope, Anna. But I can't let you marry Randall, feeling the way you do about me."

"You don't want ties," she countered. "You don't want marriage or children."

"How do you know?"

"Because you've said so, time and time again!"

she cried, exasperated. She lay back heavily against the pillows. "Nina's just your style. Good company and no broken heart afterward."

"She isn't," he said surprisingly. "Good company, I mean. All she wants is to go to bed with me."

"That must be a novelty."

He pursed his lips, not offended. "Not really. You want to go to bed with me, too."

She glared at him, but she didn't deny it.

He sighed wistfully and smiled at her. "You're not fragile," he said, thinking aloud. "And if I work at it, maybe I can do something about my inhibitions. God knows, I want you," he said huskily, his eyes revealing his desire. "And I'm thirty-four, plenty old enough to be thinking of settling down."

Her heart jumped. He sounded serious. "What about Nina?"

"What about her?" he asked flatly. "That's over. Finished. So is Randall," he added, his tone commanding. "You aren't going to marry him."

"Having fun arranging my life for me?" she asked breathlessly.

"Is that what I'm doing?" he mused. He finished the cigarette and put it out. He paused beside the bed and looked down at her quietly. "Tell me you don't want me, Anna."

She tried. She really did, but the words wouldn't come. She lowered her gaze.

He bent and brushed a tender kiss against her forehead. "I'll come and get you in the morning and drive you home. Polly said it was all right. She has an early-morning appointment and I volunteered."

"Evan..."

He brushed back her disheveled hair. "What?"

Her eyes were full of doubts, fears, insecurities. "Please don't play with me," she whispered. "Don't say anything you don't really mean, just because I got hurt and you feel sorry for me."

"I don't blame you for that lack of trust, little one," he replied. "Try not to brood too much. I promise you, this is no game. It isn't pity, or guilt. All right?"

She sighed. "All right."

"Good girl." He winked lazily at her. "I'll see you tomorrow."

Evan left, and as he walked out of the hospital, he seemed to relive the past few days with a vengeance. It was all catching up with him. He'd been living on nervous energy since he'd walked into the hospital with Harden. Only today was he rested enough to consider the potential consequences of what had happened to Anna, to realize how close to death she'd really come. And her last memory of him would have been painful, wounded. His eyes closed and he groaned softly. Thank God it had worked out like this. He had a second chance. Now he had to make sure he didn't blow it, even if it meant coming to grips with a lifelong fear of his own strength and size.

The next morning they wheeled her out to Evan's car in a wheelchair, and he lifted her from its confines, placing her gently in the passenger seat. It was the first time he'd ever carried her, and the sensation was odd, pleasant.

"You're terribly strong," she said breathlessly.

His jaw tautened. "I know."

He put her down and she looked into his eyes. "I like it, Evan," she whispered softly, to reassure him.

His face changed. He seemed disconcerted. He fastened her seat belt and busied himself putting her flowers and Hubert in the back seat and saying goodbye to the nurses who'd accompanied them.

They were on the way home before he spoke to Anna again. He was smoking like a furnace, something she could hardly miss.

"You never used to smoke," she remarked.

"I've been living on my nerves for several days," he replied without looking at her. "When you're back on your feet, I'll quit."

"I'm sorry you've been worried about me."

He smiled. "It isn't just worry that's done this to me, Anna," he said bluntly. "It's being near you."

She didn't know quite how to answer that, so she didn't say anything. She just stared at him, drinking in the perfection of his profile.

He glanced at her and then back at the road. "Haven't you ever wondered why I went to such lengths to avoid you? Even to the point of dragging Nina everywhere, like a shield?"

"I thought you were driving home the point that you didn't want me chasing you," she said matter-of-factly.

"Nothing quite so simple." He put out the cigarette. "I had to keep you from getting too close."

"It worked, didn't it?" she asked dully. "I got engaged to another man...."

"And I hated it," he said shortly, glaring at her. "The thought of Randall touching you the way I had made me murderous. He's damned lucky I didn't hunt him down and kill him, especially after he let you get hurt."

"He didn't..."

"If it had been me, you wouldn't have been in the car in the first place," he said shortly. "Or if you were, I wouldn't have let you out of my sight. But then, I know you better than Randall does. I would have anticipated how easily you might be tempted to leave the car."

She knew that, and it hurt. She averted her eyes to the landscape, watching it fly past the window.

"Talk about it."

She shrugged. "There isn't much to tell. He was very big and scary, and even while I was fighting him, I knew I couldn't stop him. But I thought it was me he wanted and not the jewelry."

"He might have," he said curtly. "But Randall did come along in time to prevent that, thank God."

"Yes."

"I thought you might be afraid of me at first," he said out of the blue. "The doctor said that I was apparently about the same size as the man who attacked you."

She looked at him wryly. "As if I could ever be afraid of you," she said with resignation.

He thanked God for that. He glanced at her. "About Randall..."

"We broke the engagement yesterday, Evan," she admitted finally. "He said that I'd changed since we'd been going together, and he wanted me to be happy again. He knew it wouldn't work out."

"Wise man," he said, more relieved than he could believe. "I didn't think he'd noticed the difference in you. I had," he added darkly. "But I still thought what I was doing was in your own best interest. Then you got hurt, and I realized how empty my life had been without you in it. Harden said *I'd* changed, too." He glanced at her hopeful expression. "I guess I had. Hurting you gave me no pleasure."

She stared out the window. "I'd hounded you pretty badly. I felt guilty about that."

"Hell, I loved it," he said huskily. "It was my own hangups I was fighting. When you stopped looking for me, I think I stopped living."

She smiled gently. "I'm glad."

"Yes. But we're not over the hurdles yet, little one," he said grimly. "In fact, we've hardly faced them."

"But we will," she said.

He reached over and touched her hand lightly. "Do we have a choice?" he asked heavily.

He didn't sound terribly pleased, and she worried at the strained look on his face.

"Louisa scarred you, didn't she?" she asked unexpectedly.

He hesitated. "I suppose so," he said heavily. "One of the things I vividly remember her saying is that a woman would have to be suicidal to take me on in bed." His jaw tautened as he told her. He'd never told anyone else, not even Harden.

Anna searched his rigid face. "Surely you've... been with other women?"

"With experienced women," he corrected curtly.

"But you still think you'll scare me to death?"

He stared straight ahead. "Maybe I was afraid to take the chance." He glanced at her and his eyes softened. "You're very young, Anna. You've been sheltered. More so than most women."

"That's true." She smiled gently. "But when you touch me, does it show?"

His heart beat heavily as he recalled how it had been when he put his hands on her, and his breath drew in sharply.

"It doesn't, does it, Evan?" she asked quietly, watching him. "In fact, I seemed to shock you in the gallery, when you opened your shirt and taught me how to excite you."

"For God's sake!" he groaned, and his hands gripped the steering wheel so hard that they turned white as he remembered her ardent, headlong response.

"Being innocent doesn't make me totally hopeless," she said, as she sat back against the seat. He didn't love her, but he wanted her just short of madness. She felt reborn, whole again. She shivered inside just thinking what it would be like to seduce Evan, to lie in his arms and let him love her.

At the same time she thought of the consequences, and the smile faded. She bit her lower lip hard. She couldn't have an affair with him. Sure as the world, she'd get pregnant.

She didn't realize she'd said it aloud until the car jerked sideways and she heard Evan curse.

"What?" she asked dazedly.

"Unless you want to end up in a ditch, could you please stop talking about babies?" he asked shortly.

That could mean he wanted them, or that he didn't. She was afraid to ask which. She started talking about the weather instead, delighted that he picked up on it and began to relax with her.

She couldn't know, and he wasn't going to tell her, that the thought of a child made him go rigid with a kind of desire he'd never felt before. He hadn't allowed himself to think about children for years, because it was only Anna who made him want them. But now he wondered how she'd look with her belly swollen, her face radiant, her eyes full of dreams. He wanted her in ways she didn't realize, to come home to after a hard day's work, to talk to about his dreams and fears, to hold in the darkness when he felt alone. He wanted her so badly that his body suddenly went rigid with the force of it, and he didn't want her to see, to know how vulnerable he'd become. First he had to be sure that he could overcome his hang-ups. If he couldn't, they might not have a future.

The weather was the best diversion of all, because he could concentrate on it and his body would relax. He focused on it all the way back to Jacobsville, refusing to allow himself to even think about Anna in maternity clothes.

Chapter Nine

Lori, the small, graying housekeeper, was waiting for them at the front door when they pulled up. Evan had forgotten the housekeeper, but he was grateful that she was in residence. He hadn't liked the idea of leaving Anna alone, and being around her tested his self-control to the limits. Only her condition kept him from going right over the edge, and it wasn't—as she thought—guilt and pity that drove him. He wanted her desperately, in every way there was.

He lifted her gently and carried her into the house, following Lori down the hall to the bedroom.

"Lord, it's so good to have you home!" she enthused, smiling at Anna. "We've all been so worried. And to have Mr. Duke home again and Miss Polly fussing over him..."

"I'm glad to be back," Anna agreed. She was trying to hide what it was doing to her to have Evan hold and carry her. She could feel the heavy thump of his heartbeat against her breasts, where they pressed into his chest, and she knew from the hardness of his face that the feel of her soft breasts was arousing him. She was shivering by the time he got into her bedroom, and grateful for Lori's presence.

"That reminds me, I've got to get to the store," Lori said suddenly.

"No!" two voices echoed.

Evan and Anna stared at each other, both faintly flushed, before they burst into laughter.

Lori stared at them. "My goodness, what was that all about?" she asked absently, frowning because her mind was already on what she needed at the store. "If you'll stay with her just a few minutes, while I run down to the supermarket, Mr. Evan?" Lori asked.

"I'll stay," he said with resignation as he laid Anna gently on the floral cover of her canopied bed.

"I'll be right back!" Lori grinned. "Anything special you want, Miss Anna?"

"Fish," Anna said. "And cheese crackers and tomato juice."

"I'll fetch them. I won't be long." She pulled the bedroom door shut, making everything much worse, and seconds later the back door closed. Then they heard Lori start Polly's car and drive off.

Evan looked down at Anna as she raised up on her elbows, her blond hair around her face in beautiful silky swirls, her blue eyes wide and soft.

He'd left his Stetson in the car. His head was bare.

He was wearing a blue-printed Western shirt with jeans and boots. The shirt was taut across the muscles of his broad chest, and she watched it rise and fall with the rough unsteadiness of his breathing.

Her eyes slid further down, to his belt and the unmistakable bulge below it. She flushed a little as her eyes slid down the powerful, muscled length of his legs and back up to his broad shoulders and darkly tanned face and glittery dark eyes.

His own gaze had gone to her legs and slowly up to the hard-nippled thrust of her breasts under the thin dress. It lingered there while his face grew visibly tauter and paler with the strain of staying where he was.

"You're aroused," he said huskily.

"So are you," she replied breathlessly.

"I haven't been any other way since you grew up," he said surprisingly. "It amazes me that you never noticed."

"I noticed that you avoided me."

He nodded.

She gnawed at her lower lip, her heart shaking her. "What happens now?" she whispered.

"We pray that Lori hurries back," he said with icy humor. "Before I do what we both want."

Her breath came out in jerky little spurts. She slowly lay back on the bed, on the floral pillow sham, her arms beside her head, her body softly trembling.

He was trembling as well, his body in anguish. But he knew all too vividly what he was going to do if he dared to touch her. They were both too aroused already to be able to stop. If he so much as kissed her, he'd take her.

"Evan," she whispered, her voice, like the soft eyes that met his, questioning. She drew up one long leg, deliberately letting the skirt fall to her upper thigh so that he could see the pale, graceful length of it.

His breathing became more audible. "Stop it."

"You want to," she whispered.

"Yes. More than you know. But it can't...happen like this," he said harshly, and deliberately turned away.

"Why?"

He leaned against the closed door, his forehead pressing there, the coolness easing the fever she'd aroused. "Because I'm desperate for you," he said huskily. "It can't be like that...the first time."

"I...wouldn't mind," she whispered, on fire to have him soothe the ache in her body.

"You would," he replied, regaining his almost-lost control. He turned, leaning his back against the door while he fumbled a cigarette into his mouth and lit it. His eyes met hers, solemnly. "Close your eyes and try to relax until it passes."

She let her eyelids fall, shivering as her taut body rippled with unknown sensations, desires, tensions.

He watched her, delighting in the knowledge that she felt exactly as he did, that her hunger could match his despite her naïveté. If Louisa's reaction to him in total intimacy hadn't scarred him so much, he

wondered if he could have kept his distance from
Anna.

After a minute or two, she sank into the mattress
with a gentle sigh, and the tension seemed to ease
from her.

"Better?" he asked quietly.

"Yes." She turned her head on the pillow and
looked at him. "Is it usually like this?"

He shook his head slowly. "I've never experienced anything half as powerful in all my life."

That had to be a point in her favor. She smiled at
him. After a minute he smiled back.

The door opened suddenly at his back and he
moved just as Polly came in. She laughed at Evan's
surprised face.

"Didn't you hear me drive up?" she asked, smiling. "How are you feeling, darling?"

Relieved, Anna almost said, because if Evan had
done what her body had begged for, a very embarrassing confrontation could have ensued.

"I'm feeling tired," Anna said evasively, smiling
back. "But much better. Lori ran to the store. Evan
said he'd stay with me."

"Nice of you, Evan," Polly said gently.

"Yes," he replied evenly. "If you're going to be
home for a while, I need to get some work done."
He smiled at Anna. "I've let things go lately."

"I wonder why?" Polly mused. "Thank you for
bringing her home," she added seriously.

"No problem." He glanced at Anna, trying not to
show how much he hated leaving her, even for a day.

"I promised to help Harden shift some cattle this afternoon, but I'll be back tomorrow. I've got some videos you might like to watch."

She managed a smile. "That would be nice."

"Yes, it would," Polly said. "Duke wanted to take me out tomorrow, but I hesitated, because I hated leaving Anna alone. We're going fishing," she added. "Duke and I want to talk."

Anna brightened. "Really?"

"Don't get your hopes up too high," Polly said. "But cross your fingers."

"I'll do that little thing," she promised.

"And I'll baby-sit," Evan said with a mocking smile.

Anna had to fight not to blush at the images he was conjuring up with that sensuous tone, but she reminded herself that she mustn't read too much into his innuendoes. He wanted her. Maybe it had blinded him to reality.

"Then I'll buy those new jeans I saw today." Polly grinned. "Evan, you're sure you don't mind?"

He looked at Anna and had to fight down another wave of throbbing heat. "No," he said huskily. "I don't mind."

Anna wanted to beg him to stay, because her scruples were beginning to give under the weight of her desire. But when he came tomorrow, he might lie beside her while they watched television, and with no one in the house—since tomorrow was Lori's day off—anything might happen. She knew she could never say no to Evan if he really wanted her. But giving in to him would be a big mistake, she realized sadly as reality punctured her bright dreams. His sense of honor might even force him into marriage if he compromised her. She didn't want a reluctant bridegroom. Love on one side would never be enough.

Evan smiled, but he didn't look at her again. He left, and Polly went back to her daydreams, unaware of Anna's rising fears.

That night she got up long enough to have supper with her parents, enjoying the way they talked to each other and to her. She felt part of a family for the first time in years. And Polly was actually radiant.

Later she excused herself and went to lie down, leaving Duke and Polly alone together. When she fell asleep after hours of daydreaming about the day ahead and Evan, they were still sitting in the living room talking.

Evan arrived late the next morning with two newly released movies in his hand, looking rakish and barely awake in denim and a checked Western shirt. He also looked half out of humor.

"I was up late doing book work," he explained to Polly, forcing a smile. In fact, he'd lain awake worrying about what he was going to do if he lost control with Anna and scared her half to death. He knew his fears were irrational, but he'd lived with them far too long to be able to dismiss them now.

Duke had stayed the night at the house, but he was dressed and ready to leave before Polly awoke and got dressed herself. Lori had served breakfast and gone out with friends to see a movie.

"How's my girl?" Duke asked Anna, as he joined his wife and daughter and Evan in Anna's bedroom where she lay, dressed in a long red skirt and a red-and-gold patterned blouse, stretched out on top of her covers with her long blond hair soft around her face and her pretty feet bare.

Anna kissed his tan cheek when he bent down. "Doing fine. I hope you and Mom catch a lot of fish."

"I'll settle for one pretty one," Duke murmured dryly, and Polly actually blushed.

Anna smiled at them. "Go away and enjoy yourselves."

They exchanged glances, but they didn't argue.

"Don't worry about her," Evan told them solemnly. "I'll take good care of her."

He was saying more than the words implied, and they knew it. Polly saw Duke relax visibly, and after a brief conversation, they left.

Evan walked them out and then returned to Anna's room, pausing in the doorway to look at her. She looked delicious. His heart began to run wild, just at the sight of her.

"Do you feel like watching these?" he asked, holding up two tapes of just-released movies.

"Yes," she said huskily, thinking how sweet it would be if he lay down with her on the bed and let her lie against him. Her face flamed with desire.

He had to turn away from that expression. He was

glad the housekeeper was around. If she hadn't been, he wasn't sure he could manage to keep his hands off Anna.

"Lori's here, isn't she?" he asked tautly, to make sure, while he loaded the first movie into the VCR and turned on the television before he started it.

"Well...no," she said. "It's her day off."

His jaw tautened. He actually shivered.

"Will it help if I promise not to seduce you?" she asked with a lightness she didn't feel. Her heart was racing.

He felt his body tauten as he looked at her across the room, his eyes falling helplessly to her blouse. "You wouldn't have to, don't you know?" he asked on a harsh laugh. "All you have to do is touch me."

Her heart ran wild. The truth of it was in his face, and all her dreams seemed to come true at once. She held out her arms to him, burning up with need.

He groaned, but he couldn't help himself. He went to her, feeling her cold hands curve around his neck as he bent, easing her back on the bed. It was wrong, he shouldn't. But her body was yielding and soft and exquisitely formed, and he felt himself going rigid long before his mouth lowered to her parted lips.

His body went down alongside hers on the mattress, his mouth fitting over hers with warm, slow mastery as they sank back onto the quilted coverlet.

It was heaven. Anna nibbled eagerly at his lips, loving the taste of him, the warmth and strength of his body against hers. But just as he deepened the kiss and his arms tightened, she gasped, and he drew back instantly.

"Did I hurt you?" he asked curtly, his eyes worried. "My God, sometimes I hate my own size!"

"You didn't hurt me," she said and lowered her eyes to his hard mouth. "I go hot all over when you kiss me like that," she whispered huskily.

He relaxed. His fingers traced her cheek. "All that worry, wasted," he mused with forced lightness.

"Do you really think I could ever be afraid of you, Evan?" she asked unsteadily. "Don't you know already that you could do anything to me and I'd let you?"

His eyes flashed. He bent hungrily to her lips as one big arm slid under her and lifted her against him. His mouth caressed and withdrew, brushed and lifted, as he aroused her with maddening skill until she was clinging and following his lips with her own, trying to make him end the torment.

"What do you want?" he whispered.

"Kiss me!" she moaned.

His teeth nibbled lazily at her lower lip. "Isn't that what I'm doing?"

"Do it right. Open your mouth and do it...!"

He did, at the same time shifting his big body so that his hips were squarely over hers, his arousal hot and blatant as it rested on her soft belly.

She gasped at the intimacy.

He lifted his mouth from hers and looked into her shocked eyes. He didn't move for a long moment, but that wasn't fear in her eyes. He moved softly and she grimaced.

He realized then that it was embarrassment, not distaste, and he smiled gently as he levered his body to one side. She smiled back, her face coloring delicately.

He eased one powerful leg between both of hers and she stiffened.

He shook his head. "No. This is part of lovemaking. I want you to know everything there is to know about my body. You have to, before we go any further."

She had to fight her own shyness, but after a minute she relented and let him rest against her.

"Don't be afraid," he said, his voice deep and sensual. "I'm letting you learn me, that's all."

She relaxed even more, and as the shock of intimacy slowly wore off, she began to enjoy the feel of his body.

He knew that she had no experience by which to judge him. That relaxed him a little. There was so much that she didn't know, but at least, thank God, there was no apprehension in her face. He'd never been able to make Louisa lie with him like this at all. In fact, she'd found intimacy with him almost distasteful. He still remembered how she cringed when he touched her breasts, and she'd never liked his mouth on them.

He drew his fingers slowly over Anna's breasts, the sound of flesh against fabric loud in the tense silence as he gently teased around the nipple that suddenly became taut. He held her eyes the whole time, heard her breathing change even as she allowed him the caress with damning generosity.

She gasped and arched toward his hand, trying to make him end the torment as he touched everywhere except against the hardness that ached for him.

"Gently," he whispered. "I'm going to do what you want me to, but let me make you burn for it first."

She colored, but she didn't protest his touch. She lay back against the pillows, her face flushed, waiting, trembling, as he built the torment almost to anguish and she moaned.

His big hand tensed under her, and he leaned closer, his dark eyes filling the world. "Is it bad?" he whispered.

"Yes!" Her nails bit into his shoulders as she let him see the helpless reaction of his body to his caress. "Evan, please! Oh, please!"

He drew his nose softly against hers, his breath on her cheek, her lips, and still his knuckles brushed with maddening slowness just at the very edge of her taut nipple.

Then, very gently, he caught the hard nub in his fingertips. She felt a rush of heat in her belly, and a long shudder rippled through her. She could barely see him through a blur of anguished desire, her expression one of taut abandon as she arched upward and gasped at the unbelievable pleasure.

Evan watched her with indulgent tenderness. "So hungry," he whispered. "I could almost satisfy you just by putting my mouth on you, couldn't I, little one?"

The intimacy of the statement made her flush, but she didn't protest when he began to flick open the buttons of her blouse with careless deftness.

"Lie still," he said when she touched his wrist in a faint protest. "Let me look at you."

"I've never," she began shakily, her eyes enormous.

"My God, don't you think I know?" he asked huskily. His eyes flashed as he pulled the blouse gently aside and then snapped the front catch of the bra. He drew it away from her swollen breasts and caught his breath at the beauty of her creamy body with its mauve nipples.

"I'm so...big," she whispered, almost apologetic.

"You're as self-conscious about your size as I am about mine," he said quietly. He touched her, as lightly as a breath, watching her face as she gave herself up to his hands. "You please me," he said, his voice deep and exquisitely tender. "You arouse me as no other woman ever has, ever will. You're delicious, Anna," he breathed, bending toward her breasts with unbearable slowness. "I want to eat you up..."

His mouth settled over the hard-tipped mound and began to pull at it, nibble at it, with tender absorption. Anna cried out. The pleasure she experienced was so overwhelming that tears stung her eyes. She clung to him, her shaking hands grasping his thick hair, pulling him closer, closer...!

One big hand was under her skirt. Dimly she registered its progress, felt his touch on her slender legs and then on her flat belly.

"Anything," she gasped at his ear. "Anything you want...Evan!"

His hand contracted on her soft flesh and just for an instant, he gave in to the need that was consuming him. His mouth grew rough, like his insistent hands, and Anna yielded completely. His strength delighted her, his ardor made her weak all over. She bit his shoulder in her own oblivion, hard.

He caught his breath and jerked up, his face unfamiliar in passion.

"I...I'm sorry," she faltered, embarrassed at the expression in his eyes. "I bit you."

"Yes." There was something unfamiliar in the way he was looking at her, in the set rigidity of his face. His eyes fell to her body, to the faint redness where his hungry mouth had touched it. He actually shuddered.

"I thought you'd be afraid of me like this," he said quietly.

"Why?" she whispered.

"I could hurt you," he ground out. He grimaced at the marks he'd left on her breast. He touched it softly. "I didn't mean to lose my head like this!"

That she could make him lose it gave her a sense of wild elation. "It doesn't hurt, you know," she said with a gentle smile. "In fact, I liked it."

"Dangerous, to say that to me," he said huskily.

"I'm not antique glass, Evan. I won't break if you're a little rough with me."

She moved closer to him, her eyes searching his as she slid her leg gently against his and laid her hand flat against his shirt.

"What do you want?" he asked softly, delighted and overwhelmed by her desire for him.

"Can I touch you, here?" she whispered.

He hesitated for only a minute before he gave in to the need for her hands on him. He snapped open the pearly buttons and tugged the shirttail out of his jeans, holding her eyes while he threw the shirt onto the floor.

She rested her forehead against the broad, hair-roughened expanse of muscle and her hands caught in the hair, tugging it sensuously. "Like this?" she whispered, wanting nothing more than to please him. "Isn't this what you like?"

"Yes," he said in a choked tone. His hands slid into her hair, moving her forehead against him. "Kiss me the way I kissed you. Here," he emphasized, guiding her mouth to one side of his chest.

She caught her breath. It had never occurred to her that men had nipples or could be aroused by having them touched. The possibilities made her dizzy. She slid her lips through the thick hair until she found the hard thrust of a flat male nipple. She nuzzled it first with her nose, then with her lips, then with her teeth. Evan's big body went rigid and shuddered when she took the nipple in her teeth. She loved the way he responded to her. Her mouth nuzzled all over

his chest as he eased onto his back to give her the
total freedom of his body. His eyes closed, his chest
rippled as she touched it. Her lips pulled softly at the
other nipple and he actually groaned. Amazing, she
thought, delicious, to be able to make him even mo-
mentarily at the mercy of his need for her. She drew
her lips daringly down to the wide belt at his hips
and bit him delicately just below his navel.

He shuddered and arched, crying out. Anna lifted
her head, shocked and a little frightened by his reaction to so gentle a caress.

She didn't recognize him when she saw his face.
His eyes were tormented, his face dark with passion,
his mouth a thin line.

"I'm sorry," she said quickly. "Evan, I'm sorry,
did I hurt you?"

"For God's...sake...Anna!"

He whipped her over beside him, pausing just long
enough to strip the open blouse and bra from her,
throwing them carelessly on the floor, and then he
arched above her and looked down, his big body
shivering with need.

Her breasts were big; full and firm with dark
mauve tips that quickly grew hard as he looked at
them.

Instinctively her arm moved to cover herself, but
he caught it and pulled her up into a sitting position.

"No," he said gruffly. "You belong to me. Let
me look."

After a minute, she gave in and sat trembling,

flushing as he stared at her breasts. This kind of intimacy was new, and a little scary.

"Only you," she whispered unsteadily.

"Only me," he said, his voice deep and slow and husky. His eyes darkened. "God, you're beautiful, Anna," he said roughly. "Absolutely beautiful!"

She seemed to blossom at the words, her back arching unconsciously. "Evan," she whispered, shivering. "Evan, I'll die if you don't touch me…!"

He felt the same way. He reached for her hungrily. "So much for patience," he managed. His jaw clenched as he held her upper arms tightly and let his eyes feed on her beauty. "This is where we could get in over our heads very quickly," he said through his teeth, and he brought her breasts suddenly against the thick rasping mat of hair that covered him from throat to stomach. "I don't even know if I can stop," he bit off against her mouth as he took it hungrily.

Anna stiffened and shivered at the contact of her taut breasts with his bare chest, the most intimate she'd ever experienced. Evan held her by the rib cage and slowly, torturously began to drag her breasts against that thicket of hair with sensuous movements that were like setting a match to dry wood.

She hadn't known that her body could shudder with ecstasy from just the feel of a man's hairy chest against her bare breasts. But her nails bit into Evan's big shoulders and she moved with him, her body shivering as the delicious contact aroused her to fever pitch.

"Do it…hard," she whispered hoarsely, her eyes

closed as she swayed against him. "Rub me against you...very hard!"

He wasn't even thinking now. His body was reacting predictably to the ardor she aroused in him. He looked where they touched, watching her hard nipples drag against his warm chest, feeling them like brands on his body. He bent her across him and increased the ardent pressure, moving her from side to side now, hearing her shaky moans, feeling the bruising bite of her fingernails. She sobbed and her mouth pressed hard against his bare shoulders. She bit him again, quite hard, her tongue drawing circles on his skin in helpless passion.

One of his hands had slid to her lower spine and was grinding her rhythmically into the taut heat of him while his mouth suddenly bent to hers and possessed it fiercely.

At that moment, she would have let him do anything he liked to her. When his mouth lifted, she let her body arch backward, her firm breasts jutting toward his lips, her eyes closed as she yielded her body to him completely.

The action made Evan shiver. He knew what she was saying, without words. She would give him anything he wanted, do anything he asked of her. He could lay her down on the bed and strip her and make her his, and she would allow him to.

That submission stopped him, when nothing else would have. He lifted his head slowly, his eyes focusing hungrily on her breasts. He was faintly aware of the stab of her nails into his shoulders, but it was her flushed, hungry face that caught his attention. He'd never seen her look more beautiful.

He eased her cheek against the reckless throb of his bare chest and gently held her there, fighting for sanity.

She rubbed her breasts against him helplessly, her lips pressing soft kisses against his throat.

"Don't," he whispered, stilling her. "The feel of you is driving me out of my mind."

"I know." She nibbled at his chin. "We could make love," she whispered unsteadily. "Right here."

His big hands firmed on her shoulders. "No."

"You want me," she said.

"Viciously," he agreed. "But we can't make love on your bed in the middle of the day, when Lori or your parents could come home unexpectedly and find us."

"We could lock the doors," she moaned.

He lifted his head and tilted her chin up to his. "Take deep breaths," he said quietly. "Let yourself relax. I'm not going to use you like a woman I've bought for the night, Anna. Cheap sex isn't what I'm after, despite the fact that our lovemaking got a little out of hand just now."

She let her eyes fall to his bare chest. "A little?" she whispered on a nervous laugh.

"I told you how it would be," he reminded her. He held her eyes and slid one big hand up her body to cup and caress her firm breasts. "You really are a big girl," he whispered, smiling gently. "Just my size."

She blushed, but she smiled, too, arching so that his hand moved to encompass her even more fully.

"Like it?" he asked huskily.

"Don't you know?" she countered.

He bent his head and the hand at her back moved her so that he could put his mouth over the breast he was cupping. He suckled at it gently, nibbled, caressed, bit, until she curled into him with a helpless moan. She loved the moist heat of his mouth on her skin, remembering the first time he'd ever done it with a layer of fabric in the way.

She held him when he started to lift his head. "Just...a little more, please," she whimpered. "Bite...me...!"

And he'd been afraid of frightening her, he thought ironically as he gave in to her pleas. He laid her back on the bed and fed on her breasts like a starving man, delighting in her cries of pleasure, the clasp of her arms, the trembling vulnerability of her yielded body.

His mouth slid back up to her open lips and without thinking of the consequences, his body slowly levered over her, one powerful leg insinuating itself between hers so that he could bring them into total intimacy.

She caught her breath and clutched at him, shivering. He lifted his head then and looked into her wide eyes.

"It will probably hurt like hell," he said flatly,

one lean hand going under her to press her hips up into his. "Especially if you've never even played at intimacy before."

"I haven't. But if it isn't you," she whispered, "it won't be anybody, ever. I love you!"

He groaned and his eyes closed. She made all his fears seem groundless. She loved him. He began to wonder if Louisa ever had, or if she'd only wanted him for his position, his wealth. Anna had insinuated as much, as Harden had years ago, and now he had to face the fact that it might have been true.

He brushed his mouth gently over her bare shoulders, her throat, her lips. "I'll be rough with you," he said in something like anguish. "I won't be able to help it, don't you understand? I lose control so easily with you. Oh, God, I've probably left bruises on you already...!"

She kissed him softly, rubbing her nose lovingly against his. "You haven't seen your shoulder yet, have you?" she asked tenderly, and smiled.

He laughed softly. "Yes. You bit me, didn't you?"

"Very hard," she whispered shakily. "I didn't know it was going to feel like that, or that you'd do what you did to me." She dug her fingers into the thick hair that covered his chest. "I thought I might faint when you started rubbing your chest against me."

"There are times when I'm not sorry about this thicket," he admitted against her lips. "You were very, very aroused."

"I still am," she said softly. "I wish we could make love."

"So do I. But we can't, like this."

"You could undress," she suggested half-humorously.

"You don't understand." He moved to her side and stretched a little jerkily, pulling her down against him with her cheek pillowed on his chest. "What we're doing is something that belongs in the confines of marriage." He searched her eyes quietly while his fingers gentled on her breast. "If I give you a baby, it's going to be after we're married, not before."

She didn't think she could have heard him properly. "You don't want to get married," she faltered.

"Oh, but I do," he said doggedly. He lowered his mouth to hers and kissed it slowly, hotly. "I'll take the chance, if you will. Say yes, Anna," he breathed.

"Yes!" The word burst from her like a rainbow of sound and Evan took a long breath and damned the consequences.

"No long engagement, either," he whispered. "We'll get the license tomorrow."

"So soon?" she gasped.

"I can't bear to be away from you for five minutes lately," he said, his eyes glittering with barely leashed passion. "I want you with me all the time, day and night. I want you under me in bed, Anna," he whispered sensually, nibbling her lower lip while he played with her lips and stroked her breast. "I want your naked body writhing under the hardness of mine...!"

She met his mouth halfway, her body turning, accepting the crush of his, begging for more. It was all he could do to get away from her. He rolled away and got to his feet, keeping his back to her until he could stop shuddering. He reached for a cigarette, but they were in the shirt he didn't remember discarding. He reached down and retrieved it from the floor, along with her blouse and bra.

Anna was sitting up, breathing raggedly, and his eyes went pointedly to the thrust of her pretty breasts.

"Exquisite," he whispered breathlessly. "I could look at you like that for the rest of my life. But in the interests of your chastity, I think you'd better cover them up. Quick."

He tossed her garments to her, watching her flush and jerk trying to get them back on again.

The droll humor soothed her embarrassment. She was a little shy of him now. He seemed to sense it, because he pulled her up from the bed and held her gently. "You still don't know exactly what you could be letting yourself in for. I was in control most of the time today. But when I lose control, and eventually I will, you might not like what happens."

"I'm still trying to figure out what it is that I'm supposed to be so afraid of."

"I'm oversized," he said quietly. "I've always had to pull my punches, ever since I was a boy. Even now..." He broke off. "I keep remembering Louisa," he admitted finally, and he winced.

This, she thought, was going to take time and patience. But if she was careful, maybe she could heal those scars. "I'm not fragile," she said, her voice soft and hesitant. "I want you as much as you want me. And I love you."

His hand touched her lips with exquisite tenderness. "You make all my worst fears sound ridiculous."

"They are," she replied. She closed her eyes while he kissed her with something like reverence. "Are you going to stay with me?"

He laughed softly. "How can I stay away?" he countered. "There aren't that many women in Jacobsville who worship the ground I walk on."

She glared at him. "Go ahead, rub it in."

"I wasn't. I feel pretty arrogant and smug right now, if you want to know." He nibbled at her mouth. "Now let's sit down, in the living room," he emphasized, "and watch some movies, before we end up in bed again."

"We will, eventually," she said doggedly.

He sighed. "Eventually," he agreed. "First I have to work up the nerve," he said under his breath. He brushed a careless kiss against her forehead and, minutes later, started the VCR in the living room. Evan settled her in the curve of his arm and wondered quietly how he was going to go on living if she ever turned away from him out of fear.

Chapter Ten

Evan wasn't wasting much time arranging the wedding, Anna discovered the next morning, when he came to pick her up to apply for the license. They'd told Polly and Duke the day before and decided to wait overnight before they started the paper work, but nobody was surprised by the news. The other couple only grinned.

Anna was as close to heaven as she'd been in her life. Evan was openly affectionate now, kissing her when he came into the house, wrapping her up against him when they walked. If he didn't care about her, he was certainly a good actor.

After they applied for the license and had a blood test, Evan took her out to lunch at a restaurant downtown.

"You aren't eating much," he observed when she barely touched her roast beef.

She looked up at him, her eyes soft and loving. "I'm still in shock," she confessed. "I can hardly believe it, even now."

His dark eyes slid over her face possessively. "I'd never thought about marriage before," he confessed. "Not seriously, at least, even if I did lip service to the idea of wanting a home and a family."

"You used to say that they all trampled you trying to get to Harden," she recalled with a smile.

His big shoulders rose and fell. "In a way, it was true. Harden hated women, so naturally they all loved him. Especially Miranda, fortunately for him," he added with a grin.

"I used to think that if Harden could get married, anybody could," she admitted. "He was a real woman hater."

"No less than Connal, until Pepi came up on his blind side," he agreed. He caught her hand in his and turned it over, stroking her ring finger absently. "I haven't even bought you a ring," he remarked.

The license and the blood test had convinced her that he was serious, but the mention of a ring made her heart beat faster. That was commitment.

She looked up into his eyes with pure joy.

"Do you want a diamond, Anna?" he asked gently.

"I'm not sure..."

"Don't, for God's sake, tell me you want an emerald," he said, his dark eyes flashing. "I won't buy you one."

He sounded viciously jealous of the emerald Randall had given her. She had to hide a smile. "No, I don't want an emerald," she admitted. "I don't suppose colored stones are a very good investment, are they?"

He scowled. "Honey, I'm not buying it for an investment," he said gently. "This isn't a business deal."

"I'm sorry." She couldn't very well tell him that she didn't understand why he was marrying her. She was sure that he cared, a little. It was just that she wanted him to be in love, as she was. He was attentive and kind and even affectionate, but she wasn't sure of him.

What she didn't know was that he hadn't abandoned his fears. He was going ahead with the wedding despite them, mostly out of worry that she might go back to Randall. He was taking a terrible chance on her age and innocence, despite her confession of undying love.

She sensed his reservations. Nina still bothered her. That old flame had turned into a raging fire just before Anna was attacked. How could she be sure that Evan didn't feel something for Nina? How could she be sure that he wasn't marrying her out of pity and guilt and helpless desire?

She sipped her coffee absently, her eyes avoiding his.

In answer to all her unspoken worries, Nina walked in the door of the restaurant, alone, and spotted Evan.

He saw the woman coming and cursed viciously

to himself. His manners outweighed his anger, so he pushed back his chair and stood up, but his eyes weren't welcoming.

"Well, hello," Nina gushed. She went up to Evan and blatantly kissed him, despite his obvious reticence. "How are you, darling? I haven't seen you for ages! What have you been doing?"

"Getting engaged," he said flatly. "Anna and I are going to be married."

Nina actually froze. She didn't move or speak for a long moment, and then she laughed harshly. "You're marrying Anna? After all the time you spent running from her? Well, well, what did you do, Evan, get her pregnant?"

"That's enough," Evan said coldly.

Nina stared at Anna with pure hatred in her eyes. "You aren't stupid enough to think he loves you? All he's capable of is wanting! I should know!" She was almost shaking with rage, and attracting the attention of half a dozen other diners as well. "I gave him everything I had, and I couldn't hold him!"

"Nina, stop it," Evan said quietly. "You're making a spectacle of yourself."

Her lower lip trembled as she stared at him. Despite her embarrassment, Anna felt a terrible sympathy for her. Nina had been in love with Evan. It was painfully obvious.

"Just my luck...to be the wrong kind of woman to get you to the altar," Nina sobbed at Evan. "Everybody said experience appealed to you, but it wasn't true, was it? You're robbing the cradle at that…!''

She whirled suddenly and ran out of the restaurant, still crying.

Evan sat back down heavily. "I'm sorry about that," he told Anna, his voice strained but tender.

"She loved you," Anna said softly.

"Yes," he agreed. "But I didn't love her. You can't force yourself to care about somebody, Anna. That's life."

She knew that. She looked at Evan with horror. She was marrying him, and he didn't love her any more than he loved Nina. What kind of relationship could they build on a one-sided attraction? Eventually even desire would wane, and what would be left?

Evan cursed roundly when he got a good look at her face. He helped her up and went to pay the check, ignoring the curious stares of the other patrons. Nina had destroyed Anna's radiant mood, and his own. He'd thought the woman realized when he didn't call that he was no longer interested. It was his own fault. He'd used her to keep Anna at bay and she'd misunderstood his continuing attention. He should have had a long talk with her, but Anna's situation had claimed all his faculties.

He escorted Anna back to the car, his whole demeanor quiet and preoccupied.

"I think we'll wait and get the rings in the morning, if you don't mind," he told her when he pulled up in front of her house. "I have some things to take care of."

"It's all right with me," Anna replied. "The day's been rather spoiled anyway."

He cut off the engine and turned toward her. He winced at her bleak expression. "I'm sorry," he said huskily.

"You can't help it that women fall all over themselves trying to get to you." She laughed bitterly. "After all, I'm one of them, aren't I?"

"No," he said flatly. "You're not one in a crowd. I've asked you to marry me, Anna, not to spend a few feverish hours in bed with me!"

"I do realize what a great honor you're doing me." She looked at him with something approximating panic. "What kind of life will we have, falling all over your discarded lovers every time we go out to eat? Evan, I don't want this," she said wildly. "I can't marry you...!"

His hand shot out and caught her arm, dragging her over against him so that her head fell back against his shoulder.

"No, you don't," he said huskily. "You're not backing out."

"Yes, I—!"

He stopped the frantic words with his mouth. She fought him, but only for a few seconds. The heat and mastery of his mouth slowly began to weaken her struggles. She couldn't resist him. Her lips parted and her arms went up and around his neck, as she gave him back the long, slow kiss. Her pulses began to throb with the sweetness of being in his arms.

"You aren't playing fair," she whispered, shaken, when he finally lifted his head.

"I'm not playing, period," he replied, his dark eyes piercing, steady on hers. "Nina knew the score from the very beginning. I made no promises, ever."

"You used her," she whispered miserably.

His face tautened. "Yes," he admitted curtly. "I did. At the time, I thought I was protecting you. I used her shamefully. She had every right to be upset about that, but she can't pretend that she didn't know what I was doing. She was willing."

Her lower lip trembled. "You slept with her!" she accused huskily.

"Years ago, if you have to know," he replied flatly. "Not since. Certainly not since she's been back in town. I told you before, I can't even get aroused by other women, least of all Nina!"

Her breasts rose and fell in a slow, heavy sigh. She let her cheek rest against him. She stared past him out the window. It was misting rain and cloudy. Like her life, she thought.

"Why do you want to marry me, Evan?" she asked finally.

He lifted his head, scowling. "What?"

"Why do you want to marry me?" she repeated. "Is it pity, or guilt, or desire, or a little of all three?"

"My God, you still don't trust me, do you?" he asked. He sounded almost defeated. "I can't blame you, but if you have so little faith in my motives, why are you willing to go through with it?"

She looked up at him. "Because I love you," she said simply.

He touched her loosened, disheveled hair. "You aren't sure of me," he replied. "If you loved me, wouldn't you be?"

Her eyes grew sad. "Not really. It's hard to be sure of someone when you don't know how they feel."

He let his eyes fall to her mouth. "How do you think I feel?" he hedged.

"I don't know. You've been very different since the accident," she replied. "Before, you made it clear how you felt about me, that you wanted me out of your life. Then I got hurt and all at once, you were willing to marry me."

"You make me sound fickle, Anna," he said, but he couldn't deny the truth of what she was insinuating.

"Not fickle. Just uncertain. You can't blame me for feeling the same way. You've never really told me what you felt."

And he couldn't. Not just yet. He still had too many misgivings, too many fears.

He touched her mouth lightly with his forefinger. "Will words convince you?" he asked quietly. "Somehow, I don't think so. You've got it fixed in your mind that I'm only sorry for you. Nothing I say is going to change that. You're just going to have to wait and see."

Fear flickered under her eyelashes. "You'd be tied

to me, don't you see?'' she asked gently. ''You'd
hate it!''

His mouth covered hers. He lifted her into a
warmer, closer embrace, his lips driving every worry
out of her mind. His hand slid inside her blouse,
under the bra, with blatant mastery. She felt his fingers against her soft, bare flesh. She stiffened and
gasped at the surge of pleasure it gave her.

His teeth caught at her lower lip, gently teasing it.
''We're going to have the most unusual wedding
night in history,'' he said with black humor. ''It will
probably be the first time that the groom has jitters.''

She drew back a little. ''Are you afraid to make
love to me?'' she asked hesitantly.

''Isn't it obvious?'' he asked darkly. ''My God,
I've fought this. And in the end, I couldn't give you
up, not even for your own good.''

''Evan, it's not going to be that bad,'' she said,
trying to reassure him. He looked…she couldn't
quite decide how he looked. ''I can see the doctor
before we're married. If he thinks there's going to be
any, well, any difficulty, he can take care of it for
me.''

His jaw tautened. ''Your virginity isn't what con-
cerns me.''

''Then what?''

He drew in a rough breath and looked down at the
bulge of his hand under her blouse. Absently his fingers caressed her, loving the softness of her skin.
''Anna, I could hurt you so badly,'' he said huskily.
''It might bring back terrible memories of the night

you were attacked. And quite frankly, past a certain point, a man can't stop.''

She reached up and nibbled at his mouth. ''Then you'll have to make me crazy first, won't you?'' she whispered. ''Like you did...yesterday when you opened your shirt and held me against you...Evan!''

His mouth bit into hers. She arched closer, her fingers pressing his intruding hand to her breast. For a few seconds, he actually seemed blind and deaf, his mouth devouring and sweet.

He groaned and pulled her across his lap, turning her so that her belly pressed against his hardness. He ground her into him, feeling her tremble.

''Yes,'' she whispered into his mouth. She moved deliberately, loving the feel of him, the raging arousal that she seemed to kindle in him so effortlessly.

His hand tangled painfully in her hair as his tongue drove into the softness of her mouth. His free hand, at the base of her spine, rocked her rhythmically against him, sending ripples of pure ecstasy through his rigid body.

He felt her soft trembling with wonder, felt her submission. His fingers went to her blouse and began to unfasten it. Thank God the yard was deserted and Polly's car was gone. They were totally alone.

He lifted his head long enough to get the blouse out of his way and unclasp her bra.

''Yes,'' she murmured. She sat up, impatiently helping him rid her of the unwanted fabric. But then her hands went to his own shirt and unfastened the pearly snaps.

"Anna..." he began, fighting for control.

"I want to feel you against me," she whispered hungrily. She linked her arms around his neck and brushed the tips of her breasts against his hair-roughened chest.

"Anna!" he groaned harshly.

She saw his face contort and recognized the rigid mask of pleasure.

"Is this how to do it?" she whispered, moving her torso even harder against his. "Teach me, Evan. Show me how to make love."

"My...God, you don't...need lessons!" he managed.

"Here," she said, tugging at his head as she arched back against his arm, her eyes half-closed. "Do...what you did to me yesterday. Do it hard!"

He was out of his mind. He barely realized it as his mouth settled helplessly on one dusky hard-tipped breast. He suckled at it, feeling her body ripple with pleasure as he fed on her softness. His fingers cupped her, caressed her while he discovered the hard tip with his tongue, his lips. And she lay there and let him, vibrating with pleasure, her soft sighs lost in the rough groans that burst from his mouth.

"Evan, it feels so good," she moaned feverishly. Her hands tangled in his thick hair, holding him to her hungry body "It feels so good, so good!"

"You taste of rose petals." He lifted his head and

looked at her, at the soft flesh with its deep flush that his mouth had caused. He took a slow breath and let his hand slowly caress her. "I want you."

"I want you, too." Her back arched gently, her eyes glazed with desire. "Can't we...go somewhere and be alone?"

His jaw tautened. "Risky," he managed.

"I don't care. I want you to look at me," she said dizzily. "I want to look at you!"

He wanted to scream. He had to think. He had to protect her. She arched her back again and rubbed her breasts slowly against him.

"All right," he said shakily.

He made her sit up, helping her into the blouse again. He started the car without a word. He didn't dare look at her or he'd wreck it.

He drove quietly, and quickly, to the Tremayne lake. It was deserted during the week, and no one ever went there. He stopped the car, turned off the ignition, and got out.

Anna lifted her arms as he bent to carry her down to the grassy bank of the lake.

"This is insane," he whispered as he laid her down in the grass and went down beside her. "We'll go too far."

"It's all right," she said softly. She pulled off her blouse and let him look at her, totally without inhibitions. He was going to marry her. She loved him. Now she had to convince him that she wasn't frightened of him.

Evan could hardly breathe for the pounding of his heart as he stared at her soft, swollen breasts.

"You're a virgin," he groaned.

"Would you rather I let Randall see me like this?" she whispered.

His eyes flashed. "No. I would not." He stripped off his shirt and his belt before he laid her back on the grass and spread his broad, dark chest over her breasts. He held her eyes as he began to move his torso sensually over hers, letting his hair-roughened muscles drag arousingly over the hard tips of her breasts.

Her nails dug into his powerful upper arms as the motion kindled a sudden, shocking desire. She gasped jerkily.

"And this is only the beginning, Anna," he said roughly. "It gets worse. Much worse."

He bent to her mouth. He'd never kissed her like this, in such a deliberately arousing way. He teased and tormented her soft mouth until she was openly begging for his, driven half mad by the sensual movements of his body against her bare breasts.

She was almost in tears by the time he finally relented, and his tongue penetrated her mouth in one deep, smooth motion. She was so aroused that she actually cried out and went rigid, pulsating with feverish need as the kiss she thought would satisfy her only aroused a deeper hunger.

Her legs moved against Evan's helplessly. He felt her anguished need and his big body levered over hers. He eased her legs apart and slid slowly between them.

He lifted his dark head. His eyes were black with arousal, his swollen lips parted on jerky breaths. He rested his weight on his forearms and held her dazed, hungry eyes while he deliberately pushed down.

She felt him in an intimacy that she'd never shared with anyone before. Her eyes dilated and her lips parted on a gasp as she felt the full force of his desire.

He watched her, certain that it was going to be just as it had been with Louisa. She was going to run…

Even as he thought it, her long legs began to tangle shyly with his. Her hips lifted, very gently. He stiffened and shuddered, even though his eyes never left hers.

She did it again, her face radiant as she watched his helpless reaction.

"This is very, very dangerous," he bit off. "If you arouse me enough, I won't be able to stop."

"I don't mind."

His big hand caught her thigh and stilled her under him. "You don't understand. I could make you pregnant."

She smiled gently. "You don't understand," she replied. "I want a baby with you."

He actually shuddered. For one mad instant, he looked into her eyes and gave in to her. His hand moved from her thigh to the base of her spine and he pushed her legs further apart as he settled completely between them in a blatant urgency that made her moan sharply.

"This is what you're inviting," he said roughly, and pushed, hard. "It will hurt like hell if I'm this aroused when it happens!"

That was when she first began to make sense of all the warnings, all the misgivings. She relaxed under his weight and her eyes held his fierce black ones.

"Oh," she whispered.

He was trembling. "Seen the light, have you?" he choked. "I hope to God you haven't seen it too late. Lie still!" he bit off, anchoring her with a merciless hand. He looked at her, shivering with reaction as he fought to control himself.

She watched him, shaken by his vulnerability, by her own ability to affect him. Sex had been a vaguely frightening mystery, but now it was a wonderous surprise. She had a pretty good idea of what it entailed and exactly why Evan was so afraid of his uncontrolled strength.

He was breathing unsteadily, his eyes closed, his forehead resting against hers.

She smoothed the dark hair at his nape gently and relaxed completely, absorbing his formidable weight. He was calming. The rigidity of his muscular body was slowly giving way.

"So that's what it's like," she murmured, awed.

Her tone dragged a strained laugh from his throat. "Didn't you know?"

"Not really," she confessed. Her eyes closed. "Puzzles," she said.

He caught his breath at the word picture she evoked. "Yes," he managed. "Except that this particular one can be difficult to fit together, unless it's put into place with exquisite tenderness."

Her arms linked around his neck. His chest was damp and cool against hers as the heat began to die out of them.

"Am I too heavy?" he asked.

"Oh, no. I like the way it feels."

He nuzzled his face against hers. "How about a swim, while we're here?"

"I don't have a bathing suit," she said absently.

He lifted his head. "Neither do I. We're being married in two days, Anna. I want you to know it all before I put my ring on your finger."

The thought of seeing him without his clothes disturbed her, but she sensed that for him this was an obstacle that frightened him. As he said, they were going to be married. Many engaged couples did much more together than just swim without their clothes.

"All right," she said softly.

Evan caught his breath. "Are you sure?"

"Yes." She touched his mouth with her fingertips. "I love you."

So she said. But he wanted proof. If she could look at him without fear, one hurdle would be out of the way. Louisa's face still haunted him.

"So be it," he said quietly.

He got to his feet and helped her up, noticing her shy reluctance to undress in front of him. He smiled gently. "I'll walk down the path a bit. Yell when you're in the water."

She sighed. "Thank you, Evan."

"You'll get used to it," he replied. He brushed a kiss across her mouth and moved away.

She was in the water when he came back, and she kept her eyes averted while he took off his own clothes. Seconds later there was a splash as he landed close beside her.

"Not so difficult, was it?" he asked with a grin as she trod water beside him.

"I guess the first time is the hardest," she mused.

"And the most necessary. Come on, chicken. I'll race you."

She laughed, catching up with him. They played lazily. The feel of the water against her skin was exquisite. She closed her eyes and floated, glorying in the sense of freedom she felt.

Evan watched her with hungry eyes, his heart pounding as he got fascinating glimpses of her creamy body under the water. When she arched her back and began to float, her taut nipples breaking the surface of the lake, he was totally lost.

"Oh, God," he groaned softly.

He reached for her, pulling her body totally against his as he bent to her lips.

She let him kiss her, feeling for the first time the touch of his body with no fabric to conceal its power and strength. She hesitated, and he lifted his head.

"Afraid of me like this?" he whispered.

"Not afraid, really," she confessed. Her blue eyes searched his dark ones. "I've never been without my clothes in front of anyone since I grew up—not even my mother."

He held her waist in his big hands and searched her eyes. "I won't hurt you. Try to remember that."

As he spoke, he lifted and turned her, carrying her toward the bank. She gasped and buried her embarrassed face in his cool throat.

His mouth slid across her cheek to her lips and he began to kiss her with exquisite tenderness. After a minute, she forgot her nudity and gave in to the delicious pleasure of skin against skin.

She felt the jolt of his body as he walked, then the cool air on her body and the softness of the grass on her back as he laid her down.

He knelt over her, waiting for her eyes to open.

She looked at him, flushed and looked away.

He stiffened. "Don't you want to scream and run?" he asked tersely. "She did."

The bitterness in his voice knocked the shyness right out of her. She forced her embarrassed eyes back to his powerful body, reminding herself that in two more days he was going to be her husband. She had to grow up, very fast.

Her lips parted as she looked at him, and her heart began to race. She'd never seen a centerfold, but she was certain that he would have made a perfect one.

Her rapt stare drained some of the apprehension

from him. Her eyes were shy and frankly fascinated, but not afraid.

He was doing some looking of his own. A woman's body was no mystery to him, but Anna's was enough to make a hardened womanizer crazy. Her soft curves were perfect, all of her, from the thrust of her breasts to the sweeping curve of her hips and her long, elegant legs.

The sight of her aroused him, and he didn't turn away or try to hide the effect she had on him. She had to face that as well.

Her breath came unsteadily through her lips. "Oh, my," she whispered.

He lifted an eyebrow, waiting to see if she was bluffing.

After a minute, her gaze lifted from his body to his eyes. "You thought I'd be afraid if I saw you like this," she said suddenly.

"Yes."

She smiled shyly. "I'm sorry to disappoint you," she said, watching the way his eyes followed hungrily the sensuous lines of her body. "Why don't you come down here and kiss me?"

He could barely breathe, much less speak. "Because if I do, I won't be able to stop."

"We're going to be married day after tomorrow."

"Yes," he agreed. "And we're going to have a wedding night. A conventional one, with all the trimmings."

He managed to drag himself to his feet. He fished

a couple of towels out of the trunk of his car and tossed one to a subdued Anna.

"Spoilsport," she managed with a shy laugh.

With a muttered curse of pure frustrated anguish, he pulled on his clothes and lit a cigarette while she was still fumbling with hooks and snaps.

She watched him quietly when she had finished. He was remembering the past, she knew. She'd always thought of him as a gentle giant. The idea of Evan hurting anything or anyone deliberately had never occurred to her.

"You can't be afraid of people you love," she said gently.

He grimaced, glancing at her. "Can't you? She was."

She went close to him. "There's something you don't know yet, Evan."

"What?" he asked huskily, remembering the incredible beauty of her body as he looked down at her.

"If Louisa had loved you—really loved you—she couldn't have been afraid of you in bed."

He flushed. "She loved me," he said doggedly.

"Did she?" She turned and picked up the towels, folding them neatly. He was preoccupied all the way back to the car.

He put her in the front seat and got in beside her. There was a terrible truth in what she'd said. He hated the implications of it, that he'd wasted years of his life, years of happiness he might have had with Anna, brooding over a love affair that must have been nothing more than a brief infatuation for Louisa. His great love affair had ended in tragedy, only because he couldn't recognize what Anna seemed to know instinctively—that Louisa had never loved him in the first place. It was a hard pill to swallow.

Chapter Eleven

They were married on Friday afternoon, with Evan's entire family in attendance. It was a brief but beautiful ceremony, and Anna could hardly believe she was actually marrying Evan, even after he had slid the diamond-studded gold band that matched her solitaire onto her finger and kissed her tenderly.

But despite that tenderness, he was worried. During the small reception at the Tremayne home, he was preoccupied. Anna alone knew why. He was dreading his wedding night, so haunted by the past that he was certain he was going to send her screaming from him. She knew better, but she had to convince Evan that his great strength wasn't dangerous in intimacy.

"It was a beautiful wedding, darling," Polly told her daughter just before Anna and Evan left on their brief honeymoon to New Orleans. "I hope you'll be happy."

"I will be," Anna replied. She kissed and hugged her mother, then glanced toward her father, who was talking to Evan and Harden. "How about you and Dad?"

Polly grinned. "He has to fly back to Atlanta tonight."

"Oh." Anna's face fell.

"I'm flying back with him," Polly continued, laughing at Anna's shocked face. "He's going to ask for a transfer to Houston so that he can be home nights when he's not scheduled on flights. We're going to be a family again, Anna. And when Duke retires—which he's planning to do next year—I may get out of the real estate business and travel around the country with him."

"It's almost too good to be true," Anna sighed, smiling through tears. "I'm so happy!"

"So am I," Polly replied. She dried Anna's tears. "Go and have a nice honeymoon. When you're back, with both feet on the ground, we'll talk. Take care of yourself."

"You, too."

Minutes later, Anna was sitting beside Evan as he drove them to the airport.

"Happy?" he asked gently, glancing at her.

"Very. Are you?"

"Ask me in the morning," he said with a rough laugh.

"Oh, Evan," she sighed. "Am I going to have to get you drunk and seduce you?"

He didn't laugh. His face hardened. "That wasn't funny."

"I'm not afraid of you," she said gently.

"I hope not. Because tonight, you'll get to prove it."

She gave up trying to reassure him and stared out the window. Her wedding day had fallen flat, and the honeymoon had barely started.

New Orleans was brassy and colorful, and once Anna had rested for a few minutes, she and a subdued Evan went out to explore the French Quarter and Bourbon Street. It was late afternoon when they got back to the hotel, and Evan herded her right into the restaurant for supper before they went up to their room. During the meal she tried to make conversation, but he was heavy weather. And if she thought things couldn't be worse, she was mistaken.

When they got up to their room, she turned to kiss him, but he actually backed away.

"No," he said shortly, his dark eyes antagonistic. "Not now."

"We're married, Evan," she said gently. "It's all right."

"The hell it is." He grabbed up his Stetson and went toward the door. "I've got a business meeting. I'll be late, so don't wait up."

"A business meeting? On our honeymoon!" she wailed.

He wouldn't look at her. He'd let his anxiety build until he was terrified to touch her. He couldn't admit that. The next best thing was to invent an excuse to get away from her until he could get a grip on himself.

"Sorry," he replied. "It couldn't be helped. I'll be back when I can. Good night."

He closed the door. Anna sat down on the bed with a thud and gaped after him. She wondered how she was going to survive marriage with a man who was afraid to touch her. Damn Louisa!

She finally slept, but not until the wee hours of the morning. When she drifted off, Evan still hadn't come to bed, and she'd cried until her eyes were red.

Meanwhile, Evan was sitting in a bar, drinking whiskey, trying to convince himself that he wasn't King Kong. Anna loved him. She wasn't Louisa. But she was innocent, and he knew all too well how delicate an innocent woman's body was. He was helpless when he started kissing her. If he lost control, he knew he was going to hurt her. He loved her until he thought his heart would break. He took another swallow, and another, brooding over all the times his strength had intimidated men and women alike. Before he knew it, the bar was empty. He paid for his drinks and went slowly up to their room, wondering whether Anna was asleep yet.

The next morning, she woke, vaguely aware that she wasn't alone in the bed. She rolled over and found Evan.

With a faint sigh, she propped up on her elbow and looked at him. Asleep, he seemed younger and much less dangerous. Poor, tormented man. She couldn't really blame him for those mental scars. A man's ego was his most vulnerable spot, after all.

But they really couldn't go on like this.

It seemed underhanded somehow to take advantage of a man in his sleep, but Anna knew instinctively that Evan's irrational fear of hurting her was going to make any other course of action impossible.

She tugged off her nightgown and smiled as she looked down on his sleeping face. With any luck at all she could make him believe he was only dreaming. Of course, she'd have to do it just the right way....

Dawn was only beginning in the eastern sky, so that there was barely any light in the room. Carefully she pulled the sheet down and threw it off the bed, her breath catching at the sight of Evan's body. He was already aroused, and he began to move restlessly, as if just the brush of the sheet had excited him.

She eased down, her mouth slowly touching his broad chest, teasing his nipples. They were already hard, and she felt his breathing change as she nibbled at them. Her hands slid over the broad expanse of his hair-roughened chest and down his flanks to his hard thighs. As her hands moved, so did her mouth. She kissed him tenderly, nipped at him with her teeth, until she reached his navel and the sudden rippling of muscles just beneath it.

His back arched sensuously and he moaned. She turned her face, so that her long hair brushed across his hips and thighs, and he whispered her name.

She nipped at his waist with her teeth while her fingers slowly, torturously made their way up his powerful legs to his flat stomach.

Seconds later, she felt herself lifted and turned, felt his mouth catch and half swallow her breast, his tongue rough on the hard nipple as he began to suckle her.

She shivered with delight, holding his head to her body. His hands were smoothing over her, learning her. One slid between her thighs and coaxed her legs apart.

He touched her then in a way he never had before, and she gasped at the unexpected surge of pleasure the exquisitely slow movements of his fingers aroused. All the while, his mouth was warm on her taut breast, drawing the nipple into the moist darkness with devastating expertise.

Her eyes closed as she let the pleasure wash over her. Her body twisted sinuously under his hands and mouth, soft moans whispering out of her throat while the minutes grew hotter and more feverish.

His mouth gently covered hers while his fingers trespassed in a new and frightening way. There was a brief flash of pain and she moaned, but his mouth gentled her, moving lovingly from her lips to her closed eyelids while his hand began to rouse her all over again. The pain was quickly forgotten as her hips began to lift toward those tormenting fingers.

She felt his breath on her lips, just before he whispered her name. Her eyes opened slowly, half-dazed, and met his.

Holding them, he moved slowly between her legs, levering down carefully. "No, don't look away," he said shakily.

She swallowed, because she could feel him now in an intimacy unlike anything they'd ever shared. He was much more potent than she remembered, powerful and a little intimidating.

"Hold on," he murmured. "Dig your nails into me, if it helps."

She gasped as his hips arched down into hers, very carefully. He pushed, softly, and she tensed despite her resolve.

"Shh," he whispered, his eyes tender. "You knew it would be difficult. But you can take me. Try to relax. Try to let your body absorb mine. Think of a stone falling into water," he said softly as he moved. "Absorb me, little one. Take me...inside you."

The imagery was arousing. She drew her eyes down to their bodies and caught her breath at what she saw.

"No, don't look there," he said gently, convinced even now that she was going to panic. "Look at me, Anna."

She lifted her eyes back up to his, but there was no fear in them. She arched her back, her breath catching, her eyes misty now with desire. "I watched," she said unsteadily. "Evan, I saw...!"

She pushed harder, absorbing him. There was a burning sensation, a stabbing pain. She cried out, but she pushed harder. And then it was easy. Slow. Soft.

Her breathing began to quicken and she managed

a smile as she sought his eyes. "Oh...yes!" she moaned, shaking as she experienced the full power of his masculinity.

He let out a ragged breath. "Yes." He bent to her lips as his body began the slow, familiar rhythm. He nibbled her mouth as his muscles tautened, as his hips lifted and fell with exquisite tenderness.

Her fingers slid to the base of his spine and lingered, stroking him. He shuddered. She liked that, so she did it again.

"Stop," he ground out. "You'll make me lose control."

"I want you to," she whispered with a tiny smile, arching her mouth up to his. "Let go," she breathed at his lips. "Let go, Evan. It's all right, darling, you won't hurt me. It's all right. Let go, Evan...let go...!"

"Anna!" Her name was a tormented groan as he gave in to her coaxing and suddenly drove feverishly for fulfillment. He lost his fear of hurting her and every vestige of control, in the violent need to experience ecstasy, to satisfy the throbbing, savage ache in his loins.

Even through her own building pleasure, Anna watched him achieve it. As she felt the crush of his arms and the weight of him, she saw his torso lift, his back arch tautly, his face contort as if with the most incredible kind of agony. He threw back his head and cried out, shuddering against her so violently that she thought he might actually lose consciousness.

When he stiffened and fell heavily against her, she was still shivering with her own unsatisfied need. She clutched at his broad shoulders, biting him helplessly as she moved under his weight. When he started to lift his hips, she caught them with her nails and held him there.

"No, please…!" she sobbed.

"Almost, but not quite, is that it, sweetheart?" he whispered huskily. "Give me your mouth, little one, and hold on tight. I'll satisfy you completely, now."

She turned her face up and he kissed her gently, his tongue suddenly stabbing into her mouth as his hips rose and fell slowly.

It took only seconds. She sobbed her pleasure under his mouth, so racked by ecstasy that she could only cling to him while the rhythm wrung every last silvery bit of strength out of her.

He kissed the tears away, but she still wouldn't let go of him.

"All right," he whispered, smiling through his exhaustion as he settled back over her, his forearms catching his weight. He kissed her gently, soft kisses that calmed and soothed and comforted. All that worry, he thought ruefully, and for nothing! He hadn't killed her after all, even if, for a few delicious seconds, she had sounded as though she were dying.

"Don't go away," she whispered. "Hold me."

He kissed her very gently. "It was for your own sake that I was moving away, not for mine. I thought you might be uncomfortable. It was difficult for you."

Her arms contracted. "I love you," she whispered. "It was heaven."

"For me, too." He sighed softly and rested his cheek against hers, his eyes closed as he savored her softness under him. "Are you all right? It didn't hurt too much?"

"No." She nibbled at his earlobe. "Now will you stop running from me?"

"Do I have a choice?" He looked down at her tenderly. "You took me without fear," he said, his voice coloring with pride and pleasure.

"Yes." She blushed a little and dropped her eyes to his mouth.

"None of that." He tilted her face up and searched her shy eyes. "I didn't hold back. I couldn't. We never discussed precautions..."

Her face brightened. "I could be pregnant."

The way she said it made his heart lift. "Yes." He smoothed back her long, soft blond hair. "You're very young."

"Not that young." She lifted herself to his mouth and began to kiss him, slowly, seductively.

"It's too soon," he said huskily. "You need time to get over what we just did."

She did, but she hated the thought of giving up the closeness they were sharing. Her eyes told him so.

"Come here." He wrapped her up against him and pulled the sheet over them, pausing to brush a kiss across her nose before his arm contracted around her, bringing her even closer. "We'll sleep a bit longer."

"And then?" she whispered.

He smiled. "And then."

She closed her own eyes, sliding into a deep and dreamless sleep. When she awoke, the smell of beignets—little square sugar-dusted doughnuts—and jam and fresh coffee filled the room.

"Hungry?" Evan asked. He was wearing his slacks and nothing else, and he looked younger and lighthearted and totally loving. That could have been a trick of the light, of course, she told herself. But she could dream.

"I'm starved," she confessed, sitting up.

He pulled the sheet away and looked at her, his eyes darkening with possession. "My God, you are so beautiful," he said, his voice deep and uneven.

"Flatterer," she whispered softly.

He sat down beside her, his eyes searching hers while his hands stroked slowly down her body. She caught her breath and stiffened with pleasure and he bent to kiss the hardened tips of her breasts.

But when she tried to trap his mouth against her, he shook his head and pulled away. "It's too soon for you," he said, his eyes full of tender wisdom. "We've got the rest of our lives to love each other in bed."

"It felt like that," she said softly. "Like…loving, I mean."

"Shouldn't it?" he asked, his eyes holding hers. "When two people love each other as much as we do?"

Her heart stopped beating. "You...don't," she whispered.

"Then why did I marry you, little one?" he asked quietly. "If sex was all I wanted, any woman would have done."

She thought she might faint.

"I was trying to spare you what Louisa suffered at my hands." He smiled bitterly. "She never loved me, Anna. And I never knew it. Until you told me."

Her breath was trapped somewhere in her throat.

He touched her face with a big, gentle hand. "I was sacrificing my happiness for what I thought was yours. After what Louisa had said to me, I was terrified of hurting you like that. And you were so young... But when Randall told me you were marrying him, I thought I'd go mad," he choked. "That was bad enough. But you were mugged, and I didn't even know it until hours later. You could have died, and I wouldn't have been there, with you. Your last memory of me would have been of the way I'd hurt you," he said roughly.

Tears stung her eyes. What he felt was naked in his face, in his voice. Why hadn't she seen it, known it? "You...love me!" she exclaimed, awed.

"Love. Adore. Worship." He framed her face in his hands and kissed her with aching tenderness. "Oh, God, you're the very breath in my body!"

He bore her down on the mattress, his mouth ardent and faintly rough with passion, his hands insistent on her body as he kissed her. She gave unstintingly, loving him so deeply that it hurt.

"I love you," he whispered finally, his mouth against her throat. "I'll die loving you."

She held him, her eyes closed, her heart overflowing. "I love you, too, Evan," she said drowsily. "Endlessly."

He bent again to her mouth, the look in his eyes before he kissed her so adoring that she melted under him. The kiss went on and on and on, into levels they'd never touched before.

Finally he managed to drag himself away. "You'd better eat something," he murmured, his voice faintly unsteady. "I have to build up your strength for the next few days, after you've had time to recuperate."

She laughed and looked up at him. "That goes double for you," she murmured demurely. "You're not the only one with expectations."

He burst out laughing. A minute later he picked her up in his big arms and carried her to the breakfast table. For the first time he gloried in his strength, in her trusting submission to it. All the ghosts were laid to rest, now. He looked down at her, so soft in his arms, and felt as if he had everything. He sat down at the table with Anna cuddled in his lap. Not content with that, he spoon-fed her every single bite.

From that moment on, they were inseparable, and every day brought a new and ardent memory. Anna's nightmares faded, and her painful experience with the mugger became nothing more than a bad dream. Weeks later, a big, brutal man was found in a back alley dead of a drug overdose. He was a suspect in several violent robberies in Houston, the paper said, and at least one rape. A violent end for a violent man, but his death gave Anna peace.

Polly and Duke settled down to a happy life together, while Anna and Evan moved into a newly remodeled house on the Tremayne ranch, a wedding present from Evan's brothers. It included a studio for Anna, and she went back to her painting with a vengeance. But in addition to her landscapes she did one portrait—of her new husband.

"Do I really look like that?" he asked dryly as he clasped her loosely by the waist and looked over her shoulder at the very flattering painting.

"To me, you do," she said, her eyes full of love.

He smiled before he bent to kiss her. The old specter of his size and strength were gone forever. Secure in the warmth of Anna's love, he couldn't have asked for another single thing, a sentiment she echoed with her whole heart.

* * * * *

DONAVAN

For a special reader—Peggy

Chapter One

Fay felt as if every eye in the bar was on her when she walked in. It had been purely an impulse, and she was already regretting it. A lone female walking into a bar on the wrong side of town in south Texas late at night was asking for trouble. Women's lib hadn't been heard of this far out, and several pairs of male eyes were telling her so.

She could only imagine how she looked in her tight designer jeans, her feet encased in silk hose and high heels, a soft yellow knit sweater showing the faint swell of her high breasts. Her long dark hair was around her shoulders in soft swirls, and her green eyes darted nervously from one side of the small, smoke-filled room to the other. There was a jukebox playing so loud that she had to yell to tell the bartender she wanted a beer. That was a joke, too, because in all her twenty years, she'd never had

a beer. White wine, yes. Even a piña colada down in
Jamaica. But never a beer.

Defiance was becoming expensive, she thought,
watching a burly man separate himself from his com-
panions with a mumbled remark that made them
laugh.

He perched himself beside her at the bar, his narrow eyes giving her an appraisal that made her want
to run. "Hello, pretty thing," he said, grinning
through his beard. "Wanta dance?"

She cupped her hands around the beer mug to stop
them from shaking. "No, thank you," she said in her
soft, cultured voice, keeping her eyes down. "I'm...
waiting for someone."

That was almost true. She'd been waiting for
someone all her life, but he hadn't shown up yet. She
needed him now. She was living with a mercenary,
social-climbing relative who was doing his best to
sell her to a rich friend with eyes that made her skin
crawl. All her money was tied up in trust, and she
was stuck with her mother's brother. Rescue was certainly uppermost in her mind, but this rowdy cowboy
wasn't her idea of a white knight.

"You and me could have a good time, honey,"
her admirer continued, unabashed. He smoothed her
sweater-clad arm and she withdrew as if his fingers
were snakes. "Now, don't start backing away, sweet
thing! I know how to treat a lady."

No one noticed the dark face in the corner suddenly lift, or saw the dangerous glitter in silver eyes
that dominated it. No one noticed the look he gave
the girl, or the colder one that he gave her companion

before he got gracefully to his feet and moved toward the bar.

He wore jeans, too. Not like Fay's, because his were working jeans. They were faded and stained from work, and his boots were a howling thumbed nose at city cowboys' elegant footwear. His hat was blacker than his thick, unruly hair, a little crumpled here and there. He was tall. Very tall. Lean and muscular and quite well-known locally. His temper, in fact, was as legendary as the big fists now curled with deceptive laxness at his sides as he walked.

"You'd like me if you just got to know me—" The pudgy cowboy broke off when the newcomer came into his line of vision. He became almost comically still, his head slightly cocked. "Why, hello, Donavan," he began uneasily. "I didn't know she was with *you*."

"Now you do," he replied in a deep, gravelly voice that sent chills down Fay's spine.

She turned her head and looked into diamond-glinted eyes, and lost her heart forever. She couldn't seem to breathe.

"It's about time you showed up," he told Fay. He took her arm, eased her down from the bar stool with a grip that was firm and exciting. He handed her beer mug to her, and with a last cutting glare at the other man, he escorted her back to his table.

"Thank you," she stammered when she was sitting beside him. He'd left a cigarette smoking in the dented metal ashtray, and a half-touched glass of whiskey. He didn't take off his hat when he sat down. She'd noticed that Western men seemed to have little use for the courtesies she'd taken for granted back home.

He picked up his cigarette and took a long draw from it. His nails were flat and clean, despite traces of grease that clung to his long-fingered, dark hands. They were beautiful masculine hands, with no jewelry adorning them. Working hands, she thought idly.

"Who are you?" he asked suddenly.

"I'm Fay," she told him. She forced a smile. "And you...?"

"Most people just call me Donavan."

She took a sip of beer and grimaced. It tasted terrible. She stared at it with an expression that brought a faint smile to the man's hard, thin mouth.

"You don't drink beer, and you don't belong in a bar. What are you doing on this side of town, debutante?" he drawled.

"I'm running away from home," she said with a laugh. "Escaping my jailers. Having a night on the town. Rebelling. Take your pick."

"Are you old enough to do that?" he asked pointedly.

"If you mean, am I old enough to order a beer in a bar, yes. I'm two months shy of twenty-one."

"You don't look it."

She studied his hard, suntanned face and his unruly hair. With a little trimming up and proper dressing, he might be rather devastating. "Are you from around here?" she asked.

"All my life," he agreed.

"Do you...work?"

"Child, in this part of Texas, everybody works."

He scowled. "Most everybody," he amended, letting his eyes linger pointedly on her diamond tennis bracelet. "Wearing that into a country bar is asking for trouble. Pull your sleeve down."

She did, obeying him instantly when she was known for ignoring anything that sounded like a command at home. She flushed at her instant deference. Maybe she was drunk already. Sure, she mused, on two sips of beer.

"What do you do when you aren't giving orders?" she taunted.

He searched her green eyes. "I'm a ranch foreman," he said. "I give orders for a living."

"Oh. You're a cowboy."

"That's one name for it."

She smiled again. "I've never met a real cowboy before."

"You aren't from here."

She shook her head. "Georgia. My parents were killed in a plane crash, so I was sent out here to live with my uncle." She whistled softly. "You can't imagine what it's like."

"Get out," he said simply. "People live in prisons out of choice. You can always walk away from a situation you don't care for."

"Want to bet? I'm rich," she said curtly. "Filthy rich. But it's all tied up in a trust that I can't touch until I'm twenty-one, and my uncle is hoping to marry me off to a business associate in time to get his hands on some of it."

"Are you for real?" he asked. He picked up the whiskey glass and took a sip, putting the glass down with a sharp movement of his hand. "Tell him to go to hell and do what you please. At your age I was working for myself, not for any relatives."

"You're a man," she pointed out.

"What difference does that make?" he asked. "Haven't you ever heard of women's lib?"

She smiled. At least one person in the bar had heard of women's lib. "I'm not that kind of woman. I'm wimpy."

"Listen, lady, no wimpy girl walks into a place like this in the middle of the night and orders a beer."

She laughed, her green eyes brilliant. "Yes, she does, when she's driven to it. Besides, it was safe, wasn't it? You were here."

He lifted his chin and a different light came into the pale, silvery eyes. "And you think I'm safe," he murmured. "Or, more precisely, that you're safe with me?"

Her heart began to thud against her ribs. That was a very adult look in his eyes, and she noticed the corresponding drop of his voice into a silky, soft purr. Her lips parted as she let out the breath she was holding.

"I hope I am," she said after a minute. "Because I've done a stupid thing and even though I might deserve a hard time, I'm hoping you won't give me one."

He smiled, and this time it was without mockery. "Good girl. You're learning."

"Is it a lesson?" she asked.

He drained the whiskey glass. "Life is all lessons.

The ones you don't learn right off the bat, you have to repeat. Get up. I'll drive you home.''

"Must you?" she asked, sighing. "It's the first adventure I've ever had, and it may be the last."

He cocked his hat over one eye and looked down at her. "In that case, I'll do my best to make it memorable," he murmured dryly. He held out a lean, strong hand and pulled her up when she took it. "Are you game?"

She was feeling her way with him, but oddly, she trusted him. She smiled. "I'm game."

He nodded. He took her arm and guided her out the door. She noticed a few looks that came their way, but no one tried to distract him.

"People seem to know you in there," she remarked when they were outside in the cool night air.

"They know me," he returned. "I've treed that bar a time or two."

"Treed it?"

He glanced down at her. "Broken it up in a brawl. Men get into trouble, young lady, and women aren't always handy to get them out of it."

"I'm not really handy," she said hesitantly.

He chuckled. "Honey, what you are is written all over you in green ink. I don't mind a little adventure, but that's all you'll get from me." His silvery eyes narrowed. "If you stay around here long enough, you'll learn that I don't like rich women, and you'll learn why. But for tonight, I'm in a generous mood."

"I don't understand," she said.

He laughed without humor. "I don't suppose you

do." He eyed her intently. "You aren't safe to be let out."

"That's what everybody keeps saying." She smiled with what she hoped was sophistication. "But how will I learn anything about life if I'm kept in a glass bowl?"

His eyes narrowed. "Maybe you've got a head start already." He tugged her along to a raunchy gray pickup truck with dents all over it. "I hope you weren't expecting a Rolls-Royce, debutante. I could hardly haul cattle in one."

She felt terrible. She actually winced as she looked up at him, and he felt a twinge of guilt at the dry remark that was meant to be funny.

"Oh, I don't care what you drive," she said honestly. "You could be riding a horse, and it wouldn't matter. I don't judge people by what they have."

His pale eyes slid over her face lightly. "I think I knew that already," he said quietly. "I'm sorry. I meant it as a joke. Here. Don't cut yourself on that spring. It popped out and I haven't had time to fix it."

"Okay." She bounced into the cab and he closed the door. It smelled of the whole outdoors, and when he got in, it smelled of leather and smoke. He glanced at her and smiled.

He started the truck and glanced at her. "Did you drive here?" he asked.

"Yes."

He paused to look around the parking lot, pursing his lips with faint amusement when he saw the regal blue Mercedes-Benz sitting among the dented pickup trucks and dusty four-wheel-drive vehicles.

"That's right, you don't need to ask what I drove here in," she muttered self-consciously. "And yes, it's mine."

He chuckled. "Bristling already, and we've only just met," he murmured as he pulled out into the road. "What do you do when you aren't trying to pick up strange men in bars?"

She glared at him. "I study piano, paint a little, and generally try to stay sane through endless dinner parties and morning coffees."

He whistled through his teeth. "Some life."

She turned in the seat, liking the strength of his profile. "What do you do?"

"Chase cattle, mostly. Figure percentages, decide which cattle to cull, hire and fire cowboys, go to conferences, make financial decisions." He glanced at her. "Occasionally I sit on the board of directors of two corporations."

She frowned slightly. "I thought you said you were a foreman."

"There's a little more to it than that," he said comfortably. "You don't need to know the rest. Where do you want to go?"

She had to readjust her thinking from the abrupt statement. She glanced out the dark window at the flat south Texas landscape. "Well...I don't know. I just don't want to go home."

"They're having a fiesta down in San Moreno," he said with an amused glance. "Ever been to one?"

"No!" Her eyes brightened. "Could we?"

"I don't see why not. There isn't much to do except dance, though, and drink beer. Do you dance?"

"Oh, yes. Do you?"

He chuckled. "I can when forced into it. But you may have trouble with the beer part."

"I learned to like caviar," she said. "Maybe I can learn to like beer."

He didn't comment. He turned on the radio and country-western music filled the cab. She leaned her head back on the seat and smiled as she closed her eyes. Incredible, she thought, how much she trusted this man when she'd only just met him. She felt as though she'd known him for years.

The feeling continued when they got to the small, dusty town of San Moreno. A band of mariachis was playing loud, lively Mexican music while people danced in the roped-off main square. Vendors sold everything from beer to tequila and chimichangas and tacos. The music was loud, the beer was hot, but nobody seemed to mind. Most of the people were Mexican-American, although Fay noticed a few cowboys among the celebrants.

"What are we celebrating?" Fay asked breathlessly as Donavan swung her around and around to the quick beat of the music.

"Who cares?" He chuckled.

She shook her head. In all her life, she couldn't remember being so happy or feeling so carefree. If she died tomorrow, it would be worth it, because she had tonight to remember. So she drank warm beer that tasted better with each sip, and she danced in Donavan's lean, strong arms, and rested against his muscular chest, and breathed in the scent of him until she was more drunk on the man than the liquor.

Finally the frantic pace died down and there was a slow two-step. She melted into Donavan, sliding her arms around him with the kind of familiarity that usually came from weeks of togetherness. She seemed to fit against him, like a soft glove. He smelled of tobacco and beer and the whole outdoors, and the feel of his body so close to hers was delightfully exciting. His arms enfolded her, both of them wrapped close around her, and for a few minutes there was nobody else in the world. She heard the music as if through a fog of pure pleasure, her body reacting to the closeness of his in a way it had never reacted before. She felt a tension that was disturbing, and a kind of throbbing ache in her lower body that she'd never experienced. Being close to him was becoming intolerable. She caught her breath and pulled away a little, raising eyes full of curious apprehension to his.

He searched her face quietly, aware of her fear and equally aware of the cause of it. He smiled gently. "It's all right," he said quietly.

She frowned. "I...I don't quite understand what's wrong with me," she whispered. "Maybe the beer..."

"There's no need to pretend. Not with me." He framed her face in his lean hands and bent, pressing a tender kiss against her forehead. "We'd better go."

"Must we?" she sighed.

He nodded. "It's late." He caught her hand in his and tugged her along to the truck. He was feeling

something of the same reckless excitement she was,
except that he was older and more adept at controlling it. He knew that she'd wanted him while they
were dancing, but things were getting ahead of him.
He didn't need a rich society girl in his life. God
knew, one had been the ruin of his family. People
around Jacobsville, Texas, still remembered how his
father had gone pell-mell after a local debutante
without any scruples about how he forced her to
marry him, right on the heels of his wife's funeral,
too. Donavan had turned bitter trying to live down
the family scandal. Miss High Society here would
find it out eventually. Better not to start something
he couldn't finish, even if she did cause an incon-
venient ache in his body. No doubt she'd had half a
dozen men, but she might be addictive—and he
couldn't risk finding out she was.

She was pleasantly relaxed when they got back to
the deserted bar where she'd left her Mercedes. The
spell had worn off a little, and her head had cleared.
But with that return to reality came the unpleasant-
ness of having to go home and face the music. She
hadn't told anyone where she was going, and they
were going to be angry. Really angry.

"Thank you," she said simply, turning to Donavan after she unlocked her car. "It was a magical
night."

"For me, too." He opened the door for her. "Stay
out of my part of town, debutante," he said gently.
"You don't belong here."

Her green eyes searched his gray ones. "I hate my
life," she said.

"Change it," he replied. "You can if you want to."

"I'm not used to fighting."

"Get used to it. Life doesn't give, it takes. Anything worth having is worth fighting for."

"So they say." She toyed with her car keys. "But in my world, the fighting gets dirty."

"It does in mine, too. That never stopped me. Don't let it stop you."

She lowered her eyes to the hard chest that had pillowed her head while they danced. "I won't forget you."

"Don't get any ideas," he murmured dryly, flicking a long strand of hair away from her face. "I'm not looking for complications or ties. Not ever. Your world and mine wouldn't mix. Don't go looking for trouble."

"You just told me to," she pointed out, lifting her face to his.

"Not in my direction," he emphasized. He smiled at her. The action made him look younger, less formidable. "Go home."

She sighed. "I guess I should. You wouldn't like to kiss me good-night, I guess?" she added with lifted eyebrows.

"I would," he replied. "Which is why I'm not going to. Get in the car."

"Men," she muttered. She glared at him, but she got into the car and closed the door.

"Drive carefully," he said. "And wear your seat belt."

She fastened it, but not because of his order—she

usually wore a seat belt. She spared him one long, last look before she started the car and pulled away. When she drove onto the main highway, he was already driving off in the other direction, and without looking back. She felt a sense of loss that shocked her, as if she'd given up part of herself. Maybe she had. She couldn't remember ever feeling so close to another human being.

Her father and mother had never been really close to her. They'd had their own independent lives, and they almost never included her in any of their activities. She'd grown up with housekeepers and governesses for companionship, and with no brothers or sisters for company. From lonely child to lonely woman, she'd gone through the motions of living. But she'd never felt that anyone would really mind if she died.

That hadn't changed when she'd come out to Jacobsville, Texas, to live with her mother's brother, Uncle Henry Rollins. He wasn't well-to-do, but he wanted to be. He wasn't above using his control over Fay's estate to provide the means to entertain. Fay hadn't protested, but she'd just realized tonight how lax she'd been in looking out for her own interests. Uncle Henry had invited his business partner to supper and hadn't told Fay until the last minute. She was tired of having Sean thrown at her, and she'd rebelled, running out the door to her car.

It had been almost comical, bowlegged Uncle Henry rushing after her, huffing and puffing as he tried to match his bulk to her slender swiftness and lost. She hadn't known where she was going, but she'd wound up at the bar. Fate had sent her there, perhaps, to a man who made her see what a docile child she'd become, when she was an independent woman. Well, things were going to change. Starting now.

Donavan had fascinated her. She tingled, just remembering how he hadn't even had to lift a hand in the bar to make the man who'd been worrying her back down. He was the stuff of which romantic fantasies were made. But he didn't like rich women.

It would be nice, she thought, if Donavan had fallen madly in love with her and started searching for her. That would be improbable, though, since he didn't have a clue as to her real identity. She didn't know his, either, come to think of it; all she knew was what he did for a living. But he could have been stretching the truth a little. He hadn't sounded quite forceful when he'd said he was a foreman.

Well, it didn't really matter, she thought sadly. She'd never see him again. But it had been a memorable meeting altogether, and she knew she'd never forget him. Not ever.

Chapter Two

The feedlot office was quiet, and Fay York was grateful for the respite. It had been a hectic two weeks since she started this, her first job. She was still faintly amazed at her own courage and grit, because she'd never thought she'd be able to actually do it. She'd surprised her Uncle Henry as much as herself when she'd announced her plans to get a job and become independent until her inheritance came through.

It had been because of Donavan that she'd done it. Her evening with him had changed her life. He'd made it possible for her to believe in herself. He'd given her a kind of self-confidence that she hadn't thought possible.

But it hadn't been easy, and she'd been scared to death the morning she'd walked into the office of the gigantic Ballenger feedlot to ask for a job.

Barry Holman, the local attorney who was to han-

dle her inheritance, had suggested that she see Justin
Ballenger about work, because his secretary was out
having a baby and Calhoun Ballenger's wife, Abby,
had been reluctantly filling in.

She could still remember her shock when she'd
gone to Mr. Holman to ask for a living allowance
until her inheritance came through, something that
would give her a little independence from her overbearing uncle.

That was when the blow fell. "I'm sorry," Holman said. "But there's no provision for any living
allowance. According to the terms of the will, you
can't inherit until you're twenty-one. Until that time,
the executor of your parents' estate has total control
of your money."

She gasped. "You mean I don't have any money
unless Uncle Henry gives it to me?"

"I'm afraid so," he said. "I realize it probably
seems terribly unfair to you, Fay, but your parents
must have thought they were doing the right thing."

"I can't believe it," she said, feeling sick. She
wrapped her arms around her body. "What will I
do?"

"What you originally planned. Go ahead and get
a job. You'll only need it for a couple of weeks, until
you get your inheritance."

The statement helped her fight out of her misery.
Involuntarily, she smiled, liking the blond attorney.
He was in his early thirties, very good-looking and
successful. He was married, because on his desk was
a photograph of a young woman with long, brown
hair holding a baby.

"Thank you," she said.

"Oh, it's my pleasure. Don't worry, you won't even have to look far for a job. I just happen to know of an opening. Know anything about cattle?"

She hesitated. "Not really."

"Do you mind working around them?"

"Not if I don't have to brand them," she murmured dryly.

He laughed. "It won't come to that. The Ballenger brothers are looking for a temporary secretary. Their full-time one was pregnant and just had a complicated delivery. She'll be out about two months and they're looking for someone to fill in. Calhoun Ballenger's wife has been trying to handle it, but you'd be a godsend right now. Can you type?"

"Oh, yes," she said. "I can handle a computer, too. I took several college courses before my parents died and I had to come out here to comply with the terms of their will."

"Good!"

"But surely they've found someone..."

"There aren't that many people available for part-time work," he said. "Mostly high-school students, and they don't like the environment that goes with the job."

She grinned. "I won't care, as long as I make enough to pay my rent."

"You will. Here." He scribbled an address. "Go and see Justin or Calhoun. Tell them I sent you. Trust me," he added, rising to shake hands with her. "You'll like them."

"I hope so. I sure don't like my uncle much at the moment."

He nodded. "I can understand that. But Henry isn't a bad man, you know. And there could be more to this than meets the eye," he added reluctantly.

That statement gave her cold chills. The way Uncle Henry had been throwing her headlong at a rich bachelor friend of his made her uneasy. "I suppose so." She hesitated. "Do you know just how my uncle's been managing my affairs in the past two months?"

"Not yet," Barry Holman replied. "I've asked for an accounting, but he's refused to turn over any documents to me until the day you turn twenty-one."

"That doesn't sound promising," she said nervously. "I understood my father to say he had at least two million dollars tied up in trust for me. Surely Uncle Henry couldn't have gone through that in a few weeks, could he?"

"I hardly think so," he assured her. "Don't worry. Everything will be all right. Go and see the Ballengers. Good luck."

"I think I'll need it, but thanks for your help," she said as she left the office.

The Ballenger feedlot was a mammoth operation. During the short time she'd been in Jacobsville, Fay had never gotten a good look at it. Now, up close, the sheer enormity of it was staggering. So was the relative cleanliness of the operation and the attention to sanitation.

It was Justin Ballenger who interviewed her. He

was tall and rangy, not at all handsome, but kind and
courteous.

"You understand that this would only be a temporary job?" he emphasized, leaning forward. "Our
secretary, Nita, is only going to be out long enough
to recuperate from her C-section and have a few
weeks with their new baby."

"Yes, Mr. Holman told me about that," Fay said.
"I don't mind. I only need something temporary until I get used to being on my own. I was living with
my uncle but the situation was pretty uncomfortable." Without meaning to, she went on to explain
what had happened, finding in Justin a sympathetic
listener.

Justin's dark eyes narrowed. "Your uncle is a mercenary man. I think you did the right thing. Make
sure Barry keeps a close watch on your holdings."

"He's doing that." She gnawed her lower lip worriedly. "You won't mention it to anyone...?"

"It's nobody's business but yours," he agreed.
"As far as we know, you're strictly a working girl
who had a minor disagreement with her kin. Fair
enough?"

"Yes, sir," she said, smiling. "I'm not really
much more than a working girl, since everything is
tied up in trust. But only for a few more weeks."
She smiled. "Money doesn't really mean that much
to me. Honestly I'd rather marry someone who loved
me than someone who just wanted an easy life."

"You're a wise girl," he replied quietly. "Shelby
and I both felt like that. We're not poor, but it

wouldn't matter if we were. We have each other, and our boys. We're very lucky.''

She smiled, because she'd heard about Shelby Ballenger and the circumstances that had finally led to her marriage to Justin. It was a real love story. ''Maybe I'll get lucky like that one day,'' she said, thinking about Donavan.

''Well, if you want the job under those conditions, it's yours,'' he said after a minute. ''Welcome aboard. Come on and I'll introduce you to my brother.''

He preceded her down the hall, where a tall blond man was poring over figures on sheets of paper scattered all over his desk.

''This is Fay York,'' he said, introducing her. ''Fay, my brother, Calhoun.''

''Nice to meet you,'' she said sincerely, and shook hands. ''I hope I can help you keep things in order while Nita's away.''

''Abby will get down and kiss your shoes,'' Calhoun assured her. ''She's been trying to keep one of our boys in school and the other two in day care and take care of the house while she worked in Nita's place this week. She's already threatened to open all the gates if we didn't do something to help her.''

''I'm glad I needed a job, then,'' she said.

''So are we.''

Abby came barreling in with an armload of files, her black hair askew around her face, her blue-gray eyes wide and curious when they met Fay's green ones.

''Please be my replacement,'' she said with such

fervor that Fay laughed helplessly. "Do you take bribes? I can get you real chocolate truffles and mocha ice cream..."

"No need. I've already accepted the job while Nita is out with her baby," Fay assured the other woman.

"Oh, thank *God!*" she sighed, dropping the files on her husband's desk. She grinned at Calhoun. "Thank you, too, darling. I'll make you a big beef stew for dinner, with homemade rolls."

"Don't just stand there, go home!" he burst out. He grinned sheepishly at Fay. "She makes the best rolls in town. I've been eating hot dogs for so many days that I bark, because it's all I can cook! This has been hard on my stomach."

"And on my stamina." Abby laughed. "The boys have missed me. Well, I'll show you what to do, Fay, then I'll rush right home and start dough rising."

Fay followed her back to the desk out front and listened carefully and made notes while Abby briefed her on the routine and showed her how to fill in the forms. She went over the basics of feedlot operation as well, so that Fay would understand what she was doing.

"You make it sound very easy, but it isn't, is it?"

"No," Abby agreed. "Especially when you deal with some of our clients. J. D. Langley alone is enough to make a saint throw in the towel."

"Is he a rancher?"

"He's a..." Abby cleared her throat. "Yes, he's a rancher. But most of the cattle he deals in are other people's. He's general manager of the Mesa Blanco ranch combine.''

"I don't know much about ranching, but I've heard of them.''

"Most everybody has. J.D.'s good at his job, don't get me wrong, but he's a perfectionist when it comes to diet and handling of cattle. He saw one of the men use a cattle prod on some of his stock once and he jumped the man, right over a rail. We can't afford to turn down his business, but he makes things difficult. You'll find that out for yourself. Nobody crosses J.D. around Jacobsville.''

"Is he rich?''

"No. He has plenty of power because of the job he does for Mesa Blanco, but it's his temperament that makes people jump when he speaks. J.D. would be arrogant in rags. He's just that kind of man.''

Abby's description brought to mind another man, a rangy cowboy who'd given her the most magical evening of her life. She smiled sadly, thinking that she'd probably never see him again. Walking into that bar had been an act of desperation and bravado. She'd never have the nerve to do it twice. It would look as if she were chasing him, and he'd said at the time that there was no future in it. She'd driven by the bar two or three times, but she couldn't manage enough courage to go in again.

"Is Mr. Langley married?'' Fay asked.

"There's no woman brave enough, anywhere,'' Abby said shortly. "His father's marriage soured him on women. He's been something of a playboy in past years, but he's settled somewhat since he's been

managing the Mesa Blanco companies. There's a
new president of the company who's a hard-line conservative, so J.D.'s toned down his playboy image.
There's talk of the president giving that job to a man
who's married and settled and has kids. The only
child in J.D.'s life, ever, is a nephew in Houston, his
sister's child. His sister died." She shook her head.
"I can't really imagine J.D. with a child. He isn't
the fatherly type."

"Is he really that bad?"

Abby nodded. "He was always difficult. But his
father's remarriage, and then his death, left scars.
These days, he's a dangerous man to be around, even
for other men. Calhoun leaves the office when he's
due to check on his stock. Justin seems to like him,
but Calhoun almost came to blows with him once."

"Is he here very often?" Fay asked with obvious
reluctance.

"Every other week, like clockwork."

"Then I'm very glad I won't be around long," she
said with feeling.

Abby laughed. "Not to worry. He'll barely notice
you. It's Calhoun and Justin who get the range language."

"I feel better already," she said.

Her first day was tiring, but by the end of it she
knew how many records had to be compiled each
day on the individual lots of cattle. She learned volumes about weight gain ratios, feed supplements,
veterinary services, daily chores and form filing. If it
sounded simple just to feed cattle, it wasn't. There

were hundreds of details to be attended to, and print-outs of daily averages to be compiled for clients.

As the days went by and she fell into the routine of the job, Fay couldn't help but wonder if Donavan ever came here. He was foreman for a ranch, he'd told her. If that ranch had feeder cattle, this was prob-ably where they'd be brought. But from what she'd learned, it was subordinates who dealt with the lo-gistics of the transporting of feeder cattle, not the bosses.

She wanted badly to see him, to tell him how big an impact he'd had on her life with his pep talk that night she'd gone to the bar. Her horizons had en-larged, and she was independent for the first time in her life. She'd gone from frightened girl to confident woman in a very short time, and she wanted to thank him. She'd almost asked Abby a dozen times if she knew anyone named Donavan, but Abby would hardly travel in those circles. The Ballengers were high society now, even if they weren't social types. They wouldn't hang out in country bars with men who treed them.

Her uncle had tried to get her to come back to his house when word got out that she was working for a living, but she'd stood firm. No, she told Uncle Henry firmly. She wasn't going to be at his mercy until she inherited. And, she added, Mr. Holman was going to expect an accounting in the near future. Her uncle had looked very uncomfortable when she'd said that and she'd called Barry Holman the next morning to ask about her uncle's authority to act on her behalf.

His reply was that her uncle's power of attorney was a very limited one, and it was doubtful that he could do much damage in the short time he had left. Fay wondered about that. Her uncle was shrewd and underhanded. Heaven knew what wheeling and dealing he might have done already without her knowledge.

Pressure of work caught her attention and held it until the early afternoon. She took long enough to eat lunch at a nearby seafood place and came back just in time to catch the tail end of a heated argument coming from Calhoun's office.

"You're being unreasonable, J.D., and you know it!" Calhoun's deep voice carried down the hall.

"Unreasonable, hell," an equally deep voice drawled. "You and I may never see eye to eye on production methods, but while you're feeding out my cattle, you'll do it my way."

"For God's sake, you'd have me out there feeding the damned things with a fork!"

"Not at all. I only want them treated humanely."

"They *are* treated humanely!"

"I wouldn't call an electric cattle prod that. And stressed animals aren't healthy animals."

"Have you ever thought about joining an animal rights lobby?" came the exasperated reply.

"I belong to two, thanks."

The door opened and Fay couldn't drag her eyes away from it. That curt voice was so familiar...

Sure enough, the tall, lithe man who came out of the office in front of Calhoun was equally familiar. Fay couldn't help the radiance of her face, the softness of her eyes as they adored his lean, dark face under the wide brim of his hat.

Donavan. She could have danced on her desk.

But when he turned and saw her, he frowned. His silvery eyes narrowed, glittered. He paused by her desk, his head cocked slightly to one side, a lit cigar dangling from his fingers.

"What are you doing here?" he asked her bluntly.

"I'm filling in for Nita," she began.

"Don't tell me you have to work for a living now, debutante?" he asked in a mocking tone.

She hesitated. He sounded as if he disliked her. But she knew he'd enjoyed the fiesta as much as she had. His behavior puzzled her, intimidated her.

"Well, yes," she stammered. "I do." And she did. For the time being.

"What a hell of a comedown," he murmured with patent disbelief. "Still driving the Mercedes?"

"You know each other?" Calhoun asked narrowly.

Donavan lifted the cigar to his mouth and blew out thick smoke. "Vaguely." He glanced at Calhoun until the other man sighed angrily and went back to his office with a muttered goodbye.

"You've been driving by the bar fairly regularly," he remarked curtly, and she blushed because she couldn't deny it. She'd been looking for him, hoping to have a chance to tell him how he'd helped her turn her life around. But he seemed to be putting a totally different connotation on her actions. "Is that where you found out I did business with the Ballengers?" He didn't even give her time to deny it.

"Well, no go, honey. I told you that night, no bored debutante is going to try to make a minor amusement out of me. So if you came here hoping for another shot at me, you might as well quit right now and go home to your caviar and champagne. You're not hard on the eyes, but I'm off the market, is that clear?"

She stared at him in quiet confusion. "Mr. Holman told me about the job," she said with what dignity she had left. "I don't have a dime until my twenty-first birthday, and I'm living on my own so I have to pay rent. This was the only job available." She dropped her gaze to her computer. "I drove by the bar a time or two, yes. I wanted to tell you that you'd changed my life, that I was learning to stand on my own feet. I wanted to thank you."

His jaw tautened and he looked more dangerous than ever. "I don't want thanks, teenage adulation, hero worship or misplaced lust. But you're welcome, if it matters."

He sounded cynical and mocking. Fay felt chastised. She'd only been grateful, but he made her feel stupid. Maybe she was. She'd spun a few midnight dreams about him. Except for some very innocent dates with boys, she'd never had much attention from the opposite sex. His protective attitude that night in the bar, his quiet handling of what could have become a bad incident, had made her feel feminine and hungry for more of his company. He was telling her that she'd made too much of it, that she was offering him affection that he didn't want or need. It was probably a kindness, but it hurt all the same.

She forced a smile. "You needn't worry. I wasn't

planning to follow you around with a wedding band on a hook or anything. I just wanted to thank you for what you did."

"You've done that. So?"

"I...have a lot of work to get through. I'm only temporary," she added quickly. "Just until Nita comes back. When I get my legacy, I'll be on the first plane back to Georgia. Honest."

His dark eyebrows plunged above the straight bridge of his nose. "I don't remember asking for any explanations."

"Excuse me, then." She turned her attention back to her keyboard; her hands were cold and numb. She forced them to work. She didn't look up, either. He'd made her feel like what came out of a sausage grinder.

He didn't reply. He didn't linger, either. His measured footsteps went out the door immediately, leaving the pungent scent of cigar smoke in their wake.

Calhoun came back out five minutes later, checking his watch. "I have to be out of the office for an hour or so. Tell Justin when he comes back, will you?"

"Yes, sir," she said, smiling.

He hesitated, his narrowed eyes registering the hurt on her face that she couldn't hide. "Listen, Fay, don't let him upset you," he added quietly. "He doesn't really mean things as personally as they sound, but he rubs everybody the wrong way except Justin."

"He saved me from a bad situation," she began. "I only wanted to thank him, but he seemed to think

I had designs on him or something. My goodness, he thought I came to work here because he did business with you!''

He laughed. "Can't blame him. Several have, and no, I'm not kidding. The more he snarls, the harder some women chase him. He's a catch, too. He makes good money with Mesa Blanco, and his own ranch is nothing to laugh at.''

"Mesa…Blanco?" she stammered, as puzzle pieces began to make a pattern in her mind.

"Sure. Didn't he introduce himself before?" He smiled ruefully. "I guess not. Well, that was J. D. Langley.''

Chapter Three

Fay got through the rest of the day without showing too much of her heartache. She'd had hopes that Donavan might have felt something for her, but he'd dashed those very efficiently. He couldn't have made it more obvious that he wanted no part of her or her monied background. He wouldn't believe that she had to work. Well, of course, she didn't, really. But he might have given her the benefit of the doubt.

It hadn't been a terrible shock to learn that he was J. D. Langley. He did live down to his publicity. Later, she'd found out that Donavan was his middle name and what he was called locally, except by people who did business with him. She certainly understood why the Ballengers hated to see him coming.

She was sorry about his hostility, because the first time she'd ever seen him, there had been a tenderness between them that she'd never experienced. It must have all been on one side, though, she decided miserably.

Well, she told herself as she lay trying to sleep that night, she'd do better to stop brooding and concentrate on her own problems. She had enough, without adding the formidable Mr. Langley to them.

But fate was conspiring against her. The next day, she tried a new cafeteria in Jacobsville and came face-to-face with J. D. Langley as she sat down with her tray.

He gave her a glare that would have stopped traffic. He'd obviously just finished his meal. He was draining his coffee cup. Fay turned her chair so that she wasn't looking directly at him and, with unsteady hands, took her food off the tray.

"I told you yesterday," Donavan said at her shoulder, "that I don't like being chased. Didn't you listen?"

The whip of his voice cut. Not only that, it was loud enough to attract attention from other diners in the crowded room.

Fay's face went red as she glanced at him apprehensively, her green eyes huge as they met the fierce silvery glitter of his.

"I didn't know you were going to be here..." she began uneasily.

"No?" he challenged, his smile an insult in itself. "You didn't recognize my car sitting in the parking lot? Give it up, debutante. I don't like bored little rich girls, so stop following me around. Got that?"

He turned and left the cafeteria. Fay was too humiliated by the unwanted attention to enjoy much of her meal. She left quickly and went back to work.

Following him around, indeed, she muttered to herself while she fed data into her computer. She didn't know what kind of car he drove. The only vehicle she'd seen him in was a battered gray pickup truck, had he forgotten? Perhaps he thought she'd seen his car when he'd come to the feedlot, but she hadn't. The more she saw of him the less she liked him, and she'd hardly been hounding him. She certainly wouldn't again, he could bank on that!

Abby came in the next afternoon with an invitation. "Calhoun and I have to go to a charity ball tonight. I know it's spur-of-the-moment, but would you like to come?"

"Will my uncle be there, do you think?" Fay asked.

"I hardly think so." Abby grinned. "Come on. You've been moping around here for two days, it will be good for you. You can ride with us, and there's a very nice man I want to introduce you to when we get there. He's unattached, personable, and rich enough not to mind that you are."

"Uh, Mr. Langley...?"

"I heard what happened in Cole's Café." Abby grimaced. "J.D. doesn't go to charity balls, so you aren't likely to run into him there."

"Thank God. He was so kind to me the night I met him, but he's been terrible to me ever since. I only wanted to thank him. He thinks I have designs on him." She shuddered. "As if I'd ever chased a man in my life...!"

"You're not J.D.'s kind of woman, Fay," the older woman said gently. "Your wealth alone would keep him at bay, without the difference in your ages. J.D.'s in his early thirties, and he doesn't like younger women."

"I don't think he likes *any* women," Fay replied with a sigh. "Especially me. But I wasn't chasing him, honestly!"

"Don't let it worry you."

"You're sure he won't be there tonight?"

"Absolutely positive," Abby assured her.

Prophetic words. Abby and Calhoun picked Fay up at her apartment house, and drove her to the elegant Whitman estate where the charity ball was already in progress. Fay was wearing a long white silk dress with one shoulder bare and her hair in a very elegant braided bun atop her head. She looked young and fragile...and very rich.

They went through the receiving line and Fay moved ahead of Calhoun and Abby to the refreshment table while they spoke to an acquaintance. She bumped into someone and turned to apologize.

"Again?" J. D. Langley asked with a vicious scowl. "My God, do you have radar?"

Fay didn't say a word. She turned and went back toward Abby and Calhoun, her heart pounding in her chest.

Abby spotted J.D. and grimaced. "I didn't know," she told a shattered Fay. "I swear I didn't. Here, you stick close to us. He won't bother you. Come on, I'll introduce you to Bart and that will solve all your problems. I'm sorry, Fay.''

"It wasn't your fault. It's fate, I guess," she said dryly, although her eyes were troubled.

"Arrogant beast," Abby muttered, sparing the tall, elegant man in the dinner jacket a speaking glance. "If he were a little less conceited, you wouldn't have this problem." She drew Fay forward. "Here he is. Bart!"

A thin, lazy looking man with wavy blond hair and mischievous blue eyes turned as his name was called. He greeted Abby warmly and glanced at Fay with open curiosity and delight.

"Well, well, Greek goddesses are back in style again, I see. Do favor me with a waltz before you set off for Mount Olympus, fair damsel."

"This is our newest employee, Fay York," she introduced them. "Fay, this is Bartlett Markham. He's president of the local cattlemen's association."

"Nice to meet you," she said, extending a hand. "Do you know cattle?"

"I grew up on a ranch. I work for a firm of accountants now, but my family still has a pretty formidable Santa Gertrudis purebred operation."

"I don't know much, but I'm learning every day," Fay laughed.

"I'll leave her with you, Bart," Abby said. "Do keep her away from J.D., will you? He seems to think she's stalking him."

"Do tell?" His eyebrows levered up and he grinned. "Why not stalk me instead? I'm a much better catch than J.D., and you won't need preventive shots if you go out with me, either.''

Insinuating that she would with J.D., she thought. Rabies probably, she mused venomously, in case he bit her. She smiled at Bart, feeling happier already.

"Consider yourself on the endangered species list, then," she said.

He laughed. "Gladly." He glanced toward the band. "Would you like to dance?"

"Charmed." She gave him her hand and let him lead her to the dance floor, where a live band was playing a bluesy two-step. She knew exactly where J. D. Langley was, as if she really did have radar, so she was careful not to look in that direction.

He noticed. It was impossible not to, when she was dancing with one of his bitterest enemies. He stood quietly against a wall, his silver eyes steady and unblinking as he registered the fluid grace with which she followed her partner's steps. He didn't like the way Markham was holding her, or the way she was responding.

Not that he wanted her, he assured himself. She was nothing but another troublesome woman. A debutante, at that, and over ten years his junior. He had no use for her at all, and he'd made sure she knew it. Their one evening together had sent him tearing away in the opposite direction. She appealed to him terribly. He couldn't afford an involvement with a society girl. He knew he was better off alone, so keeping this tempting little morsel away from him became imperative. If he had to savage her to do it, it was still the best thing for both of them. She was much too soft and delicate for a man like himself. He'd break her spirit and her heart, because he had nothing to give. And his father's reputation in the community made it impossible for him to be seen in public with her in any congenial way. He'd accused her of stalking him, but gossip would have it the other way around. Another money-crazy Langley, critics would scoff, out to snare himself a rich wife. He groaned at just the thought.

He didn't like seeing her with Markham, but there was nothing he could do about it. He shouldn't have come tonight.

He turned away to the refreshment table and poured himself a glass of Scotch.

"You aren't really after Donavan, are you?" Bart asked humorously.

"He flatters himself," she said haughtily.

"That's what I thought. Like father, like son," he said unpleasantly.

"I don't understand."

He made a graceful turn, carrying her with him as the music's tempo increased. "After Donavan's mother died, Rand Langley got into a financial tangle and was about to lose his ranch. My aunt was very young then, plain and shy, but she was filthy rich and single, so Rand set his cap for her. He kept after her until he seduced her, so that she had to marry him or disgrace her family. She was crazy about him. Worshiped the ground he walked on. Then, inevitably, she found out why he really married her and she couldn't live with it. She killed herself."

Fay grimaced. "I'm sorry."

"So were all of us," he added coldly, glaring at J. D. Langley's back. "Rand didn't even come to the funeral. He was too busy spending her money. He died a few years later, and believe me, none of us grieved for him."

"That wasn't Donavan's fault," she felt bound to point out.

"Blood will tell," came the unbelieving reply. "You're well-to-do."

"Yes, but he can't stand me," she replied.

"I don't believe that. I can't imagine J.D. passing up a rich woman."

"How many has he dated over the years?" she asked with faint irritation.

"I don't keep up with his love life," he said tersely, and all his prejudices showed quite clearly. Fay could see that he wouldn't believe a kind word about J. D. Langley if he had proof.

"The two of you don't get along, I gather."

"We disagree on just about everything. Especially on his ridiculous theories about cattle raising," he added sarcastically. "No. We don't get along."

She was quiet after that. Now she understood the situation. It couldn't have been made clearer.

She danced with several eligible bachelors and several married men before the evening ended. It surprised her that J. D. Langley was still present. He remained on the fringes of the dance floor, talking to other men. He asked no one to dance. Fay was sadly certain that he wouldn't ask her.

But in that, she was surprised. The band was playing a soft love song and she watched Bart glance in her direction. But before he could get across the room, Donavan suddenly swung her into his arms and onto the dance floor.

Her heart skipped wildly as she felt the firm clasp of his hand on her waist, his fingers steely as they linked her own.

"This is not a good idea," she said firmly. "I'll think you're encouraging me."

"Not likely. By now Bart's filled you in, hasn't he?" he replied with a mocking smile.

She averted her eyes to the white ruffled shirt he wore under his dinner jacket. On another man it might look effeminate. On Donavan, it looked masculine and very sexy, emphasizing his dark good looks. "I got an earful, thanks," she replied.

He shook her gently. "Stiff as a board," he mused, looking down at her. "Are you afraid to let your guard down? There's very little I could do to you on a dance floor in front of half of Jacobsville."

"You've made your opinion of me crystal clear, Mr. Langley," she said without looking up. "I haven't been stalking you, as you put it, but you're free to think what you like. Do try to remember that I didn't ask you to dance."

"That was the whole purpose of the exercise," he said carelessly. "To make sure you didn't set your cap for me."

"Then why are you dancing with me?"

His lean arm whipped her close on a turn, but he didn't let her go afterward. His dark face was all too close, so that she could smell his tangy after-shave, and his silver eyes bit into hers at point-blank range. "Don't you know?" he asked at her lips.

Her heart tripped as she felt his breath. "Oh, I see," she said suddenly. "You're trying to irritate Bart."

He lifted his head and one eyebrow quirked. "Is that it?"

"What else?" she asked with a nervous laugh, averting her eyes to a fuming Bart nearby. "Listen, I'm not going to be used for any vendettas, by you or your hissing kin."

His fingers curled into hers and drew them to his broad chest. It rose and fell heavily, and he stared over her dark head without seeing anything. "I don't have any vendettas," he said quietly. "But I won't be accused of following in my father's footsteps."

She could feel the pain in those terse words, but she didn't remark on it. Her eyes closed and she drank in the delicious masculine scent of him. "I won't be rich for another week or two," she murmured. "Until the legal work goes through, I'm just a temporary secretary."

He laughed in spite of himself. "I see. For two weeks you're on my level. No Mercedes. No mansion. No padded checkbook."

"Something like that." She sighed and snuggled closer. "How about a wild, passionate affair? We could throw the coats on the closet floor and you could have your way with me under somebody's silver fox stole."

He burst out laughing. His steely arm drew her close as he made a sudden turn, and her body throbbed with the sensations it caused in her untried body.

"Hasn't anyone told you yet that I belong to two animal rights groups?"

"So you're one of those people who protest lab animal experiments that save little children's lives and throw paint on people who wear fur coats?" she asked, her temper rising.

"Not me. I'm no fanatic. I just think animals have the right to humane treatment, even in medical facilities." His arm tightened. "As for throwing paint on fur coats, a few lawsuits should stem that habit. The idea is to stop further slaughter of wild animals. A fur coat is already a dead animal."

She shivered. "You make it sound morbid."

One silver eye narrowed. "Do you wear fur?"

She chuckled. "I can't. Fur makes me break out in hives."

He began to smile. "A rich girl with no furs. What a tragedy."

"I have plenty of velvet coats, thanks very much. I think they're much more elegant than fur and they don't shed." She moved closer, shocked when his hand caught her hip and contracted painfully. "Ouch!" she protested.

He moved her back an inch. "Don't push your luck," he said, his voice low and faintly threatening, like his glittery eyes. "You're pretty sexy in that little number you're wearing, and I'm easily aroused. Want me to prove it?"

"No, thanks," she said quickly. "I'll take your word for it."

He laughed as he spun her around in a neat turn. "For a sophisticated debutante, sometimes you're a contradiction. Is that a blush?"

"It's hot in here."

"Ah. The conventional excuse." He leaned close and brushed his cheek against hers. "Too bad you're rich."

"Is it? Why?" she asked in a tone that sounded, unfortunately, all too breathless.

He nibbled gently on her earlobe. "Because I'm dynamite in bed."

"Do tell?" She hid her face against him. "Are you?" she whispered shakily.

His lean hand slid up her back and into the coiled hair at her nape. He caressed it gently while he held her, the music washing over them in a sultry silence.

"So I've been told." His chin rubbed softly against her temple, his breath coming roughly. "But why take someone else's word for it?"

She forced a laugh. "Isn't this a little sudden? I mean, just a day ago you were giving me hell for eating lunch in the same restaurant with you."

"I'm sure Bart told you the problem. Rich, you're right off my Christmas list. Poor, you're an endangered species." His hand contracted, coaxing her face up to his glittery eyes.

"Should I cut and run?" she asked, her voice husky.

"Do you really want to?" he whispered.

As he spoke, he moved closer, and his powerful thighs brushed hers. Even through all the layers of fabric, she felt the imprint of them, the strength. His hand slid down her back to her waist and pulled, very gently, so that she was pressed right up to him, welded from breast to thigh. He watched her eyes and something masculine and arrogant kindled in his gaze as he felt the faint shiver of her soft body.

"Do you like Chinese food?" he asked.

She nodded.

"I like to drive up to Houston for it. There's a good restaurant just inside the city limits. How about it?"

Her heart jumped. "Are you asking me out?"

"Sounds like it," he mused. "Don't expect steak and lobster. I make a good salary, but it doesn't run to champagne."

She colored furiously. "Please, don't," she said quickly. "I'm not like that."

He touched her face gently. "Yes, I know. It makes it harder. Do you think I enjoyed hurting you?" he asked harshly, and for an instant something showed in his eyes that startled her. He looked away. "There's no future for us, little one."

She felt him hesitating. Any second, he was going to take back that supper invitation.

"Just Chinese food," she prompted, one slender hand poking him gently in the ribs.

He started, and she grinned at him. "And no moonlight seduction on the way home," she added. "As you said, it isn't wise to start things we can't finish."

"I could finish that," he murmured dryly.

She cleared her throat. "Well, I don't take

chances. I'll risk my stomach with you, but not my heart.''

He cocked an eyebrow. "Does that mean that making love with me might enslave you?" he teased.

"Exactly. Besides, I never sleep with a man on the first date.''

There was the faintest movement of his eyelashes. He averted his gaze to a point beyond her head. He couldn't admit that it bothered him, thinking of her with other men. She was a debutante and filthy rich, surely there had been a steady stream of suitors. She might have more experience even than he did. He'd never thought about a woman's past before. It had never occurred to him to wonder how experienced his lover of the evening actually was. But with Fay, he wondered.

"What's wrong?" she asked curiously.

He glanced down at her. She looked very innocent until she smiled, and then her eyes crinkled and there was a sophistication in them that made him feel cool. "Nothing."

"That's usually the woman's line, isn't it?"

"Equal rights," he reminded her. "Friday night. I'll pick you up at six."

"I don't live with Uncle Henry anymore," she began.

"I know where you live," he replied. "We'll eat Chinese food and you can show me what you know. It should be quite an experience..."

Long after the dance was over and she was back in her apartment, she worried over that last statement.

She felt as if she were about to get in well over her head.

She wanted Donavan more than she'd ever wanted anything in her life. A date with him was the gold at the end of the rainbow. But she'd pretended to be something she wasn't, and she didn't know what she was going to do if he took her up on it.

Abby noticed Fay's preoccupation the next day when she stopped by to see Calhoun.

"You're positively morose!" Abby exclaimed. "What's wrong?"

"Donavan asked me out."

Her eyebrows went up. "J.D. asked you out? But he hates rich women."

"Yes, I know. I told him I was going to be poor for two more weeks, so I guess he thought it was safe enough until my inheritance comes through."

"I see." Abby didn't say anything, but she began to look worried herself. "Fay, I never thought to mention it, because J.D. was giving you such a hard time, but he's something of a womanizer..."

"I figured that out for myself," she murmured with a smile. "It shows."

"He's a gentleman, in his way. Just don't give him too much rope. He'll hang you with it."

"I know that, too. I'll be careful."

Abby hesitated. "If it helps, I know how you feel. I was crazy about Calhoun, but he liked a different kind of woman altogether. We had a very rocky path to the altar."

"He's crazy about you, though. Anyone can see that."

Abby smiled contentedly. "Of course he is. But it wasn't always that way."

"Donavan already said that he doesn't want commitment. I'm not going to get my hopes up. But an evening out with him... Well, it's going to be like brushing heaven, you know?"

"I do, indeed." Abby smiled, remembering her first date with Calhoun. She glanced back at Fay, her eyes wistful. She only hoped their newest employee wasn't going to be badly hurt. Everyone locally knew that J. D. Langley wasn't a marrying man. But Abby would have bet her prize bull that Fay was as innocent as Abby herself had once been. If she was, she had a lot of heartache in store. When J.D. found out, and he would, he'd drop Fay like a hot rock. Innocents were not his style.

Fay went through the motions of working like a zombie for the next week, with a dull and tedious weekend in between that did little for her nerves. Donavan didn't come by the feedlot at all, and when she left the office the next Friday afternoon, she still hadn't heard from him. For all she knew, he might have forgotten all about her.

The phone was ringing even as she got in the door, and she grabbed up the receiver as if it were a life preserver.

"Hello?" she said breathlessly.

"I'll be by in an hour. You hadn't forgotten?" Donavan drawled.

"How could I?" she asked, adding mischievously, "I love Chinese food."

He chuckled. "That puts me in my place, I guess. See you."

He hung up and Fay ran to dress. The only thing in her closet that would suit a fairly casual evening out was a pale green silk suit and she hated wearing it. It screamed big money, something sure to set Donavan's teeth on edge. But other than designer jeans and a silk blouse, or evening gowns, it was all she had. The cotton pantsuit she'd worn to work today was just too wrinkled and stained to wear out tonight. It wouldn't have been suitable anyway.

She teamed the silk suit with a nice cotton blouse and sat down to wait, after renewing her makeup. She only hoped that he wasn't going to take one look at her and run. If he didn't throw her over entirely, she was going to have to invest in some medium-priced clothing!

Chapter Four

Just as Fay had feared, Donavan's first glimpse of her silk suit brought a scowl to his face.

"It's old," she said inadequately, and looked miserable. She locked her fingers together and stared at him with sadness all over her face.

He shoved his hands into the pockets of his gray slacks. He was wearing a white cotton shirt and a blue blazer with them, a black Stetson cocked over one eye and matching boots on his feet. He looked nice, but hardly elegant or wealthy. Her silk suit seemed to point out all the differences between the life-style she was used to, and his own.

"You look very nice," he said quietly.

"And very expensive," she added on a curt laugh. "I'm sorry."

"Why?"

"I didn't want you to think I wore this on purpose," she said, faltering.

He lifted an eyebrow and smiled mockingly. "I'm taking you out for a Chinese dinner. A proposal of marriage doesn't come with the egg roll."

She blushed furiously. "I know that."

"Then why bother about appearances?" He shrugged. "A date is one thing. A serious relationship is something else." His silver eyes narrowed. "Let's settle that at the outset. I have nothing serious or permanent in mind. Even if we wind up as the hottest couple in town between the sheets, there still won't be anything offered in the way of commitment."

"I knew that already," she said, steeling herself not to react to the provocative statement.

"Good." He glanced around the apartment, frowning slightly. "This is pretty spartan, isn't it?" he asked, suddenly realizing how frugally she seemed to be living.

"It's all I could afford on my salary," she told him. She wrapped her arms across her breasts and smiled. "I don't mind it. It's just a place to sleep."

"Henry doesn't help you financially?" he persisted.

"He can't," she explained. "He's got his own financial woes. I'll be fine when he turns over my affairs to Mr. Holman and I can get to my trust."

Donavan didn't say a word, but suddenly he was beginning to see things she apparently didn't. If Henry was having money problems, surely his control of Fay's estate would give him the means of solving them, even if he had to pay her back later. The fact that he was suffering a reversal didn't bode well for Fay, but she seemed oblivious. Perhaps like most rich women she didn't know or care much about handling money.

He was aware that he'd been silent a long time. He took his hands out of his pockets and caught her slender fingers in his. They were cold, like ice. "We'd better go," he said, drawing her along with him.

Fay had never realized how exciting it could be to hold hands with a man. He linked her fingers into his as they walked, and she felt the sensuous contraction all the way to her toes. It was like walking on a cloud, she thought. She could almost float.

Donavan was feeling something similar and fighting it tooth and nail. He hadn't really wanted this date at all, but something stronger than his will had forced him into it. Fay was a delicious little morsel, full of contradictions. He'd always liked puzzles. She was one he really wanted to solve, even if his inclination was to get her into the nearest bed with all possible haste.

She had to be experienced. She'd never denied that. He wondered if pampered rich boys were as anemic in bed as they seemed when he saw them at board meetings. His contempt for the upper classes was, he knew, a result of his father's ruthless greed.

He could still barely believe the whole episode, his father running pell-mell after a woman half his age when his wife of twenty years was just barely in her grave. It had disgusted and shocked him, and led to a confrontation of stellar proportions. He hadn't spoken to his father afterward, and his presence at his father's funeral two years later was only a nod to convention. It wasn't until much later that he'd learned why Rand Langley had been so ruthless. It had been to save the family ranch, which had been Langley land for three generations. Not that it excused what he'd done, but it did at least explain it. Rand had wanted Donavan to inherit the ranch. Marrying money had been the only way he could keep it.

"You're very quiet," Fay remarked on the way to Houston. "Are you sorry you asked me out?"

He glanced at her. "No. I was remembering."

"Yes?"

He was smoking one of the small cigars he favored, his gray eyes thoughtful as they lingered on the long road ahead. "My father disgraced himself to marry money, to keep the ranch for me and my children, if I ever have any. Ironic, that I've never married and never want to, because of him."

She folded her hands primly in her lap. It flattered her that he was willing to tell her something so personal.

"If you don't have children, what will happen to your ranch?" she asked.

"I've got a ten-year-old nephew," he said. "My sister's boy. His father's been dead for years. My sister remarried three years ago, and she died last year. Her husband got custody. But he's just remarried, and last month he stuck Jeffrey in a military school. The boy's in trouble constantly, and he hates his stepfather." He took a long draw from the cigar, scowling. "That's why I was sitting in that bar the night you walked in. I was trying to decide what to do. Jeff wants to come out here and live with me.''

"Can't he?"

He shook his head. "No chance. His father and I don't get along. He'd more than likely refuse just to get at me. His new wife is pregnant and he doesn't seem to care about Jeff at all.''

"That's sad," she said. "Does he miss his mother?''

"He never talks about her.''

"Probably because he cares too much," she said. "I miss my parents," she added unexpectedly. "They died in a plane crash. Even if I never saw much of them, they were still my parents.''

"What do you mean, you never saw much of them?''

She laughed softly. "They liked traveling. I was in school, and they didn't want to interrupt my education. I stayed at home with an elderly great-aunt. She liked me very much, but it was kind of lonely. Especially during holidays.'' She stared out the window, aware of his curious stare. "If I ever have kids, I'll be where they are," she said suddenly. "And they won't ever have to spend Christmas without me.''

"I suppose," he began slowly, "there are some things money won't buy.''

"An endless list," she agreed. "Beginning and ending with love.''

He chuckled softly, to lighten the atmosphere. He glanced sideways at her. "Money can buy love, you know," he murmured.

"Well, not really," she disagreed. "It can buy the illusion of it, but I wouldn't call a timed session in bed 'love.'"

He burst out laughing. "No," he said after a minute. "I don't suppose it is. They say that type of experience is less than satisfying. I wouldn't know. I couldn't find any pleasure in a body I had to pay for."

"I can understand that."

There was a pleasant tension in the silence that dropped between them. Minutes later, Donavan pulled up in front of a Chinese restaurant and cut off the engine.

"This is it," he said. He helped her out of the car and escorted her inside.

It was a very nice restaurant, with Chinese music playing softly in the background and excellent service.

Donavan watched her covertly as he sampled the jasmine tea the waitress had served. "Tell me about your job. How does it feel to work for a living?"

Her eyes brightened and she smiled. "I like it very much," she confessed. "I've never been responsible for my own life before. I've always had people telling me what to do and how to do it. The night I met you at the bar really opened my eyes. You made me see what my life was like, showed me that I could change it if I wanted to. I wasn't kidding when I said you turned my world around."

"I thought the job was a means to an end," he confessed, smiling at his own folly. "I've been chased before, and by well-to-do women who saw me as a challenge.''

"You're not bad looking," she said demurely, averting her eyes. "And you're very much a man. But I meant it when I said I wasn't chasing you. I have too much pride to behave that way.''

Probably she did. He liked her honesty. He liked the way she looked and dressed, too. She wasn't beautiful, but she was elegant and well-mannered, and she had a big heart. He found himself wondering how Jeff would react to her.

They ate in a pleasant silence and talked about politics and the weather, everything except themselves. All too soon it was time to start back for Jacobsville.

"How are you and your uncle getting along?" Donavan asked on the way back.

"We speak and not much more. Uncle Henry's worried about something," she added. "He gets more nervous by the day.''

He'd never thought of her uncle as a nervous man. Perhaps it had something to do with Fay's inheritance.

"Suppose you inherit only a few dollars and an apology?" he asked suddenly.

She laughed. "That isn't likely.''

"But if it was?"

She thought about it seriously. "It would be hard," she confessed. "I'm not used to asking the price of anything, or denying myself a whim purchase. But like anything else, I expect I could get used to it. I don't mind hard work.''

He nodded. That would make her life easier.

He turned off onto a farm road just at the outskirts of Jacobsville.

"Where are we going?" she asked, glancing around at unfamiliar terrain.

"I'm going to show you my ranch," he said simply. His eyes lanced over her and he smiled wickedly. "Then I'm going to shove you into the henhouse and have my way with you."

"Do you have a henhouse?" she asked excitedly.

"Yes. And a flock of chickens to go with it. I like fresh eggs."

He didn't add that he often had to budget in between cattle sales, even on the good salary he made.

"I guess you have your own beef, too?" she asked.

"Not for slaughter," he replied. "I like animals too much to raise one to kill. Mesa Blanco has slaughter cattle, but I don't spend any more time around them than I have to."

The picture she was getting of him didn't have a lot to do with the image he projected. An animal lover with a core of steel was unusual.

"Do you have dogs and cats?"

He smiled slowly. "And puppies and kittens," he said. "I give them away when the population gets out of control, and most of mine are neutered. It's criminal to turn an unneutered animal loose on the streets." He slowed as the road curved toward a simple white frame house. "Ever had a dog or cat of your own?"

"No," she said sadly. "My parents weren't animal lovers. My mother would have fainted at the thought of cat hair on her Louis Quinze furniture.''

"I'd rather have the cat than the furniture," he remarked.

She smiled. "So would I."

His heart lifted. She wasn't at all what he'd expected. He pulled up in front of the ranch house and cut off the engine.

There were flowers everywhere, from shrubs to trees to beds of them right and left around the porch. She could see them by the fierce light of the almost-full moon. "How beautiful!" she exclaimed.

"Thank you."

"You planted them?"

"Nobody else. I like flowers," he said defensively as he got out and helped her out of the car.

"I didn't say a word," she assured him. "I like flowers, too."

He unlocked the front door while she glanced covetously along the long front porch at the old-fashioned swing and rocking chair. Somewhere nearby cattle made pleasant mooing noises.

"Do you keep a lot of cattle here?" she asked.

"I have purebred Santa Gertrudis," he told her. "Stud cattle, not beef cattle."

"Why doesn't that surprise me?" she teased.

He laughed, standing aside to let her enter the house.

The living room was done in Early American, and it looked both neat and lived-in. For a bachelor, he was a good housekeeper. She said so.

"Thanks, but I can't take all the credit. My foreman's wife looks after things when I can't."

She was insanely jealous of the foreman's wife, all at once.

He saw her expression and smiled. "She's fifty and happily married."

She blushed, moving farther into the room.

"Look out," he warned.

Before the words went silent, her foot was attacked by a tiny ball of fur with teeth.

"Good heavens!" she exclaimed, laughing. "A miniature tiger!" she kidded.

"I'm training her to be an attack cat. I call her Bee."

"Bee?"

He grinned. "Short for Beelzebub. You can't imagine what she did to the curtains a day or so ago."

She reached down and picked up the tiny thing. It looked up at her with a calico face and the softest, most loving blue-green eyes she'd ever seen, with black fur outlining them.

"Why, she's beautiful!" she exclaimed.

"I think so."

The kitten's eyes half closed as it began to purr and knead her jacket with its tiny paws.

"She'll pick that silk," he said, reaching for the kitten.

She looked at him curiously. "That doesn't matter," she said, surprised by his comment.

His silver eyes registered his own surprise as they looked deeply into hers. "That suit must have cost a small fortune," he persisted. He extricated the kitten, despite her protests, and carried it into the bedroom, closing the door behind him.

"Want some coffee?" he asked.

"That would be nice."

"It will only take a minute or so." He tossed his hat onto the hat rack and went into the kitchen.

Fay wandered around the living room, stopping at a photograph on the mantel. It was of a young boy, a studio pose. He looked a lot like Donavan, except that his eyes were dark, and he had a more rounded face. He looked sad.

"That's Jeff," he told her from the doorway. He leaned against it, waiting for the coffee to brew. His long legs were crossed, like his arms, and he looked very masculine and sexy with his jacket off and the top buttons of his shirt unfastened over a thicket of jet black hair.

"He favors you," she remarked. "Did your sister look like you?"

"Quite a lot," he said. "But her eyes were darker than mine. Jeff has his father's eyes."

"What does he like?" she asked. "I mean, is he a sports fan?"

"He doesn't care much for football. He likes martial arts, and he's good at them. He's a blue belt in tae kwon do—a Korean martial art that concentrates on kicking styles."

"Isn't that a demonstration sport in the summer Olympics?"

He smiled, surprised. "Yes, it is. Jeff hopes to be

able to participate in the 1996 summer games in Atlanta.''

''A group of Atlantans worked very hard to get the games to come there,'' she recalled. ''One of my friends worked in the archives at Georgia Tech—a lot of the people on campus were active in that committee.''

''You don't have many friends here, do you?'' he asked.

''Abby Ballenger is a friend,'' she corrected. ''And I get along well with the girls at the office.''

''I meant friends in your own social class.''

She put the picture of Jeff back on the mantel. ''I never had friends in my own social class. I don't like their idea of fun.''

''Don't you?''

He moved closer. His hands slid around her waist from behind and tugged her against him. His cheek nuzzled hers roughly. ''What was their idea of fun?''

''Sleeping around,'' she said huskily. ''That's... suicidal these days. All it takes is the wrong partner and you can die.''

''I know.'' His lips slid down her long, elegant neck. His tongue tip found the artery at her throat and pressed there, feeling it accelerate wildly at his touch. His fingers slid to her slender hips and dug in, welding her to his hard thighs.

''Donavan?'' she whispered unsteadily.

His hands flattened on her stomach, making odd little motions that sent tremors down her long legs and a rush of warmth into her bloodstream.

She didn't act very experienced. The camouflage

was only good at long range, he thought as he drank
in the gardenia scent of her skin. He should have
been disappointed, because he'd wanted her badly
tonight. But something inside him was elated at his
growing suspicion that she was innocent. He had to
find out if it was true.

"Turn your mouth up for me, Fay," he whispered
at her chin. "I want to taste it under my own."

The words sent thrills down to her toes and curled
them. Blind, deaf, she raised her face and turned it,
feeling the sudden warm pressure of his mouth on
her parted lips.

It wasn't at all what he'd expected. The contact
was explosive. He'd been in complete control until
he touched her. Now, suddenly he was fighting to
keep his head at all. He turned her in his arms and
caught his breath as he felt her body melt hungrily
into his.

It shouldn't have happened like this. He could
barely think. His hands bit into the backs of her
thighs and lifted her, pulled at her, needing the close
contact as he'd never needed anything. His legs began to tremble as his body went taut and capable,
and his hands became ruthless.

Fay moaned. Never at any time in her life had she
felt such a sudden, vicious fever of longing. She
could always pull back, until now. With a tiny gasp,
she lifted her arms around his neck and gave in completely. She felt him against her stomach, knew that
he was already painfully aroused. She couldn't manage enough willpower to deny him, whatever the

cost, whatever the risk. He was giving her a kind of pleasure she'd never dreamed of experiencing.

He invaded the silk jacket and the blouse she wore under it. He unbuttoned them and drew the fabric aside seconds before his mouth went down against the bare curve of her breast above her lacy bra. She'd never been touched like that. She clung to him, shivering as his lips became ruthless, his face rubbing the bra strap aside so he could nuzzle down far enough to find the hard, warm nipple.

She cried out. It was beyond bearing, sensation upon hot sensation, anguished joy. Her fingers tangled in his thick, dark hair and pulled at it as he suckled her in a silence throbbing with need.

"You taste of gardenias," he breathed urgently. "Soft and sweet...Fay...!"

His hands were as urgent as his voice. He unfastened her bra and slid it, along with her half-unbuttoned jacket and blouse, right down to her waist. His glazed eyes lingered for one long minute on the uncovered pink and mauve beauty of her naked breasts with their crowns hard and tip-tilted. Then his mouth and his hands were touching them, and she was glorying in his own pleasure, in the sweet delight of his ardor.

"So beautiful," he whispered as he drew his face over her soft breasts. "Fay, you make my body throb. Feel it. Feel me..."

One hand went to gather her hips close to his, to emphasize what he was saying. She moaned and searched blindly for his mouth, inviting a kiss as

deep and ardent as the hand enjoying her soft breasts
in the stillness of the room.

"Little one," he said huskily, "do you know
what's going to happen between us now? Do you
want me?"

"Yes!" she whispered achingly, hanging at his
lips.

His body shivered with its blatant need. It had
never been so urgent before, with any woman. He
bit at her mouth. "Do you have anything to use? Are
you on the pill?"

She hesitated. "No."

No. The word echoed through his swaying mind.
No, she wasn't protected. He could have her, but he
could also make her pregnant. Pregnant! He said
something explicit and embarrassing, then he put his
hands on her upper arms and thrust her away from
him. He went blindly toward the kitchen and
slammed the door behind him.

Fay sat down on the sofa, fastening hooks and buttons with hands so unsteady that she missed half the
buttons and had to start over. It was a long time
before she was back in order again, and only a few
seconds after that, Donavan came in with a tray of
coffee.

She couldn't look at him. She knew her face
looked like rice paper. She was still trembling visibly, too, her mouth red and swollen, her breathing
erratic and irregular.

He put a cup of black coffee in front of her without
saying anything.

She didn't raise her eyes when she felt the sofa

depress near her. She reached for the cup, barely able to hold it for the unsteadiness of her icy fingers.

A big, warm hand came to support hers, and when she looked up, his eyes weren't angry at all. They were faintly curious and almost affectionate.

"Thank you," she stammered as she sipped the hot, black liquid.

He smiled. A real smile, not the mocking ones she was used to. "You're welcome."

"I'm so sorry...!" she began nervously.

He put a long finger over her soft lips. "No. I am. I shouldn't have let it go so far."

"You were angry," she said hesitantly, her eyes glancing with sheer embarrassment off his before they fell to her cup.

"I was hotter than I've been in years and I had to stop," he said simply, and without anger. "It doesn't put a man in a sparkling mood, let me tell you."

"Oh."

He leaned back and sipped his own coffee, his eyes quiet and faintly acquisitive. "Why are you still a virgin?" he asked suddenly.

The coffee cup made a nosedive, and she only just caught it in time. Her gaze hit his with staggering impact. "What did you say?"

"You heard me," he accused softly. "You can't even put on an act, can you? The second I touch you intimately, you're mine."

She flushed and looked away. "Rub it in," she invited.

"Oh, I intend to," he said with malicious glee. "I'm not sure I've ever made love to a virgin in my life. It was fascinating. You just go right in headfirst, don't you? There's not even a sense of self-preservation in you."

She glared at him. "Having fun?"

"Sure." He rested his arm over the back of the sofa and his gaze was slow and thorough as it fell to her breasts and watched their soft rise and fall. "Pretty little creature," he mused. "All pink and dusk."

"You stop that, J. D. Langley," she muttered hotly. "It isn't decent to even talk about it."

One eyebrow went up. "This is the nineties," he reminded her.

"Wonderful," she told him. "Life is liberal. No more rules and codes of behavior. No wonder the world's a mess."

He leaned back, chuckling. "As it happens, I agree with you. Rules aren't a bad thing, when they prevent the kind of insanity that's gripping the world today. But periodically, people have to find that out for themselves. Ever heard of the Roaring Twenties?" he added.

"Gin flowed like water, women smoked, sexually transmitted diseases ran rampant because everybody was promiscuous..."

"You're getting the idea. But it's nothing new. People had cycles when rules were suspended even back in the Roman Empire. There were orgies and every evil known to man thrived. Then society woke up and the cycle started all over again. The only certain thing in life, Miss York, is change."

"I suppose so. But it's discouraging."

"Maybe you haven't heard, but the majority of people in this country feel exactly the same way you do," he said. "America is still a very moral place, little one. But it's what's different that makes news, not what's traditional."

"I see." She smiled. "That's encouraging."

"You come from wealth. Odd that you don't have an exaggerated sense of morality to go with it."

"You mean, because I was rich, I should be greedy and pleasure-loving and indifferent to my fellow man?" she teased. "Actually, that's a stereotype."

"I get the picture." He stared at her silently, his eyes growing dark with memory. "I wanted you like hell. But in a way, I'm glad you aren't on the pill."

She eyed him curiously. "You didn't sound glad."

"Wanting hurts a man when he can't satisfy it," he explained matter-of-factly. "But you weren't on the pill and I didn't have anything with me to protect you from pregnancy. That's one risk I'll never take."

She smiled at him. "I feel the same way."

His eyes warmed. "We'd better not create any accidental people," he said softly. "That's why I stopped. That," he added, "and the fact that I'm too old-fashioned to dishonor a chaste woman. Go ahead. Laugh," he invited. "But it's how I feel."

"Oh, Donavan, you and I are throwbacks to another time," she said heavily. "There's no place for us on earth."

"Why, sure there is, honey," he disagreed. "I'll carry you to church with me one Sunday and prove to you that we're not alone in the way we think.

Listen, it's the radicals who are the minority.'' He leaned closer. "But the radicals are the ones who make news.''

She laughed. "I guess so. I'd like to go to church with you,'' she said shyly. "I haven't been in a long time. Our housekeeper used to let me go to services with her, but when she quit I had no way to get there. It was before I was old enough to drive.''

"Poor little rich girl,'' he said, but he smiled and the words sounded affectionate.

She smiled back. Everything had changed, suddenly. She looked at him and knew without question that she could love him if she was ever given the chance.

He reached out and tapped her cheek. "Let's go. And from now on, stay out of lonely ranch houses with amorous bachelors. Got that?''

"You were the one who dragged me here,'' she exclaimed.

"That's right, blame it all on me,'' he agreed after he'd put the coffee things away and then escorted her out the door. "It's always the man who leads the sweet, innocent girl into a life of sin.''

She frowned. "Isn't it the woman who's supposed to lead the innocent man into it?''

He raised both eyebrows as he locked the door. "There aren't any innocent men.''

"A likely story. What about priests and monks?''

He sighed. "Well, other than them,'' he conceded.

"I like your house,'' she said.

He opened the car door and put her inside. "I like it, too.'' He got in and started the engine, pausing to glance her way. "We may be heading for a fall, but I'm game if you are."

"Game?" she asked blankly.

He slid a lean hand under her nape and brought her face under his, very gently. He bent to kiss her, with tenderness and respect. "In the old days," he whispered, "they called it courting."

She felt a wave of heat rush over her. Wide-eyed, she stared helplessly up at him.

He nodded, his face solemn. "That's right, I said I didn't believe in marriage. But there's always the one woman who can make a man change his mind." His eyes dropped to her mouth. "I want Jeff. If I'm married I have a good chance of getting him. But you and I could give each other a lot, too. If you're willing, we'll start spending time together and see where it leads."

"I'm rich," she began hesitantly.

"Don't worry. I won't hold it against you," he whispered, smiling as he kissed her again. What he didn't mention was that he had his own suspicions about her future. He didn't think she was going to inherit anything at all, and that would put her right in his league. She'd be lost and alone, except for him, when the boom fell. She was sweet and biddable and he wanted her. Jeff needed a stable environment. It wouldn't hurt his chances with the new president of Mesa Blanco to be a settled family man, either, but that was only a minor consideration. Jeff came first. He'd worry about the complications later. Right now, he was going to get in over his head for once without looking too closely at his motives.

Chapter Five

It was all Fay could do to work the next day. She was so lighthearted that she wondered how she managed to keep both feet on the floor.

Her dreams of being with Donavan honestly hadn't included marriage because he'd said that he didn't believe in it. In fact, he'd given her hell for chasing him. How ironic that she'd landed in his orbit at all.

Probably, she had to admit, he needed a wife so that he could gain custody of his nephew, and to help him get ahead in his job. He didn't want a rich wife.

But why, then, was he paying her any attention at all? She'd been honest with him. She'd told him that in a couple of weeks she stood to inherit a fortune. Hadn't he believed her?

Work piled up and she realized that she was paying more attention to her own thoughts than she was to her job, so she settled down to the job-related problems.

"How's everything going?" Abby asked when she came by to meet Calhoun for lunch.

"Great!"

Abby lifted a curious eyebrow. "Really?"

She glanced around her and leaned forward. "Donavan's taking me out."

"J.D.?"

"Don't look so horrified," Fay laughed. "He's serious. He was the perfect gentleman last night and he actually talked about a commitment."

"J.D.?"

Fay nodded. "J.D. Did you know he had a nephew and there's a custody suit in the offing?"

"Yes," Abby said, sobering at once. "The poor little boy's had a hard time. I don't like J.D. a lot, but I'll give him credit for caring about Jeff. He really does." She frowned. "Is that why he's talking seriously?"

"Probably," Fay said, then she smiled. "I don't have any illusions that he's suddenly discovered undying love for me. But he might learn to love me one day. Love takes time."

"Yes," Abby said, remembering. "But you're still rich."

"He said it wouldn't matter."

Abby didn't say another word, until she was alone with Calhoun. "I'm afraid Fay's heading for a bad fall," she told him when they were sharing a quick lunch. "J.D. doesn't seem to mind about her inheritance, but you know how he is about rich women."

"I think he's got some suspicions that her Uncle Henry isn't telling her everything. I have some of my own," he added. "I wonder if Fay has anything left to inherit."

"I had the same feeling. Poor Fay. J.D. doesn't love her, I know he doesn't. He's too much of a womanizer to feel anything deep for a woman."

Calhoun lifted an eyebrow and pursed his lips. "He may be a reforming womanizer." He covered her hand with his and clasped it affectionately. "We all meet our Waterloo eventually. God, I'm glad I met mine with you!"

"Oh, so am I, my darling," she said softly. She leaned forward and kissed him tenderly, despite the amused looks from other diners. "You and the boys are my whole life."

"We've had a good beginning," he agreed. "And the best is still yet to come. We're very lucky."

"Very. I hope Fay fares as well," she added before she concentrated on her food instead of her sexy husband.

Fay didn't see Donavan again for a few days. He'd phoned just to say that he was going out of town on business and that he'd call her when he got back. He hadn't sounded anything like an impatient lover, although he had sounded impatient, as if he hadn't wanted to call her in the first place. She'd been morose ever since, wondering if he'd had second thoughts. Her joy deflated almost at once.

From the day Donavan left, her life went downhill. Two days later she had to go to see Barry Holman about her inheritance. A nervous Uncle Henry was in the office when she got there, and Mr. Holman didn't look very happy.

"Sit down, Fay," Barry said quietly, standing until she was seated.

"It's bad news, isn't it?" she asked, looking from one of them to the other with quick, uneasy eyes.

"I'm afraid so," Barry began, and went on to tell her the bad news. She was penniless.

"I'm sorry, honey," Uncle Henry said heavily. "I did my best, honest to God I did. I pushed you at Sean because I hoped the two of you might hit it off. Sean's rich." His shoulders moved helplessly. "I thought if you married him, you wouldn't have to give up so much."

"Why didn't you tell me?" she asked miserably.

"I didn't know how," he replied. "Your father was a speculator, but for once, he picked the wrong thing to speculate on. I didn't know until a few weeks ago myself, when I tried to liquidate the stock. It fell almost overnight. There's nothing left. Just nothing." He spread his hands. "Fay, you can always come back and live with me..."

"I have a job," she said thinly, remembering almost at once that it was only a temporary job and would soon end. She felt like crying.

"You still have the Mercedes," Barry said surprisingly. "Your father had the foresight to take out insurance that would pay it off if he died. That's yours, and it has a high resale value. I could handle that for you, if you like. Then you'd have a little ready capital and enough over to buy a smaller car."

"I'd appreciate that," she said dully. "I'll get the papers together and bring them by in the morning, if that's all right."

"That will be fine. There are just a few more details, and I'll need your signature in several places..."

Fay hardly heard anything else that was said. She felt numb. In shock. Just a week ago, she'd been in Donavan's arms with a whole future to look forward to and an inheritance to fall back on. Now she had nothing at all. Even Donavan had seemed to have second thoughts, because he'd certainly dropped her flat.

What if he'd only wanted her for the money in the first place? she thought with hysteria. Or to help him provide a settled home so that he could get custody of his nephew?

The more she worried it in her mind, the worse it got. Donavan hadn't wanted her when she was rich, he'd made sure she knew it. Then all at once, about the time he decided to fight for custody of his nephew, he became suddenly interested in her.

It all fit. The only thing that didn't was his abrupt lack of interest. Had he decided he didn't need her after all? Well, she wouldn't do him much good now, she thought wildly. She was just another member of the working class, and what was she going to do when her job folded?

She went through the motions of her job for the rest of the day, white-faced and terrified. Calhoun noticed, but when he asked what was wrong, she only smiled and pretended it was a headache.

That didn't fool him. He knew too much about women. He picked up the phone and called Barry Holman.

"I know it's all confidential and you can't tell me anything," Calhoun said. "But you can pause in significant places. I only want to help. Fay didn't get a damned thing did she?"

There was a long pause.

"That's what I thought," Calhoun said quietly. "Poor kid."

"She really needs that job," Barry replied. "Knowing it's only temporary is probably eating her up. She's never had to depend on herself before."

"No problem there," Calhoun returned, smiling. "Fay's got a job here as long as she can type. We'll find a niche for her. Damn Henry!"

"Not his fault," Barry said. "A bad investment gone sour, that's all. The old story, but a tragic one for Fay. All she's got left is the Mercedes. And you didn't hear this from me," he added firmly.

"Of course not! I'll just sort of mention that she's working out too well to let go and we want to keep her on."

Barry chuckled. "She'll appreciate that."

"We appreciate her. For a debutante, she's a hell of a hard worker." His eyes narrowed. "See you," he said, and hung up. He had another call to make.

He dialed J. D. Langley's number.

"Hello?" came the abrupt reply.

"I thought you were out of town," Calhoun said curtly.

"I was. I just got in fifteen minutes ago. I was

having a cup of coffee. What's wrong?" he asked.
"Something about the cattle?"

"Something about Fay York," Calhoun said.

There was a deathly hush. "Has anything happened to her?" he asked, feeling as if the ground had been cut out from under him. "Is she all right?"

Calhoun felt relieved. That was genuine concern in the other man's voice. Of course, and he hated himself for thinking of it, it could be that J.D. was counting on Fay's money to help him get his nephew. If he was, he was going to do Fay a big favor.

"I'm going to tell you something I'm not supposed to know," he said. "You aren't supposed to know it, either, so don't let on."

"What?"

"Fay didn't get a penny. Her father lost everything. All she inherits is the Mercedes."

J.D. didn't say anything, and Calhoun felt sorry for Fay. Until the sound of soft laughter came over the line and eased his mind.

"So she's busted," Donavan said warmly. "I had a feeling it would work out like that. I'm sorry for her, but I'm damned glad in a way. I wouldn't want people to think another Langley was taking the easy way out with a rich wife."

"You're really serious about her?" Calhoun asked, surprised.

"Why is that so hard to believe? You must have noticed that she's got a heart as big as all outdoors," he replied. Then he spoiled it all by adding, "She's just the kind of foster mother Jeff needs."

"You aren't going to marry her over a custody suit?"

"Whatever it is, is none of your business, Ballenger," J.D. said with icy politeness. "If Fay wants to marry me, that's her affair."

"And if she loves you, what then?"

"She isn't old enough to love anyone yet," Donavan said carelessly. "She's infatuated with me, and she needs a little security. I can give her enough to make her happy."

Calhoun called him a name he wouldn't have wanted Abby to hear. "You're lower than I gave you credit for," he added coldly.

"And it's still none of your damned business. I'll be in to check on the Mesa Blanco stock in the morning." He hung up, leaving Calhoun furious.

After hanging up on Calhoun, Donavan sipped his coffee without really tasting it. He was fond of Fay, and physically she appealed to him as no other woman had. She was innocent, and that alone excited him. He could make her happy.

But the thing was to get Jeff, to rescue the boy who was his sister's only child from the hell he was living in. It had taken all his powers of persuasion and a lot of tongue-biting to get his venomous brother-in-law to let Jeff come up here just for the spring holidays. Possession was nine-tenths of the law. He had Jeff and he was going to keep him. He'd already talked to the lawyer he shared with Mesa Blanco about filing for custody, so the wheels were turning.

"Are you sure you won't mind having me around, Uncle Don?" Jeff asked from his sprawled position in the armchair. With his crewcut and husky physique, he looked the very picture of a boy who was all boy.

"No, sport, I won't," Donavan said. "We get along pretty good most of the time."

Jeff smiled. "Sure we do. Can we go riding tomorrow?"

"Maybe. First we have to go to the feedlot and check up on the feeder cattle. There's someone I want you to meet."

"Fay, right?" he asked, smiling again at his uncle's surprise. "She was all you talked about on the plane," he added.

Donavan lit a cigar and didn't look at the boy. He hadn't realized that he'd been so transparent. He'd missed Fay, but he didn't like admitting it even to himself. He'd been footloose all his life. Even if he married Fay for Jeff's sake, he didn't intend giving up his freedom.

"Aren't you going to call her?" Jeff asked.

"No," Donavan said, frowning. He did want to, but he wasn't going to give in to his impulse. Better to start the way he meant to go on, and acting like a boy with a crush wasn't going to keep him in control of his life.

"It's nice here," Jeff said after a minute. "I hate military school. You can't do anything without permission."

"Don't expect to be able to run wild here," his uncle cautioned.

"No, I don't. But you like me, at least. My step-father hates my guts," he added coldly. "Especially now that he's married *her* and they're expecting their own child. He didn't even love my mother, did you know?"

Donavan's face hardened. "I knew," he said. He didn't elaborate on it, but he knew very well that his brother-in-law's blatant affairs had all but killed his sister. She'd loved the man, but his womanizing had depressed her to the point of madness. A simple case of pneumonia had taken her out of this world, out of her torment, leaving a heartbroken brother and son behind to mourn her. Donavan had hated Jeff's step-father ever since. Better his sister had stayed in mourning for her first husband than pitch headlong into a second marriage that was doomed from the start.

"What did she see in him?" Jeff asked miserably. "He drinks like a fish and he's always off some-where. I think he's running around on his new wife already."

It wouldn't surprise Donavan. After all, he thought viciously, he was running around with his current wife while he was still married to Donavan's sister.

"Let's forget he exists for a few days," he told Jeff. "How about a game of chess?"

"Super!"

While Donavan and Jeff were playing chess, Fay was trying to come to grips with her new situation. She'd always secretly wondered how she would cope if she ever lost everything. Now was her big chance, she thought with black humor, to find out. If she could conquer her fear of having her livelihood depend on her own efforts, she could manage. Thank goodness Donavan had made her take a good look at herself and start learning independence. If she'd still been living with Uncle Henry now, she really would have been terrified.

She understood now why her uncle had been so eager to push her at his business associate, Sean. It had been out of a misplaced protective instinct. He'd hoped she'd marry Sean and be secure when she found out there was nothing left of her parents' estate.

Even though she was grateful for his concern, she wished he'd told her sooner. She put her face in her hands. Well, she could always write to Great-Aunt Tessie and beg for help if things got too bad. She and the old lady had always kept in touch. In fact, there was no one else who loved Tessie just because of her sweet self and not her money. Fay always remembered the elderly woman's birthday. She wondered if anyone else ever had. Certainly not her parents.

She wiped the tears away and wondered when Donavan was coming back. He might not want her now. She had to face the fact that without her wealth, despite what he'd said about not wanting a wealthy woman, he might walk away without looking back. Time would tell. For now, she had enough to keep her busy. She got up from her chair and went to find the paperwork on the Mercedes. At least it would bring a tidy sum, and give her a badly needed nest egg.

The next morning after she'd dropped the papers off at Barry Holman's office, she was working away when the office door opened and Donavan Langley came in with a dark-haired boy at his side.

So he was back. And that had to be Jeff. Her heart ran wild, but she pinned a polite smile to her face as he approached her desk.

"Good morning," she said politely.

"This is Jeff," he replied without answering her. "Jeff, this is Fay York."

"Nice to meet you," Jeff said. He was watching her with open curiosity. "You're pretty."

She flushed. "Thank you."

Jeff grinned. "My uncle likes you."

"That's enough," Donavan drawled. "Go out and look at the cattle. But don't get in the way, and stay out of the pens."

"Yes, sir!"

He was off at a dead run, barely missing one of the amused cowboys. "Keep an eye on him, will you, Ted?" Donavan called.

"Sure thing, Mr. Langley," the cowboy replied, and turned on his heel to follow Jeff.

"He's impulsive and high tempered," Donavan told her. "I have to watch him like a hawk so that he doesn't hurt himself." He searched her eyes with no particular expression on his lean face, but his silver eyes were glittery with contained excitement. She stirred him up. He'd missed her more than he wanted to admit. But she wasn't receptive today. That smile was as artificial as the ficus plant in the pot beside her desk.

"Did you have a nice trip?" she asked for something to break the silence.

He nodded. "Jeff and I got in last night."

And he hadn't called. Well, now she knew where she stood. The fixed smile didn't waver, even if she had gone a shade paler. "He's a nice looking young man."

"He favors his mother. How about lunch? You can go with us to the hamburger joint."

She wanted to, but it was better to break this off now even if it killed her. Things could only get worse, and her life was in utter turmoil.

"I can't today, but thanks anyway."

He started. "Why can't you?"

"I have to see Mr. Holman about selling the Mercedes," she said with stiff pride. "You'll find out sooner or later, so I might as well tell you. I don't have any money. My parents left me without a dime." She lifted her chin and stared at him fearlessly. "All I have is the Mercedes and it's going on the market so that I'll have a nest egg for emergencies."

He didn't like the way she said that. She made it sound as if his only interest in her was what she had. Didn't she know it was her wealth that had stood between them in the first place?

He scowled. "The money didn't matter."

"Didn't it?" she asked bravely.

His gray eyes narrowed. "So you did believe Bart after all. You think I'm as money-crazy as my father." His expression went hard with contained rage. He'd thought she knew him better than that. It hurt to realize that she was just like several other people in Jacobsville who tarred him with the same brush they'd used on his father. "All right, honey. If that's the kind of man you think I am, then take your damned Mercedes and go to hell with it," he said cuttingly. He turned and went after Jeff.

Fay couldn't believe she'd said such a thing to him. Not that it would make any difference, she kept assuring herself. He didn't want her in the first place, so all she'd done was save herself a little more heartache.

Donavan didn't come back through the office on his way out. He took Jeff with him the back route, stormy and unapproachable, smoking his cigar like a furnace all the way to the car.

"What's eating you?" Jeff asked curiously.

"Nothing. What do you want for lunch?"

"A cheeseburger. I thought you said Fay was coming with us? Didn't she want to?"

"She was busy," he said curtly. "Get in."

Jeff shrugged. He wondered if he was ever going to understand adults.

Calhoun paused by Fay's desk, noticing her worn expression and trembling hands.

"J.D.'s been by, I gather," he said dryly.

She lifted her miserable eyes to his. "You might say that. He had Jeff with him."

"And left you here?"

She sat up straighter. "I told him I didn't have any money. He left."

He whistled. "Not a wise move, Fay," Calhoun said gently. "Donavan's touchy about money. You knew that his father—?"

"Yes, I knew," she cut him off gently. "It's for the best," she said. "He didn't really care about me. If he wanted me at all it was because he had a better chance of keeping Jeff if I was around. I'm not stupid. I know he doesn't love me."

Calhoun wanted to deny that, to reassure her, but it was patently obvious that she was right, J. D. Langley wasn't the hearts-and-roses type, but he sure didn't act like a man in love.

"It's early days yet," he told her, wanting to say something positive. "Give him time. J.D.'s been a loner ever since I've known him. He's a lot like Justin. Maybe that's why they get along so well. I have to admit, he and I have never been particularly friendly, but that doesn't have anything to do with you."

"I guess I should apologize," she began.

"Oh, not yet," he said, smiling. "Let him sweat for a while. It will do him good to be on the receiving end for once."

"You mean, he's usually the one who does the jilting," she said, sighing as she remembered how experienced he was. "I guess he's done his share of breaking hearts."

"Be careful of yours," Calhoun said seriously. "There's something I want to mention to you. I told you that this job was temporary, just until Nita came back." He hesitated, noticing her depressed look as she nodded. "Well, I want to offer it to you permanently. I need a secretary of my own, and Nita works a lot better with Justin than she does with me. What do you say? We've been thinking of adding a secretary, but until you came along, we weren't sure exactly what we wanted. You suit me and we seem to work pretty well together. Besides," he added on a chuckle, "Abby might divorce me if I let you go. She thinks a lot of you."

"I think a lot of her." Fay brightened magically. "You really mean it?"

"I mean it. If you want the job permanently, it's yours."

"And Nita won't mind working just for Justin?"

"I've already asked her. She almost kissed my feet. It seems that she's only been putting on a brave face about handling the workload for both of us. Getting some relief has given her a new lease on life. She said she was actually thinking of staying home with the baby just to get away from the work."

"Then I'd love the job, thank you," she said brightly. "You have no idea how much I enjoy working here. Besides," she confessed, not realizing that he already knew her situation, "I'm afraid I'm going to have to work for the rest of my life. My parents didn't leave me anything. I'm flat broke."

"In that case, we'll be helping each other out," he said. "So welcome aboard."

"Thanks, Calhoun," she said, and meant it. "Thanks very much."

"My pleasure."

She turned her attention back to her computer with an improved outlook. At least she had a job, even if she didn't have J. D. Langley. But that might still be for the best. She'd only have been letting herself in for a lot of heartache. It was better not to even begin something that was blighted from the start. And it wasn't as if he loved her. She had to keep remembering that.

The man driving back toward home was trying to keep it in mind himself, while he fumed inwardly at Fay's attitude. He wasn't mercenary, but she thought he was. Like father, like son. He groaned inwardly. Would he never be free of the stigma?

Jeff hadn't said a word, and Donavan couldn't bring himself to tell the boy why Fay wouldn't come to lunch with them. She thought he'd only been keeping company with her because of her money, when he'd already told her he didn't like rich women.

But in all honesty, he had to admit that he'd given her no real reason to think she was of value to him as a person. He'd talked much more about getting custody of Jeff than of wanting her for herself. He'd made love to her lightly, but even that could have convinced her that it was desire mingled with the need for a woman to aid his case to keep Jeff.

He frowned. He hadn't given her any chance at all. To compound it, he'd told her that he'd been back in town for almost a whole day and hadn't even bothered to phone her. He groaned inwardly. He'd made so many mistakes.

Worst of all, he hadn't considered her feelings. She'd just been told that she'd lost everything. All she had to her name was a Mercedes-Benz that she was going to have to sell. It was more than an inheritance she'd lost—it was her whole way of life. She had to be terrified at being responsible for herself. She was only twenty-one, and so alone, because she and her uncle weren't close. She'd needed comfort and help, and he'd told her to go to hell.

"You look terrible, Uncle Don," Jeff broke the tense silence. "Are you sure you're okay?"

"Not yet. But I will be," he said, and abruptly turned around in his own front yard and headed right back toward town. It was quitting time, so Fay would most likely be at home. He didn't know what he was going to say to her. He'd think of something.

Chapter Six

Fay had thought about staying late at the office, just to keep her mind busy, but in the end she decided she would be equally well-off at home. She said good-night to her co-workers and drove the short distance back to her apartment house.

The Mercedes felt uncomfortable now that she was a working girl. It was just as well that Mr. Holman was going to help her sell it. There would be no more luxury cars, no more shopping sprees that didn't include looking at price tags. There would be no more designer clothes. No bottomless bank account to fall back on. She could have cried. She would make it. She knew she would. But getting used to her circumstances was going to take a little time.

She got out of the car and was walking onto the front porch when she heard the roar of a vehicle and saw Donavan driving up next to the Mercedes with Jeff beside him.

Not another fight, she prayed silently, her wan face resigned and miserable even if her eyes did light up helplessly at the very sight of him when he got out and approached her.

He stopped just in front of her, his own expression somber. She looked bad. The camouflage she'd hidden her fears behind had vanished now, because she was tired and her guard was down. He reached out and touched her mouth, dry and devoid of lipstick.

"I'm sorry," he said without preamble. "I didn't think about how you must feel until I was back home."

The unexpected compassion, on top of the emotional turmoil she'd been through, cracked inside her. Tears poured down her cheeks.

"I'm sorry, too," she managed brokenly. "Oh, Donavan, I didn't mean it…!"

His breath caught at her vulnerability, and he was glad he'd made the decision to come back. Without a word, he bent and lifted her in his hard arms and started back toward his car, kissing the tears away as he went, whispering comforting things that she didn't quite hear.

Jeff saw them coming and, with a grin, moved into the back seat. Donavan winked at him before he slid Fay into the passenger seat and trussed her up in her seat belt.

"Stay put," he told her. "We're kidnapping you."

"What will my landlord think?" she asked with a watery smile.

"That you're being kidnapped, of course. We'll take her home and hold her prisoner until she cooks

supper for us," he told Jeff, who was smiling from
ear to ear. "If she's a good cook, I'll marry her right
away."

Fay was trying not to choke. "But you told me to
go to…!" she began.

"Not in front of the boy," he said with a mock
glower. "He isn't supposed to know words like
that."

"What century is *he* living in?" Jeff asked, rolling
his eyes. "Gimme a break, man!"

"Too much TV," Donavan said. "We'll have to
take a plug out of the set."

Fay's head was whirling. "But, Donavan, I can't
cook. That is, I can," she faltered, wiping at her eyes.
"But only omelets and bacon."

"No problem," he said as he started the car. "I
like breakfast. Don't you, Jeff?"

"Sure!"

She gave up. In the scant minutes it took them to
get to the ranch, she'd dried her tears and managed
to gather her composure. She still didn't understand
what had prompted Donavan to come after her, despite the way she'd insulted him, but she wasn't going to question a kindly fate.

Jeff was in a flaming rush to get to the living room
for one of his favorite TV programs, leaving Donavan to escort a worn Fay into the kitchen.

"Mind Bee," he murmured, stepping around the
kitten as she rushed toward them.

"I'll take care of her, Uncle Don," Jeff interrupted. He scooped up the kitten, popped back into
the living room and closed the door behind him. The

blare of the television could be heard even through it.

"The noise takes a little getting used to," Donavan said slowly. He studied Fay, whose hair was straggly as it came loose from its neat chignon. "Why do you wear it like that, anyway?" he asked gently, moving far too close to her. His lean hands deftly separated hairpins from upswept strands, loosening the dark cloud of her hair around her shoulders. "That's better," he whispered. "Now you look like my Fay again."

A tiny sob broke from her lips at the tenderness. Somehow she'd never associated it with him until now.

"I said such terrible things to you," she whispered back, her eyes eloquent.

"I said such terrible things back," he murmured, smiling. "We had a lovers' quarrel. Nothing to lose sleep over. Everything's all right now."

"We aren't lovers," she protested.

His eyes searched hers. "We're going to be, though."

She flushed. "I'm not like that."

He bent and drew his lips with aching tenderness over her own, gently parting them. His hands went to her hips and brought them firmly into the cradle of his, so that she could feel every vibrant muscle and tendon of him close, close against her softness.

"Come on, baby," he breathed into her open mouth. "Don't make me fight for it...."

She lost the will to protest the second she felt his tongue going past her lips, into the darkness beyond.

A white-hot flash of sensation rippled her body in his arms, stiffened her. She caught her breath and then released it in a long, shuddering sigh that he could feel and taste.

"Yes," he said huskily. "That's it. That's it!"

He lifted her by the waist, turning her deftly to the wall. He pinned her there with his body, his long legs pushing between her thighs as he penetrated her mouth with quick, hard thrusts that simulated a kind of joining she'd never experienced.

When he finally lifted his head, she couldn't see anything except his swollen mouth. Her body was throbbing, like the tiny breaths that pulsed out of her, like her heart in her throat.

He leaned closer and bit her lower lip, not hard enough to hurt, but quite hard enough to make her aware of the violence of his passion.

She couldn't move. He had her pelvis completely under his, her legs supported by his, her breasts pinned beneath the heavy pressure of his chest. Behind her, the wall was cold and hard, not warm and alive like the man who had her helpless.

"I think you'd better marry me, Fay," he said huskily. "I don't know how much longer I can protect you."

"Protect me from what?" she asked, dazed by passion.

"Do you really need to ask?" he murmured against her bruised mouth.

"Marriage is a big step," she said weakly.

"Sure it is. But you and I are getting more explosive by the day. I want you like hell, honey, but not in the back seat of my car or some out-of-the-way motel when time permits. You're a virgin. That puts you right off limits.''

"I'm poor," she said. "No, don't look like that," she pleaded, touching his thick eyebrows where they clashed to smooth away the scowl. "I mean, I'd be a burden on you. I'll work, but I can't make much…''

"How do you think other couples manage?" he asked. "For God's sake, I don't care if you're poor! So am I, in a lot of ways. You're much more desirable to me without money than you were with it, and I think you know why.''

"Yes. I shouldn't have said what I did. I was so afraid that you wouldn't want me anymore.''

He lifted an eyebrow. "Does it feel like I don't want you?'' he asked pleasantly.

He hadn't moved, but what he felt was rather blatant and she blushed.

He laughed softly as he let her slide down against him until her feet touched the floor. He loomed over her as he searched her flushed face with indulgent amusement.

"You're priceless," he murmured. "Will you faint on our wedding night, or hide in the bathroom? I'll wager you've never seen a naked man, much less an aroused one.''

"I guess I'll get used to it," she replied gamely.

He chuckled. "I guess you'll have to. Yes or no?''

She took a deep breath. "Yes, then," she said, refusing to worry about his motives or even her own.

She wanted him and he wanted her. She'd worry about the rest of the problems later.

He didn't speak for so long that she was frankly worried that he was regretting the proposal. Then he lifted her hands to his mouth and kissed them with breathless tenderness, and the look in his silver eyes made her feel humble. Whatever he felt right now, it wasn't reluctance. Her heart lifted and flew.

Jeff was called in minutes later and told the news. He literally jumped for joy.

"When?" he asked them.

Fay hesitated. Donavan didn't. "Next week," he said, his eyes daring Fay to challenge him.

"Then," Jeff said, as if he was reluctant to put it into words, "can I stay for the wedding?"

Donavan studied him in a silence that became more tense by the second. "As far as I'm concerned, you can stay until you're of legal age."

"That goes for me, too," Fay said without prompting.

Jeff looked embarrassed. He colored and averted his eyes. Like his uncle, very little showed in his face unless he wanted it to. But his uneasiness was a dead giveaway.

"I'd like that," Jeff said. "But wouldn't I be in the way?"

"No," Donavan said tersely. "We won't have time for a honeymoon right away, and you'll need to be registered in school here, even though it's almost the end of the school year."

Jeff's eyes widened. "You mean I won't have to go back to military school?"

"Not unless you want to," Donavan told him. "I've already started custody proceedings for you."

"Gosh, Uncle Don," Jeff said enthusiastically. "I don't even know what to say!"

"Say okay and go back and watch television with Bee," Donavan mused, glancing warmly at Fay. "I haven't finished kissing Fay yet."

"Oh. That mushy stuff," Jeff said with a sly grin.

"That mushy stuff," Donavan agreed, smiling at Fay's wild-rose blush. "You'll understand in a few years."

"Don't bet on it," the boy murmured. He reached down to retrieve Bee, who was tangling his shoelaces. "I'd like to stay here," he said without looking at them. "I'd like it a lot. But my stepdad won't ever agree."

"Let me worry about that," Donavan told him. "We'll call you when supper's ready."

"Okay. I won't hold my breath or anything, though," he added dryly, and closed the door behind him.

Fay stared up at Donavan and felt as if every dream she'd ever had was about to come true. She had nothing. But if she had Donavan, she had the world.

She said so. He looked briefly uncomfortable. She didn't know that he was unsure of his own reasons for wanting to marry her. He wanted to keep Jeff. He felt a furious physical longing to make love to Fay. But beyond that, he was afraid to speculate. He'd done without love all his life. He wasn't sure he knew what it was.

"I haven't embarrassed you?" she asked worriedly.

He moved forward and drew her slowly into his arms. "No," he said. His eyes searched hers. "It's going to be hard for you getting used to my life-style. I like my own way. I budget like a madman. There's no provision for pretty dresses and expensive cosmetics and a trip to the hairdresser once a week..."

Daringly, she put her fingers against his hard mouth. "I won't miss those things." She traced his lean cheek and his firm mouth and chin, loving the way he tolerated her exploration. "Oh, glory," she said on an unsteady breath. "I'll get to sleep with you every night."

He stiffened at the way she said it, as if being in his arms would lift her right up to heaven. He brought her closer and bent to kiss her with slow, expert thoroughness.

She reached up to hold him back, giving in with exquisite delight pulsing through her body, loving him as she'd never dreamed she could love someone.

He lifted his head feverish seconds later and clasped her shoulders firmly while he looked down at her. "I hope I'm going to be man enough to satisfy you in bed," he said on a husky laugh. "You are one wild little creature, Fay."

She flushed. "I hope that's a compliment."

"It's a compliment, all right," he replied, fighting for enough breath to talk. She confounded him. For an innocent, which he was almost certain she was, there was no reticence in her when he started kissing her. She made his knees weak. In bed, she was going to be the end of his rainbow.

She studied him with soft, worried green eyes. "I haven't ever slept with anyone," she began nervously.

He smiled gently. "I know that. But you've got promise, honey. A lot of it." He leaned close and brushed his lips over her nose. "I'm glad it's going to be with me, Fay," he whispered huskily. "Your first time, I mean."

Her heart ran wild. "So am I."

His lips probed gently at her mouth, teasing it open. "Do you know what to expect?" he breathed.

"I...think so."

His eyes opened at point-blank range, silver fires that burned while she felt his coffee-scented breath on her lips. "I've never been gentle," he whispered. "But I will be. With you."

"Donavan," she breathed, her eyes closing as she pulled him down to her.

He didn't know if he was going to survive the soft heat of her body, the clinging temptation of her mouth. He groaned under his breath as the kiss went on and on, burning into his very soul.

"I can't bear it," he groaned at her lips. "Fay...!"

The tormented sound gave her the willpower to pull gently out of his arms and move away. Her knees felt weak, but he looked as if he was having a hard time standing up straight.

"It's like being thirsty, isn't it?" she asked breathlessly. "You can't quite get enough to drink."

"Yes." He turned away from her and lit a cigar with hands that were just faintly unsteady.

She stared at his long back lovingly, at the body that would one day worship hers. He was going to be her man, her very own. Losing her fortune seemed such a tiny sacrifice to make to have Donavan for the rest of her life.

She smiled to herself. "If you'll show me where the eggs are, I'll make you and Jeff an omelet," she offered. "I'm sorry I can't cook anything else just yet, but I'll learn."

"I know that. Don't worry about it," he added with a fairly calm smile. "I can cook."

"You can teach me," she mused.

"To cook," he agreed. His eyes fell to the visible tautness of her breasts. "And other things."

She smiled with barely contained excitement as she followed him to the refrigerator.

Supper was a gleeful affair, with Jeff laughing and joking with his uncle and Fay as if he'd never had a solemn, sad day in his life. He rode back with them when Donavan eventually drove Fay home and sat in the car while they walked to the door of Fay's apartment house.

"I can't believe the change in Jeff," he remarked as they paused on the darkened porch. "He's not the same boy who came out here with dead eyes and even deader dreams."

"Does his stepfather care about him?"

"Not so anyone would notice," he replied. "He was always jealous of the way my sister got along with Jeff, always resentful of him. He made Jeff's life hell from the very beginning. Since my sister died, it's been much worse.''

"Will he fight you over custody, do you think?''

"Oh, I'm convinced of it,'' Donavan said lightly. "That's all right. I don't mind a good fight.''

"That's what I've heard,'' she murmured dryly.

He chuckled. "I grew up swinging. Had to. My father made sure of that.'' His eyes darkened and the smile faded. "You'll have that to live down, too, if you marry me. Some people won't know that you've lost your inheritance. There will be talk.''

"I don't mind,'' she murmured. "While they're talking about me, they'll be leaving someone else alone.''

"You don't get depressed much, do you?'' he asked quizzically.

"I used to, before you came along.'' She toyed with a button of his shirt, loving the feel of him close to her, the warm strength of his hands on her shoulders. She looked up, her eyes shadowed in the darkness of the porch. "I'm much too happy now to be depressed.''

He frowned. "Fay...I've been alone a long time. Jeff's taking some getting used to. A wife...well, I may make things difficult for you at first.''

"Just as long as you don't have women running through the house in towels or anything,'' she said with an impish smile.

He chuckled. "No chance of that. I've kept to myself in recent years.'' He bent and brushed her mouth lightly with his, refusing to let the kiss ignite this time. "Good night, little one. Jeff and I will pick you up for lunch tomorrow."

"Cheeseburgers, right?"

"Right," he murmured. "I wish we were already married, Fay, and that we were completely alone. I'd carry you up those steps and take an hour stripping the clothes off you."

"Hush!" she giggled. "I don't wear *that* many!"

"You don't understand, do you?" he whispered. "You will."

"That first time we went out, you wouldn't even kiss me," she recalled suddenly.

"I didn't dare. I wanted it too much." He smoothed back her hair. "I figured you'd be addictive, Fay. I was right, wasn't I?"

"I'm glad I am," she said fervently.

"So am I. Good night, sweet."

He turned and left her, and he didn't look back, not even when he'd started the car and drove away. Jeff waved, and she waved back. But Donavan hadn't even glanced in the rearview mirror.

It made her nervous, realizing that he didn't seem to look back. Was it an omen? Was she doing the right thing to marry a man whose only feeling for her was desire?

She worried it all night, but by morning, the only thing she was certain of was that she couldn't live without Donavan. She went into the office resolute, determined to make the best of the situation.

"Is it true?" Abby asked the minute she came in the door later that morning, looking and sounding breathless.

Fay didn't have to ask any questions. She laughed. "If you mean, am I going to marry J. D. Langley, yes."

"Fay, you're crazy," Abby said gently. She sat down beside the younger woman. "Listen, he wants custody of Jeff, that's all. I'll absolve him of wanting your money, but if you think he's marrying you for love…"

Fay shook her head. "No, I'm not that crazy," she assured her friend. "But I care too much to refuse," she added quietly. "He may learn to love me one day. I have to hope that he will."

"It's not fair," Abby argued worriedly.

"It's fair to Jeff," Fay reminded her. "He stands to lose so much if he has to go back to live with his stepfather. He's a great boy, Abby. A boy with promise."

"Yes, I know. I've met him." She sat down on the edge of Fay's desk with a long sigh. "I hope you know what you're doing. I can't see J.D. passionately in love. Calhoun said he was actually cussing you when he left here yesterday."

"He was," she replied dryly. "And I was giving as good as I got. But we made up later."

Abby raised an eyebrow at the blush. "So I see."

"I can't say no, regardless of his reasons for wanting to marry me," Fay said urgently. "Abby, I love him."

The older woman didn't have an argument left. She looked at Fay and saw herself several years before, desperately in love with Calhoun and living on dreams. She knew that she'd have done anything Calhoun had asked, right down to living with him.

She smiled indulgently. "I know how that feels," she said finally. "But I hope you're doing the right thing."

"Oh, so do I!" Fay said with heartfelt emotion.

When Donavan came to pick her up for lunch, the office was empty. Calhoun and Abby had their midday meal together most of the time, and the office girls took an early lunch so that they could be back during the regular lunch hour.

"Where's Jeff?" she asked, surprised that the boy wasn't with him.

"Gone to the movies," Donavan told her, smiling. "He thinks engaged people need some time alone. That being the case," he murmured, tugging her up by one hand, "suppose we buy the ingredients for a picnic lunch and find a secluded spot down by the river where we can make love to each other after we eat?"

She blushed, smiling at him with her whole heart. "Okay."

He chuckled as he pulled her along with him, standing aside to let the first of the office crew back in the building before he escorted her out to his car.

"We're raising eyebrows," he murmured. "Do they know we're engaged?"

"Everybody seems to," she replied.

"Small town gossip. Well, it doesn't matter, does it?"

She shook her head. "Not at all."

They stopped by a grocery store in a nearby shopping center and bought lunch at the take-out deli, adding soft drinks and ice for a small cooler. It wasn't a fancy or expensive lunch, but Fay felt as if it were sheer elegance.

"You look like one of those posed pictures of a debutante at a garden party," he remarked, his eyes on the way her gauzy white-and-green patterned dress outlined her body as she lay across from him on a spot of grass.

"I feel that way, too," she mused, tossing her long hair as she arched her back and sighed. Her eyes closed. "It's so peaceful here."

"If that's a complaint..."

The sound of movement brought her eyes open just in time to find Donavan levering his jean-clad body over hers. He was smiling, but there was a kind of heat in the smile that made her body begin to throb.

His elbows caught his weight as he eased down on top of her, his long legs cradling hers in a silence tense with promise. His eyes dropped to her mouth.

"This is as good a time as any for you to start getting used to me," he whispered. His hips shifted slowly, first to one side, then to the other. The faint movement aroused him and he tensed as the familiar heat shot through him like fire.

Fay watched his face contort slightly even as she felt the changing contours of his body. Her lips parted on a held breath.

"A hundred years or so ago, when I was young and hot-blooded, that was a frequent and worrying occurrence. These days," he mused, watching her flushed face, "it's more of a delightful surprise. I like the way my body reacts to you."

"It doesn't...react to other women like this?" she asked, torn between embarrassment and curiosity.

He shook his head. "Only to you, apparently. I must be getting old. Either that, or a diet of virginal shock is rejuvenating me."

"It isn't shock. Well, not exactly," she faltered.

"No?" He bent and gently parted her lips. One long, powerful leg began to ease its way between hers, parting them and spreading her skirt on the cool ground. He felt her gasp and lifted his head. "We don't have a lot of time for courtship," he breathed. "We need to get used to each other physically before we marry. It will make it easier."

"I've never done this," she said nervously.

"Not even this far?" he asked, surprised.

She shook her head. "My parents were very strict. So were the relatives I used to stay with. They all said it was a sin to let a man do what he liked to a woman's body."

"Perhaps in some respects it is," he replied quietly. "But you and I are going to be married. One day, I'm going to put my seed deep in your body and you're going to have my baby. That won't be a sin of any kind."

The words, so carelessly spoken, had a very uncareless reaction on Fay. Her eyes went wide and watchful, and her face went scarlet.

He felt her sudden tension, saw it in her face. "That excites you, does it?" he whispered huskily. His eyes fell to her breasts, and he watched the nipples go hard with quiet pride before he caught her shocked eyes again. "You have pretty breasts."

The blush exploded and he chuckled. "I shouldn't tease you, Fay. Not about something so profound. But it's irresistible. As irresistible as…this."

And as he spoke, he bent suddenly and put his open mouth over the hard tip of her breast.

Chapter Seven

Fay thought that if she died and flew into the sun she couldn't have felt any greater explosion of heat. The feel of Donavan's hot mouth on her body, even through the cloth, was incredible.

She arched against him and made a sound, half gasp, half groan, while her nails bit into his hard shoulders.

His teeth nipped her delicately, before his tongue began to swirl around the hard tip and make it unbearably sensitive to the moist heat of his mouth.

"Please," she whispered huskily. "Please, please, please…!"

He barely heard her through his own need. His fingers were quick and rough on her bodice, painful seconds passing before he managed to disarrange the hated fabric that kept her soft skin from his mouth. He found her with his lips and his hands simultaneously, and she clung to him, no thought of protest

in her whirling mind as she fed on the feverish tasting of his mouth, the hot sensuality of his hands on
her body.

"Don...avan!" she sobbed.

He lifted his head abruptly and looked at her.

"My God, you're beautiful, Fay," he said unsteadily. "The most beautiful creature unclothed that
I've ever seen in my life!"

"I want you," she said weakly.

"I want you, too."

"Here."

He shook his head, fighting for sanity. He had to
drag his eyes away from her body to meet her own.
"No. Not now. We aren't married, little one."

"It...doesn't matter!" she wept, her body racked
with need.

"Yes, it does." Gently he disengaged her hands
and put her clothing to rights. When she was dressed
again, he rolled onto his back and pulled her down
into his arms. He held her while she cried, his voice
soothing, his hands gentling her while the storm
passed.

"I'm a lucky man, Fay," he said when she was
quiet again. "A very lucky man."

"I think I'm the lucky one," she said breathlessly,
clinging.

He bent and kissed her, his silver eyes looking
straight into hers while his lean hands framed her
flushed face gently. "We're taking a big step together," he said then, and looked solemn. "I hope
for both our sakes, and Jeff's, that it's the right one."

"It will be," she assured him. Somehow, she

knew it. But it didn't escape her notice that he looked unconvinced.

The next week went by in a pleasant haze. Fay spent every free moment with Donavan and Jeff, taking just time enough to go shopping with Abby for her wedding gown. She chose an oyster-hued suit, which was sensible, because it would go with everything she had left in her wardrobe. She splurged on a hat, too, and a veil to drape over it. She worried about the amount of money she'd spent, because it was no longer possible to buy without looking at price tags. But Donavan only smiled when she mentioned that, and told her that getting married certainly warranted a little splurging.

The ceremony was held at the local church where Donavan was a member, and half the population of Jacobsville turned out for the occasion. Most everyone knew by now that Fay had lost everything, and even Donavan's cousin Bart was civil to him.

Jeff stayed with the Ballengers while Donavan drove himself and his new bride all the way to San Antonio for their two-day honeymoon. They had supper on the paseo del rio, where lighted barges went past with mariachi bands and music filled the flower-scented air.

"There can't be any place on earth more beautiful than this," she commented when she finished the last bite of her apple pie à la mode and looked at her new husband with quiet possession.

He cocked an eyebrow, very handsome in the pale gray suit he'd worn to be married in. He hadn't changed. Neither had she. She was still wearing her off-white suit, because they hadn't wanted to take the time to change earlier.

"Aren't you disappointed that I couldn't offer you a week in Nice or St. Tropez?"

She smiled and shook her head. "I'm very happy. I hope I can make you that way, too."

His returning smile became slowly wicked. "Suppose I take you back to our room now? I want to see how many times I can make you blush before I show you what physical love is."

Her heart beat faster. "All right," she whispered with barely contained excitement, and was unable to meet his eyes as he paid the bill and led her out into the sweetly scented night.

"Are you afraid of it, Fay?" he asked in the elevator, where they were briefly alone.

"A little, I think," she confessed with a nervous laugh. She looked up at him. "I don't want to disappoint you. I know you aren't innocent..."

He smiled gently. "I've never been married, though," he reminded her. "Or had a virgin to initiate." The smile faded. "I'll try not to hurt you too much."

"Oh, I'm not worried about...that," she faltered.

"Aren't you?" he mused knowingly as the elevator stopped.

They entered the room and he locked the door behind them, but when her cold hand went toward the light switch, he caught it.

"It will be easier for you in the dark," he whis-

pered as he brought her gently close. "I don't want
you to see me just yet."

"Do you have warts?" She laughed, trying to
make a joke of it.

"No. You'll understand a lot better in the morning. For now," he said, swinging her up in his arms
as he started toward the bed, "let's enjoy each
other."

She'd never dreamed that she could lie quietly
while a man took her clothes off, but she did. Donavan made what could have been an ordeal into a
breathless anticipation, kissing her between buttons
and catches, stroking her body gently to relax her
while he slowly and deftly removed every stitch she
had on. Then he pulled her against him, and she felt
the faint abrasion of his suit while he began to kiss
her.

"You...you're still dressed," she whispered.

He bit at her mouth with lazy delight. "I noticed.
Open your mouth a little more. That's it." He kissed
her very slowly and his hand smoothed down over
her taut breasts, making her gasp, before it left a
warm trail down her flat belly to the soft inside of
her thighs. "Don't faint," he whispered as he
touched her intimately for the first time and felt her
tense. "Relax, Fay," he breathed at her lips as he
trespassed beyond even her wildest and most erotic
dreams. She cried out and he made a rough sound,
deep in his throat. "My God, this isn't going to be
the best night of your life. Listen, sweetheart, do you
want to wait until you can see a doctor?" he asked,
lifting his head. "I don't want to frighten you, but

this barrier isn't going to be easily dispensed with. You know, don't you, that I'm going to have to break it before I can take you?''

"Yes." She swallowed. "Will it hurt you, too, if you do?"

"More than likely." He rolled onto his back and pulled her close, his body pulsating with its denied need while he fought his inclination to say to hell with it and go ahead. He needed her, but he didn't want to hurt her, to make intimacy something that would frighten and scar her.

"I didn't know," she said hesitantly. "I've never had any female problems, and I didn't think I needed a prenuptial checkup..."

He smoothed her long hair gently. "I'm not fussing, am I?" he murmured.

"I'll bet you feel like it," she said miserably. She laughed and then began to cry. "I've ruined everything!"

"Don't be absurd." His arms tightened and he rolled over against her, his mouth warm and soft and slow as his hand moved down her body again. Instead of probing, this time it touched, lightly, sensually. She gasped and instinctively caught his hand, but it was already too late. The pleasure caught her by surprise and for minutes that seemed never to end, she was oblivious to everything except her husband.

A long time later, he got up, leaving her wide-eyed and more than a little shaken on the bed. He turned the lights on and looked at his handiwork, from the drowsy, sated green eyes to the pink luxury of her sprawled body. She was too fulfilled to even protest the intimacy now, and his expression was just faintly smug.

"No need to ask if you liked it," he murmured unforgivably and began to take off his clothes.

She watched him with visible pleasure. He had a stunning body, very powerful and darkly tanned, except for a pale band where she imagined his swimming trunks normally rested. He was lightly feathered all over with dark, curling hair, except for his chest and flat stomach, where it was thickest. He turned toward her and she caught her breath, unable to take her eyes off him. Even like this, he was any woman's dream. Especially like this.

He knelt over her, his eyes glittering with unsatisfied desire. "Now it's my turn," he whispered, easing down beside her. "I want what I gave you."

"Anything," she choked. "Teach me…!"

His mouth covered hers, and lessons followed that banished her shyness, her fear, her inhibitions. When he cried out a second time and was still, she lay against him with drowsy pleasure and closed her eyes in satisfied sleep.

They went back home the next morning. Donavan murmured dryly that he wasn't spending another night playing at sex when they could have the real thing after she saw the doctor. She did, first thing Monday morning, although the minor surgery was a little embarrassing. The doctor was pleased at Donavan's care, because, he added, it would have been an unpleasant experience for both of them if her new husband had been impatient. He sent her home with a smile and she dreamed for the three days it took for the discomfort to pass.

It was going to be the most exciting night of Donavan's life, Fay promised herself as she got everything ready. She'd already asked Abby to keep Jeff for that one evening, without telling her why, and Jeff had agreed with a murmured dry remark about newlyweds needing some privacy. Nobody knew that the marriage hadn't been consummated. But tonight it was going to be.

Fay had a bottle of champagne chilling. She'd cooked a special meal and made a crepe dessert, things she'd had Abby show her how to do. Everything looked delicious. Even Fay, who was wearing one of the only sexy dresses she possessed, a little strappy black satin number that showed off her full breasts and her long, elegant legs in the nicest possible way. She'd left her hair loose around her shoulders, the way Donavan liked it, and sprayed herself with perfume. He'd been exquisitely patient and caring for the past few nights, contenting himself with a few gentle kisses and the feel of her in his arms and nothing more. Tonight, she was going to make him glad he'd been so considerate.

She heard his car pull up in the driveway, very impatiently, and heard the vicious slam of his door. Something must have upset him at work, she thought as she quickly lit the candles on the table. Well, she had the cure for that.

She turned as he threw open the front door and came in. That was when she realized that what had upset him wasn't the job. He was staring at her with undisguised fury, his whole look accusing and violent.

"You didn't tell me you had a great-aunt who could buy and sell Miami Beach."

She blinked and had to think hard. "You mean Great-Aunt Tessie," she faltered. "Well, yes, but…"

His face hardened. His lean hand almost crushed the hat he'd just swept from his damp hair. "Your uncle Henry had a call a few minutes ago. He wanted me to break the news to you." He took a steadying breath. "Your great-aunt died last night. You inherit everything she owned, and that includes millions of dollars."

He was white in the face. Now she knew why. She sat down heavily. "Tessie is dead? But I had a letter from her just last week. She was fine…"

"You didn't tell me," he ground out. "Why?"

She lifted her eyes. "I never thought of it. Honestly," she said dully. Tears stung her eyelids. She'd been very fond of Tessie. "I loved her. Her money never made any difference to me. I expected she'd leave it to charity. She knew I didn't need it."

"Didn't, as in past tense." He nodded. "But now you're not a woman of property. Or are you?"

"I can always refuse it," she began.

"Don't bother. I assume you'll want to fly down there," he said shortly. "Your uncle will go with you. He said he'd make the travel arrangements and let you know later." He tugged at his tie, glaring at her.

"It's not my fault," she said huskily, tears pouring down her cheeks.

"Don't you think I know that?" he replied, his eyes cold and dark. "But it changes everything. I won't stay married to you. Not now."

"What about Jeff?" she gasped. "The custody suit?"

"I don't know…"

He was uncharacteristically hesitant. She went closer to him. "We don't have to tell anyone," she said. "I'll swear Uncle Henry to secrecy. We can stay married long enough for you to get Jeff away from his stepfather. Then we can get a…a divorce."

"Divorce?" he asked with a curt laugh. "An annulment." She flushed. "Had you forgotten, baby?" he asked mockingly. "We played at sex, but we never had it. Now it's just as well that we didn't. No harm done. You can find yourself some society boy in your own circle and get married again."

"And you?"

He shrugged indifferently and turned away before she could see his face. "I'll have Jeff."

"You don't want me?"

"What I want or don't want doesn't enter into it anymore," he said coolly, careful not to let her see his face. "The last thing I can afford is to have Jacobsville start gossiping about another Langley marrying for money, especially when I've got Jeff's future to think about."

"Oh, I see."

She did, painfully. Donavan would never want her with millions. He was a proud man. Much too proud to withstand the snide remarks and gossip. Even if he was less proud, there was Jeff. The boy shouldn't have to suffer for things he'd never done.

"I'll...just phone Uncle Henry," she said, but Donavan didn't answer her. He went out and closed the door.

The next morning, he drove her and her uncle to the airport and put them on a plane. The Ballengers had been very understanding about her absence from work for a couple of days, and Abby was glad to fill in for her under the circumstances. They all put down Fay's apathy to her fondness for her great-aunt, so it was just as well they didn't see her with Donavan. His fierce scowl might have changed their minds.

"Thanks for driving us here," Henry said uncomfortably. "Fay, I'll wait for you on the concourse."

"Yes." She watched him go with dull eyes before she lifted her own to Donavan.

"You haven't slept, have you?" he asked formally. And he had to ask, because he'd moved out of her bedroom the night before without a word.

She shook her head. "I was fond of Great-Aunt Tessie. We were good friends."

"I wasn't very sympathetic last night," he said stiffly. "I'm sorry..."

Her chin lifted proudly. "I haven't asked for anything from you, have I, Donavan?" she asked with expression. "And I won't. I'll stay with you until the custody hearing. Then, as you suggested, we can get an annulment."

"What will you do?" he asked.

She only laughed. She felt a million years old.

"What do you care?" she asked without looking at him. She picked up the case he'd been carrying for her. "I haven't told the Ballengers about what I'll inherit, and I hope you won't," she said over her shoulder. "Until I talk to her lawyers, nothing is really certain."

"Don't make some stupid decision about that money out of misplaced loyalty to me," he said coldly, forcing himself to smile as if he didn't give a damn about her. Letting her give up millions to live a modest life-style with him, out of nothing but desire, would be criminal. "I only married you to get Jeff. Maybe I wanted you, too," he added when she looked at him. "But bodies come cheap, honey. I've never gone hungry."

Her face went, if possible, a shade paler. "It's nice to know that I'll be leaving you heart-whole and unencumbered. Goodbye, Donavan."

"Not goodbye," he said carelessly. "So long."

She shook her head. "No, I meant it. I'll come back. I'll stay, for Jeff. But in every other way, it's goodbye." Her eyes fell away from his and she tried not to feel the bitter wound of rejection that made her insides hurt. Every step was one less she'd have to repeat. She thought about that as she counted them. She didn't look back, either. She was learning, as he apparently already had, not to ever look back.

The trip to Miami was long and tiresome. She and Uncle Henry spent two days dealing with Great-Aunt Tessie's possessions, saving keepsakes and arranging for disposal of everything else. The very last stop was the lawyer's office, where Fay sat beside her uncle with dead eyes, hardly aware of her surroundings.

"I know the will seems cut-and-dried," the attorney said apologetically, glancing at Fay and grimacing, "but I'm afraid it was altered just recently without my knowledge. Tessie's maid found the new will in her bedside table, witnessed and properly signed."

Henry's eyebrows raised. "Did she leave the whole shooting match to her cats?" he asked with a chuckle.

"Oh, it's a little better than that," the attorney returned, reading over the document. "She left it to open a chain of hostels that would house the families of children with incurable cancer. It seems her housekeeper's sister had a child with leukemia and was having to drive a hundred miles a day back and forth because she couldn't afford to stay in a hotel… Mrs. Langley, are you all right?"

Fay was aghast. Delighted. Unbearably pleased. She looked at the attorney. "You mean, I don't have to take the money?"

Her wording shocked him, when very little ever had. "You don't want it!"

"Oh, no," she agreed. "I'm quite happy as I am."

"Well, I'm not," Henry muttered. "She could have left me a few sticks of furniture or something."

"But she did," the attorney recovered himself enough to add. "There's a provision for the contents of her apartment to be sold at public auction and the proceeds split between the two of you. I should say it will amount to very nearly a quarter of a million dollars. There is, too, her jewelry, which she wanted to go to Mrs. Langley—provided none of it is sold. Heirlooms, you know.''

Fay smiled. "Some of the pieces date back three hundred years to European royal houses. I'd never sell it. It should go to descendants.'' She realized that she wouldn't have any now, and her face fell.

"At least we got something,'' Henry told her once they were outside. "I don't feel so bad that your inheritance didn't come through, now.''

"There was nothing you could have done,'' Fay assured him. "I don't have any hard feelings.''

He stared at her curiously. "You didn't want Tessie's money?''

She shook her head as they walked back to the rented car. "Not at all. Donavan would never have married me in the first place if I'd been rich.''

"Yes. He does have a sore spot about his father.'' He glanced at her. "Well, this slight in Tessie's will should make your marriage a little more stable. I can imagine what J. D. Langley would have thought if you'd inherited all that money.''

"Yes. Can't you, though?'' Although she was thinking that if he'd loved her, money wouldn't have mattered at all. He'd tossed her out on her ear because he thought she was inheriting Tessie's money. He didn't want her rich. Well, that was all right with her. A relationship based on money—no matter if it was too much or too little—wasn't the right kind. She'd go on with her job at the feedlot and tell him that her inheritance was going to be tied up for a

time. Beyond that, he didn't really need to know anything else. He'd thrown her out. She had to consider
that maybe he'd done her a favor. She was falling
more in love with him by the day. But aside from
his need to keep Jeff and his desire for her, there was
nothing on his side worth fighting for. As he'd already said, he could have all the women he needed.
What would he want with Fay?

She did feel somewhat responsible for Jeff,
though, since she'd agreed to the marriage in the first
place partly to help rescue him from his stepfather.
She liked the boy. For his sake, she wasn't going to
walk out on J. D. Langley. She'd stick with them
until the court case was settled one way or the other.
Then she'd make whatever decisions had to be made.

It was ironic, though, that she'd gone to her marriage bed a virgin and left it still a virgin, even if she
had learned quite a lot about pleasure in the process.
She wondered if she could get into *The Guinness
Book of Records?*

She packed her things and got ready to head back
to Jacobsville. She didn't seem fated to be rich anymore, and she was rather glad about it. It was one
thing to be born into money, quite another to learn
to make it in the world without a big bankroll to fall
back on.

If Donavan had loved her, she'd have had everything. She remembered so many good times with
him, so much sweetness and pleasure. He'd genu-
inely seemed to like her at times, and his desire for
her had been quite unmistakable. But desire wasn't
love.

She couldn't settle for a man who looked at her as an infrequent dessert that he could live without. She wanted to be loved as well as wanted, to be cherished just for herself. Donavan had put conditions on their relationship that she couldn't meet. Be poor and I'll want you, he'd as good as said. If he'd loved her, whether she was rich or poor wouldn't have mattered. And all the gossip in the world wouldn't have made any difference.

Donavan had never loved, so he couldn't know that. But Fay did. She had to go back to him now and pretend that she didn't love him, that they were simply two people living together for the sake of a child. They weren't even legally married, because the marriage hadn't been consummated. She laughed bitterly. Jeff's stepfather could have had plenty of fun with that charge in court, but nobody knew except Donavan and herself, thank God.

She closed the case she'd been packing and went to phone the bellhop station. She had to go home and face Donavan, and the future.

Chapter Eight

When Fay and her uncle arrived at the airport, it was a shock to find Donavan waiting for them.

She shot a curious glance at her uncle, but he looked as surprised as she did.

"We could have gotten a cab," she began, her very calm voice belying the turmoil that the sight of Donavan engendered in her.

"It was no hardship to pick you up," he said easily. He was smoking a cigar, wearing working clothes that were clean if not new. His Stetson was cocked over one eye so that it wasn't possible to see the expression on his lean face. Just as well, too, he thought, because he wasn't ready for Fay to find out how glad he was to see her. The days had been endless since she left, and his conscience was hurting him. He'd been unkind to her at a time when she'd needed compassion and a shoulder to cry on.

"This is decent of you, Donavan," Henry said as

he shouldered cases and followed Donavan out to the car. "I hate cabs."

Fay didn't comment. She clutched her purse and her overnight bag tightly, not returning Donavan's quiet, close scrutiny. She didn't care what he did or said anymore, she told herself. He'd hurt her for the very last time.

He dropped Henry off and not a word was spoken until he escorted Fay into the house.

"Jeff's in school," he told her when she noticed the sudden hush in the house. Only Bee, the kitten, was in evidence when Donavan came back from depositing her bags in her room. He picked her up with a faint smile and deposited her in a chair.

"You enrolled Jeff in school here, then?" she asked.

"Yes." He stopped just in front of her, his silver eyes probing as he looked down at her in the off-white suit she'd been married in. It brought back painful memories.

"How are you?" he asked.

"Still kicking," she replied dryly. "I'm not bleeding, Donavan, so you don't need to worry over me. I won't be a problem. Now, if you'll excuse me, I'll unpack and change. Then I'll see about starting something for supper."

"You don't have to..." he began irritably.

"I don't mind." She turned away, cutting him off before he could sway her resolve. "You've said it all already," she added without turning. "Let's just leave it alone. Have you heard from your lawyer about the custody hearing?"

"Yes," he said after a minute. "It's scheduled for next week."

She didn't know what else to say, so she nodded and left him there. It was some small consolation that he seemed as ill at ease as she felt. Their marriage was over before it had even had a chance to begin. She wished they could start again. But she doubted that Donavan believed in second chances any more than she did herself.

It was a silent meal. Jeff looked from one of them to the other with curiosity and faint uneasiness.

"I'm sorry about your great-aunt, Fay," Jeff said when they were eating the pudding she'd made for dessert. "I guess you're still sad."

"Yes," she agreed without argument. "Great-Aunt Tessie was special. She was a renegade in a day and age when it wasn't popular."

"Was she really rich?"

Fay hated the question, but she couldn't very well take out her wounds on the boy. "Yes, Jeff, she was. Very rich. But money isn't the most important thing in the world. It won't buy good health or happiness."

"Yeah, but it sure would buy a lot of Nintendo games!" he enthused.

She laughed despite herself. But Donavan was silent all through the meal, and afterward.

While Fay was washing dishes, he came into the room. His hands were dangling from the thumbs in his jeans pockets, his silver eyes watchful in a face like a carving in a stone cliff.

"I heard you call Abby Ballenger just before supper. Why? Did you tell her you were resigning?'' he asked slowly.

"I'm not resigning. You do realize that paperwork and so forth takes time?'' she added, playing for time. "I don't automatically inherit. Neither does Uncle Henry.''

"You wouldn't have known that by the way he was talking on the way to his house,'' he reminded her with a calculating smile. "He's already got his money spent. Or he will have, by the time he actually gets it.''

She didn't speak. He made her nervous. It was impossible to be in the same room with him and not remember how it had been between them that one night of their honeymoon. Even without the ultimate intimacy, she'd had a taste of Donavan that still could make her head spin. She loved him with all her heart. It wouldn't have mattered if he'd owned several multinational corporations or only a rope and an old horse. She loved him so much that his circumstances would never have made any difference. But he didn't feel the same about her, and she didn't need him to put it into words. She had money—or so he thought—and he didn't, so he didn't want her. Nothing would alter his opinion one iota, and she knew that, too.

"I should have stayed there with you, shouldn't I?'' he asked unexpectedly. "You look worn to a nub, Fay. All that grief and your uncle to deal with at once. I suppose all the details were left up to you.''

It was a question, she supposed. "Yes,'' she replied. "Uncle Henry was able to make the funeral arrangements, though, with the attorney's help. I sorted out the things in the apartment—'' She stopped, blinking to stay the tears. She washed the same plate again, slowly. "It was so empty without her.''

He hesitated. "So was this house, without you in it,'' he said gruffly.

She swallowed. She didn't dare turn around. "Thanks, but you don't have to pretend. I haven't lived here long enough to make any real difference in your life, or Jeff's. You're a better cook than I am, and you've had people to help you straighten up. I'm just a temporary convenience. Nothing more.''

He was conscious of a terrible wounding in her and in himself. Had he made her feel so inadequate that she thought he was better off without her than with her?

"The boy wants to see that new adventure movie that just came out. It's playing at the Longview. Want to come with us?''

"Oh, no, I don't think so,'' she forced herself to say. "I'm very tired. You two go ahead, and enjoy yourselves. I just want to go to bed and sleep the clock around.''

He hesitated. "Fay, we can wait until you're rested.''

"I don't like movies, honestly,'' she said quickly. "But thanks all the same.''

He moved closer, his eyes narrow and concerned. "You've had a rough time lately, and I haven't been much help. Listen, Fay...''

"I don't need pity,'' she said, her voice steady

despite the turmoil his nearness aroused. She dried her hands and sidestepped away from him. "I'm learning to stand on my own two feet. I won't pretend it's easy, but I think I'm finally getting the hang of it. After the custody hearing next week, I may see about moving back to my apartment house."

"You're assuming that I'll win it," he said formally. "There's a good chance that I won't. And if you tip out the front door hours later, Jeff's stepfather may appeal the court's decision even if I do win. Proof of an unstable home life would cost dearly."

Incredible that he sounded so determined to keep her with him, when she knew that wasn't what he wanted at all. Of course, it was for Jeff's sake. He loved the boy, if he loved no one else.

"All right," she said, sounding and feeling trapped. She sighed deeply. "I'll stay as long as you need me."

"If you stay that long, you'll never leave," he said curtly.

He turned and left the room, with Fay staring after him in a daze, not quite sure that she'd really heard him right. Probably, she thought later, it was only wishful thinking on her part.

They fell into a routine as the days passed. Fay went back to work, despite Donavan's comment that she was taking a job that someone else might really need, and Jeff went to school each day and began to look the very picture of a happy boy.

Fay worked harder than she ever had before, deliberately putting in late hours and paying more at-

tention to detail than ever. Calhoun and Justin Ballenger were complimentary and appreciative of her
efforts. Donavan was not.

"You do nothing but work!" he complained one
evening when she wasn't working late—a rarity in
recent days. "Don't Jeff and I count with you?"

"Uncle Don, Fay has to do her job right," Jeff
pointed out. He grinned. "Besides, Mr. Ballenger
says she's saved them plenty with all that hard
work."

Donavan finished his dessert and reached for the
carafe, to pour himself a second cup of coffee. "So
I hear."

"You don't work any less hard yourself," Fay accused him. "And I don't complain."

His silver eyes met hers with cold impact. "Most
brand-new wives would."

He was making an insinuation that, fortunately,
went right over Jeff's head. But Fay knew what he
was really saying, and she flushed.

"Yes, well, ours is hardly a normal situation."

"It could be," he said, startling her into looking
up. There was no teasing, no mockery in his expression. He was deadly serious.

Fay flushed. "There's no time."

He lifted an eyebrow. "I beg your pardon?"

The flush grew worse. Jeff finished the last of his
dessert and excused himself. "I want to get out of
the line of fire," he said dryly, and closed the door
into the living room. Seconds later, the TV blared
out.

"Turn that damned thing down!" Donavan raged.

"You bet!" Jeff said irrepressibly and barely touched the knob.

Donavan, placated, was still glaring at Fay. "We're husband and wife," he reminded her. "There's no reason on earth that you can't share a bed with me."

"There's a very good one," she differed. She put down her napkin. "When Jeff's situation is resolved, I don't plan to stay here any longer than I have to. I won't risk getting pregnant."

His face drained of color. He looked...wounded. Cut to the bone. Fay felt sick at the careless comment when she saw its results. She hadn't even meant it. She loved him, but he only wanted her. She was fighting for her emotional survival, with the few weapons she had left.

"I didn't mean that," she said stiffly, averting her eyes. "Not like it sounded. But you must realize I'm right. A baby right now would...would complicate things."

"You don't think children can be prevented?" he asked with cutting sarcasm.

She lifted her eyes to his. "I won't be around that much longer," she said quietly. "I realize I must be stifling your sex life, and I'm sorry, but very soon I'll be gone and you can... Your life can get back to normal."

He grew colder in front of her eyes. He threw down his napkin and slowly got to his feet. "So that's what it's come down to in your mind. I'm hot for a woman and you're someone I can use in the meantime, until I'm free."

She went scarlet. "You can't pretend you feel anything other than desire for me," she said proudly. "After all, I'm rich."

His gaze averted to the table. He stared at it for a long moment. "Yes." He'd almost forgotten. Memories came back, of his father's greed, the censure after Rand Langley's second wife had committed suicide.

He left without another word. After a few minutes, Fay got up and cleared away the dishes. Well, what had she expected him to do, deny it? She laughed at her own folly and then had to bite back tears.

The court hearing was only two days away now, and both Jeff and Donavan were looking as if the pressure of it was giving them some problems.

Fay went by the video rental store and found three movies that would probably appeal to the two men in her life—both of whom were adventure fans—and presented them after supper.

"Wow!" Jeff enthused. "I've wanted to see these for ages! Thanks, Aunt Fay!"

"I didn't think you liked adventure films," Donavan remarked.

She shrugged. "I can take them or leave them. But I thought they might take Jeff's mind off court." She looked up at him curiously. "Have you heard anything from his stepfather, even through the lawyer?"

He shook his head. "It wouldn't surprise me to find that he's having us watched, though."

"Why?"

"Looking for anything to further his case." He laughed coldly. "It would be like him."

"Neither of us has been indiscreet," she reminded him primly, but with a nervous glance.

He glared at her. "I told you, I don't have women on the side. As long as we're married, you're it."

She averted her face. "Thank you."

"I hope that I can expect the same courtesy?"

Her eyes on his face were explosive and expressive. "You don't have to worry about that. I don't attract too many men now that I'm not rich anymore!"

The slip caught Donavan's attention. "You just inherited a fortune," he reminded her.

"Oh. Oh, yes," she faltered. She turned away quickly. "Nevertheless, I'm not going to break my wedding vows."

"I never thought you would, Fay," he said unexpectedly. He moved close behind her and caught her waist gently in his lean hands. "You needn't flinch like that." His voice was quiet, tender. "I may be a 14-karat heel, but I wouldn't hurt you physically."

"I know that," she said breathlessly. "And I don't think you're a heel. You love Jeff very much, don't you?"

He heard the jerky sound of her breathing and moved even closer, his powerful body all but wrapping around hers from behind. His face eased down so that his cheek was against hers, his warm breath sighing out at the corner of her mouth.

Her cold hands rested uneasily atop his, tremulous

as the spell of his nearness made her pulse race wildly.

"It's easy to love a child," he said heavily. "Even a neglected, temperamental one. A child accepts love and returns it. Adults know better than to trust it."

"I see."

His hands tightened and his mouth dropped to her soft neck, pressing there hotly. "You see nothing," he said huskily. "Lift your mouth. I want it."

She started to protest, but the stark need of his mouth silenced her. His lips parted hers ruthlessly. He whipped her around against him, his body hardening as he held hers possessively to it. He groaned softly, and the sound made her even weaker.

With a tiny sigh, her mind let go and made her vulnerable in his arms. She reached up, opening her mouth to the rough, insistent probing of his tongue. The sensations he was causing made her knees tremble, and eventually it was only the crush of his arms that kept her on her feet at all.

The sudden silence in the living room was as blatant as a gunshot. Donavan reluctantly lifted his head just as Jeff's footsteps impinged on the silence.

Fay tried to pull back, but Donavan wouldn't let go.

"He isn't blind," he said unsteadily. "Stay put."

She didn't quite grasp what he meant until he moved deliberately against her, making her realize at once that his hunger for her was blatant and easily seen.

She subsided and laid her cheek on his broad

chest, relaxing against him as Jeff pushed open the kitchen door, and made an embarrassed sound.

"Sorry," he faltered. "I needed a soft drink."

"Help yourself," Donavan said, chuckling. "We are married, you know," he added, lightening the atmosphere.

"It's about time you started acting like you were," Jeff murmured with a grin. He got his soft drink and closed the door behind him with a faint wink at Fay.

"I'll remind you of the same thing," he told her when he stepped back and her face flamed before she was able to avert her eyes. "And you've seen me with a hell of a lot less on, in this condition."

"Will you stop?" she moaned.

"You're very easily embarrassed for an old married woman." His eyes narrowed as he paused long enough to light a cigar. He watched her closely. "I'll keep you from getting pregnant. I want you in my bed tonight. Hear me out," he added when she started to speak. "Sophistication is the one thing you can't fake. If even Jeff realizes we aren't living like married people, his stepfather might realize it as well. We could still lose Jeff."

She hesitated. "I realize that."

"You can pretend all you like," he added, "but you want what I can give you in bed. You're as excited right now as you were in the motel room the night after we married. The difference," he said sensually, "is that now we can experience each other totally, Fay. I can satisfy you totally."

Her lips parted. She could still feel him on them,

taste him on them. He looked at her and knew, at once, that she was totally at his mercy.

Slowly he put out the cigar. He opened the door. "Jeff, we're going to have an early night. Bed by eleven, got that?"

"What? Oh, sure, Uncle Don," he said distractedly, his eyes on the TV screen. "Sleep well."

"You, too."

He closed the door and caught Fay's cold hand in his. He tugged her with him to the hall door, opened and closed it behind them, and then led her into the darkness of his own bedroom.

He closed that door, and locked it. Seconds later, in the warm dark, Fay felt him lever down completely against her, pushing her back against the cool wood of the door as the heat of his muscular body overwhelmed her.

While he kissed her, his hands slid under the dress she was wearing and played havoc with her aroused body. Long before he began to take her clothes off, she was barely able to stand alone.

Later, she lay quietly, trembling, in his bed while he removed his own clothes. She could barely see him in the faint light from the window, but what she saw was devastating, and her breath caught.

"You know what to expect already," he whispered as he eased down beside her and began to arouse her all over again. "Except that this time," he whispered into her mouth, "I'm going to fill you..."

She cried out. His mouth hurt, his body was hard and heavy, but she didn't notice, didn't care. She welcomed the warm weight of him, the fierce passion of his mouth and hands. She even welcomed the faint flash of pain when he came into her, her body arching up to receive him, her eyes wide with shock and awe as he slowly completed his possession and then paused, hovering with her on the brink of some sensual precipice.

One lean hand had her hip in its steely grasp. He looked at her, breathing unsteadily, his silver eyes glistening with excitement, beads of sweat on his lean, swarthy face.

His hand contracted and he moved, sensually, just enough to make her feverishly aware of how intimate their embrace was.

She caught her breath and he laughed, deep in his throat.

"Yes," he whispered roughly. "You didn't realize just how intimate it was going to be, did you, little one?"

"N-no," she got out. She looked at him in astonishment, feeling him in every cell of her body. It was embarrassing, shocking, to talk to a man in the throes of such intimacy. And he was laughing. "It isn't funny," she choked.

"I'm not laughing because I'm amused," he whispered, and bent to nibble with barely contained hunger at her softly swollen lips. His hips curled down into hers and lifted, creating a sudden sensual vortex that coaxed a cry of shocked pleasure from her lips. "I'm laughing because you're the most sensual little virgin in the world, and because despite the newness and fear, you're giving yourself to me without a single inhibition. Lift your hips. Let me feel you as close as you can get.''

She obeyed him, her body on fire. Her dreams had never been so explicit. Her nails bit into his broad shoulders as he began to move with exquisite delicacy.

"I may be a little rough with you now," he whispered into her mouth. "Don't be afraid of my passion. If you give yourself to it, to me, I'll give you a kind of pleasure you can't even imagine. Match me. Match my rhythm. Don't pull back. That's it." His teeth clenched and he groaned as his body stiffened. "Oh, God, I'm losing it...!"

He did. He lost it completely, before he could give her the time she needed to experience fulfillment. He arched above her, his face contorted and terrible in its unearthly pleasure, and he bit off something explicit and harsh as he gave in to the silky convulsions.

"I'm sorry," he whispered, lying drained and heavy over her. "My God, I'm so sorry!"

"Sorry that you made love to me?" she asked in a curious whisper.

"Sorry that I didn't satisfy you!"

"Oh." She stroked his dark hair gently. "You mean, the way you did the night we were married?" She smiled. "Now you can, can't you?"

He stared at her poleaxed. "You think that what just happened was only for my benefit?"

She frowned. "Wasn't it?"

He pulled her close and his arms tightened.

"You're one in a million, do you know that? Lift this leg...yes!"

She gasped as his body suddenly became part of hers. She hadn't expected this again so soon. Weren't men supposed to be incapable for several minutes after intimacy?

He moved slowly, exquisitely, and her breath caught. She clung to him, as the most astounding sensations worked through her tightening body.

"Donavan," she began, and suddenly cried out at the unexpected spasm of staggering pleasure.

"Be quiet, sweetheart," he whispered at her mouth, his hips moving with more insistence now, more purpose. "Hold on tight. Yes, Fay, feel it, yes...yes!"

She wept brokenly as the pleasure burst inside her like an overfilled balloon. She had no control whatsoever over her body or the vicious contractions that convulsed her under his openly watchful eyes.

He whispered to her, words of encouragement, praise, flattery, while his mouth touched quickly over her flushed, taut face. It went on and on. She shuddered and clung, convulsed and clung, experiencing sensations beyond her wildest dreams of perfection.

At last, the world stopped rocking and whirling around her. She trembled helplessly in the aftermath, drenched in sweat, weeping softly from the onrush of pleasure and its abrupt loss.

Donavan cradled her in his hard arms, smoothing back her damp hair as he comforted her.

"This," he said after a few minutes, "is what intimacy really is."

"I thought…before, at the motel…" She couldn't quite find the words.

"An alternate way of making love," he said quietly. "But nothing like the real thing. Was it, Fay?"

He wasn't mocking, or teasing. His voice was soft and deep and matter-of-fact.

"We…were like one person," she whispered into his cool, hair-roughened chest.

"Yes." His cheek moved against hers and he kissed her, very gently.

Her body felt pleasantly tired. She went boneless against him and slid even closer, her legs tangling with his. "Can I stay with you?" she asked drowsily.

His arms tightened. "Let me put it this way—just try to get away."

She smiled sleepily. "I don't think I want to."

He bit the lobe of her ear softly. "I want you again, right now," he said huskily, feeling her heart jump under his palm. "But we'll wait until in the morning. It didn't hurt? Even the first time?"

"No," she lied, and snuggled closer. It hadn't hurt very much. And the second time had been heaven.

"Fay," he said hesitantly. His fingers threaded through her soft hair. "Fay, I forgot to use anything."

She didn't stir, or answer. He looked down and realized belatedly that she was asleep.

He bent and kissed her closed eyelids. "Maybe it's just as well that you didn't hear me," he whispered. His lean hand found her soft belly and rested there possessively. "You'd love a baby, Fay. So would I. Maybe it's already happened. If it has, perhaps I can convince you that it would be a bonus, not a complication.''

Fay was wavering between consciousness and sleep. She heard Donavan say something about a bonus, but her mind was already headed for oblivion. She clung closer and gave in to it.

Chapter Nine

Fay was humming softly to herself when Donavan
came in from the barn. He'd gone out without waking her, and she was disappointed. She'd been hoping
that the night before might have coaxed him to want
her again, but obviously that hope had been doomed.

She stopped humming when he walked in, her
eyes a little shy and nervous. "Good morning," she
began, searching for the right words.

He paused in the doorway, and he could have been
playing poker for all the expression in his face. Her
stiff composure told him things he didn't want to
know. He'd pleased her in the night. He'd hoped that
things would change between them now that she
knew what married life could be. But he wasn't reassured. She looked uncomfortable and poised to run.
If she felt anything for him, it didn't show. And he
needed some reassurance before he paraded his own

feelings in front of her; his pride would take a mighty blow if she didn't care anymore.

"Good morning," he replied with equal formality. "Breakfast ready?"

"Almost."

He turned. "I'll call Jeff."

And not a word was said, either about the night before, or about what he felt. Fay watched him surreptitiously, hoping to see some flicker of warmth in those silver eyes. But they never met hers. He was polite, nothing more. Fay left the table resolved not to expect anything from that encounter in the darkness the night before. It was just as well, because that night he didn't come near her.

The next morning, they went to church, and then spent a lazy afternoon in front of the television watching old movies. There had hardly been three words spoken in front of Jeff, who looked worried.

"Something bothering you?" Donavan asked curtly after supper.

Jeff looked uncomfortable. "Yes, sir. Sort of."

"What is it?"

"It's you and Aunt Fay," he said miserably, wincing at Fay's shock and Donavan's quick anger. "I'm sorry, but if you two go into court tomorrow looking like you do right now, I guess I'll be back in military school by the next morning. Could you pretend to like each other, just while we're in court?"

"No problem there," Donavan assured him. "Now you'd better get your bath and go to sleep. We've got a big day ahead tomorrow."

When he left the room, Donavan got up and turned

off the television. His eyes lingered on Fay's flushed cheeks for a few seconds before he spoke.

"He's dead right," he told her. "If we don't present a united front, he won't be able to stay here."

"I know." She folded her hands in her lap and clenched them, staring at her nails. "I don't want him to have to leave, Donavan, whatever you think."

His broad shoulders lifted and fell in an offhand gesture. He lit a cigar and stared at its tip. "I shouldn't have lost my head night before last," he said tersely. "It made things worse between us."

She didn't know how to answer that. She picked at one of her fingernails and didn't look up. "It was my fault, too."

"Was it? You didn't seduce me, honey," he drawled.

She sighed heavily. "I'm not on the pill," she said.

He hesitated. "Yes, I know."

"And you...well, you didn't do anything..."

"That's right," he replied. "Keep going."

She cleared her throat, glancing up at him. "You might have made me pregnant."

One corner of his mouth curved gently. "There's an old family christening gown around here somewhere. My great-grandmother made the lace it's edged in. There's a high chair and even a cradle that date back to the first settlers in Jacobsville."

Fay's green eyes softened as they met his. Her cheeks warmed as she looked at him. "I...I have a baptismal set, too. The furniture's all gone. But there's one antique that Great-Aunt Tessie kept—a silver baptismal bowl. I saved it from the auction."

The mention of her deceased relative made his expression become grim. He averted his face and smoked his cigar, still pacing slowly. "You inherited a lot of money," he said. "Can't you keep the furniture, or don't you want it?"

"I have no place for it in my apartment," she said simply.

He spun on his heel, glaring at her. "This is your home. There's no way on earth you're leaving here until I know if you're pregnant."

She started. "It's unlikely..."

"Why? Because it was the first time?" he asked with mocking amusement.

His sophisticated attitude angered her. "Can't we talk about something else?" she asked stiffly.

"Sure." He raised the cigar to his firm lips. He felt optimistic for the first time. She still reacted to him. She couldn't hide the way he affected her. It made him feel proud to realize that she was as helplessly attracted to him as he was to her.

Now, if only her heart was involved...

"Why don't you sleep with me tonight?" he asked sensuously. "After all, one more time isn't going to make much difference now."

"You don't want me to stay here," she said. "I don't want a child who has to grow up without his father."

"I didn't say I didn't want you to stay here," he returned.

"You did so!" she raged, standing. "You said that

you didn't want me anymore because my great-aunt died and left me rich again! You let me go to Florida all by myself—''

"Not quite. Henry went with you," he pointed out.

She continued as if he hadn't interrupted "—and then you said I could find somewhere else to live!"

"I didn't say that," he murmured dryly. "Surely not?"

"Yes, you did!"

"That was before I slept with you, of course," he pointed out, letting his eyes punctuate the flat statement. "Now I'm hopelessly addicted."

"Any woman would do," she muttered.

"Not really, or I'd have had a few in the past year or so. I'd all but lost interest in sex until you came along and knocked my legs out from under me."

"A likely story, after the things you did to me night before last...!"

She stopped very suddenly, her hand going to her mouth as she realized what she'd said. She sat down again, hard.

"I had experience, Fay," he said softly.

She flushed. "I noticed!"

"You might consider that those early encounters made your life a little easier."

She stared at her feet, still smoldering. "You did things to me that I never even read in books."

"I'll tell you a secret, honey," he mused, putting out his cigar before he came to kneel between her legs where she sat rigidly on the sofa. He was almost on a level with her shocked eyes as he looked into them. "I've never done with anyone some of those things I did to you. And never could."

"C-couldn't you?" she whispered.

"No." His hands caught her waist and pulled gently, suddenly overbalancing so that she landed breathlessly on his chest. He rolled, pinning her under him on the big throw rug. As he held her eyes, one long leg inserted itself between both of hers and he moved slowly.

"I want you again. Now," he told her, his body screaming it in the intimate embrace. His lean hand smoothed blatantly over her soft breast and then began to slip buttons out of buttonholes.

"But the door..." she began.

"Isn't closed. I know." He slid his hand inside her bodice and under her soft bra, to find even softer flesh. His fingers gently caressed it, and she arched, gasping. "I'm going to carry you to bed now," he breathed. "And I'm going to do all those things I did two nights ago. Right now."

He got to his feet and picked her up, shifting her gently as he carried her down the long hall and into his bedroom. He placed her on the bedspread and went to close and lock the door. Then he stood at the foot of the bed, his black hair half in his eyes, his face devoid of expression, his body blatantly aroused.

She eased up onto her elbows, feeling feminine and hotly desired, her green eyes lost in the glitter of his gray ones. He nodded slowly. And then he moved toward her.

But just as he reached her, bent over her, warmed

her mouth with his breath in a deliciously tense bit of provocation—the telephone rang noisily on the bedside table.

Donavan stared at it blankly, as if for a moment he didn't even realize what was making the noise.

Impatiently he jerked up the receiver and spoke into it.

A familiar, sarcastic voice came over the line— Brad Danner, Jeff's stepfather.

"I'm looking forward to tomorrow, Donavan," he told the angry man on the other end of the line. "If you think that sham marriage is going to make any difference in a custody suit, you're very wrong."

"It isn't a sham marriage," Donavan said tersely, without looking at Fay, who was sitting shocked and disoriented beside him now, on the bed.

"I'll let you prove that tomorrow. Take good care of my stepson, won't you? I'm looking forward to having him home again."

"Yes, it would be something of a luxury, wouldn't it?" Donavan asked icily. "When you stuck him in military school at his first show of spirit."

"One of you in a family is enough," the other man replied, obviously straining to keep his temper. "All my married life, Debbie threw you up to me. Nothing I did was ever right, ever the same thing *you* would have done in my place. My God, you don't now how I hated you!"

"Debbie always had a tendency to romanticize everything," Donavan said curtly. "After Dad died, I was all she had. As for her opinion of you," he added with mocking amusement, "I had nothing to do with it. You were a spineless complainer from day one. And don't tell me the dowry I gave her wasn't the real inducement to get you to the altar. You spent half of it the first week you were married to Debbie—on your mistress!''

The other receiver slammed down. Donavan slowly replaced his, chuckling with bitter amusement.

''Jeff's would-be guardian,'' he said, nodding toward the telephone. ''He fancies himself a man. Imagine that?''

''He might have loved your sister,'' she began.

''Really? If he did, why was he involved with another woman before, during and after the marriage? The woman he's married to now, by the way. Debbie's insurance money set them up real well. He made sure that Jeff wasn't mentioned as a beneficiary.''

''He sounds very mercenary,'' she said quietly.

''He thinks he can prove that our marriage is a fraud,'' he said. His eyes narrowed on her face. ''It's imperative that we act like lovers. You understand that?''

She nodded. Her eyes fell to his broad chest, where his shirt was unbuttoned over a thick mat of curling black hair.

''I understand.'' Her lips parted with helpless hunger, but she lowered her eyes so that he wouldn't see how she felt. ''That's why you brought me in here, isn't it, Donavan? So that it would show, in court tomorrow, that we'd been intimate.''

He hesitated, but only for an instant. ''Yes,'' he

said curtly. "That's right. I wanted to make you look loved, so that I wouldn't risk losing Jeff."

"I see."

Her defeated expression made him wild. "He might run away if he gets sent back, don't you see? He's high-strung. I can't let that happen. He's all the family I have left in the world, Fay!"

She stood up with a long, gentle sigh. "Funny," she said as she turned. "Once upon a time, I thought I was part of your family. It just goes to show how money can warp you. Being rich must have made me stupid."

He rammed his hands into his pockets. He felt guilty, and he didn't like it. She was rich. She had the world. She didn't need a poor husband and a ready-made family, anyway. Even *if* he wanted her for keeps, which he didn't. He had one scandal to live down. He couldn't take another.

He only hoped he hadn't made her pregnant in that feverish coupling. It would make her life impossible, because he knew he'd never be able to turn his back on his own child. She'd be trapped then, and so would he.

"It's just as well that Brad interrupted us," he said tersely, thinking aloud. "I've been unforgivably careless about taking precautions. It's just as well if we don't take any more risks. I'll see you in the morning, Fay."

It was a dismissal. He looked as unapproachable as a porcupine. Fay couldn't understand why he'd bothered trying to seduce her in the first place. Now he seemed concerned about not making her pregnant.

She left him there and went to bed, hurt and bitter and totally confused.

She dressed very carefully for court the next morning, in her off-white suit and leather high heels. She carried the one designer purse she had left, and wore a very becoming and very expensive spring hat. She looked what she was—a young woman with breeding who'd been raised to be a lady.

Donavan, in his pale gray suit, was openly appreciative of the way she looked. In fact, he could hardly keep his eyes off her.

"You look...lovely," he said.

She managed a cool smile. "Why thank you, darling," she said, playing her part to the hilt. Only her eyes gave the show away, because they were like two green pieces of ice. His hot-cold attitude had worn her out. She was giving up all hope of a happy marriage, but first she was going to help Jeff out of his predicament. It was a matter of honor. She'd given her word.

"Very nice," he replied curtly. "You'll convince anyone who doesn't look at your face too closely."

"I can handle that." She pulled the hat's matching veil down over her nose. "Now. One wife, properly accounted for, ready to go on stage."

He stiffened and turned away, his anger evident and blatant.

Jeff came out of his bedroom in a suit. He looked from Fay to Donavan and grimaced. "Well, I guess I'm as ready as I'll ever be, but I'm sure not looking forward to it."

"Neither are we," Donavan said. "All the more

reason to get it over with as soon as possible. Try not to worry,'' he added gently, placing an affectionate hand on the boy's stooped shoulder. ''And stand up straight. Don't let him think he's got you buffaloed.''

''Yes, Uncle Don.''

He herded Fay and Jeff out to the car and drove them to the county courthouse in a silence filled with worried looks and cigar smoke.

Brad Danner wasn't at all what Fay had expected. He was short and redheaded and looked as if he had a massive ego.

''So you're the brand-new Mrs. J. D. Langley,'' Brad said mockingly, shaking off the firm hand of a suited man who was probably his attorney. ''Well, it won't work. You might as well go back to whichever bar he found you at and throw in your chips. You'll never pull this off. I've got too much on you!''

''Have you indeed?'' Fay asked, enjoying herself now. ''Actually, Donavan did find me in a bar.'' She leaned closer. ''But I didn't work there.''

''Oh, of course not,'' he agreed amiably, and laughed as he turned back to the bleached blonde with the overlipsticked mouth who was obviously pregnant and almost certainly his wife.

Donavan motioned for Fay to sit down at the table with him. Jeff had already been taken away by a juvenile officer for the course of the hearing.

Formalities had to be observed. Once those were out of the way, Donavan's attorney—an elderly man with keen eyes and alarming dignity—offered Brad's attorney the opportunity to present his case first.

Donavan looked nervous, but Mr. Flores only smiled and winked.

Brad's attorney got up and made a long speech about the things Brad had done for his stepson, most recently having enrolled him in a top-flight educational facility, which would lead him to an admirable career.

"We do concede that Mr. Danner has no blood relationship with the boy, as does Mr. Langley. However, despite his hasty marriage in an attempt to present a stable home environment, Mr. Langley overlooked one small detail. He neglected to keep his new wife close to home."

Fay and Donavan exchanged puzzled glances. The opposing attorney opened his briefcase and dragged out several photographs of Fay with her uncle on the way to Florida, and at Tessie's apartment, where they'd stayed until the funeral was over.

"This is the kind of monkey business the new Mrs. Langley gets up to when her husband's back is turned," the attorney said haughtily, glaring at Fay as if she were a fallen woman. "Hardly a moral example for a young boy!"

Donavan chuckled.

"You find these photographs amusing, Mr. Langley? You had been married for only a matter of days, I believe, when Mrs. Langley and her gentleman friend flew to Florida alone?"

"You aren't from here, are you?" Donavan asked

the attorney. "And apparently neither is your private detective."

"He isn't a private detective, he's a friend of mine who used to be in intelligence work during the Korean War," Brad said stiffly. "But you won't lie your way out of this. That man in the photographs is…!"

"…my uncle," Fay said. She glanced at Judge Ridley, who was an old friend of her family—and who was also trying not to break up.

"I'm afraid so," Judge Ridley agreed, wiping the unjudicial smile off his face. "I've known Henry for years."

"If he's her uncle, why doesn't he have the same surname she does?" the other attorney argued.

"Henry is Fay's mother's brother," Judge Ridley explained. "Surely your detective checked?"

"He said Donavan had probably found her at a bar," Brad began.

"Mrs. Langley and her uncle went to Florida to make the final arrangements for Mrs. Langley's great-aunt," Donavan's attorney clarified. "As for your friend's assertion that Mrs. Langley worked in a bar, let me assure you that nothing could be farther from the truth. In point of fact, she was a debutante. And now, with the death of her great-aunt, she stands to inherit a large share of the estate."

Brad looked sick.

"I am also reliably told," Judge Ridley interrupted, "by the young boy whose custody is in question, that his uncle and Mrs. Langley have a warm, loving relationship, which gives him a much-needed feeling of security. Your accusation that the marriage is fraudulent hardly concurs with the home life the young man describes."

"He'd do anything to get Jeff, even pretending to be happily married. Ask him if he loves her," he challenged the judge. "Go ahead! He never lies. Make him tell her how he really feels about her!"

Fay stood up. "I know how my husband feels about me, Mr. Danner," she said stiffly. "I also know how you feel about him. Jeff is only a pawn to you. But he's a flesh-and-blood boy to Donavan. They're very happy together. Jeff will get a good education and caring company, and it won't be in a military school where he isn't even allowed weekend visits home more than twice a year! If you wanted him so badly, why send him away in the first place?"

"A good question," the judge agreed. He stared at Brad, who was slowly turning red. "Answer it, please."

"My wife is pregnant," Brad said shortly. "Jeff makes her nervous. Isn't that right, honey?"

"I fail to see why you sought custody, Mr. Danner," the judge persisted.

"Oh, tell him, Bradley," the blonde muttered. She sanded a nail to perfection. "He only wants the insurance money. He's afraid if he loses custody, he'll have to give Jeff his share of it, and he's already spent it."

"You idiot!" Brad raged at his wife.

"What's so terrible about the truth?" she asked with careless unconcern. "You were so scared of your brother-in-law finding out. Well, now he knows. Big deal. It's only a thousand dollars, anyway. If you hadn't bought that stupid boat, you could have afforded to pay it back."

The courtroom erupted. Before the fur stopped flying, Fay got a glimpse of the real Brad Danner, and she was very sorry for his second wife. By the time Fay and Donavan left the courtroom, with custody of Jeff and the promise of repayment of the insurance money Jeff should have had, Fay's head was whirling.

"Aunt Fay, I'm so relieved!" Jeff laughed, and hugged her impulsively. "I can stay, isn't it radical?"

"Just radical," she agreed happily.

"And you and Uncle Don fooled them all," he added. "Everybody thought you were the most devoted couple anywhere!"

"That was the joke of the century, all right," Fay said quietly, and met Donavan's angry eyes over Jeff's head. "Congratulations. You've got what you wanted."

"Yes," he said. "I've got everything I wanted."

She smiled coolly, grateful for the veil that hid her sadness, and put an affectionate arm around Jeff as they walked toward the car.

Donavan walked a little behind them. He didn't know how he felt exactly, but elated wouldn't have covered it. He was glad to have Jeff with him, of course, but in the process he was certain to lose Fay.

That shouldn't bother him. Fay was rich; he wasn't. Their life-styles would never mix, and everyone would think that he'd married her for her money. Hell, they probably thought it already. He laughed at his own folly. Even if he divorced her, they'd say he was after a big cash settlement in return for her freedom. They'd say like father, like son.

Suddenly the public censure that had worried him so much before fell into place. If he knew what his motives were, did it really matter what a few small-minded people thought? It was usually the hypocrites who gossiped, anyway—the people who lived public lives of high morality and private lives of glaring impurity. The few friends he had wouldn't sit in judgment on him. So why was he agonizing over his plight?

He glanced at Fay hungrily. Hell, he wanted her. He'd grown used to having her around the house. He enjoyed watching her stumbling attempts to cook edible meals. He liked the smell of her perfume when he stood close to her, and the way she fussed over him and Jeff, as if it really mattered to her that something might happen to one of them. He liked her, most especially, sliding under his body in bed, giving him her warmth and exquisite sensuality, giving him ecstasy that even in memory could make him weak in the knees. He wanted to stay with her. He wanted a child with her. Was it too late? Had he done too much damage?

"Suppose we stop off at the pizza place and get a supreme to go?" Jeff suggested. "After all, we are celebrating."

"Good idea. We'll give Aunt Fay the night off," Donavan agreed.

"He's just tired of bouncing biscuits and black

steak,'' she told Jeff with a sigh. ''I guess one well-cooked meal won't kill us all.''

Jeff laughed, but Fay didn't. Now that Donavan had Jeff, she wondered how much time she had left until Donavan wanted her out of his life for good.

Chapter Ten

The pizza was delicious. Fay enjoyed it as much as the rest of the family seemed to, but her heart wasn't in the celebration. She wanted to stand up and scream that life was unfair, that she'd been shortchanged all the way around. She'd always had money. But she'd never had love. Now it seemed that she didn't have either. Great-Aunt Tessie's legacy would be nice, but it would hardly allow her to give up her job. With some careful investing, it would grow, as long as she could live on what she made.

She worried about that for the rest of the day, trying to put on a happy face for Jeff. But Donavan saw through it. He joined her in the porch swing while Jeff played with one of three new snow-white puppies in the barn.

"We won," he reminded her as he smoked his cigar. Like her, he'd changed into casual clothes—

jeans and a cotton shirt. He propped one booted foot on the swing and glanced down at her. "Aren't you glad?"

"Of course," she said absently. "I know how worried Jeff was."

He stared out over the horizon. "There really wasn't too much to worry about," he mused. "I had a contact of mine feed his Korean War veteran buddy a few scandalous facts about you and Uncle Henry. It's not my fault the man took it for gospel and didn't double check. His loss, my gain."

"Donavan!" she burst out. "That's devious!"

"That's how I am when people I love get threatened." He looked down at her. "I'll fight under the table, any way at all, to win when someone else's life depends on it. I couldn't let that strutting rooster get Jeff. It wasn't a tug of war with me—it was Jeff's whole life."

"I know he appreciates what you've done for him."

"I don't imagine you do. I'm sorry to have made you look, even temporarily, like a fallen angel. But I had no choice."

"I understood. Even the judge was having a hard time keeping a straight face."

"Where do we go from here, Fay?" he asked solemnly.

She listened to the creak as the wooden swing pulled against the chains rhythmically.

"I'll stay until your brother-in-law is safely back

home and over his defeat,'' she said. ''We've already discussed where I'll go.''

''No we haven't,'' he disagreed. ''You said you were going to move back to the apartment house and I said you weren't. My God, buy yourself a place, why don't you?''

Her hands clasped together painfully. Didn't he know he was tearing the heart out of her?

''I might, later on.''

She wasn't giving an inch. He couldn't tell anything by her voice or her expression.

''You could stay on here,'' he remarked casually. ''There's plenty of room. Jeff likes you. So does Bee.''

''I've burned up enough good food already.''

''We haven't complained.''

She smiled to herself. Amazingly they hadn't. Only three days ago, Jeff had complimented her on one small side dish that was actually fit to eat.

''I might get the hang of it one day.''

He studied his boot. ''How about getting the hang of making formula and changing dirty diapers?'' he asked, his eyes on the horizon.

She hesitated. He sounded...serious. ''What do you mean?''

He shrugged. He lifted the cigar to his mouth and took a draw from it, blowing out a large cloud of pungent smoke. ''I mean, suppose we stayed married. If you'd let me, I think I could make you pregnant eventually. We could raise a family, give Jeff a stable environment to finish growing up in.''

She studied his profile. Nothing there. He looked as formidable as he had the first time she'd ever seen him. Just as handsome, too, she thought wistfully.

He glanced down and saw that wistfulness and one eyebrow went up. He looked at her openly now, from her forehead down to her mouth and back up to her eyes. "You're thinner. I've been cruel to you, Fay. Give me a chance to put things right."

"By making me pregnant?" she asked with pretended lightness.

"If it's what you want, yes. If not, we can put if off for a few years. You're still very young, little one. You might like to go to college or do some traveling before you get tied down with children."

"I've already done my traveling, and I don't want to go to college. I have a nice job already."

"You can resign from that," he said. "You don't need it."

She stared at him for a long moment, until he scowled. "Actually," she confessed, "I'm afraid I do."

"If you just want a way to get out of the house…"

She rested her cool fingers atop the lean hand that was propped on his jean-clad knee. "Donavan, I'm not exactly going to inherit a fortune."

"Yes, I know. Henry said you'll only get about a third, when it's all wrapped up. It doesn't matter," he said doggedly, averting his face. "I don't give a damn what people think anymore. I don't know now why I ever did. I'm not like my father. I married you for Jeff's sake, not because I stood to gain a fortune.''

She felt the impact of that statement down to her toes. If only he'd married her for love of her. She sighed, audibly.

He tilted her face up to his. "What a wistful little sound," he said quietly. "You don't like thinking that I only married you for Jeff. You liked it even less when you thought it was for money."

"It doesn't bother me," she lied.

"Sure it does," he countered quietly. "I wanted you," he said softly. "You knew that already, I imagine."

"Yes."

"You wanted me back. I didn't have to coerce you into my bed. You came willingly."

She flushed and looked down at the lean fingers that slowly wrapped around hers in a close embrace. "It was new and...exciting."

"More than just exciting, I think, little one." His voice was soft, deep, sensual. "I lost you for a few seconds just as I fulfilled you. It made me feel pretty good to know I could give you that much pleasure."

"As you said," she swallowed, "you've had a lot of experience."

"I've had a lot of *bodies*," he said with faint cynicism. "Just that, Fay, a lot of bodies in the dark. I went through the motions and learned the right moves. But it was nothing like what I had with you, even on our wedding night, when my hands were all but tied. I knew then that it was more than physical attraction. But I knew it for certain when I put you on that plane to Florida and let you walk away from me. I didn't sleep all night, for thinking how cruel I'd been. You loved Tessie, and I'd given you no comfort, no support at all. I'm sorry for that. I owed you more than that.''

"You owed me nothing," she told him dully. "We got married for Jeff, that's all."

His free hand spread against her soft cheek and lifted her face. "Haven't you been listening to me at all?" he asked softly.

"Yes," she said nervously. "You've got me on your conscience."

"Fay, listen with your heart, not your ears," he replied. He searched her face with eyes that adored it. "Can't you see it? Can't you feel it? Fay, can't you put your mouth on mine and taste it...?"

He pulled her lips under his and kissed her with such tenderness that she felt her body ripple with sheer pleasure.

His tongue probed inside her mouth, increasing the heat, making her moan. While he built the kiss, he lifted and turned her, so that she was lying completely in his arms, pressed close against the heat of his muscular chest.

Unseen, his lean hand eased inside her shirt and began to trace the warm, taut contours of her breast until he made the nipple go hard against his fingers.

He lifted his head minutes later, and looked down at her swollen mouth and dazed eyes before his gaze dropped to the taut nipple so evident under the thin fabric.

"You look as out of control as I feel," he said huskily, his gray eyes pure silver in the daylight. "If we were alone, I wouldn't even bother to strip you. I'd just get the necessary things out of the way and I'd take you like a tornado."

She shivered, pressing her hot face into his throat.

"Want it like that?" he whispered at her ear. "Rough and quick and blazing hot?" He glanced over her head at Jeff, who was sprawled in the aisle of the barn playing with the dogs while one of Donavan's older hands watched him.

Donavan stood up abruptly and put Fay on her feet. Catching the older hand's attention, he indicated that he wanted him to keep an eye on Jeff. The cowhand nodded, grinned and waved. Then Donavan turned back to Fay, his eyes glittery with intent.

"Oh…we can't," she faltered as he came toward her and she began backing toward the screen door. "Surely, you were kidding, with Jeff right outside…!"

"Like hell I was kidding," he whispered against her mouth.

He picked her up and carried her straight into his bedroom, pausing just long enough to lock the door before he backed her up against the waist-high vanity and opened the fastening of her jeans.

She gasped and started to protest, but he had her mouth under his, and she couldn't manage speech. She heard the rasp of another zipper, felt him move, and then her jeans slid off her legs. His tongue went roughly into her mouth, in quick, sharp thrusts that were unbelievably arousing.

He lifted her sharply and she felt him suddenly in an intimacy that took her breath. He half lifted her from the vanity, his body levering between her legs while he invaded her with urgent, exquisite mastery. She clung to his neck, feeling the force of his desire with faint awe as she experienced for the first time the unbridled violence of passion.

He wasn't tender, or particularly gentle, but the pleasure that convulsed her was beyond anything he'd given her before. She heard him cry out and felt him tense, then he was heavy in her arms, damp with sweat, trembling faintly from the strength he'd had to exert in the uncomfortable position.

"I like the noises that boil out of you when we make love," he said roughly. "You excite me."

"I can't stop shaking." She laughed shyly.

"Neither can I. We went high this time."

"Yes. Oh, yes!"

He drew back, finally, and looked at her. His face was solemn, his eyes quiet and gentle. He brushed back her damp hair and smiled. "That will have to last us until tonight," he whispered. "Think you can manage?"

"If you can," she teased. His eyes were telling her impossible things, too wonderful for reality. "Am I dreaming?" she asked.

"No, sweetheart. Not at all."

He lifted her, separating his body from hers, and grinned wickedly when she flushed.

"You needn't look so shocked," he chided as he rearranged his own clothing. "Five minutes ago you wouldn't have noticed if we were lying under a table in a restaurant."

"Neither would you!" she accused.

He drew her close and kissed her gently. "That's a fact," he whispered. "God, I love you, Fay."

She stiffened. She couldn't have heard that. She opened her eyes, very wide, and stared at him.

"I haven't given you much reason to believe it, but it's true just the same," he told her quietly. "You're all I want, you and Jeff and however many kids we can have together. If we can't have any, then you and Jeff will more than suffice."

"How long?" she asked gently, desperate now to believe him.

"Since the very first night we met," he replied. "I fought it. God, I did! But in the end, I couldn't do without you. After I made love to you, even light love, I was lost. I knew I'd never be able to let you go."

"Then I inherited Tessie's money," she began.

"I told you. It doesn't matter. I love you. Do whatever you like with your inheritance."

"In that case," she murmured, "I'll put it in the bank for Jeff's education. It should just about cover college."

"Where are we sending him to college—the Waldorf Astoria?"

She smiled warmly, convinced at last that she was awake and aware. "I only inherit part of the proceeds from the sale of her furniture," she told him, and proceeded to explain where the rest of the money was going.

He was surprised, and frankly pleased, that Fay's inheritance wouldn't amount to very much. "She must have been some kind of lady," he remarked.

"She was. A very special one. My share will just about pay for Jeff's college. Now you know why I wouldn't give up my job. I couldn't afford to."

"Just as well the Ballengers made one for you," he murmured. He sighed heavily. "I guess this means that I'll have to start being, ugh, nice to Calhoun."

"That wouldn't hurt," she agreed.

"And your uncle," he added irritably.

"Also a nice touch."

He searched her eyes. "I won't reform completely. You know that. I'm exactly what you see. I won't change."

"Neither will I," she replied. "I might get a little rounder eventually, and have a few gray hairs."

"That's okay," he said pleasantly. "I might do that myself." He pulled her closer. "Fay, I'll never be a rich man. But I'll love you, and take care of you when you need it. If we have nothing else, we'll have each other."

She had to fight tears at the tenderness in his deep voice. She kissed him and then reached up and locked her arms gently around his neck. "I haven't said it," she whispered.

"You said it the night you gave yourself to me completely," he replied, surprised. "Don't you remember? You said it over and over again while you were trembling in my arms at the last."

"I must have been half out of my mind. Loving you does that to me," she whispered with her heart in her eyes.

"And to me," he replied. He bent, fusing her mouth with his in a slow, sweet expression of love.

"Uncle Don!" came a loud voice from below the window.

Donavan groaned. "What now?"

He opened the window and looked down. Jeff was waiting with two of Donavan's foreman's sons, both of whom were carrying fishing poles and tackle boxes.

"Please?" he pleaded with his uncle. "I haven't gotten to go fishing since the last time you took me. I'll bring home supper, honest, can I?"

"Go ahead," Donavan chuckled. "But you'd better bring home supper."

"We'll make sure he does, sir!" one of the older boys called. "Even if we have to swim under his line and hook the fish on it ourselves."

"Thanks!" Jeff laughed.

The boys were out of sight in no time. Donavan closed the window and took the phone off the hook. He moved toward her with a wicked smile.

"Sometimes," he told a breathlessly excited Fay

as he began to caress her out of her clothing, "fate can be kind."

A sentiment that Fay would gladly have echoed, except that Donavan's mouth was hard over her own, and seconds later, she was in no condition to think at all....

The next morning, Fay was hard at work when Donavan showed up unexpectedly at the feedlot.

Calhoun, just coming out of his office, grimaced.

"No need to rush, finding excuses to get out of the office right away," Donavan drawled. "I'm reformed. I didn't come to complain. I actually dropped by to see about moving in some more cattle."

Calhoun's eyebrows went up. "You don't say!"

"I just did. While I'm about it, I might add a word of thanks about keeping my wife on," he added ruefully. "We figure her inheritance from her great-aunt will just about put one kid through college. Since we plan on more than our nephew taking up residence, every penny is going to count."

"We like the job Fay does. But it's tough luck," Calhoun ventured, "about the inheritance."

Donavan smiled lazily. "Not in my book. I like the idea of working toward something." He glanced at Fay with his heart in his eyes. "Struggling together brings two people close."

"Indeed it does," Fay agreed with a sigh.

"If you'd like to take your wife to lunch, we might be able to let her off a little early," Calhoun said.

"I was hoping you'd say that," Donavan said and grinned.

He took Fay to the local hamburger joint and they ate cheeseburgers and drank milkshakes until they were pretty well stuffed.

"You won't have an easy life with me," he said when they were outside again. He paused, catching her hand in his to stop and look down at her. "You'll probably always have to work. I can take some of the burden off you at home, because I can cook and do dishes and sweep. But when the kids come along, things could get pretty hectic."

"Am I worried?" she asked, smiling. "Am I complaining? I've got you. I don't need promises, assurances, or anything else. I'm happier than I ever dreamed of being."

"Are you sure?" he asked, and looked worried. "You've always had everything you wanted."

"I still do."

"You know what I mean," he said irritably.

"Yes. Money was nice, but it wasn't particularly easy to cuddle up to. I don't mind living like ordinary working people. In fact," she said honestly, "I really like the challenge. It's nice to feel independent, and to know that you're earning what you have. I never had to earn anything before."

"You're giving me a lot to live up to, honey," he said quietly. "I hope I won't let you down. I'm not the easiest man to live with."

"Yes, you are," she replied. She put her arms around him and pressed close. "As long as I'm holding you, you're the easiest man in the world to get along with. So suppose I just never let go?''

He laughed and let out his breath in a long, contented sigh as he pulled her close and returned the gentle embrace. ''I'll tell you something, sweetheart,'' he murmured contentedly. ''That suits me just fine!''

And she never did.

* * * * *

And so the legend grows.
Look out for more Long, Tall Texans
collections—as well as original titles!
Check the list at the front of the book
for any titles you may have missed!

FANTASTIC NEWS!

For all you devoted Diana Palmer fans
Silhouette Books is pleased to bring you
a brand-new novel and short story by one of the
top ten romance writers in America

"Nobody tops Diana Palmer...I love her stories."
—New York Times **bestselling author
Jayne Ann Krentz**

**Diana Palmer has written another thrilling desire.
Man of the Month Ramon Cortero was a talented
surgeon, existing only for his work—until the
night he saved nurse Noreen Kensington's life. But
their stormy past makes this romance a challenge!**

THE PATIENT NURSE
Silhouette Desire
October 1997

And in November Diana Palmer adds to the
Long, Tall Texans series with *CHRISTMAS COWBOY*, in
LONE STAR CHRISTMAS, a fabulous new holiday
keepsake collection by talented authors Diana Palmer
and Joan Johnston. Their heroes are seductive,
shameless and irresistible—and these Texans are
experts at sneaking kisses under the mistletoe! So get
ready for a sizzling holiday season....

Only from

Take 4 bestselling love stories FREE

Plus get a FREE surprise gift!

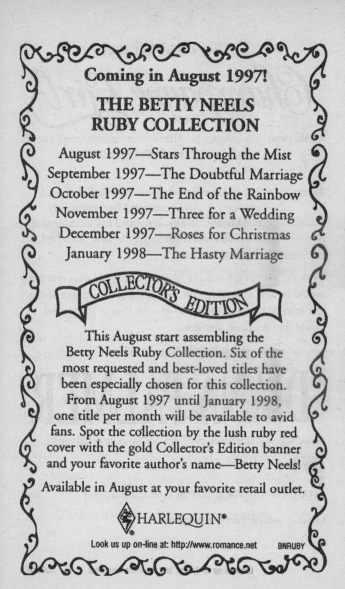

Coming in August 1997!

THE BETTY NEELS RUBY COLLECTION

COLLECTOR'S EDITION

This August start assembling the
Betty Neels Ruby Collection. Six of the
most requested and best-loved titles have
been especially chosen for this collection.
From August 1997 until January 1998,
one title per month will be available to avid
fans. Spot the collection by the lush ruby red
cover with the gold Collector's Edition banner
and your favorite author's name—Betty Neels!

Available in August at your favorite retail outlet.

HARLEQUIN®

Look us up on-line at: http://www.romance.net   BNRUBY

They called her the

Champagne Girl

Catherine: Underneath the effervescent, carefree and bubbly facade there was a depth to which few had access.

Matt: The older stepbrother she inherited with her mother's second marriage, Matt continually complicated things. It seemed to Catherine that she would make plans only to have Matt foul them up.

With the perfect job waiting in New York City, only one thing would be able to keep her on a dusty cattle ranch: something she thought she could never have—the love of the sexiest cowboy in the Lone Star state.

by bestselling author

DIANA PALMER

Available in September 1997 at your favorite retail outlet.

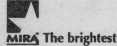

MIRA The brightest star in women's fiction

MDP8

Look us up on-line at: http://www.romance.net